michelle mckinney hammond

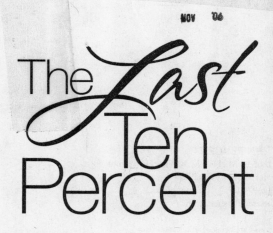

The *Last* Ten Percent

HARVEST HOUSE PUBLISHERS

EUGENE, OREGON

Michelle McKinney Hammond: Published in association with the literary agency of Alive Communications, Inc., 7680 Goddard Street, Suite #200, Colorado Springs, CO 80920. www.alive communications.com.

Cover photo © Tom Henry, Koechel Peterson & Associates, Inc.

Cover by Koechel Peterson & Associates, Inc., Minneapolis, Minnesota

THE LAST TEN PERCENT
Copyright © 2006 by Michelle McKinney Hammond
Published by Harvest House Publishers
Eugene, Oregon 97402
www.harvesthousepublishers.com

Library of Congress Cataloging-in-Publication Data
McKinney Hammond, Michelle, 1957-
  The last ten percent / Michelle McKinney Hammond.
    p. cm.
  ISBN-13: 978-0-7369-1480-2 (pbk.)
  ISBN-10: 0-7369-1480-3
  1. Dating (Social customs)—Fiction. 2. Female friendship—Fiction. I. Title.
  PS3613.C5464L37 2006
  813.'6—dc22   2005035841

Printed in the United States of America

06 07 08 09 10 11 12 13 14 / DP-MS / 10 9 8 7 6 5 4 3 2 1

For all who dare to still hope and believe in knights in shining armor, frogs turning into princes, and dreams coming true. With God all things are possible! Keep believing. Most of all, keep living life to the fullest, embracing the wind and celebrating love along the way.

Acknowledgments

To my Harvest House family who keeps pushing me out of the box. Thanks for all the encouragement, stretching, and nurturing. Where would I be without you? Perish the thought.

To Erin Healy. By jove, you've done it again—helped me birth another one. Thanks for your gentle guidance and great suggestions. You are the best. Hopefully I won't make you work so hard next time (ha!).

To all my friends and loved ones—you should know by now who you are—who put up with me being consumed by my work. You are my backbone and comfort. I love you!

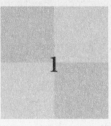

1

*H*e leaned toward her, oblivious of everything else moving around him…the waiter placing their next course before them, the other one pouring them wine, the other tables filled with chic groups and couples in various modes of repartee. The ambience of the restaurant was perfect for romance—small, European in feel, dark, and expensive. It was the type of place you brought someone to when dinner was the appetizer and they were the dessert. He kissed her as if no one else was present, much to the annoyance of a neighboring table. The couple across from them telegraphed a "get-a-room" expression in their direction while Tracy stood rooted to the spot, watching the scene through the window, allowing it to sink into her psyche that she was observing her man shamelessly groping another woman in public. She shivered, not able to discern if it was the harsh Chicago winter wind or reality slapping her viciously across her face. She didn't know how long she stood there refusing or simply unable to move until he turned toward her penetrating gaze. Their eyes locked through the glass that began to turn foggy. As tears stung her eyes, Tracy realized that her mouth was open and she was breathing hard, fighting for air as he remained frozen. *The irony of it all,* she thought. He was caught. Cool, cold, busted, trapped between two women, and of course he would take the chicken way out and simply do nothing.

She shook herself and turned on her heel away from the window, away from him. She concluded he wouldn't have the nerve to call and she wouldn't have the strength to confront him. After all, what was there to say? Again she wondered why men never seemed to have enough nerve to say when it was over. Why did they avoid confrontation, waiting for the relationship to fade to black? It seldom did without something happening that was ultimately uglier than what they were trying to avoid in the first place. But a larger question loomed in her mind. How many times could she go through this? Were there any remaining pieces of her heart left to be broken? She turned into the wind, hoping it would push her pain behind her. It didn't. Tracy could feel her tears threatening to freeze on her face. She wiped them with the back of her leather gloves and laughed for no reason at all, except for the hope of pumping air into her lungs. Perhaps if she could start breathing she could get through this.

This had certainly been an expensive shopping trip. All she had wanted was to find some shoes before meeting the girls for dinner. Little did she know her treasure hunt would culminate in finding more than she bargained for. She should have known. When a man was as smooth as Evan had been, he obviously had a lot of practice. She could imagine what her friends would say. She didn't even want to hear Muriel's mouth on the subject: "I told you he wasn't any good." She would be short and to the point. Adrian would be silently comforting, and Felicia would find a similar story from her own experiences in an effort to bond and relate with her pain. Felicia would somehow manage to make her feel even worse than she already did. But it all boiled down to one cruel fact. Once again she was one of many guinea pigs in a man's endeavor to become a certified player. Or as Aretha Franklin so aptly put it, "another link in a chain of fools."

Heading toward the lights of Michigan Avenue, which were blurred by her misery, she began to take stock of her past love repertoire. *Let's see, first there was Tony. He sure was fine.* When he entered the room heads turned and conversations stopped. So distracted was she by his good looks that she failed to notice how selfish he was. That he had anger issues was always glossed over by how contrite he was after an explosion. Making up was almost worth persevering through the storm—the operative word being *almost.* Fade.

Then there was Charles. Dear, sweet Charles. Again fine—that was always standard on her list. An actor, which should have been her first big clue, but moving on. He was so into her it made her head spin. While she was still in mid-spin he had flipped the script, focusing on his next leading lady. Again fading to black had not worked. Neither had it worked for her to find out about his new love interest in the gossip column as opposed to firsthand from his lips to her ears.

Then there was… Oh never mind. The list was too long, and the common denominator was her. *Ouch.* Tracy winced at the thought it *was* her. Why did she keep getting involved with the wrong men? What was it inside her that found them appealing? How could they all start off so right and end up so wrong? *What am I looking for, that's the question. Or am I a victim of my career?* Coming from the world of advertising where she made everyone beautiful and desirable, had she bought the lie of the perfect package? Love or perfection, did they have to be exclusive? It seemed cruel not to be able to have both, yet she had to remind herself that what appeared beautiful on screen and in the magazines had been crafted to look so.

Who would know better than she that no one really looked like that? She had firsthand knowledge of the hours spent on makeup and lighting that transformed her models into specimens of unparalleled magnificence. Add a smidgeon of retouching and *Voila!* It was a rare breed who came camera-ready gorgeous, and she managed to find them every time and miss the fact that for the most part the story line in her personal movie, as far as her leading men were concerned, always came to the same conclusion—pretty house, no one home. But it was fun to linger there enjoying the scenery until she began to want more. More substance, more stability, more love. That was when her poor choices caused her to pause for the cause and face the truth that perhaps she was her own worst enemy in her search for love.

Tracy would only admit to everyone that she was thirty plus, but to herself she knew with forty approaching more quickly than she cared to deal with, she was running out of time. It was time to get real and get serious about this thing called love. If she truly wanted a committed love relationship in her life, how would she get it? It was time to take stock of how she was contributing to her own demise. She definitely had a broken chooser. How many times had her friends told her so? She had a knack for duplicating the same theme over and over again. The results were always the same though the faces and names changed.

But what was it about her that attracted the same type of man? That was what she had to figure out. Perhaps the best way to break this cycle was to drive a wedge into it. Take a break. Yes, that is what she would do. She took a deep breath and watched it create a cloud in front of her, obliterating the avenue from view for a moment. It was time to take a step back and check herself. Truly the pain of repetition was signaling that she needed to do something different, perhaps *be* someone different. She deserved more than she was getting, but why didn't that play out in what she found herself settling for time and time again? The mystery of herself was the greatest thing she had to solve before she moved further.

Now that she had made the decision to declare a "man fast" and work on herself, she felt more ready to face her friends from a position of strength versus weakness. Being vulnerable to their opinions with no ready defense was a thought she couldn't bear in anticipation of criticism. Crossing the street, mincing through the slush, she wondered to herself why the month of March was always so unmerciful, as if giving the city a final beating before spring came to make everyone appreciate it more. This was the only time she questioned her choice of making her home in the Windy City, labeled so for the long-winded politicians as opposed to the commonly assumed reason of the blistering gusts it was also known for. But then summer would come with its hot balmy nights and endless procession of activities and festivities to remind her why she was here. She pulled her coat closer to shut out the cold that actually seemed to come from within rather than without and turned into the restaurant.

She checked her reflection in the glass door, determining she didn't look any worse for wear. Tilting her chin up as if to call her psyche and the rest of her body into alignment, she wove her way through the room in search of her friends.

The closer to the table she got the more vulnerable she felt. By the time she reached the table and sat in her chair she completely unraveled before she could even squeeze out a hello. Finally lifting a tearstained face from her hands she gazed into their faces. Adrian's beautiful, caramel-colored oval was filled with gentle concern. She reached out a hand to place on top of Tracy's and held it silently. Felicia's gray eyes were misty with empathy, soft lips parted as if waiting for an invitation to say something, anything that would soothe her cousin's pain. It was Muriel who caused her to snap out of her momentary lapse. Lips pursed, eyebrow arched, she was already angry.

"What did he do this time? No!" She held up a hand. "Let me guess. Another woman, right?"

Tracy wondered how she always knew. It also made her wonder if her girlfriend had passed by the restaurant where she had seen Evan before she did. Nah, she wasn't being clairvoyant or privy to information. She was just being her usual ornery self and assuming the worst of men.

"I remember once…" Tracy rolled her eyes heavenward as Felicia pitched in.

"Felicia." Muriel's voice should have been enough to silence her. "This is not about you right now, okay?"

"Okay." Felicia, rendered silent, waited for Tracy to say something.

After a long silence that seemed interminable for all of those waiting to hear what she had to say, Tracy drew a long shaky breath. "You know

I am not even going to dignify what I just witnessed with a long, drawn-out conversation. Suffice it to say Evan and I are finished. And I am finished for that matter."

"Why? Did something happen at work too?" Felicia looked worried again.

"Nope. That seems to be the only area of my life that I can get right. I am taking myself off the market. I am officially finished with men for a while."

"What are you going to do?" Felicia looked truly perplexed now. Then suddenly a new dawning came across her face and she sucked in her breath. "You're not going to be a lesbian are you?"

"No! Felicia, where do you get this stuff from? You've been watching too much *Sex and the City*. I keep telling you that show will mess up your brain. I'm merely taking a vacation to figure out where I keep going wrong. Declaring a 'man fast,' so to speak."

"Thank you, Jesus!" Muriel raised her hands into the air as if in the middle of a Pentecostal meeting.

"You think that's really necessary?" It was Adrian's turn to frown with concern.

"Please don't dissuade her from the first good choice she's made on the man issue in…I don't know when. Of course it's necessary!" Muriel seemed truly annoyed by Adrian's question.

"Thank you for your support." Tracy was quickly shifting from sad to irritated. She decided discussing this might not be the best idea, especially since she was still processing the decision herself. Nope. She did not need help from the peanut gallery right now. She might be fasting from men, but she was certainly not fasting from food. She turned her attention from her heart to her stomach. "So! Let's talk about something else more pleasant—like what we're eating tonight." And with that she placed the menu in front of her like a shield, warding off further opinions or questions, though she was highly aware of them all watching her. Muriel arched a brow but said nothing. Adrian studied her quietly. Felicia bit her lip and watched. *It is going to be a long night if we continue down this track,* Tracy thought as she turned her attention back to the lines that blurred before her. Blinking to beat the threatening tears back into submission, she took a deep breath and voted for introducing a new subject. She took another deep breath and lowered her menu. "So guess who I met in L.A. last week?"

Collectively the table let out a sigh of relief. Perhaps this could be a fun Friday night after all.

"Who?" A chorus of inquiry greeted Tracy's question.

"Gabriel Lawrence!"

As shrieks of delight went up from the table drawing attention from those nearby, Tracy launched into an animated delivery of her encounter with the famous movie star. *Distraction is good for the soul,* she thought. Gazing at the enraptured faces of her friends and cousin she felt back on her game. It was a bittersweet thing, her life. On one hand so successful, hobnobbing with the elite and such. From the outside looking in, anyone would have said she had the perfect life until they noticed the one missing piece. Though small in the scheme of things, it was conspicuous and she knew it because at the end of the day it was what mattered most to her. But for tonight she resolved not to go there. Doing her best Scarlett O'Hara imitation, she resolved to worry about her love life tomorrow. In the meantime, the night was young and she was a successful woman out with three of her favorite people. Tracy was back in charge, entertaining them with animated banter. If she had learned no other lessons in life, she had learned to revel in the moment at hand. And right now the jalapeño corn bread sitting in the middle of the table was calling her name. Tracy reached for the piece screaming the loudest, popped it into her mouth, and closed her eyes, letting the flavor of it fill her with pleasure. Sometimes food could be better than a man and far more available.

"Hey, you know where we have to go for lunch next? To that new place down in the South Loop…man…I can't think of the name of it," Muriel said.

"You mean 'Man Eaters'?" Tracy seemed amused.

"Yeah! They say the food is off the chain."

"It better be with a name like that!"

"Must be owned by a sister." This got a chortle out of Felicia.

"Truly a woman scorned, and I can relate."

"She sounds bitter…" Adrian didn't seem too convinced that this was healthy.

"If it makes for good food, who cares?" Tracy claimed.

This silenced Adrian though the look on her face said she was a little worried about Tracy right now.

Oh well, Tracy thought. *I can forgive Adrian for not being able to relate. After all, she has the perfect life. Beautiful home, successful, hand-some husband, designer clothes, it's all so perfect…and so perfectly out of reach for me right now.* She focused on what she could have—another bite of pleasure, short-lived but comforting for now. *If only life was a menu and you could pick what you wanted and have it served to you for a price. I'll have one good man with lots of love and faithfulness heaped on top, please!* It was a simple request, yet such a difficult order to fill. Could Adrian ever relate to that after getting married straight out of college and avoiding the entire marathon that the search for love could become? Probably not. Tracy sighed at the thought—a whole heart intact and never broken, now that was a revolutionary thought. *I wonder what that feels like?* she mused, searching Adrian's face for a clue. Finding none, she returned to burying her own pain beneath the bite of the jalapeños, turning her focus away from her emotions and on to her senses instead. She chewed slowly in an attempt to drag out dinner and the pleasure of having company as long as she could, putting off the inevitable—going home alone where the silence would tell her things she wasn't ready to hear.

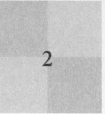

2

*F*elicia leaned forward, looking through the cab window. "You can slow down here." Her voice evaporated as her gaze swept up the building, doing the math until she calculated that she was looking at his floor. *No lights. Hmm, he still isn't home. Where can he be?* Tracy's situation had made her nervous. Even though Felicia didn't have a date with Kenny tonight in lieu of the girls, she hadn't heard from him all day either. Whenever she questioned him on his reluctance to check in, he seemed as clueless to the purpose of doing so as she did about why he wouldn't. He said she was insecure. She couldn't argue about that but, then again, he did nothing to make her feel secure either. So here she was like a silly schoolgirl skulking around in the dark for evidence of what she didn't know.

She rationalized to herself that his place was on her way home… well, almost. That really depended on one's sense of direction. Now that she was here, she didn't know what to do. Should she go and ask the doorman if Kenny was home? If he was, then what? She couldn't stop by unannounced and say she was just passing through the neighborhood. *This was a bad idea. What was I thinking?* She settled back into the seat, turning to the driver who was awaiting his next cue. "This the place, lady?"

"Um, actually I need to go back to Astor Street."

"Astor Street? But we just came from that way."

She couldn't tell if he was irritated or suspicious.

"Yes, and we are going back to Astor Street—1444 to be exact."

Whatever happened to "the customer is always right"? she thought. The driver muttered something under his breath and eased back out of the driveway. Out the corner of her eye she saw him slowly walking toward the building. "Wait!" she said a bit too loudly. The driver slammed on the brakes. "Make up your mind, lady! Are you staying or going?"

"Staying," she said. Fishing money out of her pocket she threw him a $20 even though the fare was half that and bolted from the cab. "Kenny!" He stopped in his tracks. She slowed herself in an effort to stop her heart from beating so fast. Good! He was alone. "Hey, you look tired."

"Hey, yourself. I am tired. What are you doing here?" His question had an underlying current of irritation that prickled Felicia's skin.

"Actually I was just passing by."

"Really? Where were you coming from?" He watched her face carefully.

Felicia's mind raced. There were tons of wonderful restaurants in the chic Lincoln Park neighborhood where he lived, but now the names of them all escaped her. Besides, she was already beginning to feel silly for allowing her paranoia to rise to such an escalated level that she had abandoned all reasonable facades of coolness and stooped to the desperation of stalking her absentee boyfriend. *Shoot, if this is my man, why do I have to have any reason for coming by his house, even if I didn't call first?* No, that was a lie. She had called and there had been no answer. She finally opted for honesty. Putting her arms around his neck and pulling him closer to her she whispered, "I missed hearing from you today, and I just wanted to see you so I decided to take a chance and..."

"Check on me?" His jaw tightened.

"No! I mean, well where were you? You didn't call me all day or the day before, for that matter. Kenny, what is with you?"

"What is with you, Felicia? I've been working. Isn't that what all you women want—a BMW, as you call it?" Oh now he had really stooped low, calling up the acronym for black man working. Only a guilty man could be so defensive. Felicia narrowed her eyes.

"Kenny, are you seeing someone else?"

"I said I was working!"

"Oh, don't play me. You're a plastic surgeon. Don't tell me the beauty business keeps you out this late at night unless you're having a late-night consultation, hmm?"

"I'm not even going to dignify that with an answer. We will discuss this when you're more rational!"

"So now I'm crazy?"

"If the shoe fits! You're the one standing on the sidewalk in the freezing cold hollering about what you don't know. So I'm going to help you out. I'm going home. Right after I get you a cab so you can go home."

"You're sending me home?"

"Yes, I am." His words were deliberate. His hand felt like steel closing forcefully around her arm as he steered her toward the street while hailing a cab with the other arm. Depositing her inside, slamming the door, and handing the driver cash, he curtly instructed him: "1444 Astor Street."

"I'm grown, Kenny Sample." It sounded stupid even to her, but she couldn't help herself.

"Then act like it. Go home, Felicia. I'll talk with you tomorrow."

"But…"

He was already gone, taking long, angry strides toward the lobby of his building. Embarrassed and suddenly freezing, she settled into the backseat of the cab, avoiding the gaze of the driver studying her in the rearview mirror. "Take Lake Shore Drive." She needed to avoid the darkness of the park now shrouded by night. Besides, water always made her feel better.

The lake glistened silver as they sped down the drive and back toward the Gold Coast. She chuckled to herself. *I am grown.* It was kind of an ironically funny comment. Here she was going home to the condo her parents had deposited her in on the terms that if she did well in college it would be hers. A reward for not embarrassing them, she was sure. Somewhere in the back of her mind she knew the address was probably more for them than it was for her. After all, their daughter couldn't live just anywhere. The address always raised eyebrows when meeting new suitors and giving it for the first time, and she got a special satisfaction from the knowledge that her "high cotton" address was the best possible screen she could have for romantic applicants. They knew they had to be about something or they could keep right on stepping. Well, Kenny had stopped because he was all that and a bag of chips. Fine, successful, his own man, he hadn't even blinked when she gave him her address. That was one of the things she liked about him. She had truly met her match. But the thing she liked about him was also the thing that kept her off guard and insecure. He seemed oblivious to his effect on her, growing impatient anytime she resorted to what he termed "needy" behavior. He distanced himself every time she was guilty of simply responding the only way she knew how to.

How do you stop needing what you need? Felicia hadn't been able to solve this mystery. And for this she was treated like a truant child at the ripe old age of thirty four. The wind gusting off the lake whistled around the cab with a ferocity that literally shook it. No wonder they called the Chicago wind "the Hawk." It definitely had a bite to it. The rushing wind gave way to quiet as they pulled off the expressway and turned onto the tree-lined street. All of a sudden she felt very old, very tired, and over-whelmingly alone. Why did everyone she reached out to shrink back as if she were some sort of undesirable insect? Flinching against the cold, she walked blindly toward the lobby of her building. Nodding absent-mindedly to the doorman, she voted for making a hasty escape to the elevator before he tried to engage her in late-night conversation. Tonight was not the night for light talk.

Letting herself into the dark apartment, she almost tripped over the box that had been placed inside her door. Flipping on the light, she pursed her lips as she recognized her mother's signature return label. She stepped over it, leaving it in the middle of the hallway, unwilling to deal with yet another thing that would cause her pain in the same evening. *One stab at a time,* she thought to herself. She considered going to bed without washing her face but thought better of it.

Cleansing the Kohl lining from around her eyes now suspiciously bright, she heaved a heavy sigh. *Love, that's all I want. Is it too much to ask?* But perhaps the better question was why did she want something that seemed to hurt so much? She had the feeling this puzzle would not be solved anytime soon. Sliding in between her sheets and under her down comforter, she fell back into a subconscious habit that always surfaced when she was feeling overly vulnerable. Clutching a corner of her pillow, she tucked her thumb into her mouth and began gently sucking until sleep claimed her in the embrace she had longed for all evening.

3

drian let herself in quietly, hoping not to disturb Ron. She shivered. The house felt cold. Or was she sensing something in the atmosphere? "Ron?" He didn't answer. The house was dark, yet she knew he was there. Moving toward the bedroom, she followed the sound of running water. *He must be in the shower.* She frowned. *Is he just getting home?* The water stopped as she entered the bedroom. Soft music was wafting from the small Bose stereo on Ron's nightstand, and he was humming to himself. She watched him through the open bathroom door as he wrapped a towel around his midsection, completely lost in his thoughts and the music. He sure was fine. As a matter of fact, he was finer than when she first met him on campus strutting around just as sure of himself then as he was now. Mahogany colored with a body that shouted he paid attention to it, the man was cut in all the right places. His pretty, even, white teeth lit up the room when he smiled. Confidence exuded from him in a nonchalant but "of course" sort of way. It was what had attracted her to him in college. He knew where he was going; he was in control. She had known he would be successful at whatever he chose to do. Her perfect fantasy of the man she would marry, he had made her feel safe. Adrian's heart beat just as fast now as it did the first day he gave her that look. That look that said he wanted her.

"Ron? Didn't you hear me calling you?" He turned toward her, but his eyes were distant.

"Oh hey, baby. I didn't hear you come in. How was Bible class?" he asked, stepping close to her as he grabbed a second towel.

"I wasn't at Bible class. I was out with the girls, remember?" Taking the towel from him to finish drying his back, one of her favorite things to do, she took in his scent. Running a finger down the side of his neck, she wondered why he couldn't keep her schedule straight. Why he always assumed her absence in the evening meant she could only be one place. She wasn't sure if that was his resentment speaking or if he was just distracted by his own affairs. Tonight she wouldn't linger there. She felt especially vulnerable in light of Tracy's situation. Over the years she had witnessed all the changes Felicia and Tracy went through over men, and each new drama made her even more thankful that she was not out on the block shopping for love. She already had a man, even though her man had been moody lately.

Tonight he tensed under her hands instead of welcoming her touch. Slowly stepping away from her, he took the towel, kissed her on the forehead, and headed back toward the bathroom. Adrian hesitated for a moment, wondering why he had distanced himself, but relaxed again as his voice came out of the bathroom.

"Oh? Where did you go?"

"Banderas," she answered, wondering why she felt strange. "They have jazz in the evening, and the food is really good."

"Yeah, I know. The barbeque there is serious."

"I didn't know you had been there." She still hadn't moved.

"I took the boys there when they were in town." That explained it.

"The boys" were some of the athletes Ron represented. He knew she detested sitting around with them listening to their coarse conversations about their latest exploits off the court or the field. So she and Ron had come to an understanding. She would go to Bible class alone, and he would entertain his boys alone.

He was looking at her. "I said, What did you eat?"

"Oh, the salmon. It was perfect." She wondered how long her mind had been wandering after he'd asked her the question. Now he stood before her in his customary pajama pants. Bare chest inviting her in even though he didn't. He yawned, moving past her.

"Whew, I am beat. Long day."

He said that a lot lately. Ron blamed it on difficult negotiations and players' tempers flaring, but he had endured that before without shutting her out. Again she shook off the feelings that she couldn't quite put her finger on. Gently she put her hands on his waist and steered him toward the bed.

"Why don't you just lay your body down and get some rest then." She kissed the small of his back. Again she felt the distance. "I'm going to go and take a shower, alright?" She didn't know why she was asking or even what she was asking. Was it alright for her to take a shower? Was he alright? Were they alright? The question hung in the air pregnant with possibilities. Finally he breathed, "Alright, I'll be right here." Leaning back against the headboard she could feel him watching her head toward the bathroom with detached interest.

In the safety of the shower, her mind could finally try to sort out what she was feeling. She let the water run as hot as she could stand it, as if the fiery prickles against her skin from the jets would wake her up to some profound revelation of exactly what was going on with Ron. Obviously he didn't plan to tell her whatever it was, and she felt it was her duty as a good wife to figure it out and solve the problem, whatever it may be. He'd had problems before, but they had solved them together. This was different. She felt as if she were outside looking in, a helpless spectator—except she wasn't because what affected him affected her. And right now she was feeling the full effects. There was a time when he couldn't keep his hands off of her, but lately… Though she understood no married couple could be passionate all the time, she missed his arms, his touch, the conspiratorial conversations they used to have. Now he seemed lost in his own thoughts more than he was present with her.

Adrian felt as if he was on the other side of a bridge she couldn't get across. Worse still, she couldn't quite trace when the great divide had occurred. Why she hadn't been aware, why she hadn't been watching, she couldn't say. Perhaps she never expected to be in this place. Exactly what place it was, she wasn't quite sure. Reluctantly shutting off the water, she stepped out of the shower, allowing her toes to burrow deep into the plush rug that greeted her feet. It felt so welcoming.

"I thought you were trying to go for prune status in there." Ron's sleepy voice floated toward her through the steam that was dissipating.

"Sometimes a sister just has to indulge."

"Indulge on, lady. I'm going to sleep."

"I'll be out in a minute."

By the time she had completed her toilette, lotion, potions, and all, Ron was asleep, already breathing deeply. Music was still playing. "Your body's here with me, but your mind is on the other side of town…" The words seemed to jump off the music track. She leaned over to turn the radio off. The phone rang. Ron shifted then lifted his head from the pillow, but she already had the receiver in her hand, wondering who would be calling this time of night.

"Is Ron there?"

"Excuse me?" Adrian was taken aback by a woman's voice on the other end of the line.

"Is Ron there?" Her voice was insistent.

"Who may I say is calling?"

"Amber, his assistant."

"Hold on one moment." Feeling relieved, she answered Ron's unspoken question. "It's Amber."

"Hello." He didn't seem pleased. After a beat, "That can wait until tomorrow." Another beat. "I'll take care of it." He hung up the phone without another word.

"Emergency?" Adrian asked as she settled between the sheets. Amber had never called the house before.

"Not in my opinion." Adrian got the feeling the subject was closed. Sliding closer to him, she laid her hand on his shoulder and lingered there, but it did not give in to her touch. She opened her mouth to say something but nothing came out. Her internal questions were greeted by the sound of his soft snoring. Rolling onto her back, gazing at the ceiling, still trying to make sense of the silence, her thoughts shifted to her friends. These were things she couldn't share with them. They simply wouldn't get it. How you could not be alone but still feel alone. She tried to push down the fear that was threatening to rise. *False evidence appearing real. That's what fear is.* But tonight her gut instincts pushed off the saying as a clever cliché. Something was wrong, and she knew it. Only time would tell if it was something she could fix. She glanced at Ron sleeping soundly beside her, apparently unmoved by whatever made Amber feel the need to call the house at eleven thirty at night.

"Ron..." Adrian whispered. He didn't answer.

She sighed. The greatest irony about having a man that Tracy and Felicia would never understand is how you could still feel as if you had no man at all.

4

Dear Diary,
  I just want someone to love me
      softly,
    fiercely,
  passionately,
      unconditionally
    I want to be loved in ways I can't describe
        unspeakable wishes filling my soul
  leaving my flesh
      yearning for a touch
          so deep
          so profound
          so warm
      so consuming
          I'm left breathless by the thought...
      my soul searches my heart's hidden crevices
  looking for love
perhaps misplaced
      jumping with hope at the shadows

of unrequited loves...
     reaching for arms that elude me
grasping at unfilled promises
     I grow weary in my search
wondering at the difficulty
     of such a simple wish...
I want someone to love me
     to make me giggle at nothing
to make me feel uncommonly beautiful
     to make me embrace the air just because
          just because
     I am loved...
          from the top of my head
               to the tips of my toes
                    inside and out
               gently
                    possessively
          indescribably
     totally...
          totally loved...

The words floated like luscious whispers through the remaining precious moments of sleep. The last wishes recorded before retiring for the night were the first to greet Tracy as she clung to the final seconds of warmth beneath her favorite comforter. All too soon the clock radio alarm would ring and reality would be there to greet her much earlier than she wished. Sure enough, the quiet was rudely interrupted by the crisp, studied voice of Stephanie Bee, WGNN's favorite news darling. "With the latest ratio of women to men in Washington D.C. being thirteen to one, one may wonder where do you go to find an eligible man? Well, the latest statistics indicate the top places to find eligible men are China, Alaska, and Utah, where mail order brides are back in fashion..."

Tracy's slow, raised, carefully arched brow interrupted the serene look of leftover dreams that had made her look so innocent moments before. Resentful hazel eyes glared at the radio. Reluctantly easing herself from the bed, she wondered whose brilliant idea it was to introduce such depressing news first thing in the morning. *Couldn't they save that kind of stuff for drive time in the evening when everyone was disgusted after a hard day's work anyway?* At least that way it could just mingle in with all the rest of the bad feelings accumulated throughout the day. This way...well, this will follow every lonely woman who heard the report throughout the day. It will color their every thought. Every time they encounter an undesirable single man and a desirable married man, they will be forced to reflect on these statistics and become even more depressed about their present single state.

Stephanie Bee's voice sounded as cold as the linoleum floor Tracy minced across. She wondered if she was recoiling from the floor or the unwelcome news that her fate as a single woman was sealed unless she moved to China, Alaska, or Utah. As she studied her chestnut-brown face in the mirror and distractedly reached for her toothbrush, a flurry of questions filled her mind. Did Asian men even like black women? And wasn't Utah where some racist Aryan nation people were hanging out? And if she could barely make it through a Chicago winter, how would she ever survive in Alaska?

Hoping the pulsating streams of water would help her snap out of her state of mind, she lingered extra long in the shower, letting the water massage her well-toned limbs. Still smarting from yesterday's workout, she felt entitled to a few more minutes of self-indulgence in light of this morning's report. *What is all the hard work for, after all is said and done?*

She sighed, trying to blow away the thought. Reluctantly leaving the warmth of the steamy cubicle, she speculated on what Muriel's reaction to this news would be. Since she was running late and knew she could count on Muriel to share a cab, she'd find out soon enough.

Out of second nature she punched the numbers as she reached for her favorite suit. "Hey, it's me. Wanna split a cab? I'm leaving in 15 minutes. Be on the corner." Muriel was her best bud, though nobody understood their friendship except them. As different as a circle is from a square, only they understood they somehow balanced one another between their differences in a way that fed them both. As Tracy brushed the last strands of her hair into place, she wished she could be as matter of fact about the subject of men as Muriel was. She chuckled under her breath. *That Muriel is one tough cookie.* Muriel thought she was too soft, too nice when it came to men. But Tracy believed under that strong exterior beat the heart of a pussycat who wanted love just as much as the next woman. Why she was unable to admit it remained Muriel's secret.

As the cab approached the corner, Tracy could see Muriel waiting, tall and striking, completely oblivious to the man who was openly admiring her. He leaped to open the door as she reached for the handle. In one single glide she slipped onto the seat beside Tracy without a backward glance at her admirer.

"You could've said thank you. Is that how your mother taught you to behave, young lady?" Tracy teased.

"Girl, puh-leeze. That's why I don't do buses. It's bad enough I have to get up in the morning to go to work. Can I get there in peace without some knucklehead hitting on me is all I ask. Especially before I have my coffee."

That was Muriel. Straight to the point. Tracy looked at her in total amusement. "At least they let you know you're still cute."

"Well, if that's what you need, go for it, but it doesn't pay my rent," Muriel said as impatiently as if the man was still in pursuit. Just as quickly her mood shifted and she flashed a brilliant smile. "So what's up, girlfriend! It's not like you to splurge on a cab at the beginning of the week. Are we celebrating something?"

It took Tracy a moment to recover from the sudden change in attitude. Muriel could change like the wind, this she knew, but she never got used to it. And her disdain for men disturbed Tracy even more. She wondered what was really at the root of it, but knew that was forbidden territory. "Nope, I just felt entitled to a small indulgence. I needed to fluff myself back up after listening to the news this morning."

"What news?" Muriel asked with a slight frown on her face, preparing to worry over whatever Tracy was about to relate.

"If I want to get married, I have to move to China, Alaska, or Utah."

"What!" Muriel exclaimed. She looked confused.

"Didn't you listen to the news this morning? According to the latest statistics, the only places that have eligible men left are China, Alaska, and Utah...unless you're looking for a man 65 or over, then you can go to Nevada. Think about it, Muriel. This does not bode well for a black woman in America."

"Chil', get a life! You had me thinking something was seriously wrong. Obviously you have way too much time on your hands. You couldn't possibly be upset over some numbers somebody probably made up. Children are starving in Ethiopia!" The look of confusion had quickly been replaced with high-level irritation, as if she couldn't decide if she should give Tracy a comforting pat or knock her across the head for causing her alarm. "You need to relax. God knows where you live. You better enjoy yourself while you have the freedom. Shoot, a man can make you miserable whether you have one or not. First, you spend all your time being upset about not having a man, and then you finally get one and spend all your time being upset because you can't figure him out. What did he mean when he said this or did that. Puh-leeze! I haven't got time for the pain. And besides, you're on a man fast remember? So what do you care?"

"Just because I'm on a fast doesn't mean I'm going to be on one forever. And what will be left by the time I'm done, depending on how long I choose to opt out of the love game? Eww, that's scary, hold that thought."

Tracy had been secretly hoping someone would try to talk her out of her self-imposed fast. Now with Muriel solidifying her commitment, she decided she didn't want to set Muriel off on another roll. She was relieved to see her office building looming in the near distance—a welcome escape from what could be a lengthy lecture if there was time. As Muriel took a breath in preparation for another sermonette, Tracy chose that moment as a window of opportunity to change the subject. "Don't forget we still have to decide what we're going to do for Adrian's birthday."

Muriel got the hint. "Oh, okay. Don't worry about it. I got this one," she said as Tracy dug in her purse for her portion of the cab fare.

"You sure?" Tracy knew Muriel was uncomfortable with any open display of gratitude.

"Yeah, yeah, get out of here, and try to have a nice day. Even if you don't have a man."

"Ha, ha." Tracy tried to sound as if she was not amused.

And to be perfectly honest, part of her was not. The other part of her just chalked it up to Muriel's sarcastic wit that usually tickled her funny bone. But not today. As the cab pulled off, Tracy watched Muriel settle back into her seat and wondered if she could really be that satisfied with her self-appointed isolation. Why was she so adamantly opposed to the idea that having a relationship could actually add something to her life? *Well, if Muriel feels free enough to belittle my serious heartfelt desires, I'm entitled to a few answers myself.* Tracy decided it was definitely time for a deep discussion whether Muriel liked it or not...soon, really soon.

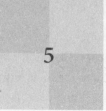

5

nd then he had the nerve to tell me that he had called but no one answered the phone. He lies so much! But he's so fine, I didn't have the heart to tell him I have caller ID." Adrian's face was the expression of complete attentiveness as Felicia related her latest male tragedy over lunch. Two weeks had passed, and everyone knew and understood that Tracy's personal business was off limits, which gave Felicia free rein to torture them with hers. Tracy felt the uncontrollable urge to laugh. Instead, she took another bite of her sandwich and wondered if she wasn't feeling slightly hysterical since mulling over the whole male issue all morning. It figures. She would get an assignment for a men's cologne now that she was feeling so vulnerable. In the past when she felt like this she always fooled herself into thinking that one of the male models or actors she met while producing an advertising campaign could actually be serious in his flirtation. After many intriguing but short-lived relationships, she had learned to leave these gorgeous smooth-talking men where she found them. Felicia, on the other hand, had not. So here they were at lunch listening to yet another tale with a predictable ending.

Again Tracy stifled the impulse to break into peals of laughter. Muriel would really have had a fit if she were here. She didn't have much patience with Felicia. She could hear her now, "Felicia is pretty, but silly. And all that amounts to in my book is pretty silly." No way would she subject herself to an entire lunch of listening to Felicia's foolish speculations about what was absurdly obvious. She had chosen to invest her heart into yet another venture that wasn't worth a dime. But Adrian was the epitome of loving patience. She was the only person Tracy knew who could listen to an entire conversation as ridiculous and pointless as this one and not, at least not seemingly so, have a judgmental bone in her body. Maybe that's why everybody ran to her with their problems. There she would sit with that calming, serene look on her pretty face while you spilled your guts endlessly. No matter how silly or horrendous the situation, you would be comforted by the nearness and the listening ear of Adrian who, interestingly enough, never seemed to have any problems of her own. Yup, definitely, Adrian was who you went to when you wanted to feel better. Muriel was who you went to when you wanted to be beat up with the truth.

As Adrian patted Felicia's hand and reassured her that any man in his right mind would want a woman like her, Tracy imagined what Muriel would say. "Girlfriend, get a grip! Who needs that kind of aggravation? Get rid of him; he's not serious."

"Tracy, what do you think?" Felicia interrupted her daydream.

"Hmm?" Tracy tried to react as if she had really been listening.

"Where were you? You're not listening! I said I think I'll try white men next. What do you think?"

Tracy looked at her as if she had just announced she was going to dye her hair chartreuse. "Felicia, you talk as if men are pieces of candy and you've decided to try a new flavor of the month."

"I didn't think of it that way, but I guess that's a good way to put it. After all, I would be switching from chocolate to vanilla." Felicia giggled at the thought, completely amused with herself.

"Why not try a Latin lover when you're in the mood for caramel," Tracy sarcastically answered, quite surprised to find herself sounding like Muriel.

"Hey! That's a good suggestion...and they are fine!"

Suddenly Tracy felt quite tired, "Felicia, do you think you could survive for one week without a man in your life?" She knew the answer would be negative before Felicia could even fix her lips to reply. Felicia had practically hyperventilated after she found out that Tracy was dating David St. Jacques. "You are not going out with that man who plays Blake Devaughn on *The Idle Rich!*" she had squealed. "Every black woman in America, well, actually any woman with eyeballs, would die to have him!" Well, Tracy had him. So did his wife, she'd just found out. Felicia's response to Tracy's state of mortified distress was to bat her eyelashes, clutch her chest, and plead, "We are talking about David St. Jacques here. This is not your average man! Just calm down, wait a minute, and see how the whole thing plays out." Tracy couldn't believe her ears. "Hello! We are discussing a married man here, Felicia. Are you trying to tell me that you believe, no matter what is going on, that something is better than nothing?"

"In this case…yes!" On that note, Tracy was too through to argue any further. Certainly she and Felicia were at odds when it came to their philosophies on men and what was acceptable behavior. Though this man fast was already proving more difficult than she had anticipated, Tracy still refused to settle for accepting bad behavior from her suitors out of desperation like Felicia did, no matter how badly she wanted a man. She never realized how much having a man—any man—in her life did for her personal validation level. Right now she was feeling pretty naked, which was not cute in the middle of spring…which was always still winter in Chicago.

But Tracy also knew that regardless of what Felicia said, she also had her boundaries. If the man wasn't good looking and loaded, he could just keep on goin' 'cause girlfriend wasn't going to give him the time of day, even if it was illuminated on her wrist. "Well, if a man is going to give you grief and aggravation, you could just as well enjoy looking at him and eat well while you're going through changes," was how she so succinctly summed it up.

"You know, Felicia, the kind of white man you would want is a tad beyond your reach," Tracy said in the most blasé attitude she could muster while feeling truly irritated.

"What do you mean?" Felicia drew her eyebrows together and down in a two-part motion.

It's amazing how she does that, Tracy thought to herself, almost allowing herself to be distracted by this oddity. But she continued, "Well, whereas a lot of successful black men feel marrying or having a white woman is an additional trophy on their list of accomplishments, in my experience, good-looking, successful, white men don't find it appropriate to marry black women. It's only chic to date them. You know, kinda like driving a Ferrari for sport and then keeping a Mercedes or a BMW for practical purposes."

"Oh puh-leeze, Tracy, that really is a stretch. I should have expected that from you, Little Miss Afrocentric USA. If you don't approve of interracial relationships, just say so." Felicia heaved a sigh as if resigning herself to complete idiocy.

"That's not where I was going, but, okay...you tell me. Give me a list of successful white men married to black women," Tracy confidently shot back without flinching.

"How about the Seagrams heir!" Felicia victoriously parried.

"Divorced. Didn't you read the latest *Time* magazine...or was it *Newsweek?* I can't remember which. But anyway, they explained away his little faux pas by saying he was young, foolish, and in rebellion against his father. He has since come to his senses, don't you know, and is presently settling down with a politically acceptable blonde number. The end. Anyone else on your list, hmm?" Tracy asked, with just a little too much syrup in her voice.

She knew Felicia hated to be outdone, and it was obvious she really couldn't think of anyone else. Suddenly her face brightened. "There's always Europe. Europeans lo-o-ove black women."

"Yeah, and old, cold apartments and rough toilet paper."

"Oh, Tracy, you do know how to find the silver lining in everything." Felicia matched sarcasm for sarcasm. Felicia skipped a beat as if something had suddenly occurred to her. "Could it be that you are just a tad bitter?"

"Bitter? Why would I be bitter?" Tracy had no idea where Felicia was going with this.

"Well, I just thought with Evan playing around on you with a white woman that's why it was such a touchy subject for you…"

Tracy felt the blood leave all working parts of her body. She shivered. "What are you talking about, Felicia?"

"I saw him. I saw him with her the other day getting out of a cab in front of Water Tower Place." She frowned. "You do realize the woman is white and not a light Beyoncé-look-alike, don't you? Why didn't you tell us?"

Tracy was watching Felicia's mouth moving, but her mind went back to the last time she had seen Evan. The lighting in the restaurant had been dim. Perhaps the thought that he had been out with anyone at all had distracted her from a taking a closer look at the woman whom she had assumed was simply a fair sister. Perhaps it hadn't computed because it had not entered the realm of possibility in her mind. This took Evan's betrayal to another level, and she wasn't quite sure she had recovered from the first. She opened her mouth, then closed it, preferring to say nothing rather than dig a deeper hole for herself. She felt seriously close to having another meltdown and was determined not to.

"Perhaps her being the other woman was the bigger issue at the time. I prefer not to waste any more breath on Evan. I believe we were talking about you." Tracy's eyes narrowed and she spoke through clenched jaws, trying to contain herself, feeling like a fool for being caught too off guard to have a good comeback. She hoped Felicia would get the hint and move on. She exhaled when she did.

"Adrian, you haven't said a word. What do you think?" Both faces turned toward Adrian.

"Well," Adrian breathed, "I think God has someone very special for both of you, and if the relationship you're in doesn't work out then the guy simply isn't ready for the gift that you are."

"I knew you were going to say that," Felicia moaned.

"The serene words of a happily married woman," Tracy added.

"I just feel that both of you have so much going for you right now that you should spend more time appreciating it instead of worrying about what will eventually work itself out at the right time," Adrian said almost apologetically.

This conversation would have had Muriel champing at the bit to scream, "Good grief! Get over it! Get a life!"—her favorite mantra for anything she termed frivolous or a waste of breath or time. Muriel was not the biblical description of patience. But there Adrian sat. As patient as ever. They could have been talking about how to grow geraniums. Her demeanor remained the same. Calm, sweet, and gentle.

But then again, Adrian had everything that she and Felicia wanted. She hadn't been able to have children yet, but she took that in stride and left that to God as she put it. The only time Tracy had ever seen a dark cloud over Adrian's face was when she expressed sadness over her husband's lack of interest in the "things of God"—whatever that meant. Other than that, Adrian seemed to live the perfect existence. Small wonder she could so calmly assess their situations and come to such a simple conclusion.

"That's easy for you to say, you already have somebody." It seemed as if Felicia had read Tracy's mind.

"Yes, that's true. But I don't have a glamorous career—running around, traveling, and buying beautiful things with other people's money—like you. Maybe that's something I would like to do. But I have a husband to take care of."

"Who says you can't have both?" Felicia and Tracy actually had a meeting of the minds in stereo. That was scary.

"Oh you can," Adrian answered, totally unruffled by their response. "I made the choice to stay at home. All I'm saying is that neither one of you have lives to sneeze at. Tracy, you get to travel and meet all kinds of interesting people, and so do you, Felicia. You both like what you do. It takes up a lot of your time. Relationships take a lot of time and work to keep them going. I don't see either one of you slowing down soon, so where does a man fit in?"

Tracy thought she had a point. It seemed Felicia did not.

"Do you think I run all over high heaven killing myself on my job because I want to? Shoot, I do this 'cause it's necessary. I have a high standard of living to maintain. If I don't have a man to provide for me, then I have to get it for myself. I can't help it if he has the nerve to be intimidated by the time he shows up because I bought a mink coat on my own, now can I?"

Tracy was getting a little disturbed. She was beginning to agree with Felicia a little too much for comfort. What did this mean? Could they actually have something in common? No, she wasn't going to allow herself to go there. *Come back, Tracy, come back!* she said to herself. *We just happen to be two single women who relate on this one point.*

"That's not what I was saying…" Adrian managed to interject, but Felicia was off and running. "I get so sick of men coppin' out on the 'I can't hang, she's high maintenance trip.' Be for real. Do they really expect us to sit on our behinds, be poverty stricken, and sheltered from glamorous experiences until they show up? Wazzup wid dat?"

Ooh, this is getting exciting! thought Tracy. Felicia was so upset she had dropped the carefully cultivated proper facade she presented to her clients and most of the world and reverted all the way back to her roots. Her sister girl 'tude had surfaced big time.

Yup, first the language changes and then the neck starts movin.' *You go, girl!* Tracy cleared her throat and interrupted for Adrian's sake. She could have watched this all day. "Hey, sorry to crack your monologue, Felicia, but I have to get back to work. Adrian, I hope you won't take this tirade personally, but obviously this 'single thing' can be a sore spot." She leaned in closer in a conspiratorial whisper, "Especially during that certain time of the month…" and then in her best white girl imitation she added, "Bye, girls!" She couldn't wait to get out into the fresh air. She had held it together long enough; perhaps the frigid cold would slap some clarity into her system and settle her swirling thoughts. She went through the motions of her ritualistic goodbyes. For the first time as she bent to give Adrian a goodbye peck on the cheek she noticed an air of sadness in her eyes. It distracted her away from her own personal drama that was raging within. *Adrian has been extra quiet during lunch….Hmm, I wonder what that's all about?* she thought as she wove her way through the restaurant toward the door. *Maybe Adrian let Felicia get to her after all. But that isn't like her.* Tracy shook off the urge to start worrying as she crossed the street, getting caught up in the rhythm of her steps on the pavement, lost again in the details of Evan's betrayal.

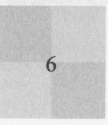

6

specially that certain time of the month." Felicia could still hear Tracy's words echoing in her brain as she stepped off the bus on her block. *The nerve of her!* she thought. *How could she be so smug? She certainly hasn't fared any better in the love department than I have!* As much as she knew Tracy would hate to admit it, they were in exactly the same place when it came down to men and the pursuit of happiness. "The type of white man you would want would be out of reach....You act as if men were pieces of candy...nyah, nyah, nyah." She caught herself screwing up her face in a childlike pout. Wait a minute! Why was she letting Tracy work her nerves? She was always like that, why should today be any different? Perhaps because those words had triggered a knot of uneasiness in the pit of Felicia's stomach that had grown to the size of a basketball since lunch.

Just as she was about to shoot back a smart answer to Tracy's PMS reference a little alarm had gone off in her head. With a slow dawning, Felicia realized she wasn't suffering from PMS. But that wasn't necessarily a good thing because she should have been. She had distractedly hugged Adrian goodbye and hightailed it back to her office to look at the calendar in her Daytimer. This caused her deeper distress. She was late. Very late. Three weeks late to be exact. How could she not have noticed? She was always like clockwork. *Okay, don't panic. It could be stress. Take a deep breath, and let's wait until we can get to an e.p.t. test,* she told all her quivering body parts.

The rest of the day was a fog. A flurry of color passed her unseen.

Her usual delight in touching, feeling, and smelling her selections before they were installed went unexperienced. Drapes were hung and carpeting put down before her very eyes, and she saw nothing. Moving on automatic, she was present only enough to confirm what she had already designed for the space and was grateful that an original thought was not required at this time because she had none. All she could think about was getting home to the safety of her own apartment. But first she had to stop at the drugstore. Though part of her mind tried to steer her to a place where she would be anonymous, habit drove her to her neighborhood place, still not wanting to believe what she was going to purchase. She avoided Mr. Webster's eyes as she placed her selections on the counter. His eyes seemed to pierce her accusingly as he put her things in a bag. Silently she grabbed the bag and headed through the door as if her heels were on fire.

She didn't even turn the light on as she headed through the entryway, stepping past the still unopened box her mother had sent her. She poured the contents of the bag into the bathroom sink. Deodorant, pantyhose, gum. All designed to distract Mr. Webster from noticing that she was purchasing a home pregnancy test. Fat chance he had missed that! Hurriedly reading the directions she proceeded. After going through the motions there was nothing left to do but wait. She lowered the toilet seat and sat, staring at the wand as if her gaze could will it to tell her something different from what she was feeling in her gut. She felt like she was in one of those TV commercials, except there was no smiling husband next to her waiting in hopeful anticipation. *Oh God, oh God!* she rolled her eyes to the ceiling. *I know I don't talk to you often, but if you get me out of this one I will. I promise.* She lowered her eyes to check the wand and expired into a horrified heap. *It is true. It really does turn blue if you are pregnant.* And she was pregnant.

She slowly opened one eye and peered at the wand again. Yup, it was still blue. *Why me? How could I have been so stupid? I don't have time for this! I'm booked to decorate people's houses for the rest of the year!* What was she thinking when she slept with Kenny without protection? What was she going to do now? Her thoughts tumbled over one another like a waterfall. She looked at herself in the mirror. Funny, she didn't look any different…same honey-colored complexion, same light ash-brown hair, same hazel eyes with green flecks that always got her into trouble with the opposite sex, and yet her life had been completely rearranged in exactly three minutes…well, not exactly.

Kenny! What am I going to tell Kenny? Absolutely nothing, she decided. He was a jerk. Tracy was right. She hated agreeing with Tracy. She couldn't understand how no matter what mistakes Tracy made in life she always came out smelling like a rose. All the way through school it had been this way. *I, on the other hand, always end up paying for the fun I have.* Tracy always warned her, she never listened, and then she plunged headlong into the consequences. *Tracy is gonna love this. It will give her the leverage she needs to show her mother that she is far more worthy of her attention than I, whom she dotes on, now that my foolishness has finally brought disgrace to our perfect little family.* Then there were her own parents. It didn't matter that she was grown and on her own; to their way of thinking everything she did was a reflection on them in the eyes of their society friends. Her father's quiet disapproval would strangle her slowly…if her mother didn't kill her first. Felicia wouldn't allow her thoughts to travel any further. The pressure was squeezing the air from her lungs. She held up the wand and shook it—as if that would make it change color…but nothing happened.

Sighing heavily, completely numb, she dragged through the hallway and plopped onto the bed like a rag doll. This had to be a very bad joke. So why did she feel like screaming instead of laughing? What was she going to do now? She had to talk to someone, but who? *I know—Adrian. She would be perfect. She won't recoil and treat me as if I were a roach that had crawled across her plate or something.* She dialed Adrian's number.

That's funny. No answer. That isn't like Adrian. Her machine is always on or someone usually answers. Oh well, maybe she and her husband are having a romantic evening and turned the phone off. How ironic, Felicia thought wryly.

Alright, I'll try Muriel. Somewhere in the midst of her blunt manner she knew she could at least count on some good advice. She gritted her teeth and dialed her number. "Hi, this is Muriel, you know what to do…" Yes, she did know what to do, but she was in no mood to leave a message. After all, what would she say? "Hi, Muriel, just calling to let you know I'm pregnant." That would go over big. No way was she leaving that message. It had taken all the nerve she had to dial Muriel's number in the first place. As far as she was concerned, you move, you lose. She had missed her big opportunity to be the first to give her a lecture.

It was a plot—a plot to make her call Tracy. She prepared herself to swallow a big "I told you so" with the tears she felt welling up inside and very slowly dialed her number. Her jaw dropped in dismay as a busy signal assaulted her ear. It actually sounded louder than usual. She muttered under her breath at Tracy and her refusal to get call waiting. Only Tracy would think it was inconsiderate to put someone on hold to see who was calling on the other line. There ought to be a law against single-line phones. What if someone had an emergency? Like me! She had never wanted to talk to Tracy so badly in all of her life. "Where is everyone when you need them?" she cried in exasperation. She put her hands over both ears as if attempting to shut out the sound of her world crashing down around her ears.

7

*A*drian stood rooted to the spot, looking through the note she was holding in her hands. The piece of paper that was now just a blur. Somewhere in the distance she could hear a phone ringing, but her legs felt like lead. She had no will within her to move. And so it rang and rang and rang. Finally it stopped, leaving an oppressive silence hanging in the air. She sighed as if trying to decide what to do with a demanding child and headed for the bedroom. She opened the closet. It was true. He was gone. Everything that once was evidence of his presence was gone except for the faint remains of his favorite cologne. She carefully hung her jacket on one of the hangers and set her purse in its customary spot. Always careful to keep everything in the proper place, that was Adrian. She woodenly went to the kitchen and began putting away the groceries she had picked up on her way home from Bible class. As she put water on to boil, she turned to see Coco and Merlot, her black Siamese cat and chocolate Labrador, staring at her from the kitchen door as if awaiting her reaction. Since she had not decided which way she should respond to the news, she had none.

Should I scream? Should I laugh? Should I cry? High emotionalism was not part of her nature. She could feel something rumbling inside her, but she was at a loss as to how to express it. Perhaps she was in shock. But she couldn't honestly say she was surprised. Five years had passed since that moment she had hurried home from church to tell Ron about her new faith in Christ. She had felt the chasm begin to grow between them, though she tried to ignore it at first. And even though he said he respected her beliefs as long as she didn't try to push them on him, he seemed more aggravated over her compliance to his wishes. Every time he caught her praying or saw the glow of refreshment on her face after a church service, the gulf between them grew wider. No matter how cherished she tried to make him feel, no matter how wonderful she worked to make his home for him, the more discontent and misplaced he seemed to be.

The more her priorities shifted and her preferences changed, the more resentful he grew. More and more it seemed they were drifting in opposite directions. She preferring the solace of her women's disciple group and church activities over the flashy, meaningless parties and endless social-izing that took place in the world of sports management. Though she still did what she deemed was necessary to support Ron, he had noticed and commented that she wasn't really present. What once impressed her no longer did, and Ron took all of this personally—seeing himself as some sort of failure in her eyes. Nothing she said or did could convince him otherwise. They had grown into different people or so it seemed at first, and then they had both found their own grooves and settled in, giving each other the space to pursue their separate interests…or so she had thought. As a matter of fact, she had congratulated herself on finding the balance between nurturing her spirit and keeping Ron satisfied.

Adrian had kept the same girlish figure she had when she and Ron first met in college. She was a fabulous cook. Their house looked like something out of *Architectural Digest*, thanks to her resourcefulness and a little help from Felicia. All of his friends commented on what a won-derful hostess she was. In essence, her entire world revolved around Ron. But that's not the way Ron saw it. Through his eyes church came first, no matter how much she tried to convince him otherwise. Short of not going at all, she didn't know what it would take to make him stop feeling as though he had to compete for her attention. Lately this had become an even bigger thing, a wide, silent yawn between them. And she didn't know how to close the gap without sacrificing what had grown to be most important to her. To conclude they had come to an impasse was inevitable, yet she had kept hoping that something would happen to turn the tide of their relationship, so she had kept treading water... hoping, wishing, praying.

Now it had come to this. Though she had tried to do all the right things to keep him happy, he was gone. And he had the nerve to think that one short note could sum up the destruction of a marriage. She couldn't help but think about Tracy and Felicia. Little did they know. This relationship thing was more than a notion. Yet it was practically all that she knew. She had never been alone in her life, except when Ron went on an occasional business trip, which had happened more often lately. She had never felt alone because she knew he was coming back. But this time he wasn't. And he couldn't even tell her to her face.

She had felt in her spirit all day that something was wrong. She just couldn't put her finger on it. She drained the water from the pasta she had made and topped it with homemade tomato sauce and sat at the kitchen table. She couldn't even taste her food as she tried to sort her thoughts and make sense of his departure. Why would a man leave a perfect home and a perfect wife? And for what? "I'm sorry, but I can't do this anymore," the note had read. "Perhaps you can find someone who can make you happy...I have. I'll have my attorney call you tomorrow. Sorry for the bad timing." *Bad timing?* She half smiled as if something was said in poor taste that she was trying to politely dismiss. *What is an upcoming birthday in the scheme of my entire life going down the drain?* She was confused. *What can't he do anymore? How can he say that? How? And who said I need someone else to make me happy? How could anyone work any harder than I did to make him happy?*

She cleared the table and washed the dishes quietly, calmly. The air was pregnant with suppressed emotions burgeoning dangerously close to the surface like the calm before the storm. After putting everything away and surveying the sparkling kitchen, she turned off the light and moved down the hallway with Coco and Merlot padding carefully behind her. Soundlessly she moved through her bedtime ritual. Shower, this time lingering a little longer than usual. Perhaps everything would be different when she stepped out of the glass enclosure. Nope, everything was the same. Uncannily still. The only movements heard were her own as she brushed her long, thick hair and pulled it to the top of her head, securing it in a bun before covering it with a scarf. She lotioned her skin and put on a fresh nightgown. It clung in all the right places and fell around her ankles. Smelling faintly of lavender and moving slowly through the bedroom toward the bed, she almost felt like an apparition, fragile in the moonlight that filtered through the shades.

She sat carefully on the edge of the bed, not a thought in her head. She reached for her Bible and opened it. No specific page. No particular passage. It didn't matter; she couldn't see the pages anyway. She closed the Bible and placed it back on the nightstand. She took a deep breath and stared into space, not looking for anything in particular. Just... waiting. A faint smile crossed her face as she finally focused on Coco and Merlot, still watching her intently from the doorway. She slowly rose and pulled back the covers, easing herself onto the mattress. She reached to turn off the table lamp and stopped to look at a picture of herself, arms wrapped around a man she thought she knew. She traced the outline of his face. He was so handsome. It seemed a hollow observance. Without changing her expression she turned off the light and lay there, cradling her cheeks in her hands.

Looking into the darkness, she heaved another sigh, this one heavier than the first. She couldn't pray. What could she say? It was as if her jaws were wired shut. She tried to open her mouth, to squeak out one word. She couldn't. She closed her eyes, trying to shut out the day, the night, everything. Slowly, ever so slowly, one solitary tear appeared in the corner of her eye. It lingered a moment and then continued its silent journey across the bridge of her nose and downward, leaving a wet line across her face until it found its place on her pillow.

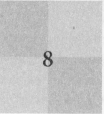

8

*M*uriel felt completely discombobulated. She reached for her Bible with one hand and the edge of her skirt with the other. What was she thinking when she left the house this morning? She knew was going to Bible class and the skirt she was wearing was a little too short for her surroundings. As she turned to slip out of the back of the sanctuary before she ran into anyone she knew, she stopped abruptly. Another step and she would have run smack dab into Carla. Dear, cute, perky little Carla. Muriel always chuckled when she thought of Carla. She was so…well, cute! She was petite, with this short, curly, auburn hair that always looked like it had a life of its own. And this cute turned up nose that Muriel was convinced the angels had received specific orders to sprinkle with freckles ever so carefully 'cause they almost seemed to be painstakingly placed instead of the usual random splash effect. Carla had the cutest lips that were always smiling and cute little eyes that twinkled continually as if she had a whole truckload of secrets that no one else knew and she certainly wasn't going to tell! The girl was vibrating perpetually. Her energy bubbled over, and her laugh was downright contagious. She was just so ca-ute! Muriel really liked her. She always told Carla, "You know, you're alright for a white girl." This would send Carla into peals of laughter.

Anyway, there she was with her husband, Al, in tow. Al was the absolute opposite. Calm, subdued, would disappear into the woodwork if Carla wasn't holding on to his hand. Where she led he went willingly, looking quite delighted to be in her presence. But then again, who wouldn't be? Muriel looked down at her with a wide smile, forgetting her discomfort. "Hey, girlfriend, what's up? Ooh, new dress?"

"Well you can't be the only show-stopper, you know," giggled Carla. Just as quickly she shifted gears. "Muriel, there's someone I'd like you to meet. One of Al's college buddies just moved here from Seattle. He's looking for a house, and I thought you would be the perfect person to help him…if you know what I mean." She spoke quickly and winked furtively. Muriel frowned. *What is Carla up to now?*

"Why, Carla, what makes you think I would be the person? I'm not a real estate agent," Muriel said carefully. If Carla was up to something she most certainly was not going to betray her to Al, who stood looking as if he didn't have a clue.

"Well, I know that you enjoy going to open houses and art exhibits and decorating, and I thought since he's doing this *all alone*…I thought you would be the perfect person. After all, Al is busy with work and my schedule is so hectic. Not to say that you are not a busy person. Anyway, he went to the restroom; he'll be here any minute, and I wanted to make sure you would agree before I brought it up," she said in one last rush as if dashing for an invisible finish line.

The girl could talk, okay? Muriel's concern deepened. *Is Carla match-making again?* That woman spent more time worrying about Muriel's single status than she did. Carla was on a mission to find her the perfect mate, but so far she had come up empty-handed.

Muriel's mind tried to rewind and replay the evening. She didn't remember seeing any eligible black men at Bible study tonight. As a matter of fact, there were no black men at Bible study tonight. That's what she got for going to a predominantly white church. That's what her mother always told her while she voiced displeasure at the fact that she had no grandchildren yet. It was Muriel's fault for going to a white church where there were no available black men. This left Muriel unfazed. "When I go to church I'm going to see Jesus. Who are you going to see?" she would always reply, effectively ending the conversation.

"I see," Muriel said slowly, studying Carla's face. She had a heart of gold. She couldn't get mad at her if she tried. Even if she was "dippin'" into her business. "I don't know if that's a..."

"Oh, here he is now!" Carla whirled around, her voice a little higher than usual. "Brad Sebastian meet Muriel James. This is the friend I was telling you about, the one who can help you find a house. She knows the market really well!" Muriel's eyes never left Carla's face; it was as if she were hypnotized. She had never seen Carla like this before. Carla was bubbly, not a whirling dervish of combustible nervous energy. *I'm going to kill her,* Muriel thought. The richest voice she ever heard interrupted her focused fascination with Carla. "Hello, I'm very pleased to meet you." Muriel lifted her head to look into the deepest blue eyes she had ever seen. She opened her mouth but no words came out. Instead she thought she heard what sounded like a sharp intake of breath. Whose, she couldn't say.

Before she could utter a word, Carla grabbed her hand and started dragging her toward the door. "I thought we could all have some coffee and a snack and discuss this further. Don't you think that's a good idea?" Muriel followed obediently, wondering what had happened to all her smart and witty ad libs. The moment they entered the restaurant she fled to the ladies' room. As she powdered her nose, freshened her lipstick, and declared war on the unruly curls at the nape of her neck, she tried talking to herself. *Calm down girl, calm down. He's not even a brother. What is happening to you? You have never been attracted to a white man in your life! And when you do, couldn't you even go for something in the mid-range with olive skin, dark eyes, dark hair? No! You've got to be an extremist and go all the way to the left. He's got blond hair and blue eyes, for crying out loud, practically the stereotype of white. But he sure is a magnificent stereotype...Oh man, I'm dizzy. How could his cologne follow me all the way back here? What is going on? And that voice!* She could still feel the warmth of his hand as he had helped her down the stairs. *That's it. I am not going back out there. Nope. No way, José.* On second thought she decided to go back before Carla came to get her—that would be even more embarrassing. Muriel took a deep breath, straightened her back, lifted her head, and yanked at the hem of her skirt. *This is it. I am woman hear me roar.* On that note she headed through the door.

As she approached the table she scanned the cast of characters seated there. Carla and Al looking very much like two pleased partners in crime. For the first time Muriel realized that Al knew much more than he let on. He only perpetuated the facade of not being in the mix. *Hmm, she was going to have to have a private conversation with Carla and find out what else she had misread about Al.* Finally her eyes rested on Brad as she slid into her seat next to him. He was truly a vision of gorgeousness, movie star quality to be exact. Again she was speechless and wondered if her smile looked as dumb as she felt.

He spoke, but his words sounded as if they were coming through a tunnel. She found herself staring at his lips. *What a wonderful mouth. Pretty teeth.*

"Carla was just telling me how talented you are."

She pinched herself under the table. "Oh, really?" She managed to squeeze the words out of a throat that was getting tighter by the minute. If she wasn't so dark she would have thought she was blushing. She shifted in her seat and the movement helped. "Now what exactly did Carla tell you?"

"Well, she told me that you are a wonderful artist and an incredible designer…and that you have an amazing collection of ethnic art from all over the world."

Now why would she tell him that? Muriel wondered. Her question was answered quickly enough.

"Brad is quite a traveler himself," Carla chimed in, happy to have so much inside information on both parties. "He spent years in Africa doing missions work." Muriel felt relieved. *Well, there you have it, good-looking and broke. I knew he was too good to be true.* Her whole demeanor changed. She was back on the block. She could feel normal conversation coming on as she reached for the creamer, missing it by inches.

"Oh! So what brings you to Chicago?" Her composure crumbled as quickly as it had been restored.

"May I?" he asked as he took the cream and began to pour it into her coffee. "Well unfortunately, after my missions project ended, there was nowhere left for me to go. So I moved back to Seattle and started a computer business, creating systems for corporations with an old school buddy of mine. It became quite successful, and a larger company bought us out. I thought about going back to Africa, but I didn't feel in my spirit that the timing was right, so I started doing research and praying about where I should go next. Everything pointed to Chicago. So here I am, in a prime location to start a new business. Uh, is that enough?" He pointed toward her coffee cup. He was still holding the creamer.

The coffee had long been forgotten. Muriel was lost in his eyes, caught up in wondering how his hair would feel curled around her fingers. He brought her back to reality.

"You did want cream in your coffee, didn't you?"

"Huh? Oh, um, yes, thank you." Oh no, now she was mumbling. And she didn't dare pick up the cup because her hands were shaking. *What is it about this man? Why is he able to make my reserve topple? Why do I feel so undone and defenseless when he directs his gaze toward me?* Muriel didn't like this at all. Uh, uh, this was not a good scenario for a control freak like herself.

She could see the telepathic conversation between Al and Carla out of the corner of her eye. Carla's eyes were alight with intuitive understanding. She could see them fighting to stifle their mirth over what they probably considered a match made in heaven based on the chemistry they were witnessing at the opposite end of the table. Muriel looked back to Brad, blindly reaching for her purse and clutching it instinctively like a shield to protect herself from him. Carla cleared her throat as if intruding on a private moment. "Muriel, I thought you and Brad could exchange numbers and make arrangements to get together...to look at houses. Brad, you'll need to do that soon, won't you? We can't have you living in a hotel forever...." Muriel didn't hear another word. She was already rising from the chair, mumbling something about an early appointment in the morning. She would be happy to help Brad anytime...

"But Muriel, you forgot to write down your number!" Somewhere in the vicinity of her back she could hear Carla's voice calling after her as she fled. Too bad. She was out of there. She didn't know what was happening. All she knew was that she felt really strange. Weird, uncomfortable feelings were overtaking her as if a dam had burst somewhere within, and she wasn't hanging around to drown in them....no way, no how! She didn't need to see the end of this movie. The night air restored her. Muriel didn't believe in love at first sight, but she decided that if any part of love felt like that, those were feelings she could live without.

9

*D*errick, you are not well." Tracy chuckled a deep throaty sound that betrayed her affection for her caller.

"Why? Because I gave you a compliment?"

Derrick had the warmest, most…male voice Tracy had ever heard. "Oh, come on! 'Do fries go with that shake?' That's a compliment? I hope you don't talk to Shirley like that." Derrick laughed at Tracy's fake show of indignation.

"Baby, Shirley likes everything I tell her. But we're talking about you. And I believe the point I was trying to make was that you are fine! Or would you prefer me to say 'You are an incredibly beautiful woman'?" Derrick switched to a nasally, very proper tone of voice for extra effect. "In other words, there's nothing wrong with you. You don't have a third eye growing out of your pretty little forehead or anything like that. You're intelligent, even fun when you're not being such a knucklehead. And your body is slammin'! So the only reason you don't have a man is because you don't want one."

"Ooh, Derrick, that is low. And you know that's not true. How can you say that? It's not that simple." Tracy tried to sound deeply wounded, but it was difficult because she was too busy grinning and lapping up the compliment. She adored Derrick. He was like a big brother. She knew she could always count on him to fluff up her ego when she was feeling as if she had lost it—whatever "it" was that made a woman attractive to a man. She had given up trying to figure men out. She had to agree with John Gray: Men were definitely from Mars.

He wouldn't think I was fine if he saw me now, Tracy thought. There she was, stretched out across her bed in her favorite scruffy, terry cloth robe. Muriel had pleaded with her to get rid of it and had even bought her a new one, but she clung to the old one with the loyalty of a child with a tattered teddy bear. The new one just didn't feel right. It was rough. This one was broken in. It had absorbed her tears and comforted her through many a lonely night. Tracy was quite a sight. Her hair was set on huge, pink, magnetic rollers, held in place with long, flat, silver clips. Her heavy old tortoise shell glasses, that told the true story of how poor her eyesight was, sat crookedly on the tip of her nose, and the wax she had applied to shape her eyebrows just before the phone rang was now cold, thick, and beginning to crack.

She cradled the phone between her shoulder and her cheek and polished her nails while bemoaning her single status to Derrick. "You know it's not just about being cute. There are a lot of attractive people out there alone."

"Well, your cousin Felicia isn't! And you're just as fine as she is, with more sense, of course." Derrick knew Tracy hated being compared with Felicia. He remembered the first time he met her. "You didn't tell me you had a cousin who looked like Vanessa Williams! Are you sure you two aren't sisters? You almost look alike except you're a couple shades darker." Tracy's face had grown dark with tension as she snapped, "And that's where the similarities end. Do not put me in the same category with her, okay? We are definitely two different people." Derrick had backed off, wondering what their history was but not daring to ask. He was very careful whenever he broached the subject of Felicia, knowing he was treading within the circumference of a time bomb.

"Okay, here we go, here we go," Tracy said rhythmically imitating the style of a rap artist. "You're right. Obviously Felicia has something I don't. So what is it about her? You're a man. Explain. What is it that is so irresistible about her?" Derrick didn't even have to think about it; he had already figured it out. "Felicia is needy. You are not. Now you're both high maintenance, but Felicia has this…vulnerable thing going on. She's like a little girl in a lot of ways. She gives off this air that makes you want to take care of her, to protect her, to give her guidance."

"Alright, alright, that's enough, cheese-on-bread, I'm sorry I asked!" Tracy realized she was overreacting, but she couldn't help herself.

"Well, you asked. I'm just being honest." Silence. "Look, you are the type of woman any man would love to have." Derrick tried to be gentle, "But you have this 'I don't need anything or anybody' 'tude that probably makes the average brother hunch his shoulders and give up before he even tries to say hello. Felicia, on the other hand, is wide open."

"She most certainly is," Tracy said with a heavy helping of disapproval in her voice. "When will she swallow more than she can handle is the question."

"Well, enough about her," Derrick said. "When are you going to come from behind that wall and let someone in?"

"I don't have any walls up!" Tracy's voice sounded unusually shrill as she struggled to defend herself. *Shoot, Muriel was the one with the wall.*

"Aren't you touchy? But I'm not letting up." Derrick refused to let this opportunity pass him by. "What about the brother who was sending you flowers and wining and dining you? What was wrong with him? Where is he now?"

"Who Evan? Oh, he was nice…he just wasn't my type." Tracy could feel herself backpedaling out of the conversation. This was always her standard line whenever she didn't want Derrick to know what had really happened. Especially in light of the fact that Derrick's initial reaction to Evan had been, "Looks like a player to me." He had since redeemed himself by doing all the right things and convincing Derrick to back off of his opinion. Perhaps she should have listened to Derrick's original opinion, but that would have been too much. Giving Derrick the satisfaction of clocking yet another man in her life was more than she could bear. She really hated it when he was right.

Derrick reeled her back into the present. "And just exactly what is your type, hmm? That's what you said about the last one before Evan, whom, I might interject, I thought was a good guy."

Tracy thought Derrick was enjoying himself a little too much. It was beginning to irritate her. "I know you're not talking about Roy!" She thought back to her one attempt to like someone who was not in her normal realm of interest. He had been nice enough, but no go. No bells, no tingles, no nothing. "I don't know, Derrick. He was nice, but something was missing. There was no chemistry. Of course I want a man who is easy on the eyes, with a j-o-b, 'cause there's definitely no romance without finance up and through here, okay? But all of that is nothing without chemistry!" Tracy couldn't understand why she was suddenly the victim of an inquisition.

"I think this whole thing about chemistry is a smoke screen for not knowing what you really want." Tracy thought he sounded a little too much like one of those talk-show psychiatrists.

"Am I too picky, scared to commit?" she sang to the tune of "Qué Será, Será." "Come on, Derrick, knock it off. I've heard that whole list before, and it's just not true. All I know is that I believe when you finally meet that special someone, somewhere deep inside of you, you both know. It's like you've known each other before in another place, another time. How did you feel when you met Shirley?"

Tracy knew how to divert the conversation away from herself, and Derrick took her cue and ran with it. "Let me just say this. I was in a different place when I met Shirley. If I had met her before I wouldn't have appreciated her. You know I went through my 'chemistry' era too. But after all the chemistry fizzled out and the smoke cleared, there was nothing left. I kept getting involved with women who were just empty shells. Pretty houses with no one home. Sometimes there weren't even lights on upstairs." He chuckled. "I could never figure out why I got bored so easily, why I was always on the prowl looking for something new."

"You actually thought about it?" Tracy was surprised. Her stomach rumbled. All this talk about love was making her hungry. She unraveled herself from beneath her comforter and headed toward the kitchen.

"Of course I did! You know, Tracy, whether you believe it or not, men go through just as many changes about relationships as women do—if not more," Derrick explained as if he were talking to a small child. "The pressure is intense. In a man's world his woman reflects how well he's got it together. His buds are checking him out and sizing him up, deciding if he's made the cut based on his career and the woman he can pull. Sometimes we end up with someone who might not necessarily be good for us because she looks good enough to play off the image we're trying to project."

"That's stupid."

"Yes, it is. But we make a lot of mistakes in search of the perfect image. And it's no more stupid than a woman who puts up with any and everything just to keep a man in her life because she doesn't feel valid without one, now is it?"

"You won't get me to argue about that. But what was different about Shirley? What happened?" Tracy was anxious to get to the point. Peering into the refrigerator, her options for a late-night snack were looking pretty dismal.

"A talk with Patrick happened."

"A talk with Patrick?"

"Mmm hmm..."

"Do you care to expound on this theme?" She was truly impatient now. *Why is he drawing this out?* Closing the refrigerator door she headed for the pantry.

"I guess I had assumed that because I was bored, everybody else was too. I couldn't understand why Patrick wasn't in hunting mode like me. He seemed so happy and cooled out—almost disinterested in other women altogether after he met Gloria. I thought she was alright, but she wasn't 'all that,' you know. So I asked him about it. I said, 'Hey, man, does this chick have your nose open or what?'"

"You didn't!" Her fingers closed around a box of crackers.

"Yes, I did."

"And what did he say?" This was getting good. She had never seen this side of Derrick. She drizzled honey on top of the crackers, creating patterns on top of her makeshift dessert.

"He looked at me and said, 'Call it what you want, but I feel like I finally found my way home. I don't need to shop around anymore.' Then he proceeded to tell me that Gloria was everything he needed in one package. His lover and his best friend, which got me insulted 'cause I thought I was his best friend. But the bottom line was she touched every part of him. His mind, his body, everything…and I realized that no one I had ever dated had done that."

"Wow, that's deep, Derrick." Tracy took great care to put the whole cracker in her mouth and chew quietly in order not to break his flow. This was getting good.

"Yeah, it was. The more I watched them interact, the more I started to see what I was missing. I never told you this, but their wedding day was the most miserable day of my life. I felt so lonely! It was like they had their own private club, and I was on the outside looking in the window at all the fun they were having."

Tracy was practically holding her breath while Derrick spoke. She could relate to this feeling. She had felt the same way as she watched Derrick and Shirley together. It was like standing across a street watching two people having a good time in a park. They just seemed to absorb one another into their own private world. And while it was sweet to watch and made her smile, it also magnified her loneliness in the moments she had spent time with them, leaving her with an ache she hadn't been able to explain.

Derrick was on a roll. "I wanted what they had. When I met Shirley, I liked her. She was fun, easy to be with, and she had a fascinating way of looking at things. I genuinely enjoyed talking to her. She was also easy on the eyes. Not super-duper fine or anything, but it was strange, every time I saw her she got cuter and cuter."

"Really?" This was a revelation to Tracy that made her bite into the second cracker loudly. The way Derrick looked at Shirley you would have sworn he thought she was the most beautiful creature in the world.

"Mmm hmm. I would have put her in the friendship file if I hadn't been in a different space. And it was still a struggle initially. The old tape playing in my head tried to remind me that women I could talk to were good to keep as friends, and women I could…, well, you know, got thrown in the lover file. My lovers were not my friends. I couldn't expose all of myself to one person. That was too much to risk."

"Get out of here! What kind of nonsense is that?"

"It may be nonsense to you, but it made good sense to me at the time. Are you eating in my ear, girl?" Derrick was trying to sound offended but Tracy knew he wasn't. This was part and parcel of their late-night talks.

"Yeah, what about it?"

"You are a mess. One day you'll get some manners. Anyway, I'm finally arriving at my point. I was different, and Shirley was different. I trusted her. And that trust helped me turn off the old tape and start a new one. One day we were sitting around talking about nothing in particular and she laughed. Suddenly she was the most beautiful and desirable woman I had ever met. I realized I wanted her in every way. It was the scariest and happiest moment all at the same time. When I followed my feelings, I found out what Patrick already knew. It was good to be home."

"Wow, Derrick!" Tracy was deeply touched. She had been given a very precious gift—access to this secret place inside her friend's heart.

"Now, if I could just get the woman to marry me," Derrick said, searching for a bit of levity.

Tracy knew he hadn't meant to get that deep. He had to be feeling pretty uncomfortable about now; he was still a dude after all.

"Hey, maybe that's what I like about her—she's hard to get without playing it."

"There's probably a lot of truth in that. Men do seem to be suckers for a good challenge. She'll come around—just be patient. Since her last experience with marriage was rough, it'll take her a while to exorcise those demons. And I doubt very seriously that she would willingly allow a good man like you to slip through her fingers. It's just a matter of time."

"The same holds true for you, Tracy. You're a good woman, and it's just a matter of time before you meet someone who will want to be your friend and your lover. But you've got to be ready. And you've got to have the right tape playing in your head or you'll let it pass you by. I have to say I believe the man upstairs knows when to send that special someone our way—when we're ready and won't destroy her or him. I don't think He's in the business of giving Rolls-Royces to two year olds."

"Boy, aren't you getting philosophical in your old age!"

"I guess so."

"Well, I gotta go and finish my beauty ritual before this special man shows up and wonders what I've done to my eyebrows."

"What do you do to your eyebrows?"

"That's none of your business. See, now you're dippin.'" Tracy laughed.

"Alright, keep your beauty secrets to yourself while I spill my guts out all over the place." Derrick had teasingly slipped into brother man dialect, which Tracy hated. Derrick continued, "Ain't no biggie. I think you fine anyway. Shoot, mama, if I didn't have a lady already I'd have to make a play. You know what I'm sayin.'"

"Now I really have to go, you're beginning to sound like a little street urchin." Tracy waffled between being disapproving and giggling at the compliment.

"Okay go on wit'cha bad self, and don't worry, be happy, all good things worth waiting for come in time. But you've got to get a hold of what I finally learned."

"And what's that?"

"That love is not a destination—it's a journey."

"Hmm, truly the wisely spoken words of a converted man."

"Sho' you right!" Derrick sounded pretty sure of himself.

"Next thing you'll be telling me you got saved or something."

"Hey, just keep in mind anything is possible." The phone clicked. "That's probably Shirley, good night, baby, keep the faith, okay?"

"I will. Good night, Derrick." Tracy laid the phone down. She could imagine Derrick and Shirley's conversation, exchanging how they spent their day. She wondered if he would tell her about their discussion. She hoped Shirley understood how lucky she was to have a man like Derrick. He was one of the small percentage of good men that were still available.

As she finished her nighttime preparations, Tracy continued mulling over what Derrick said. Perhaps he had a point. She had ignored his subtle advances when they first met at work. She liked him immediately, but she didn't like him "that way." Now in retrospect she had no idea why not. They had become close friends, bosom buddies, the date they could rely on when no one else was available, and yet she had never considered him as a possible romantic partner. At least not when the opportunity had existed. He had since given up and accepted her terms for platonic friendship, even though his teasing still held hints of unfulfilled wishes of more than a dance from her.

Perhaps she was guilty of the same thing he was. Keeping a file cabinet that separated friends from lovers. Oh well, that was all water under the bridge. At the present time she had no prospects, and she was taking a sabbatical from the tumultuous world of romantic relationships. She didn't know how long it would take or exactly what she would get out of it. She knew she was ready for a change…and change was never easy to come by. She was convinced now she was ready to do the work, to figure out why she chose the wrong guys. The end result certainly looked like it was worth it if what Derrick had just shared was true.

She fluffed her pillows and pressed her back into the headboard of her canopy bed as she reached for her diary. Why had she gotten so upset when Derrick said she didn't know what she wanted? Of course she knew! Sometimes it was just hard to verbalize to others. They might view her thoughts as silly, and she just couldn't bring herself to subject her inner dreams to public ridicule. Some things were best reserved for personal reflection only. She began journaling. It was therapeutic watching the words reach across the page, corralling her emotions and rounding them up into some sort of sensical order. She heaved a cleansing sigh and let her heart do the writing…

Dear Diary,
   I just want
      what every woman wants
         warm arms on a cold night
         promises of forever
          and wonderful todays
      silent understanding
          and kisses that leave me breathless…
   I want what every woman wants
      soft words
         in hard times

someone to read my heart
and touch my mind...
        I want
    a co-conspirator
        a treasure chest to hold my secrets
I want
    a firm hold
        when I'm losing my grip...
    someone to call me in from the rain...
    to be my shield
    my pillow
        my river
            my mountain
                my rock...
    I want a raven to feed me in the wilderness...
    I want to be rescued
            lost in an embrace
            and found not wanting...
what do I want?
    what every woman wants...
        to find her way home...

"It was good to be home," Derrick had said. Tracy mused on those words as she turned out the light. She wondered how that really felt. *Perhaps one day soon I'll find out.*

10

*C*arla carefully wiped the last remains of cold cream from her face and stood back from the bathroom mirror to assess her handiwork. With great concentration she puckered her lips and twisted her mouth as far to the left-hand side of her face as she could. Ever so slowly she twisted it all the way to the right. She had seen Jack La Lanne prescribe this simple exercise to combat laugh lines. She decided it really didn't do any good; the laugh lines were still there, yet she persisted in faithfully repeating this ritual for as far back as she could remember. Perhaps it was as much out of habit as it was the fact she still harbored a secret hope that one day she would wake up and the tiny lines she obsessed over would have miraculously disappeared...as a result of her diligent efforts, of course.

"A-a-al, you still haven't answered me!" Carla stood in the doorway pouting at her husband. He looked up from his book. "Hmm? I'm sorry, honey, what did you say?" He was still a little lost in his previous thoughts.

"I sa-aid what did you think that was all about tonight?" After assessing the blank look on Al's face she added, "You know, with Muriel?" She put her hand on her hip as she began to cross the room. She was getting a little impatient.

"O-oh, with Muriel!" The look of complete revelation crossed his face for a brief instant only to be replaced with complete befuddlement. "What do you mean? What about Muriel?"

"Well, don't you think she was behaving a little strangely this evening?"

"Honey, Muriel behaves a little strangely period."

The fact that Al was pretending to look a bit concerned that she had never noticed this very obvious characteristic of her friend did not amuse Carla. She attempted to look stern as she stood in the middle of the room in her nightgown, looking like a petite princess demanding humility from her subject. She was not going to be put off or distracted by his teasing. "Al, this is not funny! I hope I didn't overstep my bounds with her. I just want her to be happy, and I thought she and Brad would hit it off. Maybe I should have asked her first."

"No kidding!" Al retorted in mock dismay. He softened after seeing the look of contrition on her face. "I find it hard to believe Muriel could be offended by anything you would do." He reached for her as she sank wearily onto the side of the bed. She relaxed, head rolling backward, as he slowly kneaded her shoulders.

"You really think so?" she queried.

"I know so."

"How do you know?"

"Because I know you have a heart of gold and would never even hurt a fly on purpose."

"You're just saying that because you love me."

"Well, that's true but…" He ducked a mock swat at his head from her. "Muriel knows you love her and would never do anything to deliberately hurt her. However…"

"Oh, here it comes…"

"*However*…" He gripped her tightly as if to hold off any resistance. "You should have asked her first."

"But if I had asked her if she wanted to meet Brad before I introduced them, she would have said no!"

"Aha! Ladies and gentlemen, my point exactly!" Al made a sweeping gesture to his imaginary audience.

"Cut it out, Al. I'm serious."

"So am I. If you knew she would say no, why did you do it?"

"Because Muriel needs a little jumpstart in that area of her life, and she doesn't realize it."

"What area of her life?"

"The *man* area, Al. Where are you in this conversation? What is it about what I'm saying that you don't get?"

"I don't understand why you should be so concerned about Muriel's man status if she isn't."

Carla was truly getting exasperated at this point. "Because I know what's good for her! She'll get a clue later."

"I see. So tell me, what is good for her?"

"Brad is good for her."

"Oh, and could you be any more specific?" Al chuckled and shook his head. His wife was something else when she made up her mind about something. What was even worse was she usually got her way before the other parties involved had a chance to know what happened.

"Brad is *perfect* for Muriel." Carla was adamant.

"And your reasoning is?" Al was trying not to make Carla feel as if this whole thing wasn't important, but he just didn't understand why she was so intense. Muriel and Brad were two adults who could handle their own lives. And besides, Al had a better idea of how he and Carla could be using their time.

"Muriel needs a strong man in her life. No, hear me out, Al. I know you think Muriel is a strong, independent woman, but she's not as tough as you think. I see past all that surface bravado that she thrashes around. I know what that's all about because I've been there."

"Oh *really?*"

"Yes, *really.* I was just like Muriel at a point in my life before you came along. That's what a string of disappointments will do to you. In order to survive, a person builds up the walls around her heart to protect herself and keep moving."

Al was sitting up and looking at Carla. *Is there ever an end to the depths of this woman I've married?* he wondered. He would never have suspected that Carla had ever experienced anything that would affect her personality to the extent of diffusing her perpetual state of effervescence. From the very first day he met her she was so open, so warm, so…embraceable. He couldn't imagine her being anything like Muriel, whom he really liked but always felt in her presence as if he was obeying an invisible cue to keep his distance. "I have a really hard time picturing you being anything like Muriel."

"It's called staying on top of your circumstances. If you give in to how you're really feeling, you would drown in a sea of hopelessness, so you take a deep breath and just 'keep strokin',' as Muriel would say."

"But when I met you, you were not just 'strokin' your way through life. You were this beautiful, vibrant woman who seemed to be thoroughly enjoying herself."

"That's because I met a man who changed my life before you came along."

"Wait a minute! Who is this guy, and why haven't I heard of him before?" Al was getting more concerned by the minute in the face of all this new information.

"I'm talking about Jesus, silly."

"Whew, you had me worried for a minute."

"Well, not to worry. But seriously, take it from me, it takes the grace of God to keep your head above water these days. Do you know how afraid a woman gets when she looks at the list of her heart's desires for a good man, a wonderful family, and a secure life, and then compares it to the present reality? Then throw in a couple of deep wounds, add some costly mistakes and setbacks, and what have you got? A woman who feels as if she's scraping the bottom of the barrel looking for a pipe dream."

"Carla, what are you saying?"

"I'm saying you end up concluding that happiness is something that happens for everyone else, but not for you."

"Why would anyone ever come to that conclusion?"

"Because they're tired, Al. And they've come to the point of realizing that if they're ever going to find a decent, eligible man, they've got to fight with the rest of the women looking. Which means they're in big trouble on the grounds that the margin between lonely women and eligible men is extremely wide and they've only got the last ten percent of humankind to work with because the rest of the world has lost its mind."

"You actually felt like that?"

"I sure did. Thank God I allowed the Lord to do a work in my life before I met you. I don't think you would have liked me if you had met me in my 'B.C.' days."

"You mean you actually had a life before Christ?" Al tried to lighten the conversation by joking, but Carla was more serious than he had seen her in a long time.

"Unfortunately, yes," she answered.

Al wasn't sure if there was really a tear in the corner of her eye or if the light was just playing tricks with him, but her eyes looked unusually bright in the dimness of the room.

"A life filled with some very hard times. Remember when I told you you were my knight in shining armor?"

"Yes, I recall some sort of ego-gratifying statement like that being thrown my way once upon a time."

"Well, I meant it. You literally rescued me and restored my faith in human love. And that's all I want for Muriel. A man who can find the little girl in her and love her into the kind of woman who doesn't feel she has to hide her heart in her toy box and bully the world to get through life. I want someone who can be gentle with her softness, and strong enough to disarm her toughness without breaking her. Then you'll get to see the real Muriel. She's a beautiful flower who has just gotten tired of bending in the direction of the sun only to find it's ducked behind yet another cloud. She needs the kind of man you were for me. Only love can coax the wounded from the shadows they choose to hide behind for their own protection."

"Wow! Where did all of that come from, and what happened in your life to create that philosophy?"

"Oh…nothing I care to discuss tonight…" Carla's voice dropped into a husky breath as she leaned forward to kiss Al on the tip of his nose. As he moved to welcome her advances he felt for the first time since they had been married that there was something he didn't know about Carla. It was a strange and foreign feeling bordering on fear. He chose to shake it off and submerge himself in the now, the familiar being far more pleasant to embrace. He extended his arm to turn off the light as he allowed himself to be lost in the night and Carla's love.

11

*T*racy surveyed the glum faces surrounding the dinner table. Muriel poked her favorite penne with tomato and basil sauce aimlessly around her plate with a look of total perplexity etched into her pretty face. Felicia was definitely in her own private Idaho. She hadn't offered up a single word since she had distractedly murmured, "Hey, girl, nice suit," and plopped into her chair. Adrian looked like she hadn't had any sleep in over a week. Her usually flawless, honey-colored complexion was blotchy as if her tears had left permanent stains on her skin. There were dark circles under her eyes creating a dramatic frame that made the faraway look in them even more pronounced. She too had lapsed into silence after an obligatory, "How's everybody doing?"

"Well, you all are a truly live crowd today! I mean this is the jammin'est birthday party I've ever been to." There was no response. "And so I said, 'Derrick, take off all your clothes. I want you now.'" Still no response. "I give up," Tracy muttered under her breath, then in one last attempt she exploded, rapping her knuckles on the table, "Okay, what's the deal? Where is everybody?" Still not a word.

Tracy scanned the faces and decided she didn't know who she should worry about most. She had never seen Muriel at a loss for words. Felicia either, for that matter. But Adrian took the cake. Her pain was almost palpable. Tracy had never seen her look less than perfect, but today she actually looked slightly disheveled. What had been going on with this group? In hindsight, reviewing her hectic week, she realized she hadn't spoken to any of her crew as she customarily did at least every other day or so. Long hours at the office and the stress of trying to please clients who didn't seem to know what they wanted had left her too drained to do anything but collapse on her pillow and escape the events of the day somewhere between whatever was showing on Nick at Nite and her heavy eyelids.

At the last minute she had hurriedly emailed everyone the meeting place for Adrian's birthday celebration, concluding that Muriel had once again dropped the ball on reminding her. Perhaps her week had been just as crazy. It didn't matter that Tracy would be the responsible one in the group and pull it together at the last minute. But now she wondered if she had missed something in the midst of her own self-absorption. Hmm, no one had called. They had all responded to the email without the usual banter. Adrian had even left off her usual inspirational scripture for the day.

But wait a minute. Everyone was in a funk but her. Surely they wouldn't leave her out of whatever was going on. She couldn't remember when she had been the last to know anything. Her feeling of deep discomfort increased. "Adrian, are you all right?" The words seemed to come from the back of the room in slow motion as she got lost in the sadness of her dear friend's eyes. Adrian shook her head from side to side to affirm the negative. "He's gone..." a faraway voice replied from lips that didn't seem to move. Adrian expelled the answer as if she had been holding her breath all week, and now she was close to the last thread of her strength as she exhaled what she had been holding in.

Tracy didn't understand, but all of a sudden she was afraid to press for further details. Muriel's head snapped in Adrian's direction.

"Who's gone?" she demanded.

"Ron," Adrian whispered, a tear finally escaping. Tracy watched her fighting for her composure, trying not to allow her face to cave in, but it was rapidly doing so. No one dared to say a word as they watched her eyes rapidly filling and spilling her pain onto a usually flawless face now marred with emotions they had never seen there before. Tracy, speaking slowly, asked, "Gone where, Adrian?"

"Did he die? 'Cause I know he didn't leave you!" Muriel blurted.

"Muriel!" Felicia snapped, then as quickly leaned forward, her face etched with concern. "It's okay. Take your time and tell us what happened."

"He left me. He said he found someone to make him happy," Adrian whimpered, completely disintegrating to all of their dismay. Felicia cupped Adrian's hands with one hand while gently wiping her tears with a table napkin with the other, all the while shushing her as if trying to coax a fretful infant to sleep. Tracy was fascinated with this uncharacteristically caring side Felicia was presenting, then understanding quickly replaced her consternation. Of course she would be good at this. This was her specialty...getting left. But not Adrian, not sweet, dear, perfect Adrian. Something was truly wrong with this scenario.

Felicia must have thought the same thing because just as Tracy was giving her points for her wonderful tableside manner she reverted back to her usual behavior. "He didn't leave you for another man, did he?"

"Now what would make you say something as ridiculous as that?" Tracy couldn't believe what she was hearing, but at least it had yanked her from the black hole she had been in.

"Well..."

"Well *what*, Felicia?" Muriel's eyes were dark and angry as she glared at Felicia, who seemed to be growing smaller by the minute.

"Well, what woman could he possibly leave *her* for?" Tracy and Muriel looked at her with impatient disgust, awaiting her rationale for such a thoughtless statement. "I mean look at her. Well, you know, when she's in a better mood of course. All I'm saying is that what else could a man want in a woman? She's perfect. Therefore he has to be on the downlow, although I must say he never came off that way." Adrian's face was a wet mask of nonemotion. Tracy and Muriel mirrored the fact that they had all shut down in the course of Felicia's mindless dissertation. She was rambling but couldn't stop herself.

Somewhere between feeling sorry for Adrian and being able to relate to her pain, Felicia felt a strange sense of relief at the thought that she was now released from sharing her own distressing issue with them that evening. She had spent most of the afternoon rehearsing how she would say it and wondering if it would be better to do so before or after dessert, even though she wasn't sure if she could wait that long without bursting. But certainly Adrian's drama took precedence over her own predicament. "Let's face it, she's not like us. She's perfect," Felicia added.

"What do you mean by that?" Tracy's voice rose in decibels with each word. Before Muriel could get out an indignant second to the motion, Felicia held up her hands as if to defend herself. "Whether you want to admit it or not, we are flawed ladies, but Adrian here is well…perfect. It's actually a bit intimidating, you know. Sometimes it's hard to be around perfection because it uncovers all your own imperfections, if you know what I mean."

With that Adrian bolted from the table, leaving Felicia to shrivel under the glares of Tracy and Muriel. "I didn't mean…"

"Don't say another word!" Tracy threatened through gritted teeth. Slapping her table napkin onto the table like a gauntlet cast down to declare war, she headed toward the ladies' room in pursuit of Adrian. Muriel was the next to rise, looking just as dangerous. "I think it's best you stay here." With that Felicia was left to watch their backs grow smaller down the corridor that led to Adrian's emergency sanctuary.

She sighed a shaky breath and paused for reflection. How could men creep into every pore of your life and ruin even the moments that were supposed to be fun? There had to be a way to live above the drama of love. She actually felt a little frightened. After all, if Adrian couldn't make a relationship work, who could? Felicia knew why her relationships never panned out—whether she ever vocalized it or not. She just wouldn't give Tracy the satisfaction of admitting a weakness she had often accused her of, but she knew she gravitated to the wrong men. Why Felicia couldn't say, but she certainly did. She had been teased often for liking a little trash with her class, but at least she never had a dull moment—that's what she told herself anyway. Although now in her present circumstance she most certainly wished for one.

Lost in her thoughts she was snatched from her musings by the feeling that someone was watching her. Out the corner of her eye she saw him. "Fine as wine," she would have said before tonight. But now his deliberate gaze to get her attention made her stomach flip over in nausea. She could not afford to start something she couldn't finish. Not now. Felicia rose from the table carefully and headed deliberately toward the ladies' room. *Shoot, Adrian is my friend too!* She carefully opened the door to find them all sitting huddled in the powder room. She completed the semicircle around their forlorn friend. No one said anything. All of a sudden Adrian began to giggle. It was a foreign sound, a little too brittle for Adrian's usual carefully cultivated laugh, which was never too loud or too shrill. "You all look like Job's friends."

"Joe who?" Felicia asked.

"Job, stupid." Muriel spat out.

"Job was a guy in the Bible. You should read it sometime," Adrian gently explained to Felicia, happy to have a moment's distraction from her pain. But it was short-lived. "He lost everything too." With that she dissolved into fresh tears.

"Alright girl, I'm not good at all this emotional stuff, so you need to pull yourself together long enough to tell us what happened so we can figure out how to fix this." Everyone knew that Muriel was not into feeling helpless.

"There is no fixing it. He's gone; he's not coming back. He said he couldn't do this anymore, whatever 'this' is. I haven't been able to reach him because he's on a business trip. His attorney served me with papers on Tuesday."

They all listened, mirroring their disbelief as Adrian related how Ron had carefully drafted up a divorce agreement like a tidy severance package. She could keep the house, the pets, her car, and a nice portion of all their finances. Because she was a good woman and he didn't want to hurt her, he had said. "Guilt offerings," she mused. She had done some investigation work and her findings had confirmed her fears. Again she giggled. It was like a bad movie and far too obvious for her to have been so stupid. He was having an affair with his personal assistant. "So you don't need to worry, Felicia." Adrian giggled her strange giggle again, "He didn't run off with a man."

"Well, these days you do have to ask," Felicia countered. On that note they all burst into laughter, a little brighter than usual but nevertheless it felt good. At least Adrian was breathing again.

"What now?" Tracy asked.

"I don't know," Adrian replied, "but do you mind if we put off my birthday celebration for another time? I'm not very good company this evening." Three pairs of eyes stared at Adrian in complete wonderment. Only she would be thinking about how others felt at a time like this. Still at a loss for words or solutions to such an unexpected turn of events, they watched Adrian rise, lean toward the mirror, carefully powder her nose and refresh her lipstick. "No need to look a mess when you're falling apart," she said. "I'll call you in a few days. I just need a little time to sort myself out." With that she assumed her usual dignified stance and left as if her public awaited her.

"Now that's a lady," Tracy breathed as she headed toward the door. "I tell you, she's a better woman than I am. After all she's done to make that man feel like the king of his castle, I would be going off about now."

"I know that's right," Muriel amened from the rear.

"Perhaps we should just call it a night."

"Fine with me!" Muriel said a little too quickly. "And that's another fine case for keeping your heart to yourself." As the door slammed behind her, Felicia opened her mouth to say something but with no audience to address, she opted for heading into one of the stalls to throw up instead.

12

*H*ey, Muriel, this is Brad. I've left several messages…perhaps you're out of town." Muriel looked at the phone as if it were a monster and pressed seven for delete.

When was he going to get a clue that she was not going to call him back? If she didn't get anything else out of her evening with Adrian, she got the confirmation that she needed to run for cover while she still had her wits about her. She had not liked the way she felt the other evening. After her encounter with Brad, she had arrived home rattled and feeling a sense of foreboding that was difficult to shake. She prayed about it, but nothing gave her back the peace she had before meeting him. What was it about him? She couldn't put her finger on it. All she knew was that when she felt her grip loosening on any area of her life, she grabbed on tighter. She hated feeling out of control. She had compartmentalized the different areas of her life and lined them up like squares in a row, but now her perfect filing system was being scattered.

How could one encounter affect her so deeply? Since their first meeting, the image of Brad's face came up at the most inopportune times. She struggled to focus on the fabric she was draping on a model when she remembered the brush of his fingers as he had intercepted her hand to grab the cream for her coffee. "Ouch!" the girl had yelped as Muriel jabbed her with a pin absentmindedly. "Sorry," she had muttered, ruefully deciding perhaps she should stick to something less dangerous—such as sketches—until she could concentrate.

Looking up from her drawing board, Muriel surveyed her studio with satisfaction. This was the one place where she felt safe to be soft, safe to be a woman. Her fabrics could not hurt her. As a matter of fact, they were nurturing and inviting to the touch as she manipulated them into beautiful fashions that made women coo as they allowed the confections she created to embrace their frames. This was her sanctuary, surrounded by all things beautiful. Soft colors of mauve, cotton-candy pink, and taupe fell from the ceiling to the underlit, opaque white floor in sheer organza pools. These beautiful creations were backlit, hinting at female forms in various postures of dancing and praise in the circular gallery that extended off into various wings of an open office space constructed with glass and accented with soft, suede-covered furniture. Airy, light, feminine, she recalled the look of surprise when Tracy had seen her digs for the first time.

"Are you sure this is your studio, girl?" she asked.

"Of course it is. Why would I show you someone else's?" Muriel frowned.

"Wow!"

"Wow what?" Muriel countered.

"It just doesn't look like you, that's all."

"Now what is that supposed to mean? What should my studio look like?" Muriel knew what she was thinking but didn't like it even if it was true.

"Well, you know, you can come off a little tough and unapproachable if someone didn't really know you, and this is sooooo…soft and inviting. It's kind of weird; it's like the exact opposite…"

"Alright, alright. Enough of that. Do you like it or not?" Muriel had run out of patience.

"I love it, Muriel. It's beautiful! And I'm glad to discover another side of you. You need to let this side show more often."

The conversation had bothered Muriel to no end. Tracy's knack for blatant honesty was the thing she loved and disliked about her at the same time. Though she didn't like the things that Tracy said sometimes, there was always that underlying current of truth that she knew she needed to examine and deal with. And though there was merit in what Tracy said about reconciling her true inner self with her outward attitude, that was just too frightening. Didn't Tracy know it wasn't safe to put yourself out there like that? Some parts of yourself don't need to be common knowledge for everyone. That was asking for trouble.

Speaking of trouble. A frown settled over her cocoa-brown face as she watched the deliveryman weaving uncertainly behind a flawless bouquet of the most beautiful exotic flowers she had ever seen. "Muriel James?"

"Yes," she said suspiciously.

"Will you sign for these?"

Distractedly she signed while reaching for the card to find out who could possibly be sending her flowers.

"Was it something I said? Brad," the note read. Muriel groaned looking heavenward. Now what was she going to do? What if she ran into him at church again? What would she say? Something told her she was merely putting off the inevitable. The phone ringing and Roxanne, her assistant's voice on the intercom, interrupted her thoughts. "It's Carla on line one."

"Hey, Carla." Muriel tried to sound cheerful even though she was certain she knew why Carla had called.

"Muriel?" Carla sounded concerned.

"Yes?"

"Are you okay?"

"Of course. Why do you ask?" Muriel baited her, knowing exactly why she was asking the question.

"Well, Brad said he had been trying to reach you for ever. Where have you been? Why haven't you called him back?"

"Oh, I've been soooo busy, you know, getting the collection finished in time for market is overwhelming. No matter how much I plan in advance, something always happens. Fabric doesn't come in time, the pattern is off, the workers are moving slow."

"What I know is that you are avoiding him. Why, Muriel?" Carla sounded as if she would not be moved off her mission any time soon. "That's not like you. Even when you're at your most frantic you call people back. So what's really up with you?"

"Well, I'm glad you know me so well. What's up with me is I don't understand why you put me in this position in the first place. I was minding my own business, and now I have some man ringing my phone off the hook and sending me flowers. Did I ask you to set me up? I don't have time for this, Carla! I have a business to run and a life to catch."

"And exactly what kind of life is that alone, Muriel?"

"Carla, Carla, Carla! We've had this discussion before. There is nothing wrong with being single."

"Mmm hmm. You're absolutely right. There's nothing wrong with being single—if you're happy. But you're not happy."

"What? Carla, puh-leeze!"

"Don't you puh-leeze me!"

Boy, Carla can be tough when she wants to be. There was iron in her voice that silenced even Muriel.

"Now you listen to me, girlfriend. Don't give me that nonsense about being happy. I've got your address because I used to live there. Now you don't have to tell me your past, Muriel, but at some point you are going to have to face your fears. All I know is that you are one wounded sister. And believe me, playing the tough role will only play for so long before you implode. I've been there, done that, and I know keeping up the act doesn't work. At some point it's going to be curtains."

"Are you finished?" Muriel interjected.

"No, but something tells me you want me to be so I will conclude by saying, Muriel, you are a beautiful woman with a huge heart. Too huge to keep to yourself. Everything about you and your surroundings tells me you are a woman just waiting to be loved."

"What do my surroundings have to do with this?" Muriel was tired of the comments about her conflicting image and her place. "This isn't making any sense. Why don't *you* take Brad around to find a place? If he has so much money, why can't he hire a decorator? And who asked *you* to play *matchmaker?*" Muriel's temperature was rising along with her voice. Roxanne peeked around the corner, raising an inquiring eyebrow as if to ask, Do I need to break this up? Muriel waved her away as if swatting at an irritating fly.

"Listen to yourself. I think thou protesteth a bit too much. Am I pushing some buttons, hmm?"

"I tell you what, I am going to ignore this entire conversation for the sake of our relationship, 'cause I like you—even though I want to swat you right now. I don't ask much from my friends, Carla, but this one thing I do ask: Honor my personal business by staying out of it."

"Oh, I'm happy to do that, Muriel." Carla would not be bowed. "I will agree to no more matchmaking, but as your sister-in-Christ, understand and know I'm going to hold you accountable when I see you making a mistake whether you like it or not. So on that note I say call the man back; he does not deserve your rudeness."

"I'm sure he'll get over it."

"You are a coward, Muriel James. A tall, beautiful, perpetual coward."

"Oh, Carla," Muriel all of a sudden felt very tired. She hunched over her work table as if a tidal wave had just washed over her, drenching her in more exhaustion than she could bear. She knew she was weary to the bone.

"Don't 'oh Carla' me! Just call the guy. I don't care what you do after that, but my reputation is on the line."

"And who put herself in that position?"

"Are you and Al in cahoots or something?" Carla asked. "Just call him back, Muriel. It's the right thing to do."

"For whom?"

"For you. Besides, you should help a brother out."

"Are you sure you're white?" Muriel asked, chuckling at the familiar vernacular.

"Don't sidestep the issue. Caaaall him. Or should I hook us up on a conference call?"

"Goodbye, Carla!"

"Call him."

"Alright. Got to go."

"Call me back as soon as…"

"Will do, gotta go, b'bye!" Muriel pushed the off button on the phone before Carla could get out another word. She heaved a sigh of deep relief as if she had narrowly escaped a major catastrophe.

The phone rang before she could return it to the cradle. Without thinking Muriel pushed the answer button. "Carla, I really don't think…"

"Something tells me you think a lot…" a wonderful male voice interrupted.

Muriel's hand began trembling, causing a rattling sound against her earring. She clasped the phone with her other hand to still herself. Slowly a frown crossed her face, replacing the look of definite resolve she'd had a moment ago. "Who is this?" she slowly asked, already knowing the answer.

"This is Brad. Remember me? Ex-missionary and computer geek from coffee the other night? Did you get your flowers?"

"Yes, I did. They were…or should I say are, rather stunning, to say the least."

"Thank you. I picked them myself."

"That must have taken you a while." Muriel was surprised that she had fallen into the conversation so easily, all her previous angst forgotten.

"Actually no, I just sort of thought about what a woman like you would like, and I guess you could say I was *lee-ed* by the spi-rit." He finished the sentence with the flair of an affected preacher.

Muriel heard herself giggling, but it sounded far away. Now caught up in the moment, she fell into the scenario, "Why, pastor, you must really know Gawd!"

"Oh, indeed I do, dear sister," Brad chuckled and retorted with a lazy southern drawl. Then he grew serious. "Indeed I do." Just as abruptly he got to the point. "So, Muriel, how difficult would it be to get you to agree to have dinner? Nothing deep, just dinner. And this is not meant to make you uncomfortable."

"I'm not uncomfortable at all," Muriel said a little too quickly. What did Carla know? She was not running, just being careful.

"Good! Shall we say seven on Saturday then?" Brad smoothly transitioned to British politeness.

"That would be fine." Muriel fell in line, wondering why she was agreeing to this. He was slick.

"I'll pick you up at six thirty then. And now I'll let you get back to your day."

"Wait a minute—you don't know where I live." She couldn't believe she actually cared about his ability to find her.

"Oh yes I do. I've gotten all the information I need from Carla."

"I see." Muriel's stomach was sinking. *What else has Carla told him?*

As if reading her mind, Brad quickly said, "Hey, it's all good. See you Saturday. By the way, the florist said the fragrance of those particular flowers intensifies and reaches its peak in seven days, so you might want to take them home."

"Seven on Saturday, seven days of fragrance; what's up with you and sevens?"

"Ooo, you're sharp. Thanks for noticing. Seven is my favorite number."

"And why is that?" Muriel was growing more and more fascinated with this man who seemed to know how to put her at ease even against her will.

"It's the number of completion. And I never like to leave a matter unresolved." Brad's voice changed, but Muriel was unable to decipher what the change was suggesting. "See you Saturday, Lady Muriel."

"Mmm hmm. Bye." Once again Muriel was left speechless and wondering about the funny feeling that was invading her senses. She walked toward the flowers, and their haunting smell greeted her before she reached them. Rich and earthy. A little sweet, but clean. Nice, like an expensive perfume. She couldn't wait until the room was filled with their aroma in the next few days...or perhaps it was really Saturday she couldn't wait for.

13

*A*drian examined the canvas. Something was wrong. The woman she had painted looked as bad as she felt. Crouched and broken, what was supposed to look like a stance of victory looked more like a whimper for help. *Funny how art imitates life,* she thought. Broken—that is exactly how she felt. And now the very thing that she turned to in order to feel better was reflecting her pain instead of allowing her to escape from it. And yet she was determined to work her way through this.

She glanced at the papers still strewn across the couch, read but yet unsigned. The papers. The dreaded divorce papers that dared to define her life from the moment she signed them. He being the petitioner, she being the respondent. And yet she only had a vague notion of what she might be responding to. If the terminology was correct, then the papers lied. He hadn't petitioned anything of her except for a divorce. There had been no discussion of what he really wanted from her. Perhaps she would have felt better if she'd had the chance to respond as to whether she could comply with his wishes or not. No, she had not been given that chance. She'd simply been kicked to the curb for a younger, more shallow model. His assistant, some child by the name of Amber. And now Adrian was being asked to respond to a cold piece of paper, hand delivered by courier.

The wind had wrapped itself around her when she opened the door to their townhouse. Though they lived west of the lake, it seemed as if their street served as a wind tunnel proving to be quite insistent in making its power known to those attempting to step out into the world. No amount of heat from the fireplace could warm her as she opened the envelope to see the cold, hard facts written in black and white, pronouncing the end of her marriage. All she had to do was sign next to where the fastidious attorney had placed red arrows. It was all so simple…and yet it wasn't. Perhaps for him, but not for her. He was moving on to someone else, but what was she moving on to?

Was she to be placated by the tidy division of their assets and his seeming generosity? There was no amount of property appropriate to comfort her in her loss. She wondered if she would have been as devastated if he had simply left. To be left for someone else seemed a double assault against her identity as a woman. It caused her to question her desirability. And if she wasn't desirable enough, then she was totally at a loss. She had spent most of her life molding herself according to what he wanted, what would make him happy. And now she had been stripped of her identity. Who was she besides being Mrs. Ron Henderson? She no longer knew. So she stood before her easel trying to reclaim a piece of herself that had been buried under years of dust and neglect as she had gone in search of a warm body and love that came to life. It seemed that even here she had lost her touch. But she was determined to reclaim it. There was an urgency within her to identify the missing pieces of herself…and perhaps discover new ones.

Standing back, she flicked her brush at the canvas, splattering the image that was cowering on its surface. Again and again she shook the brush until the pitiful woman disappeared from sight. By the time she was finished, Adrian was as covered with paint as the canvas—but it felt good. It felt good to be a mess and admit it. There was some strange sort of redemption in the confession of this fact. Yes, confession was good for the soul. She was undone, totally undone. A tightly wound coil from within began to loosen and suddenly snapped. "God, where are You?" A wail came from deep within, sounding foreign but bringing release.

Merlot and Coco raised themselves from their resting places to gaze in deep concern as Adrian bent forward, holding herself. Time and time again she cried out as if in labor, birthing tears that could not be abated. She wept as though her soul was torn...and indeed it was.

The gaping wound Ron left behind could not be filled with money and belongings. It could only be filled with the things that truly mattered to her. His breath on her face in the morning when she woke up to find herself in his unconscious embrace. The laughter they shared over unspoken observances that only they understood. The pride of standing by his side and watching the reaction of his peers as he spoke and moved through a room. The way he smiled when he ate her food. The way he always touched her before he left the room, as if to leave a lasting impression while he was away. It was the little things. Never acknowledged out loud but always noted and now sorely missed.

And now there was nothing. She felt empty and ashamed to admit it. After all, she still had something of great import. She still had God. But right now even He did not seem to be enough to help her cross this river of loss and pain. She felt empty, ugly, devoid of anything, even her faith. It was something she did not want to admit as she haltingly moved closer to the mirror hanging on the wall above her desk. Leaning in, she studied her face. It was a pretty face even though it was streaked with paint and tears. She touched her hair. Her hair had been a source of pride to Ron. Luxuriously thick and long, flowing past the middle of her back, he loved to run his fingers through it and had always dissuaded her from cutting it. *Well, he is no longer here,* she thought as she reached for the scissors.

The rush of adrenaline that came when the first handful of hair fell into her palm fueled her courage to continue. Snip by snip she let it fall to the floor. It brushed her shoulders in soft farewell as if resigning to the fate of being separated from her and no longer being her glory. Finally finished and spent with the last flourish of her tool of transformation, she stood studying herself. Her eyes looked larger, her cheekbones more prominent. The fullness of her mouth was more pronounced. Gone was the softness that lured people to seek her out as a safe refuge from trouble. Now there was an edge to her countenance. It was hard to say if it was something in her eyes or the sharpness of her jawline that was now revealed from behind her hair. Her long neck gave her a regal air. It was as if she had come out of hiding. She ran her hands down the nape of her neck. It felt good to feel the air where a curtain of hair had been. Suddenly she felt free. She didn't know what from yet, but she chose to revel in the moment. Flinging her arms wide, she twirled, laughing at the nonsensical nature of it all. *Maybe I'm cracking up!* she thought. *What do I have to laugh about? Absolutely nothing! But does everything have to make sense? Obviously it didn't. Who could make sense of a man walking out of a perfectly beautiful home, leaving behind a wife who loved him?* She stopped. She had to get past that. She couldn't keep rehearsing the same question over and over again. Only God knew the answer, and she hadn't decided if she was talking to Him yet.

Adrian stood back, gazing around the room. *Wow!* she thought. *What a fine mess. If my friends could see me now their theories on my perfection would go right out the window.* The room was a mess. Her life was a mess. And she was a mess. A conglomeration of hair, paint, and tears made her a sight to behold. Out of habit she began to clean up—and then she stopped. Nope. She wasn't going to worry about it, at least not tonight. Sometimes when you've done all you can do, the best thing to do is celebrate being totally out of control. And with that she headed toward the promise of a bubble bath. The warmth of the water would anesthetize her pain for now.

14

"Tracy, I'm pregnant," Felicia said in her most grown-up voice. Then groaning, she looked at herself in the mirror and wilted, just as she knew she would under Tracy's disapproving gaze. She could never do anything right in Tracy's eyes. No matter how much she reached out to her, she always felt as though she was living under the cloud of an offense she would never be able to rectify. Tracy merely tolerated her, and Felicia didn't understand why. Well, perhaps she did, although it seemed like such an old story line.

An only child, Felicia had been spoiled. Her parents doted on her, giving her her heart's every desire. All she had to do was be the picture-perfect daughter, which she had mastered according to her parents' specifications so they could continue being the celebrity toasts of their socialite circle, in exchange for rewards that made them look even better. She was the beautiful one with the impeccable manners. Not especially bright, but her beauty would land her a good husband and life would continue on as it always did—with all the right clothing and worldly experiences in place. And so Felicia had watched her parents shuttle from charity events to fabulous soirees to political socials from time to time, leaving her in their wake with polite acknowledgements and fabulous trinkets, but never the love, tenderness, or real attention she yearned for.

Enter Tracy stage left…with the type of parents Felicia really wanted. Caring and attentive. Not as indulgent in the material sense with Tracy as her own parents, but for what Tracy lacked in goodies and trips, her parents made up for with their presence. While Felicia was more like the poor little rich girl, Tracy led a very healthy life rich in love. Tracy's parents, Felicia's aunt and uncle, were always so kind to Felicia, considering her to be the second daughter they never had. She had felt the loss as deeply as Tracy when her father died of cancer. It was as if she had lost a father too because he had shown her the affection her own father had not. Felicia used to wonder as a child if their love was out of pity or genuine affection.

This had set up a rivalry and much tension between Felicia and Tracy. Tracy was beautiful too. As a matter of fact, they were often mistaken for sisters, which seemed to irritate Tracy to no end. In Tracy's mind, Felicia was the spoiled brat who never had to work for anything. Meanwhile, she'd had to earn everything she wanted and share her parents with someone who never seemed to want for anything. Couldn't she have just one thing to herself? And so Felicia had tried to make up for it by weathering Tracy's disdain and showering her with gifts, which Tracy accepted while still keeping her at arm's length.

But there was also the flip side of Tracy. The part of her that felt responsible for Felicia in an irritated, big sister kind of way. If Felicia needed her help she would be there, but so would that expression of "I'm only doing this because you're family." And Felicia, happy for any sort of caring, lapped up whatever attention she could get—good, bad, or indifferent. By the time they reached college, Felicia's train of thought had moved beyond parents and Tracy to men. Never wanting for their attention, Felicia chose the ones she deemed exciting, taking her soap-opera life to even higher heights of drama.

She had a knack for selecting those who reinforced her feelings of loneliness and rejection. There was something strangely reassuring about knowing what to expect. Emotional distance had become her normal, and she knew how to deal with that. Whenever someone seemed to be truly serious about pursuing a committed relationship, Felicia found herself curiously uncomfortable and unable to decipher why the very thing she wanted scared her so. It was a vicious cycle. Girl meets nice guy, runs from nice guy to bad guy, bad guy hurts her, which attracts another nice guy who wants to rescue her, who she hurts for another bad guy who hurts her again. Tracy got tired of watching and told her so…many times. Felicia wondered if she had made a mistake attending the same university as Tracy. Their parents had thought it would be a good idea. After all, they could look out for each other. But it seemed Tracy had merely appointed herself the review board for Felicia's cycle of failure in the love department.

Never mind that Tracy made her own mistakes and was probably more like Felicia than she cared to admit. She too went for the wrong kind of guys; however, she seemed to almost deliberately sabotage her relationships, though this is something she refused to admit the few times Felicia had managed to get a word in edgewise. No, Tracy could do no wrong; it was she—Felicia—who was the mess, the mess Tracy and her friends Adrian and Muriel clucked over like mother hens, seemingly forgetting they were all in the same age range. And Felicia let them. Sometimes any type of attention was better than none.

They were all artistic, and that was their common bond. Muriel was the up and coming fashion designer on campus, winning awards at every presentation. She was as vibrant and alive as her designs, with a quick laugh and an edgy wit that intrigued many a guy on campus, none of whom she took notice of except for one. And what a one he was! Captain of the basketball team. A tall glass of cool chocolate milk. They were stunning together, both statuesque and dark with stunning features. Muriel was mush in his presence and the envy of every woman on campus. Her eyes said what her lips never did, but everyone knew she was over the moon for Cedric. Then just as suddenly as he had swept her off her feet, they were finished. Muriel never explained why, stating that the subject was off limits. But it seemed to Felicia that the light went out in her eyes and never came back on. From that day on she was distant, impatient, and a bit too driven when it came to her schoolwork.

When Felicia tried to broach the subject with Tracy, she had been reprimanded and told that perhaps she too could use a dose of Muriel's dedication when it came to her own courses. On that note it was never discussed again, although from time to time Felicia still wondered what had really happened and what Cedric had done to generate Muriel's lack of enthusiasm toward the male gender ever since.

All four women had done their own bit of evolving during those college years, though Adrian's metamorphosis was much more subtle. Deeply involved in theatre, Adrian could sing like a bird and dance like Ginger Rogers. Beautiful and shapely, she was a perfect candidate for stardom. Even more appealing was that she remained humble while being so talented. And if that wasn't enough, she could paint beautiful, gallery-quality images that invited appreciation from art connoisseurs who commissioned her work.

And then came Ron interrupting her flow. Handsome and smooth, touted as one of the up-and-coming brothers who would definitely make a name for himself. He had added capturing Adrian's heart to his list of things to accomplish, distracting her away from all the glitter that awaited her, though everyone admitted the glow on her face never burned brighter. It seemed to make sense at the time. This talented woman would enjoy being the star of a home versus the stage any day, as well as the perfect trophy wife for Ron. So when she traded her cap and gown for a wedding ring it seemed natural to everyone. As long as she was happy that's all that mattered. As a matter of fact, they all envied her and wondered how they had missed the obvious graduation transition. After all, their secret goal at college was to walk away with a mate in addition to a diploma.

Felicia chuckled in retrospect. Interesting how life had turned out. Everyone had expected her to be the one who landed a man in college and become a pampered housewife. Instead she had chosen romantic experiences over commitment and barely scraped across the academic finish line. In spite of it all, she had made a name for herself in the interior design industry. Even Tracy had to grudgingly give her her props. While Tracy went left into the world of advertising, hobnobbing with celebrities and enticing the world to eat, drink, and be merry, Felicia had sailed brilliantly into what she did best—spending other people's money to make things beautiful. Now that their parents had been able to relax since both Felicia and Tracy had turned out "right," the only expectation they now had to live up to was getting along with one another. And so their reticent sisterhood had continued, more out of effort exerted by Felicia than championed by Tracy.

From her parents to Tracy to the men in her life, Felicia's relationships mirrored one another. On the surface they looked normal enough, but each had the underlying theme of distance, of not being truly satisfying connections. Yet she was determined to work at these unfulfilling alliances, secretly longing for more and yet concluding this was all there was or, worse yet, it was all she deserved. At one point she had sought counseling but quickly stopped going after being told that all her relationships were codependent and that she should get to the root of why she pursued those who didn't love her. It had been too much information too fast. She decided it was easier to deal with what she knew rather than try to navigate through the waters of the unfamiliar. What would she do with someone who truly loved her and actually wanted pieces of her that she didn't know how to give because they had never been given to her? It was all too scary, and so she had chosen to dance around the fringes of her desires rather than go for the gold and perhaps find herself incapable of really claiming it. As much as she came off as a space cadet to others, failure was her biggest fear. What constituted failure she hadn't decided yet. It usually was associated with the opinions of others. What her mother and father expected. What their friends expected. What Tracy expected. Felicia wasn't quite sure what she expected of herself. *Ah, but now,* she mused, *my unanticipated state of affairs changes everything.*

She eyed the box that had now made it to the dining room table after several weeks of sitting in the hallway. It was the only thing in her apartment that seemed out of place. It screamed for attention—attention she didn't want to give it because she already knew what was in it. Her mother's subtle hints on what was acceptable attire came in the form of boxes containing expensive designer clothes, which ended up hanging at the back of Felicia's closet until she made one of her rare trips home to model one in front of her mother at one auspicious occasion or another. The clothes were beautiful and expensive. They just weren't her. This was a conversation that would go nowhere if she tried to have it with her mom, so Felicia avoided all confrontation by complying with her mother's wishes until she was back in her own space and able to express herself as she pleased, fashion and otherwise.

Subconsciously she sucked her thumb as she sank down on her favorite satin lavender chaise, reaching for one of the pillows she caressed as if it were a baby. Clinging to it for comfort, she let her eyes travel around the room. It was soft and pretty. Shades of lavender, gray, and silver gave a feminine coolness to the room. Beautiful black-and-white photographs matted in white and framed in black added an unexpected clean edge to the surrounding softness. A classic baby grand piano that Felicia didn't know how to play anchored the room, giving the overall appearance of a gallery—artistic, perfect for a good party or a quiet evening of reclining in luxury. It was beautiful, and she had done it herself, so why was she still allowing herself to be pushed around by other people's opinions?

She might be able to dismiss her mother's fashion selections, but her current situation was different. A baby was not about outward appearance. Something was growing inside her. She would keep the baby—that was not even an issue in her mind. Perhaps this would be the chance for her to love someone fully without fear. She looked at her reflection in the mirror. She looked the same—lean and polished in her Michael Kors suit. She wondered how much her body that she took so much pride in would change. But even that did not faze her as she considered that perhaps this was a "God thing" as Muriel would call it. Felicia realized that it wasn't a "God thing" to have sex before marriage. Still, she believed that perhaps God could use the consequences of her mistake to turn her life around for the better. Finally the opportunity to give and receive the type of love she had always wanted to experience was within her reach. She would love this child unconditionally. She wouldn't overwhelm it with expectations as her parents had her. The primary issue was no longer about a man. Suddenly the priority had shifted to preserving someone who would be totally dependent on her. Could she do it? A child was not a room you could adorn until it met your liking. It couldn't be discarded or rearranged. It was what it was and would still expect to be loved.

Perhaps because she knew the sting of rejection firsthand, Felicia could give what she had never received—love and affection, pure and simple. She pulled herself up to her full height in the mirror. That clinched it. She didn't care what anyone had to say. Not her parents, not Tracy, not even Kenny, her baby's father. In her heart of hearts she had known from the beginning he would not be a permanent fixture. Now that she had resolved these issues, she was back to her original question. Since she was keeping the baby, who would she break the news to first? Her momentary courage subsided as she reached for the phone, punched the numbers quickly, and endured the rings. At the first sound of a pickup, Felicia spoke first, "Hello, Adrian, are you busy tomorrow evening?"

15

*T*racy peered through the dimness of the theatre at the couple nestling together a few rows in front of them. "Earth to Tracy! What are you thinking about so hard, girl?" Derrick's eyes followed her gaze toward the black man seated next to the white woman then swung back to Tracy. "You are ruining our date. You didn't really invite me out to ignore me, did you?"

"Hmm? Oh, I'm sorry…"

"What is up with you?" Derrick was frowning, trying to decide if he should be concerned or irritated. "Hey, you're not one of those sisters that gives a brother a hard time because he likes vanilla are you?"

"What?" His question jolted Tracy back to the present. Then catching Derrick's drift and averting her gaze before she was caught staring, she replied, "Nooo…" in an unfamiliar octave. "I don't get it, but whatever floats your boat, I suppose."

"Now see, that answer is loaded with disapproval. What don't you get?"

"I don't get why so many brothers are passing perfectly good sisters by in pursuit of white women. Isn't it bad enough that we are suffering from a shortage already? Between all the black men who are either dead, in prison, or gay, there's not that many good ones left. And for the few that remain to defect to the other side…well, I find it disturbing. That's what I don't get."

"Listen to you!" Derrick was leaning back in his seat looking at her. "Defect to the other side? Is this a war? Why don't you get that brothers want the same thing as sisters without the angst?"

"What is *that* supposed to mean?"

"Now let me preface this by saying that I love sisters, okay? Remember, I date and happen to be in love with a black woman. However, sisters could learn a thing or two from white women."

"What!" Tracy was about to lunge out of her seat. Derrick ducked as her voice level rose, attracting attention from the other several rows of people.

"What? What?" He mimicked her but wouldn't back down. "Are you not hearing me? What is it going to take for black women to learn they need to switch up their game? Cut the brothers a break? Brothers are tired, Tracy. Black women are fine, but they make loving them hard work."

"What do you mean by that?" She resisted the urge to knock him across the head.

"Ssssh!" An insistent voice behind them shushed them to silence as the movie began.

"We'll talk about this la…" Tracy began to whisper. Then, a sharp intake of air cut off the rest of her sentence. The couple in front of her had finally separated. The man's face was turning in her direction as if to second the motion of the shusher behind them. It was Evan. Evan with that woman Felicia must have seen him with. She was indeed white. Not that it should have mattered, but Tracy had to admit it did as she absorbed the feeling of being doubly rejected. He turned back toward his companion while Tracy sat transfixed, boring a hole into his profile. Derrick followed the direction of her stare, then turned toward Tracy. She knew that if she allowed him to say anything she would have a meltdown in front of him, and she simply could not bear that. Before he could say anything, she silenced him by placing her hand on his arm. "I'm alright, let's just watch the movie."

The movie was one big Technicolor blur. Tracy had looked forward to this evening all week. *Mahogany* was one of her favorite old movies. Derrick always humored her and went along on her old movie jaunts while Shirley opted out, preferring more artsy fare. Armed with popcorn and gummy bears, Tracy had settled into her seat prepared to repeat her favorite lines and lose herself in the fashion savvy of Diana Ross being pursued by that fine Billy Dee Williams. Now all she wanted to do was run out of the theatre, but pride glued her to her seat.

She could feel Derrick's concern; it was draped around her like a heavy blanket. She knew it was killing him not to say anything, but she couldn't hear it right now. No, she did not *want* to hear it. And so she sat with unseeing eyes glued to the screen. Billy Dee's words stung her as he announced to Diana, "Success is nothing unless you have someone to share it with." Shoot, she knew that. But where were the men who crossed continents to claim their woman? Who weren't intimidated by their successes? Where were the men who would wrestle a woman's heart to the floor and pin it down, claiming it for their own no matter how difficult the pursuit? What was supposed to be an evening of lighthearted flight down memory lane had raised way too many painful questions.

As soon as the credits began to roll, she made a hasty beeline for the lobby, which was out of Evan's sight. Derrick struggled to catch up.

"Whoa, hold up, girl." Grabbing her by the shoulder he whirled her around to face him, frowning as he searched her face for signs of distress. Tracy concentrated hard on creating a mask that he could not read. "Are you okay?"

"I'm fine." There was no power or breath beneath her words, but it was all she could muster.

"Breathe." Derrick was standing in front of her, motioning with his hands. As if hypnotized she followed his direction, taking in a deep gulp of air and slowly letting it out.

"Can we leave, please?" She could not take another Evan sighting.

"Of course…"

Derrick was being so understanding. Tracy felt every bit as fragile as he was treating her as she allowed herself to be led out into the crisp air. For once it felt good.

Derrick was frowning at her now, searching her face. "Why didn't you tell me about this?"

"I just couldn't, okay? Besides, you've explained to me why he would choose her over me so we can move on now."

"Aww, now you're going to take a general conversation entirely out of context. That is not fair!" Tracy could see he was gearing up for a long, drawn-out conversation she couldn't handle. Holding up her hand she cut him off. "I can't talk about this anymore. Did you know that Ron left Adrian?"

Derrick looked confused. "What? Run that by me again?"

"Ron left Adrian. Keep up with the conversation." Tracy was impatient for him to move on.

The dawning of enlightenment that he was being diverted to another topic illuminated his face.

"Really!" It was more an exclamation than a question of surprise.

"Is that all you have to say?" This was not the response Tracy had expected.

"I can't say I'm surprised."

"What?"

"You know you have really worn out that word today."

"I'm just not getting you. Why wouldn't you be surprised? I'm shocked. Adrian was the perfect wife. Easy to love, as you would put it." She couldn't resist a little dig.

"Perhaps a little too perfect."

"Hmm, that's what Felicia said." Tracy stopped to look at Derrick in dismay.

"Perhaps Felicia is smarter than I thought." Derrick chuckled at this revelation, but stopped short as Tracy's eyes began to narrow. "But let's stay focused. Let's look at the evidence. Ron has a bit of game about him, if you know what I mean. And Adrian is, well, kind of like a Stepford wife. Now don't get me wrong," cutting off Tracy as she opened her mouth to defend her friend, Derrick continued, "she's beautiful and she's nice. But be for real. Can you imagine her making love to her husband? No! That would come too close to messing up her hair."

"Derrick!"

"Well, you asked my opinion…"

"That was too much information."

"But she's the one who's the good little Christian, right?"

"What does that have to do with anything?"

"Well, that's all I've ever heard about her. What else does she do? She stays at home, she goes to church, that's it."

"What's wrong with that? I thought you men needed to be needed. Ron gets to be the hero, bring home the bacon, and feel like a man. What else could he want?" Tracy was truly getting angry now, glued to the spot with one hand on her hip. The cold air was a thick mist resembling the smoke from a cigarette as she spat her comeback to Derrick's theorizing. But Derrick was not backing down.

"He could want someone who is interesting. He's out in the high-powered world of sports management, mixing and mingling with a lot of testosterone and perfume, wheeling and dealing. That's a lot of excitement and hormones. Then he goes home. What does she bring to the party at the end of the day? What does she have to talk about? The latest recipe and the Lord?"

"Now *that* is disrespectful."

"I didn't intend it that way. My mama is a saved woman, but she didn't let it cramp her style. She stayed at home, but she mixed it up too. My father was not a bored man, okay?"

"Kudos to you for having one of the rare, well-adjusted families in America!"

Derrick ignored her sarcasm. "All I'm saying is a man needs mental stimulation. He doesn't just want a lady in the living room and a playmate in the bedroom. He wants someone who stirs him up mentally."

"Boy, the list is getting longer and longer. You know you men want a lot and give way too little." Tracy turned on her heel and began stomping up the avenue. The fashions of the chic boutiques she loved to frequent were lost on her as she made a beeline toward the corner.

"That's not true! Again, that goes back to your previous choices, but that's another conversation. I'm sure there's more to Adrian than meets the eye, but I've never seen it when I'm around her. She always seemed a little too contained to me, and Ron seemed restless. Even though she mastered most of the things a man wants, she left out the most important ingredient—being herself. And that was probably what got his attention in the first place. Somewhere along the way she decided that acting like a wife looked different from who she was as his lady, and that's when she lost the game."

"Is love a game, Derrick?"

"To some degree it is. There are a lot of unspoken rules, and wise players find out what those are."

Right now Tracy wasn't feeling at the top of her game at all, exasperated yes, wise no. "Oh forget it. It's too much information to keep up with."

"It's not brain surgery, Tracy. A woman's got to learn not to lose the important parts of herself while she's investing herself in her man. Remember, it's your flaws that make you interesting. Perfection is highly overrated. All it does is magnify your man's imperfections in his own eyes and make him feel like a failure. And that is the quickest way to push a man into another woman's arms. It might not be right, but he will find somebody to make him feel alright about himself."

Tracy was feeling more hopeless by the minute, and it showed, causing Derrick to switch channels.

"Well, enough man secrets for today. I better get you home and out of the cold."

As they walked silently into the wind toward the lakefront, Tracy didn't even notice the cold so deeply entrenched was she into what Derrick had said. He was right about Adrian. She had thought many times about it and done her own comparisons between Adrian in college and the married woman she now knew. But Tracy had chalked up Adrian's behavior to growing older and thus change was to be expected. Plus Adrian was so sweet. How could one vocalize such things in a way that wouldn't be insulting? Hurting Adrian would be like hurting an innocent child. But perhaps her neutral stand had cost her friend what could have been saved had she said something. And now here was Derrick stating the facts that could no longer be ignored.

He also said some things that cut her a bit too deeply. What was it Muriel always said? "The truth will set you free, girl." If that was the case, what was the truth about her? Was she difficult to love? How could she be something other than what she was? What did that mean for her future? Would she ever get the love she wanted without having to compromise herself?

Tracy turned the corner, relieved that home was in sight. She loved the fact that she lived in the middle of everything and that all the things she enjoyed indulging in were within a twenty-minute walking radius. It was city living at its best, especially for a single woman. She didn't even feel the blast of wind from off the lakefront as she headed into the homestretch, picking up her pace the closer she got to the entrance to her apartment building. She wanted to be inside the safe confines of her own living room should she choose to lose it completely. It was taking everything within her not to fall apart in front of Derrick. She could hear Derrick trying to keep up with her. "Good gravy, woman! Who are you racing with? Slow down…" As she reached the front of her building he grabbed her elbow, turning her around to face him. Concern was etched in his face as his eyes searched hers intently. "Tracy, you know I wouldn't ever say anything to hurt you, don't you?"

"I know that, Derrick, but sometimes the truth hurts. That doesn't mean it's any less true."

"Well, know this truth: Hard to love is definitely something you are not."

"You sure?"

"Positive. Shoot, girl, you know you my boo. That man just wasn't ready for prime-time TV—pardon the pun, with him being an actor and all." Tracy looked at him without blinking.

Derrick frowned. "I'm trying to be funny, and you are not cooperating. I know a good woman when I see one! See? You shoulda stuck with me while you had me."

Tracy was laughing and crying at the same time, embarrassed over being so vulnerable in front of him. Derrick stared at her intently. Taking her chin into his hand, he gently kissed her forehead and wrapped his arms around her, drawing her close. It felt so good to be hugged. Tracy relaxed in his embrace, breathing him in. The cell phone in his coat breast pocket interrupted their embrace. Derrick released her to answer the phone. "That's probably Shirley. I promised I'd pick her up after the show." He answered the phone. "Hey, baby, I'm on my way. I was just seeing Tracy home. Alright, in a minute. Bye." He hung up and turned his attention back to Tracy apologetically. "I'm sorry. You sure you're gonna be okay?" Tracy could see him struggling between being concerned for her while being like a car on high idle, anxious to move on.

"Yeah, I'll be fine. You better not keep Shirley waiting."

Again he studied her face, then ever so gently he ran a finger down her cheek. Backing slowly down the sidewalk, he tipped his head to the side.

Tracy mustered a brave smile and halfheartedly waved him goodbye. He waved back, and then he turned and made his way up the street. Tracy watched him go. The farther away he got, the more cold, alone, and confused she felt. Taking a long, shaky breath, she turned to go home, pondering all her past decisions and present emotions, trying to make some sense of her heart. She smiled at the thought of her psychoanalysis. Certainly it would take more than an evening to come to terms with everything.

16

*C*oming!" Felicia could hear Adrian's muffled voice behind the door, sounding a little winded. As the door swung open, Felicia stared. Adrian stood before her, hair now cut into a short boyish crop, gelled on top, and standing on end. Blue jeans, bare feet, a chipped pedicure, dirty nails, and an oversized man's white shirt with splotches of paint on it finished the picture. Felicia had never seen Adrian in blue jeans before. She couldn't even imagine Adrian ever cutting the long, thick mane she had always taken so much pride in. Or having scruffy hands and feet. As a matter of fact, she never pictured Adrian looking like this, period. "Come on in," Adrian was saying as she turned and headed back into the house. Felicia obediently followed her taking in the scene before her eyes.

"Your hair..." the words escaped Felicia before she had a chance to think of reeling them back in.

Adrian stopped, turned, and gave her a grin. "Oh, I decided I needed a change." With that she felt no need for further explanation. She headed back down the foyer and gave a wave. "Come on in," she repeated. Felicia wondered if she forgot that she had said that already. Her concern over Adrian's hair, which she decided to let rest for now, was replaced by the scene before her.

The house was mostly dark except for light coming from the den. Though nothing looked out of order, there was the sense that nothing had been touched either. A thin film of dust had settled on the coffee table and the exquisite wood pieces that added a distinctive touch to

Adrian's huge living room. *Odd.* Adrian's house was always immaculate. On any given day she made sure the rooms were aglow with light, whether it be mood lighting or functional. Often candles were lit and soft funnels of illumination streamed from strategic places to create an atmosphere that not even the latest decorating magazines could rival. Tonight there was no mood to speak of. Well, perhaps depression, but Adrian didn't seem depressed. *Odd,* Felicia thought to herself again.

"Sit," Adrian said with flair as she pointed to a love seat in front of a huge, half-finished painting. Next to the canvas was a worktable with tubes of paints and various mixtures and hues of oils. Adrian reached for her palette. "You like?"

Felicia was still trying to reconcile this vision of Adrian, unkempt and imperfect, while taking in the painting, which also seemed uncharacteristic for her dear proper friend. Although it wasn't finished, it was breathtaking. The image of a woman in a midnight flight on the back of an incredible horse. The rider was nude with flowing locks strategically placed. The light of the moon lit her face and cast shadows on the floor of the desert sand they streaked across. There was a look of sheer exuberance on her face as she gripped the horse's mane. "Um…" Felicia didn't know what to say.

"I call it 'Freedom Flight.' You don't like it…" Adrian frowned.

"No…I mean yes. It's incredible." Felicia was still trying to make sense out of everything she was taking in. "Can Christians paint nudes?"

"Of course they can! Leonardo DaVinci and Michelangelo did it all the time. Plus God created the body, and it's beautiful, don't you think?" Adrian laughed.

"When did you start painting again?"

"Oh, I've been at it for a couple of weeks now. I had forgotten what a form of escape it was for me."

"What are you running from, Adrian?"

"Pain, Felicia. What else?" Adrian suddenly sounded tired.

"I'm sorry, that was a foolish question." Felicia felt very small and very embarrassed, as if overhearing something she shouldn't have and not quite knowing what to do with the information.

"Don't worry about it. It's the first time I've admitted it—perhaps that's good."

"I'm definitely a believer in facing your feelings and keeping short accounts. It's not good for your health to keep stuff bottled up inside." Felicia was relieved to move on. She was much more comfortable when it came to dealing with anyone's pain but her own.

"I suppose that's true, but I also think it's important to have an outlet. When I paint, not only is it a release for me from all the stuff I've buried down inside, but I feel as if I'm in a deep conversation with God. Telling Him how I feel with every stroke you know?"

This was truly foreign to Felicia, who never felt as if anyone was ever listening to her except her clients. "Do you think He really hears you?" she asked, sounding like a small child.

"Of course He does! He hears even the things I don't say. I feel as if all the different colors on the canvas mirror the tears I haven't been able to cry. Yes, this is my silent communication with Him." Adrian was almost whispering now, her mind drifting beyond where she was standing.

"Does He say anything back?"

"Oh yes! He whispers all sorts of sweet promises to me. He lets me know everything is going to be alright." Adrian was looking as if she was talking about a man she was deeply in love with. Again Felicia felt at a loss for words, but she was envious of this sweet, intimate relationship Adrian seemed to be having. How she longed for that with someone. *Can God really satisfy a person like that?* she wondered. Switching the conversation to find a more comfortable spot, she focused on the painting.

"You know, this painting is quite revealing about where you are right now."

"Is that so?" Adrian arched her brow.

"Mmm hmm. It shouts unbridled passion just waiting to get out… pardon the pun."

"Ya think?"

"I know!"

"Well, you know what they say: Still waters run deep."

"I guess they do. Somehow I never got that picture of you. You were the one in the group who seemed to have it all together, more sure, more safe with a tidy life. Nothing out of place—you know…perfect."

"Yes, I recall you using that word before in another conversation." Adrian's voice changed to one of dry sarcasm.

"I didn't mean to be insulting. It's just that…well…"

"I know what you think, Felicia. And even though it hurt, I had to consider what you said. Perhaps in trying to be the perfect wife to Ron I overlooked something. Maybe it got to a point where I was going through the motions without the emotions. Kind of like being religious as opposed to having a relationship with God. I stopped hearing Ron and feeling him. I was just busy serving him. The house was always clean. Dinner was always on the table, blah, blah, blah. I think I bored myself to be honest, but I was so busy doing all the right things I didn't even notice that it wasn't fun anymore. I think a lot of wives do that with their husbands. So you weren't so far off the mark."

"I hope I'm not getting too personal, but I do have my reason for asking. How was the sex?"

"It was fine." Adrian waved her hand casually as if absentmindedly shooing away a fly. "You know, Felicia, I know you single women are always envisioning that married people have all these romantic nights, but they are not having as much sex as you think they are."

"Ooo, wrong answer. Fine? Not great or fantastic—just fine? I don't buy it!" Felicia looked horrified. "What's the point then, Adrian? If you can't have a hot romance with your husband, then who can you have one with? Excuse me for saying this, but it is an objective statement. Ron is one hot brother. I can't picture him being cool with sex that is just 'fine.' If he wasn't on you, then you should have known something was wrong. You didn't suspect anything?

"Wait a minute. Didn't God tell you anything?" Felicia asked. "'Cause if you all got it like that, it seemed like He would have pulled your coat-tail. No disrespect, but I'm trying to figure this thing out. If you can't keep your life together, then I don't have any hope." Felicia could feel herself crumbling inside so she stopped herself from going on any further. She had become distracted by Adrian's situation and provoked with a strange yearning to figure out her relationship with God and how all the pieces fit together.

The urgency underneath Felicia's questions took Adrian aback. She took a moment before answering. "Yes, I did notice a change in Ron, but I attributed it to stress on his job. I should have asked him, but I didn't. Did God tell me anything? I think He did but I wasn't listening. I was so busy praying for Ron's salvation, I kept hearing, 'Give him what he wants, not what you think he needs.' I guess I didn't get it. I would look in his eyes, and they were looking through me. I couldn't figure out how to get him back, so I just prayed and hoped for the best."

Felicia leaned in. "Adrian, tell me, just how does this prayer thing work? You talk to God; He talks to you. But isn't there more? Don't you have to do anything? I mean this is the part I don't get about Christians. They always seem to be waiting for God to wave a magic wand and *bling!* He'll make all their wishes come true. Does it really work like that? Or am I missing something? Exactly how does He talk to you, anyway? And how do you know it's Him?"

Adrian's face went the gamut from embarrassed to ironically amused in a flash before she put up her hands in protest. "Whoa! One question at a time. You're making me feel like a bad example."

"I'm sorry, I didn't mean to…"

"No, don't apologize. You just put me in spiritual check. It's all good. I will take my lashes. You're right, Felicia. As we say in Christian lingo, faith without works is dead. God does expect us to follow His instructions in order to have a better life. If we don't, well then we suffer the consequences. Where we all get into trouble is when we think God should do what *we* want Him to do instead of *us* doing what *He wants us* to do. So in the midst of me deciding what He needed to make happen in Ron's life, I failed to do what I needed to do to make my marriage work. Does that make sense?"

"I guess so. But how do you know when it's God talking and not just you thinking something?"

"When you know His personality because you read His Word and spend time learning all about Him, then when He speaks you recognize His voice. Whether it be a quiet knowing you get deep down inside or a phrase that comes alive as you read it in your Bible or something someone says that just resonates with you, you know it's Him. Our friendship is a good example. You've gathered enough information about me over the years to know my heart. If someone else told you something about me, you would know if they were telling the truth or not because you know me personally. When I call you on the phone you don't have to ask who it is. You recognize my voice. That's how it is with God."

"But can you really talk to Him about anything?"

"Anything, Felicia. That's what friends are for. And He is the one friend who will always be there and never let you down. And let me tell you, it's during times like these that you really find that out. Although Ron is gone and it hurts, I know it's not as deep a pain as it could be. It feels as if God has me in the center of His hands, holding me and reassuring me that I'm not alone."

Felicia's eyes were getting bright.

"Is everything okay, Felicia?" Adrian looked at her with great concern.

Felicia didn't want to appear desperate, and she fought to reel her emotions back in. "I'm fine. It's just interesting to me. My family wasn't religious. We didn't go to church or anything—too many late nights on Saturdays, I guess. And you seem to be taking this situation in your life so calmly that I'm trying to figure out how you're coping so well."

"I see. Are you sure something isn't bothering you? You sounded a little upset when you called, so naturally I assumed you had something on your mind you needed to talk about."

"Oh nooo…I'm fine. I was just worried about you, that's all." Felicia decided Adrian had enough to worry about and didn't need her to add another bomb to the minefield, though she seemed to be putting up a brave front, her drastic measures with her hair signaled otherwise. "Anyway, I need to get going. You keep the faith, okay?" She gently kissed Adrian on the cheek as if tenderly kissing a child good night.

Perusing the painting as she rose to go, Felicia said, "Keep up the good work, girl. I hate to say it, but if it took Ron leaving to get you back to painting, it might be a good thing. I think I have a client who would love to buy this when you're done."

Adrian chuckled. "Oh, Felicia, you always know just what to say!"

Felicia winced. "Did I do it again? And just when I thought I had fixed everything. Oh well, girl, you know I love you. Work with me."

Adrian laughed. "Do I have a choice?"

Felicia grew serious. "Yes, you do. Thanks for always being here for me, Adrian. I really do appreciate it." Then snapping out of it, she said, "Gotta go, b'bye. That's enough emotion for me. Ta ta—I'll see myself out."

And with that Felicia was gone in a flurry of fur and cashmere.

Adrian watched her rapid retreat then thoughtfully picked up her palette and brush. But the painting was blurred by her concern for Felicia. Something was not right. She could feel it in her spirit, and she refused to ignore the sensation again. However she wouldn't push her; she would wait until Felicia was ready to talk about it. In the meantime, she would pray.

17

*M*uriel ran the powder puff over her flawless skin, leaving a satiny ebony finish. Smudging black liner around her luminous chocolate eyes and squinting for good measure, she studied her face before continuing her beauty regime. Pursing her lips and applying her signature soft-pink gloss, she surveyed the final results while absentmindedly tugging at the soft curls at the nape of her neck. It was more out of habit than of need that she did this. Stepping back from the mirror she heaved a sigh. There was nothing left to do except wait for the doorbell to ring. No more distractions were available to thwart the nervousness she felt.

Why she had agreed to dinner with Brad escaped her at this moment. *Well, Carla will be happy,* Muriel told herself. *Perhaps she will leave me alone after this.* Muriel shook herself. The mixed bag of feelings that had been threatening to surface were bubbling beneath her tough-girl resolve once again. She had to admit she was ambivalent about her dinner date. Part of her looked forward to more banter with Brad; the other part of her was backpedaling with record-breaking speed. She hated this. Men seemed to always set her off kilter. There was no such thing as just having a man in your life. They came bringing the strangest mix of exhilaration and misery known to the human race. She had managed to avoid the anxiety associated with relationships for…oh…she couldn't even remember now. And what was the point anyway? She had her plate full with getting on the fast track to rapid success with her design business. That had always been the perfect excuse to hide and be shielded from the types of situations Tracy and Felicia had often commiserated about during the customary get-together meals.

Muriel couldn't bear the thought that she might be setting herself up for one of those episodes, so she had voted not to share her dating plans with anyone. That way if nothing came of it, she would be spared the disgrace of having to rehearse the details of the disaster back to them, spared the nursing, rehearsing, processing, and diagnosing what went wrong. She hated that. Even the thought of it. Anticipating a negative outcome was enough to make her consider bowing out of the evening. Perhaps she could catch him before he got to her house…but, then again, she had not taken down his number so determined had she been not to return his call.

The doorbell sounded, signaling it was too late to chicken out now. Muriel took a deep breath and a last backward glance in the mirror. She did look nice, if she did say so herself. She opened the door a little too quickly, signaling to herself there would be no turning back.

"Oh, wow!" Now it was Brad's turn to look slightly off kilter. "You look absolutely beautiful, Ms. James."

"Why thank you, pastor." Muriel voted for wit to hide her nervousness. "Would you like to come in for a glass of lemonade?" she drawled in her best southern accent.

"Don't mind if I do, young lady." Brad quickly followed her lead in tone as well as physically following her through the foyer into the living room. "Ooo, nice!" He surveyed the room. It was tastefully taupe and cream with accents of deep ebony and mahogany pieces of ethnic carvings arranged artfully. Amazing original paintings and fabric hangings looked down from high open ceilings as if to follow the visitors that viewed them. Her living room looked more like a gallery than a place where someone lived, and yet it was inviting and comfortable at the same time.

"You like?" Muriel followed his eyes.

"Absolutely! No wonder Carla suggested you help me with my place. Hey, I have that same carving! Where did you get that?" Brad zeroed in on a soapstone sculpture that looked almost suspended on a clear pedestal.

"From a vendor who goes to South Africa."

"Wait a minute—a little short guy, slightly balding, always has a story about each piece?"

"How did you know?"

"That guy makes the rounds, but he always has the best pieces you don't see anywhere else."

"Except in my living room, huh?"

"Well, great minds think alike, I suppose." Brad looked at her slyly. "Could it be we actually have something in common?"

"Perhaps we do." Muriel was suddenly uncomfortable, and the air grew thick as they stood looking at one another across the room.

"Well, I think that if we are to make our seven o'clock reservation we best be on our way. I'll have to get the rest of the tour another time." Brad chose to break the mood and get back to safer ground.

"Tour?"

"Oh, but of course! If the living room is any indication of your decorating talents, I'm ready to see the rest. And get your help with my own efforts if I pass this evening's inspection."

"Hmm, we'll see about that. The verdict is still out."

"I guess I have my work cut out for me then. Here, let me help you with that." He took her shawl from her hands and gently placed it around her shoulders.

"You do get big points for politeness." As she opened the door, Muriel felt revived by the night air.

"My mama raised me right," Brad said, leading her to the car and swinging open the door. He tucked her into his Mercedes as if she were a fragile package.

Muriel worked to get the look of being impressed off her face by the time he had settled in beside her.

The sound of one of her favorite artists surrounded her as they pulled away from the curb. "Lizz Wright! She is one of my favorites!"

"Really? Wow, two things in common. I must really be on a roll."

"Don't get ahead of yourself now," Muriel said as she smiled and leaned back into the headrest. She shut her eyes.

Brad chuckled. He adjusted the sound as the song continued, "Something about you really, really moves me..." Muriel wondered if he had purposely selected this song. *What am I thinking?* she thought. She recalled the words from one of her favorite Christian authors: "A man says hello and a woman starts imagining what color peau de soie pumps she's going to wear to her wedding." *Slow down girl, it's just dinner,* she said to herself. She had always wondered what the percentage of people getting together through the famous singles organization that arranged lunch dates for those in the market for a mate really was. It certainly hadn't worked for Felicia. "It's 'Just Lunch'! It was just a disaster," she had said, reporting that to her horror she had been set up with an exboyfriend. They had spent the entire lunch arguing over why they had broken up in the first place.

Brad cleared his throat. "Are you going to hold your thoughts for ransom or share what's on your mind?"

"That depends on how much you're willing to pay."

"I have to pay for the conversation and dinner? This could get expensive." Brad pretended to whine.

And what a dinner it was! This time Muriel didn't try to hide her look of amazement as he ushered her into one of the most exclusive restaurants in the city. She didn't know if she was more impressed with the prices on the menu or the fact that he had actually managed to get a reservation in the first place. The waiting list was at least a month long, it was rumored, thwarting any attempt from her and her crew to check it out on their monthly forays to sample food at new restaurants.

Muriel could not poke a hole in the evening if she tried. The food was delicious. The service impeccable. The owner himself had come out to say hi to Brad, completing the puzzle as to how he had been able to get in on such short notice. The two laughed and reminisced about old school days and all the trouble they had gotten into together.

She saw another side of her date as his friend shared what life was like as a single parent since the death of his wife, who had succumbed to breast cancer. The look of compassion in Brad's eyes as he covered his friend's hand in empathetic silence brought a lump to her throat that she was still trying to swallow after the owner had walked away to resume his duties.

"I really feel for him. She was everything to him." Brad's eyes had turned dark blue so filled were they with concern.

"So it seems. It has to be scary to love someone like that."

"Why do you say that?"

"Because life happens. People leave or die or do something horrible that disappoints and devastates you. I sometimes wonder if loving is really worth it if it causes so much pain."

"That's a deep statement to make, Muriel. I take it you've been hurt deeply before?" Brad asked the question ever so quietly, but nevertheless it was loaded with intensity.

Muriel hunched her shoulders and shifted in her seat uneasily. "It's all relative, isn't it? Actually, I was speaking in general terms. Have you been hurt before, Brad?"

Brad's eyes clouded then cleared. "Yes, but call me a glutton for punishment. If the chance to experience love like that presented itself, I would do it all over again."

"So you think it's better to have loved and lost than not to have loved at all?"

"You better believe it. After all, isn't that what Jesus did for us? He took a big chance on a world that didn't value His love."

"Yes, but He was Jesus."

"Oh ye of little faith! You can't tell me you don't believe in taking risks. Anyone in business for themselves is a risk taker."

"True dat, but business is different from affairs of the heart."

"Ah, but we are talking about the basic character of a person here. You can't compartmentalize your natural inclinations. You just have to encounter someone or something that you want bad enough and then boom, all that reserve will be out the window."

"Is this something you know from personal experience or psychological evaluation?"

"You might say a little bit of both. A perfect example of this fact is that tonight I took a risk and ordered our dessert before we came, hoping you would like it…but I really, really wanted it."

"Oh, so it was all about you!"

"Yes and no, but definitely my desire gave me courage."

"And are you always so presumptuous?"

"Only when I'm sure of the outcome. And I knew you would love it, so I went for it."

"So much for taking risks."

As if on cue a waiter appeared with a rolling cart bearing the highest soufflé she had ever seen. With great flourish he poured a thick sticky sauce all over it and then deftly scooped the cotton candy like confection onto their plates while the steam rose into a gray purple haze before them. Muriel took one bite, closed her eyes, and involuntarily allowed a moan to escape her lips. Brad's chuckling prompted her to open her eyes. He was looking at her with smug amusement.

"I told you you would like it."

Muriel decided to let him own this victory and laughed. "And you were right. There's something to be said for risk taking. Brad?" She turned serious.

"Yes?"

"Thank you for a wonderful dinner and a really nice evening."

"Oh don't worry, the bill is in the mail."

"Mmm…shoulda known."

"Actually, this is merely a setup, a bribe…"

"Taking more risks, Mr. Sebastian?"

"Mmm hmm. I'm thinking that if I feed you well you'll agree to help me find a place and decorate it."

"Now that I'm in debt to you, I suppose I have no choice but to work it off."

"That'll work…"

As they entered the night air, Muriel didn't know if she was more chilled by the coolness of the evening or the frigid stare a brother leveled at her as he walked by. She knew the look…as well as the sentiment behind it. She had given brothers with white women the same look. Somehow she felt black women were much more justified in feeling rejected than the brothers were. Between the lack of availability and their failure to step up to the plate, what was a woman supposed to do if she wanted a companion? But this was an ongoing argument that would probably never be resolved. She boldly stared back at him, issuing her own silent challenge: *Don't even go there with me 'cause you probably never would have asked me out.* She did an appraisal of the light-skinned woman at his side—the type you couldn't tell exactly what her ethnicity was. Lean, fashion-model-like with long wavy hair. The type those type of men always wore like trophies on their arm.

"Humph." It escaped her before she could even think to stop it. Brad, following her gaze, comprehended the silent warfare and decided to distract her instead.

"Lady, your carriage awaits."

"Thank you," she murmured, absentmindedly sliding into the car. She noted him checking out her legs and enjoyed the brush of her beautiful soft silk skirt when it slid over her skin as she adjusted herself on the seat before closing her door.

Brad got into the car and she was soon in Lizz Wright land. "Are you frightened by the fire in my eyes? It burns for you…"

They silently made their way through the city, allowing the stereo to do all the talking. As they pulled up to the front of her building, Muriel was relieved to see the doorman standing ready to open the door. In spite of her strange feelings of being attracted to Brad, she saw this silent sentry as her protection from her own emotions, whether Brad was interested in her or not. As he swung her car door open and extended his hand to help her out, she felt a bit giddy. He practically swept her from the seat in one smooth move.

"I had a really nice time, Brad."

"Me too…so shall we attempt this again?"

"Will my bill go up?"

"It most certainly will!" he said as he nodded to the doorman and walked past him.

"Perhaps we should make it a working session. I would prefer to keep my tab low."

"Why not make it a combination? Saturday after next. We could check out some lofts, have an early dinner, and take in a basketball game. The Spurs are coming to town, and I'd love to go boo Cedric Graham in person."

Muriel felt the blood run out of her feet. In a moment the magic of the evening was broken, her euphoric mood a thing of the past. Through clenched teeth she managed to croak out an answer: "That won't be possible."

Brad frowned. "What won't be possible? Us going out? Or me booing

Cedric Graham? Hey, you're not a fan of his, are you? I've heard he's quite the ladies' man." He had a mischievous glint in his eye.

Muriel snorted. "I'm hardly a fan, and I *hate* basketball!" The moment she said it she knew she had gone overboard. Brad's eyes were darkening with concern and confusion. "Excuse me, I have to go," Muriel stated quietly.

"Muriel, it's not that deep okay? We can nix the game and stick with the real estate."

She was already heading to the elevator, fighting to keep a calm facade and extricate herself from further dialogue.

"I'll get back to you."

"Like you did last time or will you really get back to me?"

"I'll get back to you." She pressed the button for her floor.

"But…"

"Good night, Brad." She got in, the doors closed, and she gazed heavenward mouthing a silent thank You to God. She felt no need to share her intimate knowledge of what she knew about Cedric Graham. Just the thought of running into him was enough to push her over the edge. Too bad Brad had to be a victim of her residual pain. He was a nice guy. *But then again, they all start off nice,* she thought. *Who is to say he will be different from the rest? Well, too bad,* she said to herself. *I'm not going to put myself in the position to find out one way or the other.*

18

Dear Diary,
   The trouble with love is
      the way it wraps you around its finger
         and then shakes you off
      as if your grip had grown too tight
   But then again sometimes it doesn't
      You just never know
Sometimes it engulfs you and sweeps you up in its tide
   carrying you away to the land of no returning
No returning to your right mind
      to who you were before you met him
   The trouble with love is
      one way or another you can never return
         to who you were before
            One way or another
         loving or losing
            you are never the same
   And there is no warning
      no premonitions
         no set of instructions
            that help you put two hearts together
               and keep them beating

to the same rhythm
singing the same song
in harmony
without the notes turning sour
or the song ending in tears...
The trouble with love
is we all want it
need it
are scared to death of it
yet couldn't live without it
Run away from it
All the while pursuing it
This elusive prize
that is scary
exhilarating
depressing
invigorating
devastating
life giving
A bundle of contradictions
Who can restrain
or define it?
Who can solve the puzzle
of the trouble with love...

Tracy closed her journal and sank back onto the pillows
that surrounded her on the couch in her den. She looked
around the meticulously kept room, and suddenly it felt

very empty. Perhaps Adrian was right and she should get a pet. At first she had scoffed at her advice, but it was beginning to make sense. Especially since she wasn't seeing anyone. A dog could be good company...as opposed to a cat. Cats were a little too independent to suit Tracy's need for a companion who would see her arrival home as an important event. She chuckled at the thought of it. What would it be like to actually have someone be happy to see you when you came home? What a novel concept.

This brought her thoughts back to Adrian. She wondered how it felt after years of coming home to someone to suddenly have no one there. The thought overwhelmed her and confused her. In spite of what Derrick had explained and her own observations, she found herself struggling to reconcile Adrian's dilemma in juxtaposition to her own life. Even if it came off as being a bit much, there was something to be said for all that Adrian did. She was flawless in her appearance. Shapely but lean, she looked fabulous all the time. Simple but elegant in her taste, she always looked as if she had stepped off the pages of *Vogue* or *WWD*. Beautiful caramel skin, the kind with the small pores that made her face look smooth like porcelain. Adrian's thick, lush hair falling past her shoulders was never out of place in Tracy's assessment. Girlfriend kept herself together. She was an amazing homemaker and cook, but it was her manner that was the most distinctive thing about her. Tracy had never met someone more empathetic. Adrian truly listened. She made you feel as if she had really heard you no matter what you said. She was never judgmental...always understanding. Tracy shook her head; she just didn't get it.

If forced to truly admit it, the scariest part of this equation for her was Adrian's faith. Though her friend had never tried to push her beliefs on her, she knew how strong her convictions were when it came to her "relationship with God." It seemed to ground her and give her this serene peace that Tracy envied. She thought back to their college days, on how Adrian had been before she became "born again." She had always been a perfectionist; that had not changed. However, she seemed more overt, more vivacious. She seemed to have settled more in later years. Tracy couldn't quite put her finger on what was missing, but it's absence was unsettling. It was what Derrick had mentioned, but she still couldn't label the specifics. But the bigger question was if Adrian had all this faith, why was she in this place? Did her faith work or not? Shouldn't God bring her husband back home? Tracy did not purport to be a Christian or spiritual in any kind of way; however, she had been curious and even a little envious of Adrian's faith because it gave her such security. Now Tracy was a bit confused. What was the difference between her life and Adrian's life at the end of the day if all of her going to church and praying didn't pay off in solving her problems?

The phone rang. Caller ID announced Felicia. Tracy frowned. It was Saturday night, prime dating night for her social cousin whom she never heard from on the weekend. She hoped nothing was wrong. "Hello?"

"Hey, girl. I thought I'd check on you since I haven't seen or heard from you in a couple of weeks."

That was interesting. Felicia had actually noticed. "Oh, I'm fine. It's just been stupid crazy at work. I've been trying to get this campaign done, and every time I think I've made headway the client changes her mind and it's back to the drawing board. I think she must be going through the change 'cause the woman is irrational."

"I've got one of those myself." Felicia giggled. "It's like she gets selective amnesia over what she chose in the last meeting. At this point I'm just saying, 'It's your money, lady, but we've got to make a decision— this is just the drapes, what are you going to do when we get to the rest of the house?'"

"I know that's right."

"Hey, I went to visit Adrian last week."

"I called but she hasn't called me back. How is she?"

"She cut her hair."

"Did she finally get bold enough to take my suggestion to get some layers?"

"No, she really, *really* cut her hair." Felicia was talking slowing and deliberately.

Tracy frowned. "Exactly what do you mean by really, really cut her hair?"

"I mean off, as in *all* off except for perhaps about an inch on the top."

"Nooo!"

"Yes! It is cute, but you could have knocked me over with a balloon."

"You mean feather, don't you?"

"Whatever. You know I always get those sayings mixed up. But do you think she's more in crisis than she's letting on?"

"It's pretty normal for a woman to do something drastic when she's been devastated, but I can't believe Adrian would cut her hair. Not 'Miss A Woman's Hair Is Her Glory'!"

"Obviously she's changed her mind about that. Oh, and check this out—she's painting again."

"Really?"

"Mmm hmm. It was a little weird though. You know how Adrian's house is always spotless?'

"Uh huh."

"Well, it was a little unkempt. Nothing really out of place, but dusty and untouched."

"That's not like her."

"And girlfriend had on blue jeans."

"Blue jeans? Stop it! Adrian doesn't wear jeans. That would be like saying Adrian cussed."

"Well, there she was in all her disheveled glory. In blue jeans. Hair short and spiked all up. Nails all jacked up." Felicia stopped. "I'm not gossiping, am I?"

Tracy chose not to answer that question in case she convicted herself. "Are you sure you were at Adrian's house? That doesn't sound like her at all."

"Oh yes, I had the right house. And she didn't even offer me anything to drink. The hostess with the mostest was gone, but the artist was back in residence. The painting was fabulous. She hasn't lost her touch after all these years, that's for sure."

Tracy chuckled to herself. Only Felicia could digress from the central point of any given conversation and end with a positive flourish.

"You don't think she's cracking up, do you?"

"No, she seemed perfectly calm."

"She's always perfectly calm."

"Well, she said God was comforting her."

"Shoot—forget comfort. Can't God get her man back?"

"I kind of asked her that."

"No!"

"Ye-ah." Felicia sounded like a valley girl. "I don't know about you, but I have to admit I'm a little freaked out by this, the whole Ron leaving thing, and I told her so."

Again Tracy noted they seemed to be having a strange meeting of the minds. "I know what you mean."

"You do?"

"It's like…if Adrian's stuff doesn't work out, then whose stuff can?"

"Exactly! And what scares me most is I don't have the answer right now."

"Me either."

"When you figure it out, will you let me know?"

"I will do that."

"You know what's interesting, Tracy?"

"What?"

"We seem to be more freaked out about this than Adrian is."

"You know, that's true. I wonder why that is?"

"She told me God was talking to her."

"What is He saying?"

"I don't know…she didn't tell me. She just feels like everything is going to be alright."

"But how can she know that?"

"I don't know. I guess it's that whole faith thing."

"I don't get it."

"Me neither. Maybe we should go to church with her once." Felicia quickly added, "You know, just to get some clarification. Maybe there's something she's not telling us. I mean, aren't you just a bit curious as to why she's so adamant about this even though she's lost her husband?"

"I don't know if we'll find any clues at church, but it might be nice to go just to support her one Sunday." Tracy wasn't sure if she was ready for church. "Hey, not to switch channels, but what are you doing home on a Saturday night? No hot date for the evening?"

"I've decided to give men a rest for a minute."

"What?" This was not the Felicia Tracy knew. Something was definitely wrong. She had felt it when Felicia first called. Tracy had allowed herself to be distracted from her first premonition by the discussion about Adrian, but now the feeling returned. She had overlooked the fact that it was a little strange for Felicia to all of a sudden be playing mother hen to Adrian. She was usually completely self-consumed. Her preoccupation with someone else's problem was highly unusual. The fact that Felicia never called on a Saturday was now overshadowed by the even more uncharacteristic decision that Felicia had just announced. "Felicia, that's not like you. Is something wrong?"

There was a pregnant pause before Felicia finally answered, and her voice sounded strange. "Thanks for asking. Everything is fine."

"Are you sure? Kenny hasn't done anything to hurt you, has he?"

"No. Not more than usual anyway, but sometimes you just get tired, you know?"

"Yeah, I know. I can truly relate."

"Do you think anybody ever gets it right?"

"Gets what right?"

"This whole love thing."

"Hard to say. I doubt if we'll solve it in a night, that's for sure." Tracy yawned, suddenly feeling exhausted by the whole conversation.

"I guess I better let you go to bed. I've pulled on your ear enough."

"Oh anytime…"

"Really?"

"Really." Tracy was worried again.

"Tracy, do you like me?"

"What kind of question is that?"

"A real question. I guess I don't call more often because I've always felt like I'm the cousin you have to put up with versus someone you genuinely like."

Tracy felt a pang of guilt. "Felicia, I love you. I mean we're practically like sisters! I admit I do get a little impatient with you when it comes to the man department because I think you sell yourself short…and I don't understand why. But perhaps that's my issue." A nagging feeling was growing in the pit of Tracy's stomach. "Are you sure you're okay? I feel like something is going on with you…"

"No, I'm just a little melancholy with a lot of things on my mind. I love you too, Tracy. Gotta go."

Tracy decided to release her rather than press the issue. "All right, girl. We'll all have to hook up soon."

"Perhaps after we get our hormonal clients off our necks?"

"Whew, sho you right!" Tracy was relieved to move on to lighter fare. "Talk to you later."

"Bye."

In the silence that followed, Tracy reflected on the latter part of the conversation. She knew that her ambivalent feelings toward Felicia were her issue. True, her parents had not done her any favors by comparing them to one another constantly while they were growing up. Felicia was not the sharpest knife in the drawer, but she had done alright for herself. She had tapped into her natural gift for making things beautiful and made it into a thriving interior design business. She was beautiful, easily attracting male admirers. However, her choices were not always the best, resulting in episodes that ranged from torrid to ridiculous that Tracy had been forced to sit through. Perhaps this was where the real issue was. Tracy envied Felicia's ability to dance between the raindrops no matter what happened. In spite of her disappointments, she was always able to bounce back and see the bright side of everything. Tracy, on the other hand, always had to work twice as hard at everything. School, work, her parents' approval, men….And when things didn't work out, she felt things far more deeply and did not rebound as quickly. This had made her more careful but also more envious of Felicia's capacity for spontaneity.

I wonder how Felicia would react if she ever had to deal with a real crisis? Tracy thought. Not that she wished one on her or anything, but still, what would her sanguine cousin do if she had to deal with something deeper than a disappointing date? Tracy yawned again. It was later than she thought. Something must really have been bothering Felicia for her to call at this time of night. Just what it was, she still didn't know— but she did know it had nothing to do with Adrian.

19

*A*drian looked at her mother standing in the doorway, the picture of immaculate chic. Nervously she double-checked her appearance in the hallway mirror before heading toward the door. She had felt confident that her new spiky, short do was cute until she found herself withering under her mother's critical gaze.

"What have you done to your hair?" her mom asked. She frowned as she entered the foyer, her heels tapping impatiently on the marble in the entryway. She scanned the living room and inspected a photograph on the mantle. Casually she ran her finger across it as she turned back to Adrian, taking in her daughter's appearance from top to bottom. Her face was unreadable as she assessed the entire situation before coming to a conclusion. Adrian's long, luxurious locks were gone, replaced by a short, tapered do that brought out her classic cheekbones and large, soft eyes. Large gold hoop earrings, an artist smock covered with smudges of paint, jeans, and scuffed mule flats gave her entire look an air of casual irreverence.

Adrian could feel her mother studying her and trying to make sense of this radical change.

"I cut it. Do you like it?" Adrian stood before her, making her own assessment of her mother. She had inherited her mother's petite frame and fabulous figure as well as her hair, which was in sharp contrast to her own right now. Her mother's hair was combed back off her face and gathered at the back of her neck into a tasteful chignon. Her St. John suit quietly screamed expensive as did her jewelry. Beautiful diamond studs, a little larger than normal, as well as one simple, bold, gold bangle adorning her wrist made it official that her mother had taste as well as the money to back it up.

"It's different, but why would you do something so drastic? Exactly what is going on here, Adrian? When was the last time you cleaned this house?" She murmured this a little softer than the rest as again her finger ran along the edge of the mantel she stood in front of. "Where's Ron?" It was the question Adrian was hoping she wouldn't ask; however, even she knew that Ron was conspicuously absent for a Saturday evening. She had held this conversation at bay as long as she could, but she knew on the day her mother finally made her way down from the suburbs her secret would be out. Though she was only thirty minutes away, Adrian's living in Chicago was not conducive for visiting frequently. The lifestyle of the city simply didn't allow it. Adrian had banked on this fact buying her some time.

"He's not here, Mother."

"Where is he? He certainly has been traveling a lot."

"He's gone, Mother; he's left me." With that Adrian turned and began walking toward the den, dog and cat in tow as if they too silently stood in support of whatever was about to transpire.

Adrian's mother followed her daughter into the room that was now truly converted into a studio. Canvases of different sizes stood against a wall awaiting their turn to be adorned. One finished work lay resting against an opposite wall, while a half-finished canvas sat on the easel before Adrian. She picked up her palette and turned toward it.

"Left you for what, Adrian?"

"I'm not sure. I believe it is for another woman, but I'm not clear on why." Adrian sounded removed from the information she was giving. She had avoided telling her mother about this development in her marriage because, perhaps, she had secretly hoped that Ron would come to his senses and come back home before she had to tell her. He had not. The only contact she had with him was the correspondence from his attorney. She had left a message at his office inviting him to come and get the rest of his belongings, things she had collected from around the house and put tidily in several boxes. Even this call had not been returned. Ron did not want to talk, did not want to face her, did not want to fight over anything. All his attorney could mutter off the record was that Ron said she was a good woman, and he didn't want to hurt her. He just wanted to get on with his life; therefore, he would not be disputing her about anything she wanted. She shared these facts with her mom.

"Well, that's decent," her mother said sarcastically. Adrian knew this story was all too familiar to her mother. She had found herself in the same situation shortly after Adrian left for college.

"What is it about men? They are such cowards." Her mother had smiled wryly at the time when sharing the news with Adrian. "Life should always be so simple, where unpleasant issues just fade to black without explanation."

Adrian decided she did not want to rehash that conversation. Adding another dab of paint to the canvas, she could feel her mother watching her as she silently set about working a cloud into the sky that outlined the woman standing at the precipice of a mountaintop. Facing the sun, kissing the wind, she seemed entranced with something invisible beyond her. It was striking and beautiful, yet calming at the same time.

Finally her mother asked her, as if reluctant to interrupt her, "And how do you feel about all of this, Adrian?"

"I'm not sure how I'm supposed to feel."

"What you're supposed to feel and how you really feel are sometimes two different things."

"I'm not sure I'm following you."

"There is a way we all like to handle things for appearance's sake, and then there's what's really going on beneath the surface."

"I suppose that's true. I certainly got my fill of training on what to do for appearance's sake from you. So tell me, how did you feel when Daddy left you?" There was a tension under her words that caused her mother to frown.

"I didn't take it very well at all!"

"You could have fooled me."

"Well, for your sake I couldn't just fall apart. I had to suck it up and move forward."

"Why?" The quiet tension returned in Adrian's voice.

"What do you mean why?"

"Why did you feel you had to be perfect in front of me? Did you think it would have been too human of you to let me see you fall apart?" Though the volume of Adrian's voice never rose, it sounded like she was shouting.

"I don't understand what you're saying, Adrian. What is this all about?"

"This is all about the sake of appearances, Mother. People just can't live like that all the time. In the end what do you have when the performance is over?"

"What performance?'

"The performance of perfection, Mother."

"What?" Adrian's mother looked truly worried now. She shifted her stance in silence, shaking her head and squinting as she tried to follow her daughter's train of thought.

"You were always so perfect when I was growing up. The house was perfect. You were perfect. I assumed your marriage was perfect too until one day Daddy was gone. I could never understand how he could leave such a perfect existence, especially for someone who was the complete opposite of you. I mean, come on, weren't you even a little insulted that he would end up with someone who couldn't dress and didn't know the meaning of housework or cooking?"

"I don't know if insulted would be the right word. I would say outdone or confused would be a better fit. But why are you so upset about this? This has been water under the bridge for a long time. There is nothing I can do about your father's choices. All I can do is know that I did the best job I could to be a good wife to him and mother to you. At the end of the day he needed something I did not have."

"But why didn't you have it?"

"Adrian, that is too great a question for me to answer. What makes any man want to leave a wife who loves him and does her best for him? If we could answer that question, we would know why Ron left you."

"Touché."

"I didn't mean it like that! All I was trying to say is there is no rhyme or reason for why a man leaves."

"I think you can say that about some men, but not all of them. Some men just have an unfaithful spirit and there is nothing you can do about it. But men like Daddy and Ron are a different breed. There had to be a reason."

"And what do you propose that reason to be?"

"Based on what they both left us for, I would say that we were both too busy being perfect to be who they needed us to be for them."

"Where did you get that from?"

"Felicia."

"Felicia! What would Felicia know about keeping a man? Are we talking about the Felicia whose love life is a revolving door?"

"I think that is beside the point."

"I don't. One does have to consider the source when receiving advice!"

"That's true. But I think Felicia had a point. Don't get me wrong, Mother. I've always admired you; after all, I did my best to become like you. I did such a good job that I got the same results. Now we are both alone. I think it's high time we take a look at the women we've become. I think we both have the same disease."

"And what disease would that be?" Adrian's mother wasn't sure she was ready for this.

"The disease of perfection. Tell me, why does a woman get up at six o'clock every morning and get fully dressed and made up when she has nowhere to go?"

"Because a man doesn't want to see a woman looking unkempt when he gets up in the morning. He should never see you looking undone. Men are visual creatures." Adrian's mother sounded as if she was repeating a well-rehearsed speech.

"Listen to yourself. Who told you that?"

"My mother."

"Grandmother! I should have known. Another example of perfection. Hmm, interesting, Grandfather left too."

"Adrian, exactly what are you trying to say?"

"I'm saying we all read the script and performed for love—except it seems we all did the wrong tricks. Tell me something. Did you wear makeup to bed, Mother?"

"What?"

"Did you wear makeup to bed?" Adrian spoke slowly and deliberately. "If a man never wants to see his woman undone, when is it okay? Were you too polite for passion? Did Daddy ever see you sweat?"

"Adrian!"

"Don't Adrian me! I'm trying to figure something out here. You're my mother. You're supposed to know how to fix this, but you can't because you've been too bound up yourself! Come on, tell the truth and shame the devil. Wouldn't you like to just let it all hang out just once? To let a strand of hair fall out of place? To go bare-faced for an entire day? To not have to suck in your gut and be prissy 24/7? To not cook a meal one night and, heaven forbid, pick up McDonald's? And so what if a table gets dusty? Is anybody really looking besides us? I guess not, because we are both alone!" Adrian crumbled into a chair reduced to tears.

"It sounds as if you've figured this out on your own, so why don't you share the conclusion you've come to, Adrian." Her mother suddenly felt drained.

"Well, as Dr. Phil says, 'How's that working for you?' I guess I've concluded it isn't. So I'm going to relax. Stop being so uptight and controlled. Go with the flow." With that she ran her fingers through her newly spiked hair.

"Be careful, Adrian. The grass is not necessarily greener on the other side, either. Trust me, you'll get where you want to go a whole lot faster taking the road in the middle. Going to the extreme can hurt you just as much as staying where you've been. I learned that the hard way."

Now it was Adrian's turn to be surprised. "When?" She had never seen anything different about her mother's behavior.

"After your father left I completely disintegrated. You were away at school so you didn't get to witness my madness. I will spare you the details; however, suffice it to say I tried to be someone I was not and hurt myself more than your father ever did. You are fortunate in the sense that you have other gifts to work with to fulfill yourself and keep you interesting. I married your father right out of school and had no other identity other than being his wife. No other skills, no other dreams. This wasn't a bad thing. I think there is something to be said for being a stay-at-home wife and mother, but I lived for that man and nothing else. That is dangerous. After David left and I came to the Lord, I realized that my husband had been my God. I think you are a little guilty of that, and if I taught you that then I'm sorry."

"I'm sorry too. I didn't mean to hurt or offend you."

"You didn't, honey, but I feel your pain. I know you're angry at yourself, but you shouldn't be. You did your best with what you knew, just as I did and my mama did. Life is a journey of learning. So here we are, and you're learning earlier than I did that the sun cannot rise and set over a man."

"Funny, that's the name of my painting, 'Sonrise.' Perhaps I should add the subtitle 'with no man in sight.'" Adrian chuckled in deep, throaty amusement.

"Just remember who you were before you met Ron and be that person, Adrian. I think you hid away too many of the fascinating things about yourself in pursuit of a perfection you could never attain. And by the way, your father did see me sweat, but it was too late. It was right before he left."

"I'm sorry…" Adrian regretted her tirade.

"Well, I'm hungry." Adrian's mother had obviously had enough. " I suppose you don't have anything to eat around this place?"

"We could go out and get something." Adrian took the cue that the conversation was over.

"Sounds good to me!"

"Done deal. I'll get my purse!" Adrian stood up and gestured toward the door with a flourish while heading for the hallway.

"Wait a minute."

"What?"

"You're not going out dressed like that are you?"

"But I thought we were going to McDonald's?"

"We most certainly are not!" Adrian's mother gave her most indignant look, drawing herself up to her full height.

"I guess some habits die hard." Adrian thought of her mother standing in line at McDonald's in her St. John suit, laughed, and headed toward the bedroom in search of a more fitting ensemble for dinner.

20

*M*uriel stretched like a cat on her sofa, thankful for the weekend. Cupping a steaming mug of coffee in her hands, she nestled into a deep recline beneath her favorite chenille throw to watch a team of home decorators turn an unsuspecting couple's home into an exotic love nest. Just as she had taken her first warming sip and entered into deep satisfaction mode, her phone rang. Checking the caller ID she frowned. Why would the front desk be calling? She wasn't expecting anyone. "Hello?"

"Miss James, you have a delivery."

"What kind of delivery?" She hadn't ordered anything.

"Flowers."

"Flowers? Are you sure you have the right apartment?" She couldn't think of anyone who would be sending her flowers. She had put such a major freeze on Brad, she knew he would be the last person to be sending her something.

"Yes, they are addressed to you. Shall I send them up?" He was beginning to sound impatient.

"Alright…" Before she could get out the rest of her sentence he had hung up. She was filled with curiosity. *Who is sending me flowers?* The wood floor was cold beneath her bare feet as she made her way to the front door to look through the peephole. She stood watching as the deliveryman stepped off the elevator with an exquisite array of flowers. So Brad hadn't given up, that was clear to see. She swung open the door prepared to tell the deliveryman he could take the flowers back to the person who had sent them. He lowered the flowers. Her prepared speech went out the window as she stared into Brad's angry eyes. He had a nerve being angry—he was the one who was an intruder.

"Didn't your mother ever tell you you're supposed to call before going to someone's house?"

"I have been calling. For two weeks to be exact. Which is more than I can say for you. I believe you were supposed to call me. What is up with you, anyway? Didn't your mother ever tell you to keep your word?"

"Don't play the dozens with me!"

"I believe you started it. Now are we going to continue to let the neighbors hear all our business or are you going to invite me in?"

"We don't have any business." Then noting the stubborn set of his jaw, she heaved a sigh of resignation. "Oh for crying out loud, come in."

"That's more like it," he said marching past her. "Now, where should I set these. Aren't they lovely, by the way?"

"Aren't you ashamed of yourself, using deceptive measures to enter a woman's apartment?"

"Hey! By any means necessary. Especially if I've been cut off for no obvious or just cause. What happened to our agreement? I'm beginning to question your integrity."

Muriel couldn't figure out if he was being serious or not. She stood glaring at him, slowly becoming amused at the fact that he was not to be intimidated. She kind of liked that…though she wouldn't make it known to him. Drawing another deep sigh she resigned herself to be tortured by him. "What do you want from me?"

"I want you to stop being a chumpette and honor your commitment."

"What do you know about chumpettes?" Muriel was trying not to laugh.

"A lot more since meeting you!"

"Ooo, touché!"

"Now, if you could get yourself together, we can still make my first appointment. I believe the agreement was we were going loft shopping together. Remember, you still have a tab to honor, and your bill is going up the more you make me wait."

Muriel had to admit she admired his boldness. She stood looking at him, trying to decide if she should push him back out the door and teach him a lesson for being so pushy and presumptuous or...oh what the heck, she was powerless in the face of his unwavering gaze. His eyes were clear and guileless, patiently awaiting her response.

"Alright! Do you always arm wrestle women out of their apartments on the weekend? Let me get my shoes." Pretending not to acknowledge the big grin spreading across his face, she turned and stomped down the hall. Ducking into the bathroom to powder her nose and check her hair, she wondered how he had managed once again to lure her out of her safety zone.

"Don't take all day, woman! Time's a wastin.'"

"Cool your jets, mister. You better be glad I'm going with you." She reappeared coat, hat, and purse bundled in her arms. She struggled to hold everything and put her coat on at the same time.

Brad watched her in amusement, and then gently emptied her arms to help her with her coat. "And *you* had better be glad I don't give up on you. It's a shame you can't even get your coat on by yourself." Then sighing dramatically he said, "I don't know what you would do without me."

"Trust me—I've had plenty of time to find out."

"And what did you find out?" He swung her around to face him, pulling her hat down over her eyes.

She adjusted it. "You are a pest, you know that?"

"But I'm such a nice pest. Aaaand, if you're nice to me, I might feed you."

"I can be bribed."

"I thought so. Let's go."

Stepping out of the building into the misty cold, Muriel could see that the month of April was lying about it being spring. She had concluded long ago there was no such thing as spring in Chicago. Just winter, summer, and Indian summer, making one wonder why people chose to stay in the Windy City…until June when the warm breezes and the endless summer festivities began. Then you remembered why you were so in love with this place. It seduced you time and time again. Just when the cold was convincing you to leave, the sun returned to talk you into staying. *Just like a bad man,* Muriel thought to herself. She settled into Brad's car and allowed him to whisk her away.

Time passed too quickly as they were absorbed into the world of pre-construction and overfriendly real estate agents. Some looked them over with far too much interest, as if trying to gauge their connection to one another. It slightly rattled Muriel but seemed to have no effect on Brad. While others, the younger buppie type, felt compelled to be overly hip and too familiar or ignore her altogether, which she also resented.

"What do you think?" Brad was looking at her, yanking her back from her discomfort.

"Hmm? Oh, nice, but I think we need to look a little more, don't you?" She didn't like the way the woman was looking at him. "After all, we did say we would take our time, right?" She lowered her voice looking into Brad's eyes, deliberately shutting out the flirtatious agent.

"Yes, we did." Brad was smiling.

Muriel shot the woman a "back off" look, then turned back to Brad. "We don't want to be late for our last appointment. Perhaps we should be going."

Brad thanked the slightly miffed agent for her time. Placing his hand on the small of Muriel's back, he gently steered her out the door. Once outside he turned to her, one eyebrow raised. "Whew! What was that all about?"

"What was what all about?" she replied, feigning innocence.

"You know what I'm talking about. You and that woman. You know we didn't have another appointment."

"That woman was trying to put the moves on you. Didn't you notice? Oh, what am I saying! You're a guy—you all never get it."

"I'll ignore that dig. Were you jealous?" He was really grinning now.

"That is not the point! She was being disrespectful. She didn't know what our relationship was, and she decided we shouldn't be having one." No way was Muriel walking into his trap.

"And what have you decided?"

"I haven't decided anything except that I'm hungry and you said you would feed me." With that she closed the car door to end the conversation.

"You are a piece of work, you know that?" Brad said, sliding into his seat beside her.

"Because I want something to eat?"

"No, because…never mind. Where would you like to go?"

"You did so well last time I will leave that decision to you."

"Do I get points for that?"

"Mmm, maybe."

"You sure make a man work hard."

"I thought a man liked a good challenge."

He was pulling up to one of her favorite places. Small and intimate, Ina's was like visiting your mother's house—good food that tasted like home cooking with a familiar atmosphere and Ina reigning over her staff as well as the customers, chiding them to turn off their cell phones. Ina waited until Brad had passed her to give Muriel a secret smile of approval, which Muriel tried to wave away. Secretly she was thoroughly enjoying herself.

Dinner was as delicious as the time spent with Brad. She marveled at how easily conversation flowed between them and how comfortable even their silences felt. All too soon it was over, and he was delivering her safely to her doorstep once again.

"Thank you, Miss James, for accompanying me on my search."

"It was fun."

"So kidnapping you was not a bad idea?"

"I am now forced to agree there is something to be said for mastering the art of impromptu outings."

"Shall we do it again...say next Saturday?"

"I think that should work. I'll have to check my schedule and have my people call your people." Muriel lapsed into a British accent and then giggled.

"Hey! What happened to mastering the impromptu?"

"Oh yes, well in that case, I simply must throw caution to the wind and say yes that would be rather lovely—brilliant in fact," she said in her best Mary Poppins imitation. Why did he bring out the silly in her? She couldn't say, but she had to admit she rather enjoyed it. It made her feel light and carefree. Now they were standing in front of the elevator. Should she invite him up or not? She ignored the sound of the doors opening.

"On that note, Miss Muriel James," Brad followed her lead, "I will speak with you later in the week to confirm our next impromptu outing." With that he took her hand and ever so lightly placed a kiss on her knuckles in proper English fashion. He performed a bow and backed toward the door. Her fingers burned where his lips had been, and she unconsciously grabbed her hand and watched his departure, finally pulling herself together to wave just before he turned toward the street. She backed onto the elevator and tried to locate exactly where her heart was. On one hand she was relieved he had not tried to really kiss her, on the other she was disappointed. Exactly what did she want to happen? She didn't really know. *Oh brother. This is the trouble with men!* Whose idea was this anyway? She shook herself as if to shake off the evening, but his presence lingered about her like a warm wrap. Mmm mmm. She wasn't telling anybody about this!

21

Felicia could feel the cold of the table against her legs as she waited for Dr. Sternberg to return. He had always been so kind to her. Old fashioned in his approach to medicine, he chose to deal with more than his patients' physical health. He was just as concerned about their emotional well-being, believing that emotions had a direct effect on overall health. Felicia loved the fact that he never rushed through her appointment, taking the time to ask her about herself and her work. He felt like a kind uncle, a sort of father figure to her. He was tall with a medium build that looked as if he worked out regularly to stay trim. He always stood perfectly straight. White hair topped his elegant frame. Yes, elegant. That was the word for him.

Felicia liked staring at him, taking him all in. It wasn't just the way he stood; it was his demeanor. The twinkling eyes, the smooth skin that was slightly rosy as if invigorated from scrubbing incessantly. He was comforting and comfortable in his manner, the type of person you could confide in. Over the years he had heard an earful. Semi-annually, like clockwork, Felicia had sat in the same spot sharing the latest episode of her romantic adventures. He always listened with deep interest without the scolding she would get from her friends, which encouraged her to go into greater detail than she probably should. He made her feel as if she had truly been heard. Without judgment he would try to give her sound advice, which she always appreciated but seldom took. It had become their ritual. He gave Felicia advice then six months later heard the outcome.

"Well, well, well, young lady." He had always called her "young lady." It made her feel the same way each time even though she was now much older. She felt as if she had reverted back to her teens. "This is a very interesting twist to a love story."

"Yes, I guess it is." Felicia suddenly felt adolescently shy.

"And exactly how does this story end?"

"End? I'm thinking this is just the beginning!"

"So you do intend to keep the baby?"

"Most definitely!"

"And you're sure about this?"

"Dr. Sternberg, the last thing I need to deal with is guilt on top of all my other issues; so yes, I'm sure. I thought you'd be proud of me."

"I am. It's a brave move, but I feel obligated to ask all the hard questions. What are your and the father's plans?"

"The father doesn't know," Felicia said quietly.

"I see. Felicia, who is the father?"

"Kenny Sample."

Dr. Sternberg frowned. "Kenny Sample...the plastic surgeon, Kenneth Sample?"

"Yes."

"And you haven't told him?" Dr. Sternberg raised his eyebrows.

"I don't intend to tell him at all."

"And why is that? He certainly seems like a fine young man. I've heard nothing but good things about him."

"He's a jerk."

Dr. Sternberg took off his glasses, intently looking at Felicia. "I hope I'm not stepping over the line here, but we've been having a running conversation for years so I feel justified in asking. Felicia, you are an intelligent, beautiful young woman. Explain this to me. If he was a jerk, why on earth were you with him?"

Felicia hunched her shoulders, shivering in the cotton smock from the air going down her back. "I don't know. Sometimes you just want someone to keep you warm."

"Did you ever consider purchasing a blanket?"

"I guess things would have turned out differently if I had, huh?"

"I would say so. But seriously, what are your intentions?"

"Well," Felicia expelled a long, loud sigh. "I intend to keep my child. I don't intend to tell Kenny. It's my problem. This is the consequence of the choices I made, but that doesn't have to be a bad thing. I can choose to be responsible from here on out."

"And what type of support system do you have in place to help you do this?"

"Right now, none. You are the only one who knows, and I don't think the reaction to this is going to be great. So to be perfectly honest, I will be doing this alone."

"A child is a major responsibility, Felicia."

"I know."

"I don't think you fully know. It's hard work being a parent, especially alone."

"You know, Dr. Sternberg, if I'm truly honest, I was alone when I was with Kenny."

"I'm sorry, Felicia."

"I'm not. I've decided perhaps this is the wake-up call I needed. All my life I've gotten caught up in relationships with men who didn't know what love was. Perhaps I didn't either, so I put up with a bunch of surface relationships. But I have to tell you. From the day I realized there was this life inside me that would be completely dependent on me, it was like something clicked. It wasn't about me and what I thought I wanted or needed anymore. All of a sudden I was more concerned about protecting and taking care of someone who hadn't been taught not to love yet. You know what I mean? A child comes into the world with no baggage, no fear of loving, then people mess him or her up. I got messed up. Now this is my chance to actually nurture someone's heart instead of suck the life out of it."

"But doesn't Kenny deserve to know about his child?"

"You mean *my* child? I'm not going to set myself up for further rejection from someone who wouldn't care anyway. And I will not subject my child to knowing what a jerk his or her father is."

"Is this about you and Kenny or your child? Every child deserves to know who both its parents are. Wouldn't you want to know?"

"Sometimes I believe you can get hurt more by knowing them than by not knowing."

"So you're sure about this?"

"Positive."

"Alright…" Dr. Sternberg glanced at his watch then back to Felicia. Pulling out a memo pad he began writing. "Well, I'm going to give you the name of a great obstetrician who will take wonderful care of you as you move forward with this. You should call her today to schedule your first appointment as soon as possible."

He had switched back to his professional persona, and Felicia was relieved. She had felt herself on the verge of caving into tears. She silently took the card he held out to her, suddenly feeling the weight of her decision. It was official. She was going to be a mother. Another emotion was partnering with her commitment—fear. *What have I just done to the rest of my life?* she thought as she watched the doctor walk through the door and close it behind him.

Suddenly she felt extremely alone. She had no idea how Tracy would respond when she finally got around to telling her. On the other hand, she knew exactly how her parents would react. She shivered at the thought as she began dressing. She glanced in the mirror above the sink and leaned closer, studying her face. Funny how you could feel so different and still look the same. Slowly she touched her stomach, searching for signs of life. Right now her stomach was still flat and taut. She tried to imagine what she would look like as the child inside her grew. The figure she had always been so proud of would change drastically, but it didn't matter. Something was now more important than her appearance. *I, Felicia Lynn Somers, am having a baby. Fancy that…*

She walked past the receptionist, wondering if she knew. But she was too absorbed in the paperwork on her desk to give any signs of knowing about Felicia's state of health. It was still her secret, with the exception of Dr. Sternberg, and until she could get up the courage to face everyone else, that is the way it would stay.

Rounding the corner of the building she almost jumped out of her skin when she heard a familiar voice call her name. "Felicia?" She swung around to run smack dab into Muriel.

"Girl, you scared me!"

"You must have been in some deep kind of thought 'cause you walked right past me."

"Did I? Chile, I'm running late. You know how that is."

"So what are you doing up this end of town?"

"Oh time for my checkup. I'm on my way back to work." Felicia looked guilty as she said it.

"Girl, how many times a year do you go for a checkup? Didn't you just have one not too long ago?"

"No…" Felicia lied again.

"Hmm, I coulda sworn you had to go for a checkup after one of our lunches not too long ago. Anyway, how have you been?"

"Fine…and you? You look great in that color—new suit?" She fought to change the subject.

"Felicia, you have seen me in this suit a hundred times. What is wrong with you? Are you sure you're okay?"

"Yeah, I'm fine. I'm sorry. I'm just a little distracted. Work stuff."

"I can understand that. I've been really busy too. Sometimes I wonder who signed me up for owning my own business—it's a trip."

"Girl, don't even go there." Felicia was relieved Muriel finally switched channels. "Sometimes I wonder what it would be like to be married and not have to work."

"We could've asked Adrian once upon a time."

"This is true. We no longer have that luxury. But you know, I think she's going to be alright."

"Of course she is. She knows God."

"Just exactly what does that mean, Muriel?"

"Let me just say this. Knowing God is definitely different from knowing *about* God. You can know about Him and still have no assurance that He's going to work things out for you because you don't *know* Him."

Felicia looked confused. Muriel continued. "It's kind of like what we say in business. It's not *what* you know, it's *who* you know. Relationship is everything, and when you're your own source, you can come to the end of yourself and your resources really fast. But Adrian has her relationship with God to draw from and see her through. Does that make sense?"

"I guess so." Felicia wasn't really sure but decided she would mull on this on her own time. "She's painting again you know."

"Really! That's a good thing. I never understood why in Adrian's mind marriage equaled putting her gifts on hold. Humph! I'll tell you this much—God sure knows how to get our attention and get us busy doing what we're supposed to be doing, even if He has to allow something drastic to happen. Ooo, look at the time! I have *got* to run. I'll see you at lunch next week."

With that Muriel was off in a cloud of caramel-and-cream cashmere, looking as if she just stepped off a catwalk. Head held high she took charge of the avenue, turning heads as she went, oblivious to the attention she was receiving. Felicia stood still in the middle of the sidewalk ignoring the stream of humanity coming and going around her.

Muriel's words echoed in her head: *Adrian has her relationship with God to draw from and see her through.* She wondered what that felt like. She had no relationship to draw from. She was her own source. And though she had made her decision, she wasn't sure how she was going to make it. She wished she could have the confidence that Adrian and Muriel had. She wanted to be that sure that everything would work out. Could it be that God was trying to get her attention too? She made her way down the sidewalk, getting her own share of attention from male passersby, but she too was oblivious, lost in thought about how to have a relationship with a God she didn't know.

22

Adrian swept through the door and onto the avenue as if she was still dancing. She threw her head back taking in the rays of the sun before making her way up the street. It was an uncommonly warm day for the end of May, and she was taking advantage of it along with everyone else in the city. There was a bounce in her step as she smiled at the melody still playing in her head. The spicy salsa rhythms that invigorated her during dance class had left their impression in her system, and it was obvious. She generated energy, turning more than a few heads as she made her way toward the block lined with art galleries. Sporting her now signature large gold hoops that made her new short haircut even more sassy, a fitted tank that showed off perfectly toned athletic arms, a gauze wrap and tangerine knickers atop hot mules that complemented her dancer's legs to the utmost, her heels tapped out their own beat on the concrete. Portfolio tucked under her arm, she stopped at the entrance to a gallery and shrugged. *Oh well, nothing beats a failure but a try,* she thought. Though Mr. Morrow was an old family friend, she didn't expect him to agree to her idea if he didn't like her work. She knew he would be honest because it was a matter of his reputation. He had admired some of the pieces she had done in college and wondered aloud as to why she had stopped painting. At the time it felt like small talk, but now she was hoping his encouragement would be more than just friendly conversation.

Though Ron had been generous in the divorce settlement, Adrian felt the need to generate her own income as part of entering the world of single living. It wasn't as much about the money as it was about having a sense of purpose, a reason for being. She refused to become a self-indulgent mess, sitting around and focusing on her woes and feeling sorry for herself. Neither did she want to become one of the number of women who, because they had nothing going on in their lives, looked to a man for validation. She was in no hurry to leap into another relationship. She had learned the hard way that a man could be here today and gone tomorrow. So much for a man being the measure of your self-worth. As a matter of fact, she still couldn't get over the fact that she had lost so much of who she really was in the midst of her marriage.

She didn't regret being a housewife. She believed that if you could you should. She had enjoyed creating a beautiful home and entertaining Ron's clients. What she did regret was forsaking all other interests, with the exception of her faith, to focus on Ron. Truly she had lost her balance. She had completely given up who she really was and how she expressed herself by trading in her paintbrush for a vacuum cleaner and her theatrical leanings for making small talk and being the hostess with the mostest. How was that for losing yourself inside of someone else? Though she could attest to there being a season for everything, she concluded she had missed the cue for when the season changed.

Adrian would have been the first one to advise anyone getting married that she believed you had to die to different aspects of your individualism in view of the goal of truly becoming one with your mate. But she would also be willing to concede that she had taken it a bit too far. Somewhere in the middle of the high ideals of becoming one and being who you are lay the fine line of keeping the best parts of yourself to offer to your partner. Marriage was the delicate mix of two people in relationship completing one big picture by exchanging their strengths for the betterment of both. In hindsight she realized she had failed to do that. Now she was on a mission to reclaim the pieces of her that had made her feel alive, productive, and fruitful. She concentrated on calming the butterflies in her stomach while reminding herself that one man's trash is another man's treasure and that art is a subjective thing. Preparing herself for either acceptance or rejection, she squared her shoulders to face whatever criticism or praise of her artwork Mr. Morrow would offer.

Glancing at her reflection in the glass door before entering, she noted she looked like an artist. As a matter of fact, she looked downright hot if she did say so herself. Breathing a quick prayer to God as well as whispering a "Here we go" to her heavenly partner, she stepped into the gallery with confidence.

Clutching her portfolio containing the photos of her completed paintings along with sketches of the rest of the series she envisioned, she extended her hand to greet her old friend who had sounded truly pleased when she informed him that she was painting again. Though he was sorry to hear the news about her divorce, he thought returning to her painting could be therapeutic for her. "You know some of the best work has been done while artists wrestled with their pain," he mentioned before hanging up the phone. Adrian believed he was right. She had learned a lot about herself as she found what she had lost in the images she rendered on her canvases. And now here she was. He greeted her warmly, excited to see what she had. She, too, was anxious to see his response.

After taking a tour around the gallery to view the latest works that he was featuring, their social talk dwindled and it was time to get down to business. It seemed only minutes later that she emerged from his office filled with visions of the future. She stopped short taking in the sight before her. There he was in all his Giorgio Armani-suited down fineness. "Ron?" she could hear her voice though she didn't feel her lips move to form his name. He turned toward her, a strange mixture of expressions crossing his face.

"Adrian?" The look had gone from that of a caught naughty child to the surprise of taking in Adrian's new look to something that resembled...could it be interest? Adrian couldn't tell.

"You two know each other?" Mr. Morrow's smiling voice came from behind them as they both took in one another in silence.

Ron coughed in discomfort, ignoring the question. "What are you doing here?"

"Oh, just making a little presentation to Mr. Morrow." Adrian blindly gestured in the direction of the man who stood behind her.

"And what a presentation it was! You are looking at our next featured artist for the gallery, so you might want to hold off on making a purchase today."

"Really?" Ron had cocked his head to the side, still not taking his eyes from Adrian's face. The woman who stood beside him shifted awkwardly.

Casting a look of disapproval at the woman standing beside Ron, Mr. Morrow dismissed her with a glance before launching into singing of Adrian's praises. The more he talked, the more strength Adrian could feel rising within her. She had seen that look in Ron's eyes before—when they were first dating. She never realized that what had fed his desire for her had been her creative gifts. Whenever she had been in a play or done a jazz set at a club or at showcases on campus, it had an aphrodisiac effect on him. Yup, he had that look. And the woman beside him was not pleased at all as she studied their interaction.

"So you're painting again, Adrian?"

"Um hmm. It's just a little something I do now that I have more time on my hands."

She watched Ron grow uncomfortable again with this subtle barb. Cupping her elbow in his hands without breaking his gaze at her, he spoke offhandedly to both of the outside observers. "Excuse us for a moment."

As he led her away to a corner of the gallery out of earshot, Mr.

Morrow muttered, "Yep, they must know each other." At that he excused himself, leaving Ron's companion standing alone, looking as if she felt very much out of place. Finally reaching a satisfactory distance from anyone who might overhear, Ron released her elbow and turned to face her. "You look incredible."

"Thank you." Adrian self-consciously smoothed the tapering hair at the nape of her neck, recalling how she had resisted the urge to cut it before because of Ron's obsession with long hair—and now it didn't seem to disturb him at all. "I always thought you didn't like short hair."

"That's true for the most part, but I must say it's extremely attractive. The earrings, the outfit," he stepped back to indicate what he was taking in with a fluid motion of his hand that almost felt like a caress to Adrian even though he had not touched her. He had that look again, the corner of his mouth turning up at the corner in a flirtatious smile. "It's quite different for you, but it's working, girl!" Then remembering the awkward circumstance between them, he dropped his head along with his voice. "Adrian, I'm sorry…"

"Why didn't you return my calls, Ron?"

"I didn't know what to say."

"And do you now?"

"To be perfectly honest, I don't. Adrian, this is not about you—it's about me, okay? And I still haven't figured it all out yet. All I know is that I wasn't happy, and I assumed you weren't either. I just wasn't there anymore and that wasn't fair to me, to you, to either one of us. Who wants to stay in a marriage where both people feel as if they're dying?"

"How could you assume so much about how I felt without consulting me?"

"Were you…happy?" With this he studied her face closely, searching for an answer.

"In hindsight no, I just didn't know it yet."

Ron looked relieved and disappointed at the same time.

"Adrian, I don't know what to say."

"I got that piece so let's not force it. When you're ready we can talk. In the meantime there's the matter of you coming to get the rest of your things."

A spasm of pain crossed his face that Adrian couldn't fathom.

"Ron, we need to get going." His patient companion had become impatient.

"I'll be with you in a moment, Amber."

At the name Adrian's head snapped in her direction and took in his partner with new eyes. So this was Amber...*the* Amber. The Amber Ron had left her for. Tall, slim, the model type, she stood silently appraising Adrian while she shifted from foot to foot, nervously looking from Ron to her.

Adrian lifted her eyebrow then turned back to Ron, who seemed to be inching backward...and reluctantly at that.

"I need to get going,"

"Sure, I understand."

"Not really—but that's on me. I want you to understand that. Do you?"

Adrian didn't answer.

"Goodbye, Adrian. And again...you look amazing."

Adrian thought that it was amazing that she had remained as cool as she had watching the man she loved walk off with the "other woman" right in front of her. Her first instinct was to turn into a vixen confronting this woman, but actually her issue was with Ron. He was the one who had chosen to be with someone else. Amber was merely accepting his attention—as would any woman who had the chance to snag someone like him. In light of this revelation, Adrian was strangely calm about the scene unfolding in front of her. All she quietly knew were two things: One, she wanted her husband back; two, she was going to get her husband back. In spite of all that had transpired, she loved him. They had literally grown up together, and that was too much history to let go of easily. They had been good together; he was all she knew. Plus she wasn't going to just let some sorry chile walk off with her man. Oh no, that just wouldn't do.

Oh yes, she was going to play it as wise as a serpent and gentle as a dove—but she would get her man back. And she would take her time doing it because she also knew she needed to deal with first things first. Right now she would get herself back on the block. Then she would invite him to her neighborhood, though something told her she might not even have to extend the invitation. *Poor Amber. Why do women allow themselves to fall prey to the deception that they could ever win when getting entangled with a married man.*

Picking up her portfolio, Adrian headed toward the door, turning back to envision the gallery filled with her paintings and people milling about exclaiming over her work. She smiled to herself. If she could see it, she could have it. And right now she was seeing it all: herself, her art, and Ron—living her dream out in spectacular color. *From my heart to God's ears!* She sighed and made her exit, resuming her salsa groove.

23

*A*re you going to tell me what's going on with you and Brad or am I going to be forced to do my own reconnaissance work?" Carla was literally vibrating through the phone. Muriel grabbed the headset from its holder, disconnecting it from the speaker. Her personal business should remain personal and not become fodder for the rumor mill at the office. Ignoring the curiosity in the eyes of her assistant, she swung around in her chair. "What are you talking about?"

"I'm talking about you and Brad Sebastian. Don't play the nut role with me! I know you've been seeing him, and I want all the dirt. Is it too much to ask since I introduced you?"

"No. But since there is nothing to report…"

"Muriel, don't try it. You've been 'apartment shopping' for two months now, and you're telling me that nothing is going on? He is completely unmindful of all the women at church hitting on him, and you're trying to tell me nothing is going on between you two?"

"Nothing is going on." Muriel was not lying. For the past two months she and Brad had fallen into the weekend routine of doing breakfast and making the rounds to all the preconstruction sites rising from the floor of the city. They would end with an early dinner and Brad leaving her at her elevator door with a customary kiss on her knuckles. It had almost become a ritual. She had continued to have mixed feelings about their encounters. Part of her wanted more, wondering what it would be like to actually kiss him and feel those wonderful arms embrace her. The other part was relieved he came no closer. She had been praying about her ambivalence but didn't quite feel comfortable enough to share her emotional confusion with anyone, not even Carla.

Muriel didn't want anyone getting excited over something that might never be more than what it was. And she didn't want to be talked into being excited either. She knew her friends. So anxious were they to get everyone matched up and married off that any man who said "boo!" became a marriage prospect. If you didn't watch yourself, you could go careening down the garden path purchasing peau de soie shoes for your wedding before the guy ever decided he really wanted to date you. Nope. It was better to guard your heart. She had watched and learned from others that premature plans for happily ever after usually ended with tearful concessions to all the hints ignored that signaled their man was a frog and not the long-awaited prince they had hoped for. In her mind the experience of having loved and lost was highly overrated.

"Carla, seriously, nothing. Read my lips through the phone—absolutely nothing is going on."

"Are you holding out on me?"

"Trust me I am not! It's true I have been seeing Brad, but not romantically. He's nice, attentive, and very interesting but nothing, I mean nothing, is going on except I am now thoroughly well versed on every single loft construction site in the city. So we eat, we talk, we have a great time checking out floor plans and models, but nothing else. Sorry to disappoint you. I will admit it's turned out to be more fun than I thought it would be."

"Hmmm…" Carla sounded concerned.

"What? Is there something I should know? He isn't gay, is he?"

"Now why is it that every time a man is a complete gentleman these days he gets accused of being gay? Boy! A man can't win for trying. Actually I was thinking it was odd that you were still looking at places when Brad told Al he thought he had found what he wanted weeks ago."

"Really!"

"Yeah…" Suddenly she broke into peals of laughter. "Well, isn't that sly of him? He's been looking at extra places just to have an excuse to be with you. Oh, that is classic. How cute is that? Wait until I tell Al." She fell out laughing again.

Muriel was not amused.

Carla noted the silence on the other end of the phone. "Muriel?"

"I don't think that's funny. As a matter of fact, I think it's downright deceitful. Why can't he just ask me out like all the other men in the world?"

"Perhaps because you've ignored and turned down all the other men in the world. Brad is no fool, Muriel. He must have sensed that you are not the easiest woman for a man to pull out of her shell, so he found something that doesn't make you feel threatened or ill at ease. Is that so bad? Look, I don't know what your issues are, but if he's willing to be sensitive to them, don't you think he gets high marks for that?"

"Now I've got issues? Is that a way to dance around the fact that this guy has been laughing at me behind my back, monopolizing all my weekends, asking me what I think about this and what I think about that, and he's already made up his mind? I don't have time to be played, Carla. I can do something else with my time. I'm a busy woman—and you know that."

"Oh, this has been a *weekend* thing? That certainly speaks volumes."

"That certainly speaks volumes." Muriel mimicked Carla. "About what?"

"I know you've been out of the loop for a while, my friend, so let me bring you up to speed. A man does not give up his weekends or holidays unless he's serious about a woman! The biggest hint that he's not that into you is his absence on weekends or holidays, you copy? Over and out."

"Carla, I really think you are inflating this whole thing. We've just gone house shopping. No romance. No kisses, no hugs, no emotional drivel, no nothing, okay?"

"Muriel, I love you. Do you believe that?"

"Uh oh. I don't know if I'm ready for this."

"Well, you need to get ready because it is time for you to come out of your cave, my dear friend. The truth is the light. And the truth of the matter is you are not the most approachable woman in the world. Now, once someone gets to know you they find out you're nothing but a big marshmallow, but they have to wade through all the other 'tough girl, I don't need nobody I'm handling my own bizness, ain't got time for love' stuff first. So I suspect that Brad is simply giving you the room to find your own comfort level before attempting to come any closer. Smart man. I knew I liked him for some reason."

"Carla, that is all just mad speculation—and you know it."

"Listen to the one who has *no one* telling the one who has *someone* what they don't know. Why do single people do that?"

"Why do single people do what?"

"Single people always want to take advice from someone who's stuck in the same situation they are instead of taking it from someone who has a successful relationship and knows the real deal."

"That's not true."

"Yes, it is. You all act as if married people have never been single before. How do you think we got married? We didn't get married doing what you all are doing, that's for sure. Haven't you ever noticed you will get entirely different feedback from a married person than from another miserable single when it comes to relationship advice? So here's my advice: Give the man a chance."

Muriel was beginning to panic. She could feel herself trying to extricate herself from her emotions except she felt as if she was in quicksand.

"I have to go."

"You always do when someone is hitting too close to home. When are you going to stop running, Muriel? When are you going to stop letting your fears run your life and keep robbing you of what you really want?"

"What do you mean by that?"

"Or maybe you're the one who is gay, and that's your business except you need to dip that under the blood of Jesus."

"Carla, I am not gay. What is wrong with you today?"

"You're the one who doesn't want to talk about or think about a man ever. It's just not normal."

"I am not going to entertain this discussion any longer, okay? This is ridiculous."

"Suit yourself, but it is a viable question. Look, all I know is that whenever someone broaches the subject of men with you, you act as if someone just spit on you. It is highly suspect. So either you don't like them or you have some unresolved issue with them. Either someone hurt you or…I don't know. I just don't get folk who are supposed to know Jesus not being able to forgive folk, let stuff go, and move on. If it happened over two years ago, there isn't even a cell present in your body that was there when whatever it was happened. Even the body knows how to slough off dead stuff. The only place your past trauma exists is in your mind, and don't you think it's time you get over it?"

"Are you finished?" Muriel's voice was dangerously low.

"Not exactly."

"Oh, I think you are, Carla. Life is not a science project. You don't know what you are talking about. You need to back off."

"I will not back off, Muriel. I am your friend. Friends hold one another accountable."

"Sounds to me like you're just being nosy. As far as I'm concerned friends know how to stay out of grown folks' bizness."

"That is not exactly the way it works when you're trying to live a godly life, Muriel, and you know it. We are our sisters' keepers."

"Don't use godliness as an excuse to dip your nose where you shouldn't. I am so glad you have had a nice little tidy existence up to now in your own life, but everyone hasn't had it as simple as you, okay? So before you talk about moving on, you need to have your facts straight."

"And just what are those facts, Muriel?"

"None of your business!" Muriel began rearranging the items on her desk.

"I agree. People should get their facts straight, especially before they go accusing people of having a nice, tidy little life. Even though this is about you, you need to understand that I've had my own struggles. Things you don't know about that completely devastated me. I could have let them get the best of me and mess me up so that I wouldn't be able to recognize a blessing if it slapped me in the face. I almost let it make me miss Al."

Muriel stopped, still holding a stapler in mid-air.

"Even he doesn't know how narrowly we almost missed happiness," Carla continued, "I'm thankful to God that He didn't allow me to destroy my future while I was mulling over my past. Don't do it, Muriel. Brad is a good guy. Perhaps he hasn't done things the way you would have liked him to, but he's doing the best he can. Cut him some slack and allow yourself to live a little. Everything in life is not as precise as the patterns you cut. There's room for giving people a little leeway, okay?"

Muriel was silent. Why she was holding her breath she didn't know. Her mind was pulled in two different directions. One side was trying to figure out what Carla could possibly have gone through. The girl was always so carefree and full of joy. She was one of the most open people Muriel knew. There was no evidence of past scars in her conversation or her mannerisms. She worshiped God and loved people with abandon. Sometimes her enthusiasm was misunderstood by those who were more reserved than herself, but her joy was so contagious everyone eventually got caught up in it. It was impossible for her to have ever experienced the type of pain Muriel had known. Or was it?

The other part of Muriel longed to embrace what Carla was saying. It sounded so simple getting over the past—could it really be that easy? She felt trapped inside her own skin, like Rapunzel held captive in her ivory tower awaiting a knight in shining armor to come and rescue her. Except she had no hair to let down. No fairy tale happy ending. Who could rescue her from herself and the nightmare she fought to put to rest but relived at the most inconvenient times? Yes, life should be so simple. Why didn't the mind renew itself the way the cells in your body did? When it came to memories, that was a whole different ball of wax.

"Perhaps I've said enough." Carla interrupted her thoughts. "I think I better go. I hope I didn't offend you. That wasn't my intention. It's just… well…I'm gonna go…"

"Yeah…" Muriel struggled to find something to say. She wasn't angry. She didn't want Carla to think she was. She was just overwhelmed by a myriad of swirling thoughts.

"Muriel?"

"Yes, Carla?" She breathed the words.

"I…I love you…you do know that, right?"

"I know, Carla. I love you back. I just need some time to myself right now."

"I understand."

"Do you?"

"I really do. And from past experience I can tell you that until the pain of where you are becomes greater than the pain of breaking through to where you want to go, you're gonna be stuck. Hopefully what you want won't pass you by before you make the leap of faith."

"I hear you."

"I hope you do. I've gotta go. Al will be home before I know it, and I haven't even started dinner. Nothing worse than a hungry man with no food in sight." She struggled to find some levity, some sign that they were all right before she hung up.

"I'm sure one of your smiles will calm him down, though I can't imagine Al ever being irate." Muriel followed her cue. She sobered. "Carla, thanks for caring, okay? And trust me—I'm not purposely shutting you out. There are just some things in life…well…"

"Muriel, you don't need to go there with me. I'm your friend no matter what. You know what? I'm just going to pray that God will give you beauty for ashes. In the meantime, you do whatever you have to do to keep on keeping on, okay?"

"Thanks, Carla."

"Keep the faith, my friend. And give the man a break!"

"Alright!"

"Alrighty then, g'bye!" And with that Carla was gone, leaving Muriel to mull over a thousand different thoughts cascading over the edges of her heart like a tumultuous waterfall. Man, how complicated did life have to get before a sister just fell apart? She thought of Adrian. Well if Adrian could handle her drama with such grace, she certainly had to follow her example for the sake of the sisterhood. Drawing a deep breath, Muriel fingered her hair at the nape of her neck, an automatic gesture whenever she was nervous or lost in thought. Checking her image in the mirror one last time, she smoothed the back of her skirt. It was truly fitting, and boy was she glad butts were in style. She smiled wryly at the thought and headed for the door. If she didn't get moving, she was going to be late for Bible class.

24

Felicia sank into the chair, gratefully lowering her armload of books onto the table before her. It seemed as if she got tired so quickly these days. Longing for some coffee but settling instead for herbal tea, she closed her eyes, enjoying the heat from the cup. Dr. Sternberg was right. Dr. Amy Stewart, the ob/gyn he had recommended was wonderful. The moment she walked into her office a peace came over her. It was amazing how much a woman's touch could set the atmosphere and promote feelings of nurturing and solace. The lobby of the office was set up like a living room, which made patients feel more like they were visiting a friend than a physician. Soft, pastel couches arranged in semiround and plush carpeting were softly illuminated by the overhead sky lighting. Music floated through the room, and lamps that resembled candles cast a warm glow from the corners. An aquarium with the most amazing assortment of tropical fish swimming effortlessly by was almost hypnotic.

Everything about the atmosphere was soothing, including the receptionist. She made you feel as if you were a guest versus a patient, offering you a drink while you waited, along with a wonderful plate of sliced fruit finished off with a piece of banana bread. Felicia thought, *I could grow to look forward to my appointments. It's like finding an oasis in the midst of all that is going on.*

And then there was Dr. Stewart. Felicia was struck by her appearance first. Tall, slender with smooth cocoa skin. She merely wore powder, a soft natural lip gloss, and mascara, needing no further help from cosmetics. Her thick, black hair was pulled back and clasped with a tortoiseshell barrette, giving her a finished look above her soft smock that was the only thing that gave away her identity as a doctor. She looked far younger than her years. With a warm husky voice that a person could listen to all day, she gently questioned Felicia on her medical history and how she had been feeling for the past two-and-a-half months. She listened intently, as if Felicia had been the first patient of the day telling her the most incredible information.

Examining her as gently as she had questioned her, Felicia felt herself relaxing as she listened to what she could expect in the months to come. You could tell Dr. Stewart really liked her job and was a mother at heart herself. Loading her up with advice on books to read, nutrition tips, even a good lotion to begin using on her breasts and hips to avoid stretch marks, she was thorough and nurturing—the way Felicia wished her mother would be. She hated leaving the comforting surroundings to reenter the real world. In order to prolong her good feelings, Felicia decided to indulge in her favorite guilty pleasure—stopping for coffee and a good book at Borders.

After flipping through most of the design magazines to see if there was anything she hadn't thought of yet, she made her way to the limited selection of prenatal offerings and the childcare section. Armed with books on what to expect while you're expecting as well as newborn baby care books, she positioned herself at a table to peruse her findings. She wondered briefly what Kenny's reaction would be if she had opted to reveal her pregnancy to him. In a moment of fancy she imagined him being happy and excited. That would be a fantasy. Kenny was by no means ready for a commitment of any sort, and definitely not an encounter of the fatherhood kind. He was on the fast track as one of the hottest plastic surgeons in the business. His job was to make people look perfect as well as keep up the perfect desirable bachelor profile. Perhaps as she began to fill out he would have become turned off by her less-than-perfect appearance. She had a momentary giggle as she remembered his consternation when she got a rare zit while they were dating. He had immediately furnished her with a cream and ordered her to let him know if the angry swelling bump was not gone in two days. *There will be no two-day cure for this bump, that's for sure!* She absent-mindedly ran her hand over her abdomen.

Though she looked the same, she certainly did not feel the same. She felt full and her breasts were so tender she found herself dressing more carefully to avoid discomfort. This was certainly going to be interesting. She had decided she would tell her parents when she got past the three-month mark. She would then be past the most iffy pregnancy stage. No need starting a scene if one didn't need to. There was something scary about harboring such a big secret, but she felt it was best for her sanity as well as her health for now.

"Felicia?" The deep voice disturbed her reverie and caused her to spill the tea she had just bent over to sip. The cup rattled on the tabletop as she set it down abruptly while whirling toward the voice.

"Kenny!" *Shoot! What is he doing here?*

"How have you been? Why haven't you returned my calls?" He sat down across from her. *He sure is fine,* she thought, distracted from her present reality for a moment. She could feel herself getting sucked into the vortex of Kenny's smoothness. Then she remembered the stack of books on the table before her. She could feel the blood draining out of her feet, rooting her to the spot. *Oh no, get back up! Get back up! You cannot sit here, Kenny!*

"I've been really busy, Kenny," she said, keeping her voice calm. "And since you were so busy that you forgot our last date, I thought you would understand. You *do* understand, don't you?"

"Yes, I do, but..." His eyes left her face and went to the table. He reached for a book.

"You've got some interesting reading choices here. Who's expecting?"

Felicia's mouth opened but no sound came out. As Kenny watched her face, the light came on in his eyes. Slowly leaning forward he studied her more closely.

Felicia's stomach sank. *He knows. Of course he knows. It's his job to be clued into everything about a woman's appearance.* Kenny could always tell when women lied, cried, or otherwise. And Felicia knew she had that pregnant look. As well as a guilty look.

Kenny waited for her answer.

"Um…I was just…"

"You were just what? Getting ready to lie and tell me you're not pregnant?"

"And why would that matter to you one way or the other?"

"It wouldn't, Felicia." That stung.

"Exactly my point."

"And what point would that be? That I haven't heard from you in a while, and now you're pregnant? I guess you've answered my question concerning your disappearance. So who's the lucky guy?"

"What?"

"Who's the lucky guy? Obviously you've moved on."

"Oh for crying out loud. What do you take me for, Kenny? Or perhaps that's the problem, you never took me for anything. You never took me seriously or otherwise. Perhaps it was just fun to date someone you didn't feel you had to fix, but you could at least learn something about the people you sleep with. There is no other guy, Kenny."

"What are you saying?"

"I'm saying this is a conversation I've had nightmares about and decided not to have with you but, just as well, the lucky guy…or perhaps you will think *unlucky* guy…is you!" There she had said it…then regretted it. Then remembered how angry she had been at his clueless accusation of her looseness and reverted back to not caring again. Let him deal with the news she had been dealing with all by herself up to this point. Why should she sweat it out alone when he had contributed to this problem? It did take two to tango, after all.

"What!"

"Let me break it down for you. I'm pregnant. You're the father. Is that clear enough for you?"

"Are you sure?"

"Sure of what? Sure that I'm pregnant? Or sure that you're the father?"

"Well, both."

"Why did I even get started on this with you? Perhaps I'm just a glutton for insults. Why do men always do that?"

"Do what?"

"Refuse to take responsibility for the fun they've had when it isn't fun anymore? Never mind. Don't you worry, my friend, I've got this covered."

"Got what covered?"

"Kenny, why are you having so much trouble following this conversation? Yes, I'm sure I'm pregnant. Yes, I'm sure it's yours. I believe the Immaculate Conception only occurred once in the history of the world. Contrary to your opinion of me, which I don't know where you got it, but perhaps I deserve for you to think of me that way because I slept with you, I don't sleep around." Felicia was aware she had just said the longest run-on sentence she had ever uttered in her life. She sucked in her breath to continue. "But let me put your pretty little head to rest. Nothing will be required of you. I got this." She now reverted back to full on sister-girl attitude. Hand on hip. Neck stiff. Jaw jutted out in angry defiance of her perceived rejection.

"You got *what?*"

"I got this baby and you don't. Nothing will be required or expected of you, capiche? Does that make you feel better? You're officially off the hook and can return to your womanizing without any obligation to me or my child."

"Womanizing! Excuse me! Did you make that baby by yourself? What is up with black women? Why are you all so angry?"

"We're angry because brothers won't step up to the plate!"

"Well perhaps if you would give us a chance we would..."

"You would do what? Accuse me of being pregnant by someone else? Add insult to injury? Tell me I brought this on myself by not taking precautions even though you didn't either?" Felicia's voice was rising.

Kenny ducked down and leaned forward at the same time, hissing, "Keep it down! It's not necessary to cause a scene."

"But this is a real scene, Kenny. This is not a fantasy, a movie, or a bad dream. This is very real."

"I understand that, Felicia, and I resent you assuming how I would feel about it. What makes you think you get to decide what to do about our baby all by yourself? Have you thought this whole thing out? I have rights too, you know."

"Our baby? *Our* baby! Excuse me! This is *my* body we're discussing. I get to decide what goes on with it! What kind of rights do you think you have? And exactly what are you suggesting?" A look of horror came over her face, and she took a deep breath. "If you think I'm going to get rid of my baby to make you feel better about yourself, you've got another thing coming, Kenny Sample." She rose from the table in one movement. "That's exactly why I had no intention of telling you in the first place. You can't even be counted on to show up for a date much less be responsible for something as significant as a child."

"And you can?"

"Yes! I can and I will." She began gathering up her books from the table.

Kenny stood up and reached out to her. "Felicia, look..."

She jumped back as if he were on fire. "Don't touch me! You've done enough, don't you think?"

"We've got to finish talking about this."

"No we don't. There's nothing else to say. It's been nice knowing you. Have a nice life. I will make sure my child does." With a toss of her head, she left him standing there, watching her make her way down the escalator. Reaching the bottom she finally let the tears flow that she had been holding at bay. Perhaps she had blown her first resolve not to tell Kenny about the baby, but she certainly would not lose on two counts. She had no intention of letting him see her cry.

Why am I so angry? That was a good question. She couldn't speak for all the black women of the world, but she could most certainly speak for herself. She was angry at herself for hoping that giving herself to a man meant he would actually love her for it. Obviously that was not the case.

So much for "making love." Whoever came up with that phrase anyhow? Obviously you can't *make* anyone *do anything*—including love you. Perhaps it was time for her to love herself. *There is no time like the present for finally getting it right,* she thought. Something in her walk had changed as she headed down the avenue completely unaware of Kenny watching her from the window above.

25

*M*uriel wove her way hastily through the throng of people milling around the church lobby, trying to make her way to the parking lot and escape before Carla or Brad caught up with her. Just as she thought she had made it through the door safely, a hand caught her elbow. The door swung back dangerously aiming for her face when another hand slammed it back open before it could hit her. She whirled around to catch herself in Brad's arms. Backing her out the door he stabilized her before letting her go.

"You certainly were in a hurry. Didn't you hear me calling you?"

Muriel was still out of breath from finding herself so close to Brad.

"What's the matter, young lady? Cat got your tongue, hmmm?" Brad was smiling broadly but his eyes were questioning.

He is so beautiful, Muriel thought. Then remembering that she was supposed to be angry at him, she whirled around and headed toward the parking lot with Brad following close behind.

"Muriel?"

She didn't answer. Aiming for the safety of her car, she figured if she could just make it into the driver's seat and speed away, she would just keep going. All she could think about was him stringing her along. Why Carla would advise her to give him a break she could not comprehend.

"Muriel!" Brad slammed the car door shut as she opened it. "I am talking to you. What is wrong with you?"

"Perhaps I should ask you that."

"And why would that be, Muriel? I believe I have been the one chasing you across the parking lot, looking like an idiot, while you choose to ignore me."

"Now you know how it feels!"

"How what feels?" Brad looked confused.

"How it feels to look like an idiot."

"Now you've lost me. What are you talking about?"

"I am talking about who the real idiot is here."

"I'm not following you…"

"Aren't you? Actually no, you're not. I have been following you around every weekend for the past two-and-a-half months."

"But I thought you were having a good time."

"Uh huh, but why have a good time on pretense?"

"Pretense?"

"What's the matter? Cat got your tongue? Rumor has it you've already found a place to buy. So why drag me around every weekend looking at buildings if you've already found something you want? Do you think I have nothing else to do with my weekends and my time?"

"Found something? Muriel, what are you talking about?"

"Did you or did you not tell Al that you found something you wanted weeks ago?"

"Ooooh!" The light of understanding came on in Brad's eyes. He began to laugh. "Oh, that is priceless!" He leaned against the car. "So much for clear communication! That's why people should never repeat things. Yes, you are right. I did tell Al I found something I wanted weeks ago."

"Well, why didn't you tell me? After all, I was the one putting a lot of time into this. And if you found what you were looking for, why were we continuing the search?"

"Because I still haven't found the place I wanted, that's why."

"I'm confused. Did you or did you not find what you wanted?"

"Yes, I did."

"Well, where is it?"

"Right here."

"Where?" Muriel frowned then looked from side to side. They had not looked at anything in this neighborhood.

"Right here, standing in front of me. I told Al I found something I want as in *you*, Muriel. I want *you*."

"Me?"

"Yes, you." He stepped closer, looking into her eyes. Muriel thought she would pass out from holding her breath. She stepped back against the car to put some distance between them so that she could think, but he stepped closer. He leaned forward to kiss her, taking her in his arms. As he embraced her, Muriel felt herself sliding backward down a black hole. Suddenly raucous male laughter filled her ears. She flailed against the hands pulling at her, screaming, "No! No! Stop it! Please! Don't!" Brad pinned her arms to her sides shaking her. Muriel opened her eyes now filled with tears and terror to focus on Brad, who looked drawn and worried. "Muriel! Muriel! What's wrong?"

Muriel put her hands to her chest fighting for air. She had broken out in a sweat and was disoriented. Brad was frozen to the spot, trying to comprehend what had happened and what to do next.

"Is everything alright over here?" A security officer jolted them both out of their state.

"Uh, I don't…" Brad didn't know what to say.

"Yes, we're fine officer, thank you." Muriel realized the situation did look suspect for Brad. She concentrated on slowing her breathing, already beginning to feel foolish about her panic attack and the attention it had drawn.

"Okay. You need to move along; your car is blocking other cars from getting out."

"Allow us a moment, officer, and we'll be on our way." Brad had not taken his eyes from Muriel's face. Now there was a look of determination in his eyes. "Muriel, we need to talk…"

"I know. I'm sorry, Brad. It's not your fault. It's just…I….It's just…" She dissolved into tears.

"Shhhh…" Brad cautiously approached, gently taking her into his arms after noting no sign of resistance this time. "It's alright," he said, as if reassuring a small child she was safe from the big bad wolf in her nightmare. He allowed her a moment to indulge in well-needed tears. Then tucking his fingers under her chin he raised her face to his. "We were not created to bear burdens alone, Muriel. Isolation is the greatest tool the enemy of our souls uses to keep us in bondage. Whatever it is that you've experienced in your past, it's high time you faced it and dealt with it. Now I have no intention of hurting you, but I do intend to get to the bottom of what just happened here. So do you want to talk about it now or later because I won't be backing down on this one. Keys, please." He extended one hand while still holding her chin with the other.

"Keys?"

"Yes. I believe I'm driving you home or to a coffee shop or wherever you want to go to continue this discussion since we are getting kicked out of the parking lot."

Obediently handing them over, she allowed Brad to lead her to the passenger side of her car and tuck her in. They didn't speak as they wove through the streets and onto the expressway. She used the beauty of Lake Shore Drive at night with the lake glistening under the moonlight as an excuse to say nothing while collecting her thoughts, as painful as they were. Where would she begin to share something she had tried to run from and snuff down so deep inside that it had become a part of the fabric of who she had become. She had been successful in running from herself for years, but now Brad forced her to face what she had not been able to before.

She knew in the moment that he had declared he wanted her that she wanted him too. Just how to cross the chasm of her past and all her fears had overwhelmed her in the moments that followed. Perhaps it was the jolting reality of his nearness and her desperation to be able to respond to him that had catapulted her back to the past with all its horror and pain. She couldn't tell. All she knew was he was right. She had to talk about what had happened and break its hold on her once and for all. She had kept this odious secret for far too long, allowing the shame of it to hold her captive. Part of her had always blamed herself; the other half fought to lay the blame on the callousness of men. Neither rationale had given her any peace, and there she remained stuck, choosing to never put herself in the situation where the same hurtful events could be repeated. Thus had begun her self-imposed exile from the land of relationships or anything that even hinted at intimacy. But now she had met someone worth fighting her fears for. She silently asked God to help her sort through the myriad emotions that were threatening to make her do what she had always done—retreat within herself and run.

After parking the car, they silently walked to her apartment. Brad opened the door since he had yet to relinquish her keys. Taking her by the hand, he led her to the sofa and indicated that she should sit. He headed toward her kitchen. After a considerable amount of opening and closing of cabinet doors, he found what he was looking for. After several minutes and more muffled movements, he emerged with two steaming coffee mugs. One he set on the coffee table, the other he handed to her. Then sitting opposite her and taking a sip of his coffee, he again set it on the table and leaned forward. "Alright. I'm listening." His eyes probed hers, and she knew she couldn't hide any longer.

Cupping the hot mug between her hands, she clung to the cup and welcomed the burn. It was something she could feel. She was amazed how the words just poured out, as if a dam had finally broken and the flood of events and emotions could no longer be held at bay. She watched Brad's face as intently as he watched hers as she related how naïve she had been in college. Coming from a Christian home, she had always led a sheltered life. She had purposed to keep her faith and the morals that went with it while she lived on campus. Then she met Cedric Graham.

Tall, handsome, captain of the basketball team, an upperclassman who was enthralled with her.

For the first time in her life she had to fight passion and take a stand for her faith. She shared with him that she didn't believe in premarital sex, and he had said that he could wait. Obviously this had become a matter of discussion among his teammates, and he succumbed to the pressure of their opinion. Muriel drew a shaky breath, finding it hard to go on. Brad leaned forward. He reassuringly squeezed her hands and waited. She continued. "One night after a game, Cedric had a party back at his dorm room to celebrate their win. I went with him and stayed to help clean up after most of the guests had left. He and a few of his teammates had had too much to drink, and Cedric began accusing me of sleeping with someone else. He said no one in college was a virgin, and I was making him look stupid in front of his boys. He would teach me a thing or two. 'No one plays Cedric Graham.'" Muriel was rocking back and forth holding herself. Brad didn't move. "And then he raped me. He raped me, and then his friends raped me, one by one. The more I begged them to stop, the louder they laughed. Can you believe that?" She looked blindly at Brad, looking past him as if seeing the horrible scene. Her face was drenched in tears. "They thought it was funny! Him and his sick, stupid friends. They wouldn't stop. I wanted to die but I couldn't, so I passed out instead." She stopped and stared at Brad, trying to assess his reaction to her revelation. His face had the most tender expression. His eyes filled with tears. But still he didn't move…as if the moment was too sacred to interrupt her.

She swallowed. "By the time I came to, the others were gone. But not Cedric. He was as arrogant as ever. He threatened me and said that if I went to the authorities I would be the one who would look bad. After all, good girls didn't hang out with a bunch of players after midnight. It would spread all over campus. I would the one who would be construed as just another loose girl inviting trouble.

"And then I thought, What would my parents think?" She shook her head recalling it all…locating the precise moment she had chosen to stop feeling. She had remained silent, her shame greater than her pain. Perhaps it was her fault. She couldn't think of what she had done to be treated this way by someone who was supposed to care for her. She had tried to process the whys over and over in her mind, finding no answers. Even God had remained silent on the subject when she sought Him in prayer. After a while she had reconciled herself to simply being numb. Erecting walls around her heart, she had never ventured past them until now. She now wondered what had taken her so long. Her confession and her tears were cleansing her, and the chains around her heart were falling away. She was finally free.

Brad held his breath as she related all that she had been through. His face mirroring his emotions that went from anger to sympathy to the sorrow of not being able to be there to save her from such a horrible experience. Taking her in his arms, he silently prayed that God would heal the wounds in her soul and free her from the power of her memories. He knew it wasn't the time to ask, but he wondered if this was the same volatile NBA player Cedric Graham. What would be the likelihood of two players having the same name? Deep in his spirit he knew it was the same one.

He shook his head. The irony! Here was Muriel bound in her past, while the one who put her in her emotional prison seemed to be excelling on all fronts. Cedric had just penned a multimillion-dollar deal, and he and his glamorous wife were expecting their first child any day now. Known for his displays of temper on the court, everyone tolerated them in exchange for his high scoring and showmanship. Arrogant and prideful, he sported an above-the-law attitude. Those who didn't like him swallowed their distaste for his attitude and kept their focus on what they really wanted—to win the game.

Where is the vengeance God promised in Scripture to carry out? Brad wondered. But at the same time, he knew that grace usually ran out when the perpetrator least expected it. Turning his attention back to Muriel, he noticed she had relaxed in his arms. Gone was the defensive edge. A new softness was in her eyes when she raised her face to look into his.

"Thank you for listening." She whispered the words.

"I'm sorry I wasn't there for you."

"But you are now."

"You better believe I am. And I will be from now on, if you'll let me."

"I'd like that. Brad?"

"Hmmm?" His voice was muffled over the top of her head.

"You knew, didn't you?"

"Yes, I did."

"How did you know?"

"I used to work in a counseling trauma center. You had that look. I can't describe it, but after a while you recognize it."

"Brad?" Her voice came softly from somewhere in the vicinity of his shoulder.

"Yes, Muriel?"

But she said nothing further. He tilted his head to study her face and smiled. She was fast asleep. Her breathing was soft and shallow, her features relaxed as if she had not a care in the world. He shifted position to place her at a more comfortable angle and tightened his grip on her slightly. *And she won't have another care in the world after this! Not if I have anything to do with it.* Somewhere in the apartment a phone began to ring. Muriel didn't move, and neither did Brad. Eventually it went to voicemail and silence returned, punctuated only by an occasional deeper breath by Muriel. Brad examined the shadows in the room, noting they no longer appeared as deep as before. And so he waited...waited for the light to come.

26

Tracy pulled her computer bag from the overhead luggage compartment, made her way off the plane, and headed toward the baggage claim. Bone weary, she was happy to be back home. Los Angeles was always fun for approximately two weeks, and then the traffic got to her and she began to long for the familiar restaurants and reality checks of home. She wouldn't trade living in Chicago for the world. It was like a mini New York, only cleaner and quieter. But as far as having everything a single woman could want in one place, Chicago was it. Oh yes, from food to culture to music to people who were real, she'd put her money on mini Europe, as she liked to call it, any day.

Stopping to adjust her purse strap and situate her computer case for easier navigation, an image on an overhead television near the gate caught her attention. A weeping woman was being interviewed, and a photo of Cedric Graham was superimposed on the upper right-hand corner of the screen. Tracy crept closer to see what the CNN update was saying. The weeping woman, Cedric's wife, was relating to the reporter the tragic occurrences of the day. Tracy couldn't believe her ears. She had not seen Cedric since they left college except to hear of his meteoric rise as a basketball star. But since she was not really a sports fan, her attention to his career had been minimal. It wasn't as if Muriel ever had anything to say about him. Ever since they had broken up in college, Cedric had been a subject that was strictly off limits. And Muriel had developed quite an aversion to basketball, so as a group their inner circle had learned to leave well enough alone and move on to other topics they could all be excited about.

Though Tracy had not seen Cedric in years, it seemed foreign to be hearing a story of this nature about someone she knew. She wondered why no one had mentioned what had been going on in the last few weeks. Tracy found herself rooted to the spot, trying to grasp what she was hearing as the reporter related the breaking story. "Last month, Cedric Graham was accused of rape by a woman he encountered on the road. Charges were filed, and he was arrested, only to be released on bond to await trial. From all indications, Mr. Graham was confident the charges would be dropped." The camera cut to Cedric addressing the press. "It was consensual, and she knows it. As a matter of fact, perhaps I should be the one pressing charges! After all, she came after me. What is it they say? Hell hath no fury like a woman scorned? She knew I was married." With that his attorney whisked him away from the line of reporters.

The story then cut to footage of Cedric going into a house with his wife. The newscaster was narrating. "He returned home and back to the court in rare form with no sign his legal woes affected his abilities." Footage of Cedric scoring drew other passersby to the monitor.

"Wow, he was something wasn't he?" one man said.

"For a while anyway," another replied.

Tracy turned her focus back to the reporter. "Things heated up as three other women, bolstered by the courage of the first woman, stepped forward to press charges, saying they too had been raped by him." The camera cut to three women giving a press conference. "The prosecutor on the case demanded that Graham not be released on bail citing a pattern of behavior emerging."

The camera then showed the prosecutor. "Obviously Mr. Graham is not a man who feels he should have to deal with the consequences of his actions. I think it is safe to consider him a flight risk."

The crowd around the monitor was all ears as the reporter continued, "The judge released him pending an initial hearing. Pursued by the media, Graham lashed out."

The camera cut to a series of outbursts from Cedric: the basketball player attacking a reporter and a photographer, picking a fight with a referee during a game, being fined and forcefully removed from the court. Then the camera revealed his wife tearfully recounting her side of the story to a reporter.

"He became more and more paranoid. He was so afraid I was going to leave him. I was afraid to stay, but I was also afraid to leave. I didn't know what he would do. He kept saying it was a conspiracy to ruin his career. I didn't know what to do." The reporter nodded understandingly while she continued to relate the current events.

On this particular morning, she had gone down to the kitchen to prepare his breakfast. They had planned to get away for the weekend to get some rest out of the glare of the media. Cedric had seemed fine and even enthusiastic about their mini vacation. Shortly after she had gone downstairs, she heard something topple and had called upstairs to see if he was all right. He said he was fine. Then a loud blast followed. This time when she called upstairs, she got no reply. She began to weep, "I ran upstairs still calling him over and over again, but he wouldn't answer me. And that's when I found him. He was on the bathroom floor, the gun still in his hand. There was so much blood. I didn't know what to do. I didn't know what to do…"

The interview was followed by others who spoke of Cedric in unflattering terms. He had always had an attitude of entitlement, always felt he was above the law. He didn't have much respect for women and was estranged from his mother and abusive to his wife. Cedric was a coward who couldn't stand to face the consequences of his actions. On and on the story went. The crowd around the monitor drifted into their own conversations as they dispersed to their various destinations.

"Man, what a jerk."

"But it's still sad."

"Can you imagine what his wife went through?"

"Honey, I would have left him!"

Tracy didn't know how long she stood not moving. A weird fascination for the details had overtaken her. Slowly she began making her way toward the baggage claim. Somewhere in the back of her mind she thought, *This could have been Muriel's life.* For what it was worth, she had been spared the embarrassment and pain of ending up with a man whose character had obviously disintegrated over the years. *How does this happen?* she wondered. *What happens in the life of a person to cause him to go left even when everything seems to be going right?* Tracy had never found out what happened between him and Muriel in college, and Muriel had made it clear not to ask. Actually Tracy had been a little relieved when they had broken up. Cedric was out of Muriel's league, just a bit too worldly for someone as innocent as she. Muriel had come from a small town, been in church all her life, and seemed untouched and pure. Quick-witted and beautiful, she made friends easily, but she had her standards and would not be swayed by the influence of others.

Tracy had been a little surprised that Muriel had allowed Cedric to sweep her off her feet. They just didn't seem to go together. He was out there and the big man on campus. But Muriel's heart had been all aflutter, apparently even good little Christian girls could get distracted by flattering attention. *Anyway, who was I to wave the caution sign when I was too busy making my own bad choices?* Tracy thought. As mysteriously as Cedric and Muriel's romance had begun, it ended. She just assumed that Muriel had made a judgment call based on her conservative beliefs and moved on. But Muriel had changed after that. She seemed to grow up overnight, becoming more jaded and pragmatic in her outlook. It was all work and no play with little patience for others who veered off course and became entangled in matters of the heart. Nothing was asked, and nothing was explained. Everyone knew not to put Muriel and Cedric in the same room together; the imagined explosion was something everyone wanted to avoid. And so they did and moved on.

Speaking of Muriel, Tracy wondered if she knew about Cedric. But then again, she knew the answer. Muriel was not the television-watching type. *I'll call her once I'm outside the airport.* Deep in thought, Tracy considered the choices she had made herself. Though she didn't know where most of the guys were that she dated during high school and college, she had heard rumors that some of the ones she had deep crushes on were either in jail or dead. The ones she ignored had gone on to become bank presidents, attorneys…and one had even become a senator. *What is up with that?* she wondered. Why do we always go for the bad boys? Now in her older, more responsible frame of mind, she had come to realize that all the chemistry in the world wasn't worth it if the guy had no character.

How many times had she allowed herself to get caught up in a smooth rap with no substance behind it? What she would give now for a solid, quiet man who would simply love her the way she wanted to be loved. Muriel had always said it though it never rang truer than now: "Girl, you don't need a bunch of men, you just need one. The one that will be there for you do or die."

"Hey, Tracy! Fancy meeting you here. Where are you coming from?" Tracy turned in the direction of the voice to face one of her greatest temptations—Edward Mann. Tall. Fine. Gucci from head to toe. Chic. Elegant. Rich. Successful. Smart. Witty. The list went on once Tracy got on a roll about him. One she left off the list but should have added was dangerous. This always lurked at the back of her mind while she reeled from his flirtations. She got ready for his rap to begin, and indeed it did.

"Well, lady, you're looking more beautiful than ever. In from a production trip? How have you been?" He leaned forward to kiss her European style on each cheek. The faint remains of her favorite cologne, Issey Miyake, made her feel slightly intoxicated. But this time she vowed to listen to the small voice within her and not get sucked into the vortex of Edward. Taking a breath to clear her head, she smiled her most charismatic smile ignoring the compliment lest she allow her love-starved ego to take over. "Yes, just got in from Los Angeles, and you?"

"Just finished up a video in New York. I'm in town to do some editing for a few days. We should get together, have some dinner." He leaned in suggestively at the invitation. Again Tracy felt slightly light-headed, but she shook it off. Suddenly Derrick came to mind. Good, stable, solid Derrick. He was right—she should have grabbed him when the getting was good. Perhaps she hadn't accumulated enough bad experiences to truly appreciate him at the time. Now she was left with this. And she had finally learned what looked good wasn't necessarily good for you. The momentary rush just wasn't worth the heartache.

"Oh, I don't know, Edward. What would your wife say about our dinner date, hmm?" She said it sweetly while smiling.

Edward frowned slightly then recovered. "Don't you know? I'm divorced. Marie left about eight months ago. I thought you and I had talked since then. But then again, I was busy reorganizing myself. But that's all very deep water under a very high bridge. Back to my question now that all obstacles have been moved out of the way. How about dinner?" Again his tone was suggestive, loaded with the promise of endless possibilities besides dinner.

For one brief moment Tracy was tempted by the news that he was now free. It would be so nice to be in the company of a charming man who knew how to make her feel as if the sun and the moon revolved around her. Edward did that well. As she wavered, she considered her options: go to dinner and find herself once again caught up in something that would ultimately pan out to nothing or actually do the right thing and keep stepping while she still had her heart intact. *That's right!* She shook herself, mad that she even considered opening herself to Edward for a moment.

Just because he was divorced meant nothing. He had already shown her who he was when he was married. He had come after her hard and strong, and she had almost drowned beneath his advances. The only thing that had saved her was the distance between them—in spite of the fact that she knew he was married. He had managed to make her feel that he was the victim in his relationship with his wife. In hindsight she knew that was definitely not the case. Unfaithful then, he would be unfaithful now. No, she could not, would not ever trust him.

"You know, that is a very tempting offer, Edward, but I'm at a different place in my life right now."

"Really? And where would that be?" He seemed amused by her announcement.

"I'm trying to think before I leap and be more responsible for my heart, as opposed to trusting others with that job. You understand?"

"Mmm, but what does that have to do with dinner?" His intentions were very clear, and he was not to be redirected.

"It has everything to do with dinner, with me, with you…you see, my history with you lets me know you simply don't fit into my new plan."

He opened his mouth to speak. Tracy held up her hand. She had to get this out, more for herself than for him.

"I've come to a conclusion in recent months that I have to honor myself much more than I have in the past. I have worked hard to become a successful woman. I've made sacrifices to accomplish my goals. Anything that led me away from my mission I have quickly cut off without a thought or a glance. But I haven't done that with men."

Again he tried to interject; again she cut him off.

"No, let me finish. You know why I've never done that with men?

Because I never consciously and deliberately set a goal about what I wanted when it came to love!" She smiled broadly.

Edward shifted uneasily, ready to move on. Tracy didn't care.

"You know what I want, Edward?"

He said nothing.

"I want a committed relationship: marriage and babies. Therefore, I am going to make choices based on that goal! Based on that conclusion, I do not believe dinner or anything else with you will be appropriate."

Edward looked at her as if she had lost her mind.

She leaned forward and kissed him on both cheeks European style before he had a chance to respond. "But you do look fabulous as usual. I wish you the best of luck with your new life. I've got to run!" With that Tracy resumed her trek toward baggage claim without a backward glance.

A conversation she had had with Muriel came to mind. For somebody who wasn't in the game, she sure had a lot to say about how it should be played. "How much is your heart and your body worth to you anyway?" she had demanded one day when she grew weary of hearing about Tracy's latest romantic fiasco. "You treat yourself like a cheap suit. When are you going to stop letting everyone try you on for free and charge what you're really worth? Either a man wants to give you his everything or he doesn't! I tell you this much, no one will be getting a piece of me until he's ready to give it all up. If you don't value yourself, that's your problem, but I do. I will not be putting my heart, my body, or my mind on discount 'cause after you do, what do you have left? Just remember, if you don't value yourself, no one else will do so either. Think about it."

Tracy hadn't wanted to think about it at the time. It was easier to find her validation in someone else rather than consider her own value, which to tell the truth, she hadn't been sure of. She envied Muriel for being so sure of herself. Who had instilled in her the idea that her love and attention were precious? Tracy had missed that life lesson and didn't know where to begin to calculate her own worth. "How can you place a price tag on yourself?" she had asked Muriel. Without batting an eyelash, Muriel had replied that if Jesus thought she was worth dying for, then a natural man would indeed have to step up to the plate and offer something more substantial than a promise. But since Tracy wasn't into Jesus and all that Christian stuff, she was a little foggy about where else she might look for an assessment of her value. And at this point she still wasn't sure. All she knew was that what she did in her past relationships didn't work or get the results she wanted. The thought of more of the same ad infinitum was more than she could bear. Now she'd finally turned the corner on her way to a new street.

Tracy smiled as she remembered the look on Edward's face when she'd turned him down. Quizzical, but with a touch of respect. There was something to be said about the peace that came from making sound, responsible choices! Once upon a time she would have thought being heart smart was as exciting as eating broccoli, but now that she was becoming acquainted with feeling good about herself, she rather liked the newfound freedom that came from saying no.

Her bag looked lonely slowly moving around the luggage conveyor. Absentmindedly she grabbed it, dragging it to the curb like an incorrigible child. Hailing a cab, she sat back in the backseat suddenly completely drained from the toll of her travels and her unexpected encounter. She was still lost in thought with a cacophony of images, questions, and vague conclusions endlessly swirling in her mind when her thoughts returned to Muriel and Cedric. *Oo, I was going to call Muriel.* Tapping out her number on her cell phone, Tracy wondered what her friend's response would be to the news. Too late now, the phone was ringing… and ringing and ringing. When Muriel's voicemail came on, Tracy frowned. It wasn't like Muriel to be out this late. *I wonder where she is? There's always tomorrow, and nothing about the news is going to change between now and then. Cedric is dead, never to rise again.* Since this was not the sort of thing to leave on someone's answering machine, Tracy opted to keep it light. "Hey, girl, just checking in. I'm back from L.A. You'd be proud of me! I kept my eyeballs and my charms to myself. This is getting scary. I think you're finally rubbing off on me. Anyway, before I forget, put next Wednesday on your calendar for lunch. Talk to ya later. Bye!" And with that Tracy let out one last sigh for Cedric. The taxi stopped and she got out. Opening the door to her apartment, she entered into the silence and thought that if she was going to continue to be so selective about the men in her life, perhaps a pet wouldn't be such a bad idea after all.

27

*T*racy lifted her face to catch the sun and enjoy the warm, dry heat that had finally taken up residence in the city, enticing everyone to outdoor seating at the restaurants that lined the street lest they waste a moment of precious summer heat on the air-conditioning inside. The waiter set down the lemonade, cutting Adrian out of Tracy's line of vision. Her eyes slowly panned the rest of the table taking in Felicia and now Muriel, who had arrived her customary fifteen minutes late, panting about some last-minute business before she left the showroom. And by the way, was it all right if Carla joined them because she had run into her on the way there, and she had always wanted her to meet them. And what was one to say to all that when Muriel, who besides being winded, seemed to be glowing. There was something different about her. As a matter of fact, Tracy had a slow dawning that there was something different about each of her friends with the exception of Carla, whom she didn't really know. She decided to take them apart one by one.

First there was Adrian. The most drastic change of all. Tracy couldn't believe her eyes when she entered the restaurant. She almost didn't recognize her. A petite vision in a turquoise turtleneck silk slip dress that was modest yet seductive in cut. Even Tracy was caught off guard by Adrian's figure. She had never realized what a fabulous body she had. Gone were the customary prim diamond studs, replaced by large gold hoops. She had a stack of bangles on one arm and sported a Cartier watch on the other wrist. And she was handling her hot signature Gucci pumps with turquoise trim as she made her way toward the table. She sat down as if she knew she was looking cute and waved an earth-to-Tracy signal in front of her girlfriend's eyes with a giggle. Then tossing her head from side to side seeking Tracy's approval, she sat back in her chair looking very self-satisfied.

Tracy had oohed and aahed until Felicia had arrived. Tracy couldn't quite put her finger on exactly what the difference was in Felicia. She seemed a bit more quiet than usual, after all she hadn't said anything about a man since she arrived, but she looked different too. As Tracy was settling in to solve this mystery, Muriel had arrived huffing and puffing with Carla vibrating behind her. Tracy came back to Felicia, but even now as she looked at her she was just as stumped as before. *Hmmm... what is it?* Felicia looked beautiful in a tailored cream linen suit. It was cut a little looser than what she usually wore, but it made a fabulous silhouette that didn't take away from her figure at all.

"Ooo, you're wearing the suit I gave you! It looks fabulous on you. I thought you said it was too big for you. I think it's just right." Muriel frowned accusingly at Felicia as she slid into her seat beside her with Carla looking on curiously.

"I think it looks great too. You know everything doesn't have to fit like a second skin, Felicia." Tracy had always felt that Felicia could give her clothes a little more room, but had backed off, checking herself for jealousy. After all, the girl did have a slamming shape.

"Well, you know how it is. A girl can never have too many sizes in her wardrobe. One day we're up, the next we're down, but thank you for the left-handed compliment." Felicia was looking a little self-conscious, and her comment didn't fit at all because everyone knew Felicia's size never fluctuated. Just as Tracy leaned forward to take a closer look at Felicia, attempting to discern what was different about her, she got distracted by Muriel's squeal.

"Aaaadrian! Wow! Look at you! Girl, that hair is cutting up."

"Thank you, my sistah! I take it you approve?"

"Approve? I give you a resounding high five. You know I told you a long time ago I thought you would look hot with a Halle Berry cut. You have the bones for it. It's amazing. I bet you if Ron saw you right now his teeth would fall out of his head."

"Actually, they almost did but he managed to keep them in."

"What! You finally saw Ron and didn't call anybody?" Tracy had choked on her lemonade. Now all eyes were on Adrian, waiting for her to spill the beans.

"There really isn't much to tell, plus I saw him yesterday so I figured I could as well wait and recite the story once. You know how I feel about nursing and rehearsing things."

"Enough already! I can't bear the suspense. Oh, here's the waiter. Let's order lunch and not hold him up." On that note Muriel proceeded to order everyone's lunch. To save time, she said, since they were all late anyway. There was no need to drag out the ritual of trying to decide what they wanted when they always ordered the same thing. Though it was Carla's first time, Muriel took the liberty of suggesting what she should have and promised to pay for it if she didn't like it. This taken care of in short order, she focused on Adrian. "So, give up the goods, girl!"

Adrian shifted in her seat and gave a mischievous smile. "Did I tell you I was painting again?"

"So I heard, and I think that is fabulous—but forgive me if I don't linger on that topic right now. What about Ron?"

Tracy was now truly confused. She didn't know if she was more interested in finding out about Ron and Adrian or what had come over Muriel. Since when was Muriel the one to champion conversations on the subject of love? She usually avoided them like the plague. Felicia was the one who usually led the inquisition on anything pertaining to personal affairs or men, yet she sat strangely silent. Looking highly interested, yes, but not uttering a word. *Hmmm,* Tracy's eyes shifted from

Adrian to Muriel to Felicia. What had happened to her friends over the last several months? It was amazing how much you could miss by phone. Something was definitely up with each one of them, and the only one she could halfway figure out was Adrian—perhaps because she was the only one talking.

"Ron is fine..."

"Oh come on, girl! Do not try my patience. I don't care about his welfare—I want to know what is going on!"

"Are you going to let me tell this my way or are you going to keep interrupting?"

"Alright, go on."

"As I said, I've begun painting again, and my pieces have been turning out far better than I expected. Felicia saw them. What did you think, Fi?"

"The one I saw was spectacular...and don't forget, I think I have a client..." Felicia quickly answered.

"Oh for crying out loud, are you trying to see if I have any fruit of the spirit? Because about now I don't! Will you please get on with the story before I lose my salvation?" Muriel was practically bouncing in her seat.

"Alright already! Anyway, I decided to see if there was any potential for showing my work at one of the local galleries. Do you know that really great one over on Huron Street? Well, I went there. Mr. Morrow is an old family friend, and he loved my work and agreed to an exhibition of the entire series I'm doing." Adrian paused for effect and then went on. "I was coming out of his office—and there was Ron!"

Felicia clutched her chest. Muriel's mouth dropped open. Tracy leaned forward. Carla's eyes looked as if she was attending a tennis match, going back and forth between all present at the table. It was obvious that Muriel had clued her in on what had happened with Adrian.

"What did he have to say for himself?" Muriel hissed.

"Not much. In fact, he seemed at a loss for words. He was with Amber."

"Who is Amber? Not that new assistant he got? I told you I didn't like her that day we stopped by the office," Muriel commented.

"You know, I had completely forgotten about that. I guess I wasn't really paying attention. To be honest I didn't even recognize her from that day," Adrian confessed.

"How could you not pay attention when someone in skimpy clothes is all over your man? I'm telling you, it ought to be against the law the way some women go to work. And they'll be the first to scream sexual harassment when they are walking invitations for groping. Not to excuse a man for acting like an idiot, you understand, but some people just set themselves up for stuff and then have the nerve to cry victim!"

"I think we've gotten off the subject a little. Let's get back to the art gallery..." Tracy wanted to get the rest of the details. "Adrian, you seem to be awfully calm about all of this. How do you feel? It had to be difficult seeing him for the first time and seeing him with another woman. What did he say? What did *you* say? What did she say?"

"Wait a minute, one question at a time! What did he say? Not much. He was taken by my new do it seems. He kept telling me I looked incredible."

"Looking fabulous has always been the best revenge." Felicia giggled.

"You got that right, but I think he was just as intrigued with the fact that I was painting again and soon to be on exhibit. Now *that* seemed to really have him going! I think he almost forgot he had company."

"Mmm, I'm sure his little girlfriend wasn't too happy about that." Muriel sounded satisfied.

"What is she like?" Felicia asked tentatively, not wanting to say the wrong thing but still allowing her curiosity to get the best of her.

"She seemed nice enough."

"Nice! Have you lost your mind? What woman can be called nice when she takes your man?"

"Muriel, she did not *take* Ron from me. In a way I kind of served him up on a platter and *gave* Ron to her," Adrian said as if patiently trying to correct a child.

"What?" The chorus rang out from the table so resoundingly that others turned from other tables to observe the women, who all appeared to be appalled by whatever information they had been privy to.

"I think I have to be honest with myself and accept part of the responsibility for what happened to my marriage. I was not paying attention; I missed the cues. I was not on my j-o-b, okay? I put my head in the sand, being happy and spiritual with Jesus and forgetting I had a natural man to take care of. So this is what I get. You can't keep a man on just prayer, you know. I set him up to be tempted."

"I know you're not trying to justify Ron's behavior because that is crazy. And I'm sorry, but you did more than pray, girl. You were a good wife, Adrian, and there is no excuse for him leaving you. And the way he did it is totally unacceptable!" Felicia objected.

Tracy couldn't believe her ears. It was as if Felicia and Muriel had switched roles. *Since when is Felicia so hard on men? She used to always make excuses for their lack of character.*

"Amber." Muriel sniffed in indignation. "Pure fluff. How typical. What was he thinking?"

"Perhaps he was thinking he wanted to feel like 'the man' again. I don't know how to explain it, but no, Felicia, I'm not trying to justify Ron's leaving. I'm also not putting the complete blame on him. Muriel, you just told me I wasn't paying attention and I wasn't. The one thing I realized when I ran into Ron yesterday was how many of the things I had tucked away that first got his attention. I was so focused on going through the motions of what I thought it took to be a good wife that I lost the girlfriend he was attracted to and fascinated by—and that is *my* fault, not his. He lost how he used to feel when he was with me. He couldn't go on that way forever. In the business he's in, he's surrounded by way too much stimuli to not fall prey to it at some point."

"Well, that's the truth, but he could have spoken up." Felicia seemed to be taking this a bit personally.

"Perhaps he did in his own way and I didn't get what he was really asking me for. Perhaps he didn't know what he wanted himself until he met Amber. Obviously she gave him what he wanted. Now, is she a temporary filler or a permanent fix? I can't worry about that. All I can do is learn my own lessons and tighten up my act."

"Wow! You're a better woman than I am!" Carla couldn't contain herself any longer. "I don't think I could be that calm about it. Excuse me for intruding since I don't really know you, and I hope I'm not speaking out of turn. But do you suppose since you feel you gave your husband away that you could figure out how to get him back?" Carla held her breath, hoping she hadn't overstepped any boundaries. "You *do* want him back, don't you?"

Tracy couldn't take it. "Why should she want him back?"

"Because God hates divorce, number one, and number two, when you've been with someone a long time…in spite of what they do, they're still a part of you. It can't be that easy to just walk away."

Tracy chose to bow out on the grounds this was not her area of expertise.

Carla turned back to Adrian. "Is it? You don't intend to take this lying down, do you?"

Adrian was unfazed by her question. "No, I don't, Carla, and that is exactly why I am so calm. Now is not the time to cave in and lose my mind. I have every intention of getting him back."

"And how do you intend to do that?" Felicia seemed to really want to know the answer to this one.

Adrian tilted her head to the side as if listening for a cue and leaned back to allow the waiter to place her food in front of her. "I don't know yet. I have to pray about it."

"But you just said that prayer doesn't work when it comes to keeping a man."

"No, that's not exactly what I said. I just said prayer *alone* won't keep him. God gives us instructions in prayer. If we don't follow them, it can look as if our faith isn't working. But that's not on God, that's on us. So I'm going to get my marching orders on how to get my husband back and follow them to the 'T.' Humph, I kinda feel sorry for Amber."

"Why?" It was Tracy's turn to feel indignant.

"I don't blame her for what happened. She's just wants what every woman wants—to be loved. She merely responded to what was accessible. Perhaps if I had been in her position and Ron came on to me, I would have done the same thing. If you place a bone in front of a starving dog, what do you expect it to do?"

"Be a dog like Ron was. I'm sorry, I know he's your man but…" Felicia was upset and looking a little queasy as she pushed her plate away from her.

"I understand how you feel, but I have to focus and deal with *my* failings, Felicia. I'm the only person I can control or fix. I can't just point the finger at him even though adultery is never justifiable in my opinion. But I also understand that some men struggle because their wives aren't meeting their needs. Cheating on their wives is not their preference unless they have unfaithful spirits from the beginning—and that is not Ron. I think it was a cry for help. I can either get bitter about it or do better."

"How do you get to the place where you can calmly rationalize these kinds of things, Adrian? I would be crazy," Tracy admitted.

"That's what having a relationship with God is all about, Tracy. Navigating through life's difficulties without falling apart. He takes the guesswork out of life because we have His promises to lean on as well as His counsel to guide us. There are some things I know He will take care of for me as long as I do what I'm supposed to do. I'm not exempt from the things other people go through just because I'm saved. I'm just better equipped to deal with it. Felicia! Are you alright?" Adrian looked alarmed as Felicia lurched back from the table slapping her hand over her mouth.

Felicia nodded frantically in a backward glance as she headed for the ladies' room at breakneck speed. The others looked helplessly at one another trying to figure out what to do. Carla bolted from the table after her, "Somebody needs to follow the girl and make sure she's okay, don't you think?" Her sharp comment snapped them all back to their senses causing them all to make a beeline after her.

They found Felicia hunched over the sink, spewing out the remains of whatever she had eaten before she came. They encircled her like sentries watching and waiting. Carla grabbed some paper towels, dampened them with cool water, and slapped them over Felicia's forehead. Finally lifting her head from the bowl, Felicia smiled sheepishly as she took the paper towel from Carla. "Sorry," she said weakly. "The smell of the tomato sauce just turned my stomach, and before I knew it…" She hunched her shoulders and turned to splash her face with cool water.

Tracy frowned. "That's weird. That's your favorite dish. You always order the penne."

Adrian took Felicia's face in her hands, studying her ashen skin and her eyes, which now looked hollow. "Hmmm, perhaps you have some sort of virus? There's been a funny bug going around. Maybe you should go home and get some rest. You did say you've been burning the candle at both ends lately."

"If you were married I'd say you were pregnant, but I suppose we don't have to worry about that one." Carla giggled, amused by her own cleverness.

Felicia froze and did not say a word.

Muriel snickered. "Since when do only married women get pregnant? Girl, you have truly been in church too long."

Felicia gave a nervous giggle, suddenly seeming extremely uncomfortable from all the attention. "I've certainly had enough excitement and attention to last me for the day. Should we get back to lunch or have I grossed everybody out enough?"

"I think we're done, girl. The memory of you hanging over the sink is now forever etched in my memory. Let's pay the waiter and be on our way. I have to get back to work anyway," Muriel answered. "Maybe you need to get a checkup, just to make sure it's nothing serious or contagious." Placing her hands over her face in mock fear, she leaned forward and hugged Felicia, then draping her arm around her shoulders she steered her out of the ladies' room and back toward the table, stopping just short of it. "Perhaps you shouldn't get too close. We don't need a repeat of what just happened."

"I think the moment has passed, Muriel." Felicia's color was returning to her face and she looked better. More clear-eyed. Still she dug into her purse and handed over the money for her portion of the bill, not getting any closer to the table just in case.

Carla was still quietly studying her face. She quickly averted her eyes as Felicia turned toward her.

"It's been nice meeting you, Carla. Perhaps we can get together again for a more uneventful meal. I've got to get going." Turning to Adrian, Felicia hugged her quickly. "Hang in there, girl, and you go for it. I think you should get your man back. Good men are hard to find. When you do find one, he's worth keeping and I believe Ron is one of them, okay?"

"Thanks, honey." Adrian gently kissed her on the cheek. "Feel better okay?"

"I will! Bye, Trace. I'll call you. That exhibit you wanted to see is coming to town next week. Maybe we could go check it out."

"Mmm hmm, you do that." Tracy was intently studying Felicia, and the wheels in her head were turning. *What is up with her? Something isn't right, and I'm not going to wait until next week to find out!*

28

*M*uriel flung her arms out and twirled around in the open space of the expansive loft. Brad chuckled to himself as he watched her. Face lifted to the sky, she looked so carefree—like a delighted little girl with not a care in the world. A sharp contrast from the wounded woman he had encountered weeks before. He wondered if his news would cause her to revert back to more painful memories.

"Say you love this one—it's perfect, don't you think?" Muriel was looking at him with a huge question in her eyes.

"Um hmmm, it'll do." Brad was teasing her now.

"It'll do? Well, I'm done! There is no pleasing you. We have now officially become experts on every loft in Chicago and Cook County proper, and you say, after seeing everything else that this 'will do.' I'm just too through with you." Muriel tried to act indignant but she was still smiling.

"I guess I should put you out of your agony and give in. I'll just have to buy this fabulous place. Oh, the pain of settling..." Brad hammed, his hand against his forehead and staggering backward.

"Really!" Muriel was squealing. "Really?" Now she was bouncing on her toes in front of him while he nodded in delight at her excitement. "Woo hoo! Yes!" Spinning on her heels, she began walking around the space, envisioning the endless possibilities. "I think we should do inset ceiling lighting over here and feature that fabulous statue of yours in this corner, don't you? Oo! And over here we should..."

"We?" Brad was smiling.

"I meant *you! You* should…" Muriel was embarrassed by her sub-liminal conversation.

"But you said *we*…" Brad began walking toward her. "I kind of like that. Does that mean we're having a relationship now?"

"I don't know, are we? I mean, isn't that your call?"

"Why? Don't you have a say in it too?"

"You know what I mean. You're the man. You ultimately are the one who gets to pick. I only get to decide if I agree with you."

"Ooo, a traditional woman. I like that."

"I don't know how traditional it is. I just know I don't believe in pursuing men. I think a real man knows what he wants and goes for it."

"Are you challenging me, Ms. James?"

"No, I am not, Mr. Sebastian. You asked me a question and I answered it."

"I see. Well, since I am the man, I declare that I think I should close both deals at the same time."

"I'm not following you." Muriel frowned.

"Well, you better learn how to. I am referring to me buying this place and you marrying me. It's all very simple from my vantage point."

Muriel sucked in her breath…then exhaled. Putting her hand on her hip, she fought to keep the smile that was rising on the inside of her from showing on her face. "Now what kind of marriage proposal is that? And don't you think you're moving a bit fast?"

"Let me give you the inside scoop on a 'real man,' as you put it. A real man knows what he wants. I knew the first moment I saw you that you were it for me, even though you were crazy." He ducked a playful swat from Muriel. "See, that's the mistake most women make—waiting around for a man to make up his mind what he wants from them. A real man pretty much knows right away. After that he's just checking to confirm what he already knows. It's been three months. I've gathered my data, so I'm moving forward as is my intentional nature. But back to your first question. I kinda blew the plan and killed the romance part of it, so if you'll excuse me I will be right back to correct that."

With that he disappeared through the front door leaving Muriel to stand in the middle of the space wondering what he was up to. Myriad emotions washed over her. She thought about what she knew to be true. She knew that from the time they met, her heart had told her there was something different about this man. She knew she thought he was as fine as white wine. She chuckled at her personal joke. She knew he was a good man—strong yet sensitive to her and all her issues. She thought back to how he had handled the drama of her past. She knew this was what she had secretly longed for but did not dare to dream of, so bound was she in her past fears. She felt very blessed.

But then reality came flooding in. Though she loved him, was she ready for dealing with all the issues of an interracial marriage? Dealing with the stares and assumptions of people when they had gone out had been eye-opening for her. One salesperson at a store assumed she was his secretary when they had gone shopping together. And then there was the hostility of brothers staring her down when they were at restaurants. Muriel faced the fact that she had not shared anything about him with Tracy because she had issues, though Muriel didn't know why. She hadn't told the others because she didn't know what their reaction would be to her going from the extreme of not dating at all and having the reputation of not being interested in love per se to the opposite side of the spectrum and dating a white man on top of it all. Now Brad was asking her to marry him. How was she going broach this subject to her friends? They would truly be through with her. How did she go from no man to "by the way I'm getting married"? *I'll have to cross that river when I get to it. There's no way I'm going to let this man slip through my fingers!*

The door opened and Brad entered carrying a large picnic basket, blanket, and a cushion. Muriel cocked her head to the side. "Wait a minute! You had all of that in the car?"

"Mmm hmm," he murmured as he bent low to spread the blanket on the floor.

"And you had this all planned out already..."

"Yup. I confess I've been here before. I knew you would like this, so I figured this would be the spot to pop the question." He rose to his feet, took her hand, and indicated with the other the cushion. "Please be seated so I can do this right since you still have not answered me."

Muriel giggled and obediently took her place on the cushion. Brad offered her an hors d'ouevre and a glass of sparkling pear juice in a champagne glass. She accepted them in true princess fashion and took a dainty bite, never allowing her eyes to leave his face. Brad lifted his glass and began his speech. "Muriel James, from the moment I saw you I knew you were crazy." He ducked a piece of cracker she threw at him. "But I also knew you were the most beautiful woman inside and out I had ever met. And though you had this tough 'I can handle it by myself' exterior, deep down inside was this little girl I wanted to protect and take care of. I knew there was a woman in there with a lot of love to offer, and I knew I wanted to spend the rest of my life making her smile. So will you marry me, girl, 'cause I can't see you any longer and stay pure!" Brad could only stay serious so long.

"You mean to tell me you've been having lustful thoughts toward me?"

"I must confess." Brad hung his head in mock shame. "But, hey, I've stayed strong and protected your honor."

"And you get high marks for that."

"I love you, Muriel."

Muriel felt she would melt from the heat and passion she saw in his eyes.

"I love you too, Brad," she whispered, as if releasing something sacred. She was amazed at how right it felt to be saying those words without reservation. Brad eased himself to her side and put his arm around her.

"Muriel, I promise I won't hurt you."

"No one can ever make that promise to another individual."

"I can."

"How can you be so sure of that?"

"Because I love God, and to hurt you would be to hurt Him, and I would never do that."

"Wow, that's deep, Brad."

"Well, I can be from time to time. Hey, you still haven't answered my question! Are you going to marry me or just eat my food?"

"Yes, I am going to marry you, old crazy man. Heaven forbid I eat all your food and then say no."

"So you only love me for my culinary finesse?" Brad tried to look wounded.

"No, I love you because you're beautiful and strong and you're my brave prince." Muriel's voice sounded foreign to her as it quivered, but she kept going, suddenly feeling free to say how she really felt. "You are the only one strong enough to rescue me from the tower I had built around my heart." Tears welled up in her eyes. "Thank you for that. I thought my knight would never come to rescue me." The tears flowed freely now, washing away the rest of the pain in her soul. "You pressed past my anger and my pain and gave me the courage to be soft and trust again."

Brad touched her face ever so tenderly. Muriel allowed her face to rest in his hand, and her breath was taken away by the passion in his eyes. Then his mood shifted. Slowly he pulled a sports magazine out of the picnic basket where he had tucked it and turned toward her, searching her eyes.

"Muriel, did you know anything about this?" He held up the magazine with Cedric's photo on the cover. The headline read, "The Tumultuous Life and Death of Cedric Graham, 1960–2005."

Muriel's hand flew to cup her mouth, her eyes filled with shock and horror. "What happened?" She was struggling for breath though her eyes never left the magazine.

"So you don't know anything about this?"

"No, what happened?" she repeated, shaking her head as if trying to clear it.

"Well, apparently he was up on charges for raping one woman when two other women stepped forward to press additional charges. He folded under the pressure and killed himself."

"What! Oh no!" She threw her head back still struggling for air.

"Muriel," Brad held her in a tight grip, "don't go there."

"Don't go where?"

"Don't blame yourself. There aren't enough bad wishes in the world to bring this on someone. And if you had turned him in all those years ago, you don't know what would have happened. Chances are the hero of a college basketball team would have gotten off, and he would have continued to be the jerk he was." The muscle in Brad's jaw was twitching, indicating how the thought angered him. "At least you should know now that it wasn't you. He was a sick man who never had to face the consequences for his actions. On top of that, he was a coward because he couldn't face them when he had to. How selfish is that? Now a woman and unborn child have to bear not just the pain but the shame he leaves behind. Not a sweet legacy."

"So tell me how you *really* feel about him, Brad." Muriel smiled a small smile, moved by how well he knew her and what she was thinking as well as how deeply Brad had thought this out in his effort to comfort her.

"I'm sorry, but guys like that make me sick. I know he didn't know God and the world can take you on a fake power trip, but I guess what bothers me is all the people around him who never held him account-able. They literally enabled him to destroy himself...and others!"

"Yeah, that's true." Muriel wondered why Adrian hadn't told her any-thing. Then she remembered that her dear friend couldn't possibly know because of her estrangement from her husband, who had to know about it being a sports manager and all. Adrian wasn't one for watching tele-vision so it wasn't any surprise the news had passed her by. Still she wanted to put a date to the closure of this whole nightmare. "When did this happen?"

"Ironically it happened the same evening you were telling me about the ordeal between the two of you."

"No!"

"Yes!"

"Now that's ironic."

"It does seem to be too strange to be coincidental. It was as if God in His knowledge of what was to come had you face your past once and for all so your memories could be put to rest with the man. I know that sounds a little dark, but his death kind of puts an end to the whole thing. There's no more need to hold on to any of it. He's gone and you're free. Free from the past, free from fear..."

"That's true..." Muriel freed herself from Brad's arms and sat straight up. "I *am* free, aren't I? Wow, it's true!"

"So what are you going to do with your newfound freedom?"

"I'm gonna decorate my new house!" Muriel leaped to her feet.

"Don't you think you should pick out a ring and get married first?"

"Ooo, I do get to pick out a ring, don't I? I almost forgot that part!"

"Well, actually you don't." Brad looked a little sheepish. "I picked it out about a month ago and had it made for you already."

Muriel was dumbfounded. "But what if I don't like it?"

"Then I guess we'll start over, but I have this feeling..."

"Hmm, we'll see...so when do I get to see it?"

"How about when we're finished here?"

"Well, then, what are we waiting for! Hand me that basket. We are so out of here!"

"Ah, so much for a romantic afternoon."

"Don't worry, there will be plenty more where this one came from." Muriel made short work of packing the basket, gathering the blanket and cushion, and was now smoothing down her dress ready to go. Heading toward the door she stopped and turned to him. "Brad?"

"Yes, my love."

"Thank you."

"Thank you? For what?"

"Thank you for so many things I can't even begin to express right now." Her eyes were filling with tears again, and his longing for her was returning.

She stepped toward him, tenderly kissing him on the lips and then pressing in as she grew hungrier. Brad could feel himself holding her closer. Breaking the moment, he playfully slapped her on the butt, turned her around to face the door, and gave her a gentle push.

"Girl, you better ack like you saved! What chu tryin' to do? Break a brotha' down?" Brad caught Muriel off guard and caused her to break into peals of laughter. Fanning herself in church-lady fashion she headed toward the car.

"Mmm mmm. Thank ya, Jesus, for keepin' a sista!" She continued fanning, leaning against the side of the car chuckling. She sobered as Brad loaded the car and her eyes fell on the magazine with Cedric's face on the cover. Picking it up she silently shook her head. Brad gently took it from her and threw it into the trunk. "That's all behind you now." He led her to the front seat, tucked her in, and closed the door.

Muriel leaned back against the seat, closing her eyes and savoring the security she felt beside Brad. "Yes it is," she breathed. And truly it was.

29

Tracy sat back in the cab contemplating how she was going to broach the subject with Felicia. Although exactly what the subject was eluded her. She tried to put together the intellectual fragmented pieces of information she had gathered to try to figure out what was going on with her, but there wasn't enough evidence to convince her of anything. She hadn't been talking about men excessively as normal. She got queasy at lunch. She wasn't wearing her usual second-skin clothing. She was unusually low key. *So what, Tracy,* she thought. It wasn't exactly as if she had seen her a lot lately to know if these were consistent trends or just fell on the day when she happened to see or talk to her. Still she couldn't shake the gut feeling that something wasn't right in Felicia's world.

Out the corner of her eye she thought she saw a familiar figure. She turned but the car moved her out of the line of sight. Hmm, that woman sure did look like Muriel....But then again it couldn't have been her. Tracy cracked up at the thought. Now that's a picture she would like to see. Muriel all wrapped up in the arms of some man. A white man at that and heading into a jewelry store! *Whew! I'm definitely seeing things to put that vision together in my mind.* But shoot, that reminded her she had forgotten to tell Muriel about Cedric. She was certain she didn't know because Muriel didn't watch television. Tracy always felt obliged to keep Muriel up on the major events happening in the world so she wouldn't appear ignorant to her clients.

"Couldn't you at least watch CNN once a week just to get an overview of where we are in history, chile?" Tracy had been a bit frustrated by the lack of understanding why someone would want to be completely oblivious to what was happening around them.

"I don't care about history. I only care about His story, okay? If I take my eyes off of the good news and start studying the bad news, it would just be too overwhelming. So I pray for the world and leave the details to the One who can handle them."

"That's exactly my point. How can you pray if you don't know what's going on?"

"God knows what's going on. I don't have to give Him an up-to-the-minute report. As a matter of fact, He knew all of this junk was going to happen. Now you can sit and freak yourself out by absorbing all that negativity if you want to, but I have to stick to what works for me."

"If being oblivious to reality and what's going on in the world works for you, then so be it. But I'm gonna jerk your chain every now and then so you don't look as crazy as I know you are."

"Thanks for sharing! Just keep the outline brief." It was then that Tracy suspected that Muriel had a more tender heart than she had first imagined. One big marshmallow, that's what she was. She couldn't convince her that all that tough talk and shooing away of sentiment didn't hide the spirit of a very sensitive soul who simply couldn't stand to see others suffer, thus the avoidance of the news. It was simply too upsetting for her; therefore, it was another thing she chose to cross off the list of interest…along with romance.

Paying her fare and jumping out of the cab, Tracy's eyes saw the magazine on the newsstand rack. Big as day, Cedric was plastered on the cover along with the news of his untimely death. Hastily paying for a copy, she whipped out her cell phone to call Adrian. Surely she must know! Oh, that's right, she and Ron weren't really talking. Cedric's death still had not penetrated her cranium or her understanding and lacked the sense of reality that made an occurrence a fact. But it was true, which made her conclude that Adrian probably didn't know either. She would have to tell Muriel right away before she heard the news the wrong way. She didn't want her to be alone when she found out, just in case she had any feelings left for her Cedric—though she couldn't imagine that would be the case. She didn't want to take any chances. Adrian's voice jerked her out of reflection mode.

"Hey, Tracy! I was just thinking about you."

Though some found it convenient, Tracy was still a little thrown off by the ability of caller ID to announce you before you announced yourself. *Whatever happened to pleasant surprises?* she thought. That and call waiting had made the world a more harried, less pleasant place from her point of view.

"Hey, Adrian, did you hear the news about Cedric Graham?"

"Cedric Graham? Now that's a blast from the past. What about him?"

"He's dead. Shot himself in the head a couple weeks ago. It was all over the news, and now it's on the cover of this month's *Sports* magazine. I've been in such a tizzy I forgot to inform Muriel, who I'm sure is still clueless. It wasn't until I saw the newsstand that I remembered. I don't want her to find out by herself, though I can't for the life of me figure out what her reaction will be. Then I thought of you and remembered you haven't been speaking to Ron so you might not know either. Do all you church people avoid the news like the plague? What's up with that?"

Adrian chuckled. "No, I watch the news, girl, but to tell you the truth I've been so caught up in my paintings and getting ready for my exhibit that I've only been listening to music. It's a wonder I come up for air and to eat…and feed the kids of course."

Tracy laughed. It always tickled her when Adrian referred to her dog and cat as the kids. "Do you suppose we should pay her a visit? I don't think this is a telephone call discussion."

"Hmm, perhaps you're right. When were you thinking of going to see her?"

"How about this evening? I'm going to meet Felicia right now to take a look at this exhibit, so perhaps we could all go over there afterward. Muriel usually turns in early on Saturdays to get ready for church, so she should be home. I'm thinking we could just get together, call her, and stop over. Why don't you meet me and Felicia at Sugar's at six, and we'll take it from there?"

"Sounds good. I'll be there. Hey, Tracy? What happened? Why did he commit suicide? That doesn't sound like the Cedric I knew."

"Apparently he raped some woman and she pressed charges. Then two other women popped up to accuse him of the same thing. I guess he didn't think he could beat the charges with them all piling up on him and couldn't stand the thought of going to jail so he took himself out."

"You have *got* to be kidding me."

"I wish it was a joke, but it ain't, my sistah."

"Who'da thunk it?"

"Who'da thunk it indeed—not me from where I was perched. Anyway, I'm getting on an elevator so I'm probably going to lose you. See you later."

"Alright. Bye."

The elevator closed, moved, and then opened to reveal Felicia thoughtfully browsing among some sculptures. All fluid and smooth, the figures hewn out of stone looked like they were in perpetual motion. They were all women in various movements of prayer and dance. Felicia was studying one of a woman holding her child close to her heart. The woman and the child were one. Felicia stood transfixed, deeply engrossed in this study of serenity and love. With one finger she traced the out-line of the baby's body ever so softly, so lovingly. "If you were married I would say you were pregnant!" Tracy didn't know why Carla's words came to mind as she watched Felicia. Tracy moved toward her, thinking the statue Felicia was examining looked a lot like her. Woman to woman they stood having a silent conversation.

"So you like that one?" Tracy jumped when Felicia jumped. "I'm sorry, I didn't mean to startle you. Where on earth were you?"

"What? Oh, girl, you scared the mess out of me!" Felicia was still winded. She broke into relieved laughter "There ought to be a law against walking up on folk like that. I was just studying the lines in this piece. Isn't it beautiful?"

"Yes, it is…" Tracy's eyes had not left Felicia's face. She was the picture of radiant beauty herself. Her skin glowed and there was a softness in her eyes that illuminated her face. Her hair was upswept in a soft tumble and complemented by chandelier earrings with bits of turquoise that matched her soft gauze empire dress. The dress was gathered beneath her breast, which seemed a little fuller than usual, then fell in soft folds to her knees. Her shoes were delicately configured with tiny straps on a small heel, very Audrey Hepburnish. Tracy marveled at how beautiful Felicia was and for a moment could understand why men sensed a vulnerability in her and were drawn to it. There were times when she had her own unguarded moments of feeling as though she wanted to protect her. This was one of those moments, and yet she was almost distracted by the growing discomfort that something was going on that she didn't know but should. She should because in spite of all their differences, she still felt responsible for her cousin in the big city. That was the unspoken family understanding, and right now she was failing her commission. She decided to just be present and see if Felicia would open up. Slowly perusing the gallery, her eyes landed on an extremely handsome man studying one of the paintings on the wall.

"My, my, my, what have we here?" Tracy was surprised Felicia had not been the one to bring him to her attention.

"Hmmm?" Felicia's eyes swept in his direction and went back to the piece she was studying completely oblivious to the magnificent specimen before her.

Tracy studied her intently. "I haven't heard you mention Kenny lately. When was the last time you saw him?"

"About a month ago. It's over. But I thought I told you that."

"You did but…well…I haven't heard you mention anyone new so I thought maybe…"

"Maybe what? That if I wasn't talking about someone new I went back to Kenny because I can't be without a man?"

"No…" Tracy was ashamed to admit that was exactly what she was thinking.

"Tracy, I told you I was giving the whole man thing a break, don't you remember?"

Tracy remembered something around that theme being mentioned by Felicia several weeks ago but had failed to file it because it was so unlike her. Besides she was the one on a sabbatical from men; it wasn't fair for Felicia to horn in on her idea. She was growing impatient. "Felicia, what exactly is going on with you? Break or no break, your 'fine man' radar cannot be broken. It's not like you not to see or flirt with a man who looks like that. He is straight up your type. He's got your name written all over him, and all you can say is hmmm? Are you sick or what?" She placed the back of her hand against Felicia's forehead, checking her temperature.

Felicia wilted under her examination. "I'm off the market, Tracy."

"Off the market?" Tracy was a little slow. Then she laughed. "Oh, you mean not in man shopping mode? I like that. I'm going to have to use it."

"No, I mean I would probably not be desirable to a man about now."

"Don't be ridiculous. Did you look in the mirror before you left home or what? You look fabulous."

"Thanks. Not bad for an old pregnant lady, huh?" Felicia was tired of holding it in. Finally she could breathe again.

"An old pregnant lady?" Tracy repeated the words but still didn't make the connection, preferring not to know what she had begun to suspect. She voted for a slow reveal.

"Who's an old pregnant lady?"

"I am, Trace. I am."

"You are? You are what?" Tracy was wondering why she felt numb, rooted to the spot. Nothing was registering.

"Pregnant, Tracy. I'm pregnant."

"No!"

"Yes!"

"What are you going to do?"

"I'm going to keep my baby. That's what I'm going to do."

"*Your* baby." It was beginning to sink in. "Is Kenny…?"

"Yes, Kenny is the father."

"Does he know?"

"Yes, he does. And that's it."

"What do you mean 'that's it'? What are you going to do?"

"As I said before, I'm going to have my baby. It may have taken Kenny to make it, but I don't need him to keep it." Felicia felt stronger for unleashing the truth. "I know you think I'm a flake, Tracy, but I'm doing this and I don't care what anybody thinks about it."

"You're sure about this, aren't you?"

"Yes, I am."

"Alrighty then." Tracy exhaled, feeling a little light-headed from holding her breath so long. She was assaulted by a million thoughts. Among them the terror of considering their parents' reactions. Wait a minute. Why should she feel terror? It wasn't her problem. And then in that moment she realized that indeed it was. She loved Felicia. And for all her maddening ways, she was still a part of her. She was more than a cousin; she was her sister too. Tracy grew angry. "Wait a minute! So what is Kenny saying? Is he going to do his part? Please don't tell me he's going to be a deadbeat dad. Don't make me have to hurt him."

"No, don't develop angry black woman syndrome. He's been calling, and I've been ignoring him. To be perfectly honest, Tracy, I didn't give him a chance to do anything. I was so shocked when I found out I was pregnant, all I could think about was keeping myself afloat. I didn't want to put myself in the position for some man to accuse me of trying to trap him or deal with the rejection if he decided to walk, so I just cut him off. He's upset about it and keeps screaming about his rights. But all I know right now is I have a right to my peace of mind. I have to take care of myself and keep drama to an all-time low. I don't want my child being upset. They say they can feel when you're upset, did you know that?"

"But if he's calling, Felicia, don't you think he deserves a fair hearing?"

"No. I think Kenny likes the life he leads, taking his pick from his patients he recreates into perfect specimens and living a high-profile, carefree life. He's still a little boy in a great big candy store."

"Even little boys grow up, Felicia. You've certainly grown in the past months. A baby has a way of sobering folk. Perhaps you should give Kenny a chance to redeem himself. Don't sabotage yourself. You're going to need a lot of help and support. Having a child is no joke."

"I'm not laughing, Tracy. But I'm going to do this. I'm going to deal with what I can handle and pace myself. Right now it's about me staying healthy and tending to the health of my child."

"Obviously you haven't told the folks yet."

"Nope, and I'll wait until I'm ready for that too, so I'd appreciate you keeping mum on the subject."

"No problem." Tracy studied Felicia, noting the look of quiet determination in her eyes, the set of her jaw, and her body language. It was as if she had metamorphosed into a protective lioness, proud and immoveable. The fine man was checking her out, and she remained oblivious. Before she would have picked up the telepathic communication across the room and been on her way, playing a game of cat and mouse from where she stood until the hunter got captured by the game. But today was a different day, and Tracy was looking at a new Felicia.

"So we're having a baby, huh?"

"*We?*"

"Yes, *we!* You don't think I'm going to let you go through this by yourself, do you? And if you even think of having someone else be its godmother, you will hear of my displeasure forever, you got that?"

Felicia grabbed Tracy tightly and held on for dear life. Tracy could feel the intensity of her relief, fear, and thankfulness to be no longer alone, a prisoner of her own secret. She hugged her back. The man was looking at them curiously. She gave Felicia a gentle nudge, clearing her throat and releasing her.

"Perhaps we should reserve our hugs for another place. Two women holding each other in the middle of an art gallery could give rise to the wrong speculation, if you know what I'm saying."

"Oh yeah, sorry." Felicia was giggling and sniffling. "I've kinda had enough anyway. Wanna get something to eat?"

"Actually Adrian is on her way to meet us. I don't know if you heard anything about this, but Cedric Graham killed himself a couple weeks ago. Now it's being blasted on the cover of the latest *Sports* magazine."

"Oh my. Does Muriel know?"

"We don't think so. We thought we ought to get over to her place and make sure she didn't get the news haphazardly."

"Most definitely! Well, what are we waiting for? Let's blow this pop stand." Her eyes strayed to the man across the room, who smiled when she looked in his direction. She smiled back then turned Tracy toward the door, following behind her. "Oo child, he *is* fine!" She sighed. "Humph. That's too bad."

Tracy giggled. It was good to know the Felicia she knew wasn't dead after all, just growing up.

30

*M*uriel held out her left hand for an awestruck Carla to examine her magnificent ring. On her wedding finger sat a spectacular display of bling. A three-carat, flawless, white, radiant-cut diamond sat suspended between four diamond-kissed, sturdy square cut pillars of platinum, giving off more light than should have been legal. "He designed it himself! Isn't it magnificent? I was a little worried when he said he had picked it out already. I thought I was going to have to hurt his feelings but I have to admit I couldn't have done better myself—and I'm the designer here! Isn't that wild?" Muriel was downright giddy.

Carla didn't know what to say. She was absolutely ecstatic for her friend but bowled over by how quickly the events had escalated. This had worked out even better than she planned. She couldn't wait until she told Al. She'd known in her spirit this was the hookup even though intellectually it had seemed a long shot. The softness in Muriel's eyes was reward enough for her. She had wanted that for her for so long. Carla had always felt Muriel was trapped inside herself, not really knowing how to get out. Afraid to be vulnerable, Muriel took the scripture about guarding your heart to a whole new level, cutting off people—especially men—from getting too close with ferocity. Carla had been determined to get past that wall and build a friendship with this woman. And so she had persevered, coming closer only when invited, taking the time to build trust. And now she looked at the fruit of her efforts and breathed a prayer of thanks to God under her breath. Truly He was able to transform the lives of people, and He had done that with her friend, answering all the prayers she had poured out for Muriel's heart to be healed and her secret wounds to be mended.

"Girl, I'm going to need sunglasses to look at that thing. Brad did quite well for himself, I must say."

"Yes, he did! You know, Carla, it's scary to be this happy. I keep thinking something is going to happen to mess it up."

"Why would you say something like that? God doesn't wave carats under our noses and snatch them away."

"I know, but life happens."

"That's true, but that's why it is so important to take it as it comes and enjoy the moments like this to their fullest."

"I suppose you're right. It would be a shame not to enjoy your present blessings because you're waiting for the other shoe to drop. How crazy is that? That is a certified way to guarantee always being miserable."

"And that certainly is not trusting God. As a matter of fact, that is pretty revealing about how one feels about God. At some point in time you have to make a decision on whether you believe He is really good or not. If He really is, can't He ensure your joy being sustained? I mean, is He in your corner or not? Or is He this capricious, mischievous character just waiting to crack you over the head if you get too happy? To think of Him that way is actually an insult. It's got to hurt His heart to watch His children struggle with trusting Him, don't you think?"

"Hmm, I never thought about it that way before, but you're right." Just as Muriel was settling in to ponder what Carla had said, the phone rang. "Hello? Oh hey, girl! Really? Well come on by. Carla and I were just sitting here talking. Okay, see you in a few minutes. Hey, should I order some food? Mmm, true dat. I've been trying not to eat after six myself. All right. See you soon." She hung up the phone and began twisting the ring off her finger. "That was the girls. They're on the way over. Don't mention anything about this to them, okay?"

"You mean to tell me they don't know anything about Brad?"

"Nope. They don't."

"When are you going to tell them? You're getting ready to get married for Pete's sake!"

"Oh, I'm going to tell them, but they're my inner circle you know. I need to break the news gently. Brad being white and all…it's a bit complicated for a sister, okay?"

"But why didn't you tell them you were seeing him? It's been months, Muriel."

"I wasn't sure how things would work out, and I didn't want to be questioned about it if it didn't. I hate getting caught up in conversations about men, you know that. And then…I felt stupid, you know. I'm the one who is over the whole man thing, and all of a sudden I'm head over heels in love…with a white man. That's a lot for the girls to digest in one bite. And I couldn't figure out the right time to broach the subject. Then in light of the fact that Adrian's situation was understandably more pressing, we all got distracted with that. In the end, the further it dragged out, the harder it was to bring up so…there you are. But don't you worry. I am going to deal with it."

"Why don't you deal with it tonight?"

"Can't I just revel in this by myself for a little while? Besides, you're here. It would be better if I told them when they don't feel they have to be on good behavior in front of a stranger."

"I'm a stranger now?"

"To them you are. And you're white."

"I am?" Carla looked at her hands and gave a small scream in mock horror. "What am I going to do? I never realized I was white. Well this just changes everything. What am I going to tell Al?"

"Tell him you're crazy while you're at it." Muriel eyes crinkled when she laughed.

"I'll make sure I do that. But seriously, Muriel, this is really an issue?"

"A *huge* issue…" The doorbell rang. "Wow! That was fast. We'll finish this discussion later—and remember, mum's the word."

"Alright, alright, alright. Should I leave?"

"No, you don't have to leave. You just have to keep a secret, okay?"

"Whatever you say…I just don't think…"

"Talk to the hand, Carla! We're not going back over this now."

"My lips are sealed."

Muriel swung open the door to examine three somber-looking faces. "Hey, ladies! Ooo, you all look as if somebody died. What's wrong?" Her mood went from exuberance to concern in the span of seconds. They stood outside the door frozen by her prophetic comment. "Well don't just stand there, come in." Silently they entered the room. Then they spotted Carla and stood in indecision, trying to decide how to proceed.

"Now you're worrying me. What's up?"

"Um…" Felicia started and stopped.

"Speaking of somebody dying, have you seen this?" Tracy displayed the magazine with the news of Cedric on it. Her eyes were fixed on Muriel.

"Ah, yes." Muriel sounded like a worldly traveler, peering at the magazine with a detached sort of interest.

"Did you know about this, Muriel?" Adrian seemed surprised that she wasn't surprised.

"Yes, I did."

"When, who, I mean how did you find out about it?"

"A friend of mine told me."

"You knew Cedric Graham?" Carla was excited. She and Al were big sports buffs.

"Oh, yes, indeed."

"They were a hot item in college." Tracy felt Carla needed to be brought up to speed before she got too excited.

"Really? Muriel, why didn't you tell me? Wait until I tell Al!"

"There really isn't anything to tell, Carla. That was then, this is now. And the now is I haven't spoken to Cedric in years."

"But weren't you shocked? I couldn't believe it. Who da thunk he would sink to such an all-time low? Rape? Suicide? It's amazing how people can change." Felicia shook her head in dismay.

"He didn't change one bit." There was a bite in Muriel's voice that caused them all to rack focus on her.

"What do you mean by that, Muriel?" Adrian's voice was quiet and restrained as if she were holding back more than she was saying.

"Whatever happened between the two of you, anyway?" Tracy picked up on her cue.

"What do you mean he hasn't changed?" Felicia was taken aback by her comment.

"I mean he didn't change. He's the same jerk he was then. The same little boy who thought he should have what he wanted. The same bully who thought he shouldn't have to suffer the consequences for what he had done. I guess he finally met someone who wouldn't be moved by his threats," Muriel spat out.

"Muriel, did Cedric rape you too?" Adrian was standing in front of her, looking gently into her eyes.

"Yes." Muriel whispered the words then hung her head in silence. She didn't even try to blink back the tears building and spilling onto her cheeks. The years of silent pain were finally released. How many times had she longed to tell them what had happened? How many years had she felt misunderstood by them as she responded to their romance issues out of her own suffering? One by one they encircled her, touching her, holding her, and finally culminating in a group hug, each one weeping. Weeping for what they had not known. Weeping for the pain she had suffered. Weeping for the understanding they had of her at last. They should have known. Perhaps they should have pressed the issue when she retreated into her silent prison—and yet they hadn't. Each one felt shame for refusing to press past the walls Muriel had erected, and then they found comfort in the fact that they were still there. Finally the truth had set them all free.

Carla watched the group in complete amazement. How could these women have been friends so long and not known something as critical as this? She didn't get it. But while she didn't get their friendship, she did finally get Muriel. All the pieces fit now. It wasn't that Muriel was angry, tough, jaded, or didn't like men. She had merely been a scared little girl fighting to protect herself. It was truly the untold stories that revealed the most about a person.

As Muriel related all that had happened that night so long ago, her friends experienced chaotic emotions. From shock, to anger, to sorrow, to amazement that she had endured such immense trauma alone. Muriel wiped the last tear from her eye on the subject and declared she was better for the telling and ready to move on to lighter fare. "So all in all, the irony of justice delayed but timely is played out once again. I'll tell you this much, just when you conclude that people get away with stuff, they really don't. I'm just glad that I'm finally in a place where I can feel sorry for Cedric instead of bitter toward him. I'm sure in the end he suffered inside his own insanity more than I did. So that is that. Somebody please tell me something good. I am sooo ready to move on."

"Well, my exhibit is scheduled for August fifteenth." Adrian's eyes were shining.

"Wow! That's right around the corner! Are you sure you'll be ready?"

"Oh yes. I've been painting day and night. I'm really excited."

"I'll have to design you something special to wear," Muriel offered.

"Ooo, I can't wait!"

"Well I have a bit of news too." Felicia sounded tentative but looked determined to share her announcement. She glanced at her cousin for support and got it silently telegraphed in Tracy's nod. "I'm pregnant."

Carla's mouth flew open and then shut again. Muriel raised an eyebrow and waited for more information. It was Adrian who moved toward her, placing one hand over Felicia's and softly asking. "Kenny?"

"Yes."

"And you're keeping it?"

"Yes."

"So when are you due?"

"In November."

"You mean you've been keeping this to yourself for four months?" Now Muriel was indignant. "Did you at least tell Kenny? And what did he have to say for himself?"

"Whoa, Muriel! One question at a time. Kenny knows but that's it. I've cut him off. I'm not really interested in him stepping up to the table or the plate. I just want him to move on to another restaurant. And I didn't mean to keep it from you. It just seemed as though there was always some other issue far more pressing whenever we got together."

"More pressing than a baby? No way!" Carla could tell that Muriel was too through with Felicia. Felicia on the other hand was grinning widely at the predictable reactions of her friends.

"I don't understand why you would dismiss the father. A child needs its father." Carla had finally found her tongue.

"Even if its father is a jerk? I don't think so." Felicia was slightly defensive.

"How much of a jerk could he be? You liked him enough to sleep with him. I'm sorry and this is none of my business, but I've got to tell you from the outside looking in I'm a little worried about you guys." Part of Carla was telling her she had said enough, the other half disagreed. The other half won out.

"Muriel suffered a devastating rape years ago and none of you knew about it until today. Felicia has been pregnant for four months and none of you knew. Do you all talk to one another or what? What kind of friendship do you have if you're not there for the stuff that really matters? Help me out because I'm struggling with this. What are friends for if you can't share these kinds of things without fear and if you can't really be there for one another no matter what is going on? And if nobody says anything, don't you ever ask questions?"

"I think that's a white thing." Felicia made a flat assessment.

"What?"

"It's a white thing. White people ask questions. I've noticed this. Black people don't, and yes I do prefer to be called black, 'cause I'm not African, I'm part American Indian and West Indian and Jesse didn't ask me to vote when he decided to rename everybody, okay? But back to what I was saying. In black culture, people don't ask questions like that. The unspoken understanding is it's rude and if it's your business you will eventually be told, until then mum's the word. You listen and allow people to pick when they want to divulge their stuff to you. But white folks, and truly I don't mean to offend you by saying this, but you all think everything is open season and you ask questions. Every time I've been somewhere social and met white people they ask a million personal questions. Black folk just don't do that. They just case you out until you're ready to tell them more. So to answer your question, I would never poke my nose where I don't think it's wanted."

"I see…" Though Carla didn't really see. "But doesn't that leave you to draw the wrong conclusions or even worse yet miss important details that you really ought to know? And does that rule apply to friends?"

"Oh, especially to friends. It's called honoring each other's space and business."

"I disagree. I call it not being transparent or accountable and leaving yourself wide open to getting into trouble. There is safety in a circle of friends who expose and challenge one another to make wise decisions and support one another through the hard times. We just were not created to walk alone, Felicia. I think it's the coward's way out not to own your stuff—especially among friends!"

At this Carla turned to glare at Muriel, who glared back in a silent confirmation that she was still not going to tell them about Brad at this point. Since she couldn't win there, Carla continued on her roll. "Now back to the baby. You're having it. I applaud you for that. However, you're not sharing this experience with the father, so exactly what do you intend to do? Have you told your parents? What type of support system do you have set up? It's not going to be easy you know."

"Well, you are one bold little sister! No wonder you're Muriel's friend. I think I like you but the jury is still out." At this Felicia smiled a brilliant smile. "Yes, I think I like you. And even though you ask a lot of questions—you do ask good ones." At this point she sobered and got teary. "To tell the truth I'm pretty scared. But I've always taken the easy way out, Carla, and I think it's time for me to grow up. This means I have to deal with what I've created. Right now I've created a baby, and I have to think about how my life will change. I have not told my parents, and am dreading the idea so I'll wait until I can do it without falling apart. Tracy has said she will be there for me."

"So will I, Felicia," Adrian chimed in.

"Me too," Muriel added.

"Me too, if you'll allow one white woman to horn in on the group," Carla added rather shyly.

"I think that would be wonderful. My child should experience diversity. Do you have another language you can teach it?"

"I'm still trying to master English." Carla laughed. "Felicia, I hope you didn't think I was being hard on you, but this is a major undertaking. It's hard enough being a parent when you're married; it's even scarier as a single woman. I don't want you to have to face that kind of pressure without help."

"Thanks Carla, I appreciate it."

This time is was Felicia's turn to experience a group hug. More tears flowed. And their bond made the air thick with commitment and love. It was more than Carla could stand. Breaking free from the circle she headed for her purse where she kept a small notebook. Whipping it out she turned back to the group, pen poised to write. "Alright! Enough warm and fuzzies. We have plans to make. Your due date is right around the corner, and time flies. There's a lot to do to get ready. Lamaze classes, nursery items, reading up on how to take care of him or her…"

"Oh my—not only does she ask a lot of questions, she makes plans. What is it with white people?" Felicia mockingly groaned.

"Hey, I'm beginning to feel like a victim of reverse discrimination here."

"Naw, it's not that deep. All I'm saying is you people certainly do insist on keeping up with details."

"'And you know that,' as you all would say." Carla put her hands on her hips and rolled her neck. "I learned that from Muriel. Diversity training 101." With that she made a circular motion with her hand, snapped her fingers, and turned her head like a true sister girl.

For a moment they all stared at her as if trying to decide how to respond. Then peals of laughter rang throughout the room. It was the laughter of liberated women. Free from secrets, free from fears, free from all that makes a woman doubt herself. There was safety in numbers and more love than they could find elsewhere. All these silent conclusions were drawn while reveling in the relief that laughter brings and the knowledge that though some work might be involved, all things would work themselves out in time and everything would be all right. And tonight that was something to celebrate.

31

Dear Diary
   The question is
does love demand an answer
      Or simply wait
         for flowers to unfold
            and share their fragrance...
      And if it waits too long
         does the aroma grow sour
      or sweeter for the longing
         of being released
            to share its pain with those who bend close
      Close enough
         to see the tears the rain left behind
      or be cut by the thorns that have grown
         in the places where wounds once were
   How insistent does love allow itself to be
      Does it press itself against hearts to overhear
         the rhythm of their hurts and fears
            Or does it wait for the dam to break

Spilling over itself
   again and again
      until there is nothing left
But the weariness that comes from unanswered questions
and vows of never again
and undisclosed pain
Perhaps it's safe to say
   that true love lives dangerously
      daring to be misunderstood because it cares enough
         to press past where it has been invited
      to slay dragons
      and rescue maidens fair
         from themselves
            and wrong conclusions
carrying them away to rainbows filled with endless hope
And the courage to love again and again...

"ello?" The telephone ring had interrupted Tracy's stream of consciousness.

"Hey, girl, what's happening? How was the exhibit?"

Tracy could always trust Derrick to check on her on the weekends. She tucked her legs underneath her and eased into her favorite position on top of the silk duvet that covered her bed. She snuggled in deep, gearing up to tell him about the whole evening. Derrick did seem to have an uncanny sense of timing for calling just after high drama had occurred. And Tracy was relieved to have him so she could tell all the intricate details because she knew he wouldn't repeat any of it. It was great to be able to gossip and watch it disappear into a black hole never to resurface again. Tracy had decided that was one of the highlights of having a male friend. Most of the things a woman wanted to talk about a man did not find worth repeating. This meant she could gossip free from guilt or the fear that her words would haunt her later.

"To be perfectly honest, the exhibit was nice and the tamest part of the evening."

"Uh oh. Did you and Felicia fall out again?"

"As a matter of fact, we did not. Believe it or not, our relationship is the best it's ever been. I don't think she would mind me telling you she's pregnant."

"She's what?"

"She's pregnant. Pregnant, pregnant, pregnant." Tracy breathed the words out, allowing them to sink into her psyche now that she was finally free and clear to digest the news.

"Whoa! So who's the father?"

"Kenny Sample."

"*The* Kenny Sample? Dr. Kenny Sample of plastic surgery fame?"

"That's the one."

"Boy, I tell you, Felicia certainly knows how to do things with style." Derrick was chuckling. Tracy imagined him shaking his head from side to side, slouched down in a chair, slapping his thigh. Derrick was a fine brother—tall, lean, and muscular. Just the right height and the right shade of mocha, with pretty, even, white teeth. When he smiled the room came alive. He wore his hair closely cropped to a fade. But it was his eyes that were his greatest feature. Luminous and warm and a deep, deep brown, they seemed to turn colors with his moods. Deeper, almost black when concerned or worried, a warmer shade of hazel that sparkled when he was amused by something as he was right now. Tracy pictured his face and briefly wondered to herself again why she hadn't paid more attention to him when he liked her. It was too late now. Shirley had him firmly in her grip now. It was a good thing she liked her.

"Yeah, you're right, if Felicia is going out, she will have somebody who can pay for it. Although I have to admit I'm proud of her. Old girl is taking total responsibility for this herself. She told brother man to walk."

"She told him to what?"

"To step. To keep on trucking." Tracy was practically crowing.

"And you think this is a *good* thing?"

Tracy could hear the underlying tension in his voice. "Yes, I do. We are talking about Kenny here."

"What is Felicia's issue with Kenny?"

"Besides the fact that he's fooling around?"

"Has she documented this as a fact? Has she caught him red-handed?"

"No, but…"

"What is she basing this on?"

"She says he never has time for her, makes plans, and then doesn't show up…and then says he was working. C'mon, Derrick, ain't that much working in the world."

"Boy, a brother can't win with you all. Why is every man a player? You want what you say to be taken at face value, but why is a man always lying? Could it be possible that he *is* actually working?"

"It could be, but…"

"But what?"

"I don't know. What are you trying to say? Obviously I've pushed a button, so let's have it."

"Well let me back up and say this. I resent it when women get on their high horses and think they are doing something impressive by excusing a father from his duty as a father. What exactly are you trying to prove?"

Tracy frowned because she didn't really have an answer.

"That you can do it on your own? You can't. Statistics show us that. And I'm sorry, contrary to popular belief, brothers *do* care about their kids and want to be a significant part of their lives emotionally, physically, and financially. These little independent rampages you all go on make me wonder who you really care about. Is it all about you…or your child? And do you think any child appreciates being used as bribe material?"

"I take it Sylvia isn't letting you see Jonathan again?" Tracy said quietly.

"Nope and it pisses me off. Just because I decided I was better off without her, she decided my child is better off without me. Why is she using a child to retaliate? This further confirms what I decided in the first place, that she is a selfish woman whom I don't want to spend the rest of my life with. She had the power to change my impression of her by how she dealt with the situation, but instead she showed me that she was a smaller woman than I thought!"

"Whoa! Wait a minute. Have you told her all of this?"

"Oh yes—and more!"

"I bet that went over big."

"Umm hmm, like a lead balloon. And in the end she is holding my child hostage. But I'm still paying child support."

"I'm sorry, Derrick."

"Hey, it's my cross to bear and that situation is not going to get solved tonight. So back to Felicia. Could it be possible that the man is actually working? Men do tend to focus on one thing at a time, which brings me to another point. Women always want a man with a ton of money and then get upset when he has to go make it. You can't have both, so decide what you want. Either you get a brother who has time to hang out and play with you and has no money or you get a man who is making money and you have to treasure the moments you get with him until he retires."

"Is this another hot button with you? Are you okay?"

"Yeah, I'm fine now that I have a woman who is a woman…"

"Ooo!"

"Yeah, ooo. Sistahs need to grow up. Some of us are out here trying to do it right, and for the most part you women make it difficult at best. It's a catch-22. If we fight for our rights, we're being insensitive. If we give up, we're deadbeat dads. What do you all want from a man? Can you all get together, decide, and then let a brother know?"

"Okay, take a deep breath, Derrick. It's gonna be alright."

"Is it? It's gonna be alright for me, but what about brothers like Kenny who get kicked to the curb for no good reason just because some chick is feeling insecure? Felicia needs to knock it off."

Tracy stifled the urge to laugh out loud, knowing Derrick would take it the wrong way.

"Now is not the time to make the pride move," Derrick said. "She needs to give him a chance to show her what he's really made of. If she didn't want high-profile risk, she shouldn't have gotten involved with a high-profile brother. Just because he's got tons of women running after him doesn't mean he's paying attention to them. When you find what you want, the rest are just distractions, just flies in the room."

"Is that right?"

"Absolutely."

"I will pass your message on to Felicia, for what it's worth. I don't think she'll be backing down any time soon. She seems bent on becoming the model of responsibility overnight, so I've committed to being there for her. The girl is going to need some help. I don't know how she is going to do this, but she might surprise me. She has so far."

"Just make sure she is being responsible and not ridiculous."

"Yes, sir!" Tracy was ready to move on to the rest of the news she had piled up. As she launched into the whole scene that had unfolded with Muriel, she thought Derrick was going to go through the ceiling. It was a lot to unload all in one night, but she was on a roll. Derrick knew of Cedric Graham because of being a basketball buff. He had been shocked by the news of Cedric's untimely demise, but now that the story had grown more personal involving people he knew, Derrick was blown away by what Muriel had been through. Tracy could picture his eyes growing dark as he asked about Muriel's state of emotions when they broke the news to her. Even he admitted he had wondered about Muriel from time to time, but now he understood fully why she was the way she was.

"Sometimes I feel like standing on a mountaintop and apologizing for all the mess that a few brothers do that make it bad for everybody else. That's why it's so important to me that I be included in my son's life, 'cause women don't raise their sons to be with other men."

"What do you mean by that?"

"Most mothers treat their sons like surrogate husbands because they're not getting the love they want from their partners. Big mistake. They just end up spoiling their sons and making them feel entitled to have whatever they want. A boy needs a man to impart manhood and responsibility into his life, and when that doesn't happen you have an overgrown boy who is not whole, with no character, who never develops into the man he needs to be. Then he gets unleashed on some poor sister and he ends up damaging her. And then when a child comes into the picture, the whole cycle starts all over again."

"That's deep, Derrick."

"Mmm hmm, it's also very sad. At some point we have to stop and look at what we're doing to each other, not just as a people, but as a society."

"You know you can wax philosophical at all hours of the night."

"And I can count on you to yawn at exactly midnight."

Tracy giggled because what he said was true. He knew her so well. "Where is Shirley anyway?"

"She's having a girly night. I'll see her tomorrow. My mother wangled us into going to church with her."

"Really? Is there something in the water lately? Felicia wants to go to church too. She's gotten all curious about Adrian talking to God."

"Speaking of Adrian, how's she doing?"

"Amazing. The girl whacked off all her hair, came out of those St. John suits, and has gotten all hot and sassy in a conservative sort of way, but she's looking good. She's painting again and getting ready to put her stuff on exhibit. Save August fifteenth for her showing."

"Really? Adrian might get her man back if she gets interesting enough. Or maybe she won't want him back—does she?"

"I think that's the plan. Though between you, me, and the doorpost, I'd kick him to the curb. I wouldn't settle for that kind of nonsense."

"We know. That's why you're by yourself. Some things are worth working through. I think Adrian's plan is a good one. At least one of your crew has some sense and knows how to do it right."

"Excuse me? What does that mean? There's something to be said for being alone—at least I'm not in the midst of any commotion."

"That's just because you're on hiatus."

"You know I'm not considering it that anymore."

"Oh? Then what are you calling it these days?"

"Simply living. I mean, do you have to have somebody to be considered a member of society? Does my value as a person decline because I'm not in a relationship? I don't think so. As a matter of fact, I think I'm getting better. I'm actually noticing a lot of stuff I would have missed before because I was focused on what was going on with me and my relationship. Now I have time to think about someone other than myself, and you know what?"

"What?"

"There's a whole world out there that I've been missing."

"So can I tell you something?"

"Sure. Since when do you ask for permission?"

"You're right, I don't! Anyway, what I was going to say was that I like you a lot more these days."

"Really? Why is that?"

"I think it's because of what you just said. I couldn't quite put my finger on it before, but you are less self involved. It's very attractive. It's made you more interesting. Do you realize we've been on the phone for quite some time, and we are just now getting to the topic of you? That is huge. Talk about a giant leap for mankind!"

"Was I that bad before, Derrick?"

"Don't get me wrong. You know I have always adored you, but there were times I wondered when you would get past the whining about someone who wasn't worth the time of day you gave him."

"Were you jealous?" Tracy couldn't resist the jab.

"Maybe, but the bigger issue is I just wanted you to get over yourself and realize that there was life beyond you, and if you took the time to contribute half the energy you burned trying to make your stuff happen and invested it in somebody else, you just might find things falling into place for yourself. I think you're getting there."

"I think that was supposed to be a compliment."

"Yes, it was. Keep up the good work."

"Thanks, Mr. Man. Well my body clock is winding down. Got to get in my eight hours or I'm no good. But, hey, thanks for sharing."

"You're welcome. Don't forget to tell Felicia what I said. Hey, I love you, girl."

"I love you too, Derrick. Good night. Tell Shirley I said 'yo' and enjoy church." She snickered.

"Yeah, right. Bye."

Easing herself off the bed, Tracy made the rounds, pulling shades and turning off the lights. Slowly she moved through her apartment taking note that the quiet felt good—real good. There was a time she would have panicked over not being out on a Saturday night. *Am I get-*

ting old? No, she decided. She was finally comfortable with herself. And that was a good thing. It was even better that she was finally appreciating the love she already had in her life. She had overlooked it for so long, so caught up was she in her misdirected quest for love. In this moment she felt as if nothing was missing. She felt rich. Good friends, a full life, a career she enjoyed. How could the presence or absence of one man subtract from all that she already had? Finally she got it. The bowl of life was already brimming over with all that she wanted. Mr. Right would be the cherry on top when he arrived, but for now she was no worse for wearing a single garment. She was alive, satisfied, and already loved. How long had she insisted on not feeling love unless it came from the source she selected?

She crawled back into bed and reveled in the folds of her satin comforter. Suddenly she bolted straight up in the bed and turned the light back on. Reaching for her journal she made one more entry.

Dear Diary,
Love is alright if you don't insist on where you put it.

32

*A*l turned the key in the door, wondering why the house was still dark. Carla should have been home by now. Stepping into the foyer he stopped suddenly and peered into the stillness. A faint sniffing sound was coming from the farthest corner of the living room. Frowning, he hesitantly stepped into the room and reached for the corner torchiere. Slowly turning up the halogen he saw her curled up in the corner of the love seat as if seeking refuge in its arm. Her face streaked with tears, Carla looked smaller than ever.

"Carla, what's wrong? What happened?"

There was no reply. Only the sound of escalated weeping. Al had never seen Carla look like this before. Her face was streaked with tears, causing her lively freckles to appear more as blotches than the usual sprinkle of whimsy. Her lashes, saturated with her pain, appeared dark against her skin, framing her eyes, causing them to look deep and empty. What could have rendered his wife to this state?

"Carla?"

"Oh Al…" More tears. He decided to wait. He sat next to her. Finally she was spent. Lying in his arms, he could feel quiet descending upon her. He lifted her face to look into his.

"Are you ready to talk about it now?"

Carla nodded weakly. "Felicia's pregnant."

"Felicia?" Al frowned, trying to place the name. Finally the light came on. "Oh Felicia!" Then frowning again. "Wait a minute—she's not the married one, is she. I thought her husband left her."

"Oh Al, you're worse than me. I guess we've both been saved too long and grown quite naïve. Felicia is single, honey. Very single."

"Hmm, I see." Al pondered this for a moment. "And besides the fact that you are worried about her being a single parent, what has you in such a state of despair?"

Carla scooted up to turn and look Al in the eye. "You know I was fine when I left Muriel. As a matter of fact, I was really excited about helping Felicia prepare for the baby and the prospect of being able to be a sister in Christ to her. She is such a sweet girl, Al, but she really needs the Lord. I thought if I could be a help to her it would be a great way to draw her to Him."

Al looked at his wife as if seeing her for the first time all over again. This was what he loved about her the most. She was always looking for ways to be a living example to others. She was such a good woman. He felt more fortunate than ever to have her as his wife. He focused back on what she was saying.

"So you know me, I made my lists and checked them twice, much to the girls' chagrin and headed home full of plans unfolding in my head. And then, blame it on the devil or just my own evil heart, halfway home this wave of melancholy swept over me, and I just landed splat in a pit of depression."

"But why, Carla?"

"Because…I realized I was soooo jealous, Al. Jealous of Felicia." Carla's face crumbled. "All of a sudden I felt angry at God. All I've ever wanted was to give you a child. I feel as if you're having to suffer for my mistakes and it's not fair." At this point she dissolved into tears. "It's just not fair."

Al moved to hold her tighter, but she wrenched from his arms to face him again, this time a look of anger on her face.

"And another thing. Felicia isn't thinking about God. Why does she get blessed with a child and I don't? I'm faithful to God, and I'm trying to do all the right things. Is it too much to ask for one thing that's no big deal for God to do? Is it?"

"Whoa, whoa, whoa! One thing at a time here." Al was trying to lift and separate what he had just heard. What mistakes? Carla had always been one to ponder her choices prayerfully and carefully make decisions. What could she have possibly done to think she was still being punished by God? This was so totally out of character for her that he was still stuck there, but now her last comment jolted him from what she had previously said. This was a totally foreign side of his wife.

"What does faithfulness to God have to do with what He chooses or doesn't choose to give you, Carla? You're sounding a little 'religious,' aren't you? C'mon, honey. You know God doesn't owe us anything. Your faithfulness still doesn't make up for what He's already done for you. At least that's what you always tell me. Did you believe that or were you just saying something that sounded good to you at the time?" Though his words were strong, Al was gently looking into her eyes and his face was filled with loving concern.

"No, I did…I mean I do. It's just that, well, why does it seem that the people who would know what to do with a blessing never seem to get it, and the ones who are oblivious to the blessing or the responsibility always seem to end up getting what they are not ready for? I just don't get it!"

"Perhaps it's not for you to get? Perhaps that's why God says His thoughts are not our thoughts. His ways are higher than ours. Perhaps He knows those people need what you want more than you do. And perhaps He uses that blessing you think they don't deserve to bring them closer to Him."

"It's an interesting theory."

"Do you have another?"

"Yes, I do."

"You mentioned God punishing you for your mistakes. I don't agree with that. I think the consequences of our actions bear out and punish us enough, He certainly doesn't need to add to it. Which is why He gives us do and don't instructions in the first place—to keep us from hurting ourselves…even though we don't always listen. Then we end up with the scars to show for disobedience, but that's not on Him, that's on us. And since I've known you, you've always been a wise and discerning woman, so I'm a little confused as to why you think God is punishing you…and me for that fact."

"You said the operative words—'since you've known me.'" Again Carla crumbled. "I haven't always been the woman you know." Haltingly but determined to clear the slate, she began to relate her turbulent teenage years. The rebellion. The drug use. Her recovery after being placed in a youth home. "That was where I met Brian. We fell in love, and for the first time in a long time I felt alive. We wanted to get married and be together, but we were both underage so we ended up having to go back to our homes. Then I found out I was pregnant. My parents hit the ceiling. They didn't want to have anything to do with a black son-in-law and a bi-racial grandchild." Her eyes were searching his face for a reaction to this revelation, but Al was careful not to show any emotion that might hinder her from telling her story. "It just didn't fit in with their social agenda." Al could hear the bitterness in Carla's tone. "That was when mother informed me that I would be getting an abortion—no ifs, ands, or buts about it. She was not going to support me and Brian or our child." Suddenly Carla looked very tired, as if reliving the events. "We were powerless. Neither one of us had a job or any money. We had no way of taking care of ourselves or a baby. We had no choice, and she knew it."

"What about his family? Couldn't they have helped?"

Carla laughed but it wasn't out of amusement. "Oh, they weren't any better. They were just as hostile, painting me to be the one who had ruined their baby boy's life. They had no plans to embrace a white girl, no matter what side of the tracks she came from. In the end his family sent him away. They were afraid my parents would press charges against him and he'd end up in jail for raping an underage white girl. Little did they know that my parents were much more interested in making the whole episode go away before their friends discovered anything and they suffered disgrace." Carla looked heavenward, the wear of telling her story beginning to show. Still she persevered. Al tentatively reached for her hand, not wanting to do anything that would stop her from getting through this.

"So dear old mom made the appointment at the clinic and handed me over to the doctor to take care of this 'unfortunate incident' as she chose to label it. I felt like a broken appliance in need of repair in time for a dinner party." Al was astounded at the anger she still harbored; it had not been evident to him before. He was astounded that she hadn't exploded before this. "She completely ignored the fact that I didn't want to give up my baby. She just wanted it gone. She told me I would get over it and thank her later…Can you believe that?"

It was clear Carla she hadn't gotten over it. Though she emerged from the operating room free from what her mother called a "burden she would come to realize she really didn't want," Carla had remained burdened with grief over the child that was ripped from her womb but never from her heart. Al's heart broke for her as Carla, face bathed with tears, looked into his eyes apologetically.

"After we got married, I thought I would finally be able to put this whole thing to rest by having another baby, but now I'm wondering if I'm still paying for not being strong enough to defy my mother and keep my child no matter what. I don't know what else I could have done. I know I should have told you, but…"

Al watched his wife dissolving into tears front of him. He witnessed the depths of her sorrow and guilt over a situation she had been powerless to resolve. He felt helpless to ease her suffering, but finally all the pieces were coming together in his mind. Her urgency to get pregnant shortly after they were married. The distance that still existed between her and her mother. Even her diligence in the pairing of Muriel and Brad. Like a mother who regretted not becoming a ballerina pushing her child to live the life she had been denied, Carla had chosen to fix her past by living it out vicariously through her friends. But now it was more important to mend his wife than to do a complete psychoanalysis.

"Carla? Do you really believe God would hold you responsible for something that was beyond your control? Listen to yourself. What's your favorite line? Is God good or not?"

"I said that to Muriel earlier this evening. Little did I know I might have to eat my words."

"So let's take this one step at a time. Have the doctors told us you absolutely cannot have children?"

"No, they just said it might be difficult."

"Is anything too hard for God?"

"I guess right now I'm struggling with that question…well actually no, I'm not. I believe God *can* do anything. I'm just wondering *will* He for me?"

"I see. In that case can you ever do enough to earn brownie trade-in points so you can cash in on your heart's desire?"

"Of course not!"

"So then what makes God decide what He is going to give to whom?"

"I suppose it has to do with His overall master plan."

"Aha! So it's really not about you then, is it? Could it be that everything that ultimately occurs in your life is part of a bigger picture than you can see? And that God's timing and purpose according to His kingdom agenda has everything to do with how things play out in our individual lives?"

"Yes, that's possible…"

"But do you believe that's true, Carla? Because everything concerning your life and your attitude hangs in the balance of what you believe. Let me ask you another question. Why do you want a baby? Do you want a child or do you want to be a mother?"

"What's the difference?"

"There's a huge difference. One is about what you get, the other is about what you *give*. Now I know that you are a generous woman, so I think I know the answer to that question. So my next question is this, If it meant that much to you to have a child, why can't we just adopt? I'm totally open to that. I want you to be happy....Now what's wrong?"

Carla was building up for another avalanche of tears, it was written all over her face.

"I'm so ashamed of myself. I never thought about it, but I have been driven for selfish reasons. I've been trying to replace what I lost all this time and redeem myself. I…"

"Baby, it's all under the blood of Jesus. God has moved on. That's the beauty of His grace. He is gracious enough to let bygones be bygones. And the glory of His mercy is He alleviates the misery of the consequences He knows we are sure to suffer. In other words, let it go."

"But…"

"But nothing. Trust God's timing. I can see His wisdom at work personally. I've been able to enjoy having your undivided attention all to myself. And when the season ends, I will be able to move on without feeling robbed of your love."

"Oh, Al! The best part of God's grace was the gift He gave me when He gave me you. Are you upset that I didn't tell you all of this before?"

"No. I understand why you chose not to, me being so innocent and all. I know you didn't want to be a bad influence on me or anything, but let's face it: You've already ruined me." He ducked as she swung to swat him across the head. "Lady Carla, all I know is the woman you are now—and you are magnificent. I love you with my entire being, and

I will fight for you and rescue you time and time again if that's what I have to do. The past is the past, and I choose to leave it there because we can. So the bigger question is now that you've told me, can you finally let it go?"

"Yes, I think I can. Humph, you know what's ironic? Out of all that pain, Brian found the Lord. His last letter to me was a prayer that I would find comfort in the Savior he had found. He's preaching now."

"Do you think either of you could have gotten to where you are now any other way?"

"I'd like to think we could have, but only God knows. But you know what, Al?" Carla's eyes were bright with realization.

"What?"

"If that was the only way to get to where I am now, I would gladly go through it again."

"And exactly where are you now?"

"Why, right here in your arms! There's no place I'd rather be." She kissed him tenderly on his nose. "Oo! I have to tell you about the rest of the night!" Before Al could say another word, she pitched into all the events as they had transpired. From Muriel's engagement to Brad to the news about Cedric Graham and Muriel's revelation about her past. By the time she ended her dissertation, Al was looking at her in complete wonder.

Where does she get so much energy? he thought. There were just too many details for him to absorb, and though he found it all completely amazing, he also was feeling completely spent.

"Well, don't you have anything to say?"

"I don't have another word left in my vocabulary. I think I used up my quota for the day."

Carla, feeling completely reenergized by her confession, had to rein in her energy. "Oh poor dear, I'm sorry. I did dump a lot on you all at one time, didn't I?" Her eyes welled up with emotion and appreciation.

She tenderly touched the tip of his nose. "You know what I love about you, Mr. Robinson?"

"No—do tell."

"I love the way you listen to me. I love your quiet strength and the way you rise to the occasion when it's needed." She was gently kissing him in between each item she listed. "I love your wisdom. I love the way you let me ramble on and on when I need to. I love your depth. I love the way you always amaze me with just the right word at the right time." She chuckled to herself. "Hmm, maybe if I talked less you would talk more."

Al was inclined to agree, but he knew now was not the time to make that sentiment known. He had decided a long time ago that it was best to store up thoughts and opinions until they were really needed or asked for. "Let's get back to the part about what you love about me."

Rising to her feet, Carla extended her hand toward Al. "I think we should continue this conversation elsewhere. Would you care to join me in the boudoir for a little fellowship and worship?"

Al's strength was returning. "Don't mind if I do, ma'am. Don't mind if I do."

33

Muriel gazed up the long driveway and took a deep breath. Unconsciously she gripped Brad's arm even tighter. He looked at her smiling broadly. "Nervous?"

"That's an understatement."

"They're going to love you."

"Did you tell them…"

"Nope! I decided to let it be a surprise."

"Brad!"

"Sorry, I couldn't resist." He gave her a mischievous grin. Then steadying her with his gaze, "Muriel, I've got you covered. You will never have to hang in the wind alone, do you hear me? My parents are going to love you because I love you. And actually you don't need me to qualify for their love because you are pretty lovable on your own, besides being awfully cute."

"Just cute?"

"That's all I'm giving you for now so your head doesn't get too big. Are you ready to do this?"

"Yes. If I fall on my sword, at least I go down with a fabulous ring."

"You know you are wrong for that."

Muriel couldn't help laughing. She was still laughing when the door swung open and Brad's mother stood before her smiling curiously. "It sounds as if I missed something I would have enjoyed."

Muriel was speechless. Gazing at Brad's mother her mind swirled with questions. Brad's mother was beautiful but there was something about her. There was a faint olive undertone to her creamy skin and a decided kink to her sandy-blonde hair that caused Muriel to wonder. She looked at Brad, who was studying her as she studied his mother who was now leading them into the living room. She left them there in search of Brad's father. Muriel turned to Brad. "Now forgive me if I'm wrong but is your mother..."

"Part African-American? Nope, but she is part African. My great-grandmother was from the Ivory Coast." With that Brad led her to the mantel of the fireplace to show her the photographs of their family tree, which had a lone black woman in the center of the lineup.

"So you were holding out on me, were you?"

"Would it have made any difference if my mother were completely white?"

"No. After all, I agreed to marry you before I knew anything different."

"So you'll forgive me for this one little test?"

"Did I pass it?"

"With flying colors."

"Whew! That was close, 'cause I just knew my family would be the glitch in this story, but they were too happy that I was finally getting married to care if you were purple or pinstriped." Then she really began to laugh. "Oh this is too classic." She walked around him with her hand on her hip, looking him up and down as if checking him out for the first time. "So you a brother, huh? I should have known."

"Watch out now. I'm not even interested in being your brother!"

"Why not? Haven't you read Song of Songs in your Bible, baby boy? Then you'd be able to kiss me in public!"

"Well, baby girl, I don't think I'll be waiting for permission to do that about now, seeing you've agreed to be my wife and all. C'mere, woman!" With that he grabbed her in a Fred Astaire move, leaned over, and kissed her.

"Well, well, well, I see I trained you right!"

Muriel struggled to stand upright and appear unflustered as Brad's mom and dad stood gazing at them both and looking deeply interested in the source of their son's happiness.

Again Muriel studied Brad's mother's face. She was a beautiful and striking woman. Tall and slim with fine features and high cheekbones, she would have been considered a classic blonde without the knowledge of her mixed heritage. Her Grace Kelly features and soft gray eyes were complemented by her hair that was swept up and back, though a few tendrils escaped to cascade down around her face and the nape of her neck. Her husband was just as striking as she was in a classic, young Paul Newman sort of way. Muriel concluded this had to be where Brad got his blue eyes and build. She wondered how his family had felt about Brad's mother. But now was not the time to ask. As Brad embraced his dad and they went through the male ritual of back slapping and teasing one another, the women bonded in silence, telegraphing their pleasure at the scene with eye contact.

"Shall we? You must be starved after that long drive." Brad's mother finally broke the silence, beckoning toward the dining room.

"It was such a beautiful drive. I enjoy getting out of the city and actually seeing trees."

"Good. Will you help me for a moment in the kitchen?"

"Sure. I'd be happy to." Muriel gave a backward glance at Brad, who was still happily engaged in lively banter with his father.

As they entered the kitchen, Brad's mother turned to her. "I hope I'm not intruding but I have to ask, How does your family feel about you marrying Brad?"

Muriel was taken aback by the question. "They're fine with it. As a matter of fact, they were more worried about your response to me."

"Really? Well, you're a lovely girl, and Brad certainly is crazy about you. But I had to make sure because I can't have my son getting hurt again."

"Again?" Muriel frowned.

"Yes. The last girl Brad was engaged to was black and couldn't get past her family's opposition." Ignoring the intake of breath from Muriel, she continued studying her. "He was devastated."

"Really! How many times has Brad been engaged?" Muriel didn't know if she was angrier about the fact that Brad hadn't told her or that she was being put on the spot like this. She was at a great disadvantage because of her lack of knowledge.

"Just once." Brad's voice came from the kitchen doorway. "Mother, was that really necessary?" His eyes were dark with annoyance.

"I can handle this, Brad." Stepping one step closer to Brad's mother, Muriel squared her shoulders and looked her straight in the eye. She had come too close to happiness to turn back now, and she would deal with Brad on her own time. "Listen, I don't mean any disrespect when I say this, but I need you to be very clear about where I stand and the type of woman I am. I understand that you love your son, but so do I. And it would take more than people's opinions—family or otherwise—to turn me around at this point. Now I believe in getting your family's blessings and all before taking a crucial step like marriage, so all I can say is her loss is my gain. I hope that sets your mind at ease that this wedding will not be called off—at least not for that reason."

Brad's mother was smiling.

Muriel turned to look at Brad. "Another test?"

"Not one that I had planned." He smiled sheepishly.

"Let's make that the last one." With that Muriel picked up a casserole dish and headed for the dining room.

Brad's mother stood behind her son, watching Muriel set the dish on the dining room table and then engage Brad's father in conversation.

"Well, I guess she told me!" Brad's mother laughed softly.

"I believe she did. I told you you would meet your match."

"I like her. She's strong."

"They say what doesn't kill you makes you stronger, and she's definitely had the chance to choose life over death."

"I'm glad she chose life for your sake."

"Me too." On that note he decided to join those who were more interested in eating than talking.

Though Brad's mother had warmed toward her, Muriel found herself still stinging from the conversation. Her food tasted like sawdust as she fought to keep the banter light while her head spun with the information that Brad had been engaged before. She had a hundred questions for him. It was with great relief that she got into the car for the drive home. As Brad's father leaned over to give her a gentle kiss on the cheek and welcome her to the family, her concerns were put on hold so distracted was she by his elegant charm.

Pulling out of the driveway she was loudly silent.

"A penny for your thoughts," Brad said, breaking through her swirling thoughts.

"That's all you have is a penny?"

"You better believe it after buying that ring, girl."

Muriel laughed and then grew serious. "Brad, why didn't you tell me you were engaged before?"

"Because it was my past, and it had no bearing on our future."

"Your mother obviously thought differently."

"My mother is overprotective."

"And with good reason, I might add. She's probably endured her own share of prejudice from both sides of the fence. Too light to be black, and legally black to white folk who stick to the one drop of black blood rule. That had to be a big mess when she was growing up, and I'm sure even now it can be difficult at times 'cause everybody ain't free if you know what I mean."

"That's very insightful of you."

"Every now and then I try to locate the one sensitive bone in my body."

"I appreciate it. I admit Mother can be a little hypersensitive on the issue. Everyone always talks about how racist white people are, but no one ever really deals with how racist black people can be too. They can be just as prejudiced against their own race as well as others. My mother learned to live with her own rejection, but she didn't do so well with mine."

"What happened? Didn't they know you were part…"

"I didn't let it get that far, Muriel. As far as I was concerned, if they couldn't accept me at face value I didn't want any part of that type of family. It was a deeper heart issue for me, and their response revealed a lot."

"I see, but was that really fair?"

"Oh it was more than fair. Look at me. Take a good look. To the rest of the world who have no knowledge of my family tree I am a white man. What was I going to do? Run around waving a flag saying I have a black great-grandmother? No! You are going to do exactly what you did today, stand next to me on the principle that you love me and you don't give a flying fig what anybody else thinks, correct? So why would I want to marry a woman who wasn't strong enough to do that? Hmm?"

"You have a point. I concede, oh great and mighty counselor. Boy, who ever said men don't talk?"

"Men talk when they find someone who actually listens."

"I'm listening, so finish telling me, How much do you love me?"

"More than before I saw you stand up to my mother."

"I wasn't too hard on her, was I?"

"No, not at all. You won her respect—and that's huge."

"Well from one tough cookie to another, I think we'll be fine. But promise me—no more tests."

"You got it. Consider yourself officially graduated."

"So do I get a bachelor's degree or a Ph.D.?"

"Can you settle for a bachelor?"

"Ah, the concessions we make for love..."

"Indeed."

With that Muriel sat back in her seat, smiling to herself. She thought of the scripture about being tried in the fire and coming out as pure gold. Right now she was feeling pretty shiny.

34

*M*uriel wondered how long it would take the others to notice her ring. Self-consciously she kept twisting it on her finger, turning the diamond inward. All of a sudden it seemed to sparkle brighter than ever, as if insisting on being seen. Now that she and Brad had both jumped through all the familial hoops, it had been agreed it was time to inform the rest of their friends. Besides, Muriel was looking forward to having a date for Adrian's gallery showing. Her customary fifteen minutes late for the lunch gathering, she took note of the group awaiting her. Hmm, was that a new suit Tracy had on? It was very flattering and the perfect shade of celadon to bring out the golden undertones of her hazel eyes. Felicia was looking softer and more beautiful than ever in a shade of blue that leaned more to white than a color. Her hair was thick and lush, slightly tousled without trying. She was a study of femininity. Though she was now rounding the corner of the end of her fifth month, she was still slim with all of her weight concentrated in her midsection. All in all, she looked like a confection.

Adrian was growing more chic by the day. She was wearing her new cut well, spiking it with gel. With her bold hoops intact, she sported a fabulous cream suit. The jacket had three-quarter sleeves and the collar was crisply upturned. Beautiful dark eyes illuminated her face beneath perfectly arched brows, and just a hint of color on her lips highlighted her natural beauty. The girl was looking fly. Muriel decided any man walking past the table would do a double take. Collectively the women were arresting. Again she found it ironic that she was now the lone one in the group with a man in her life. "Hey, ladies, sorry I'm late, but…"

"Yeah, yeah, save it. We know the drill by now. That's why we always tell you a half hour earlier so you'll arrive on time." Adrian and Felicia laughed at Tracy's annoyance and then looked guiltily at Muriel now that their plot was uncovered

"Where's Carla?" Felicia asked.

"She couldn't make it today. Kinda grew on you, didn't she?"

"I like her. She's really bubbly, and she has a good heart."

"Carla is the best. A good friend to have. Earth to Tracy, where are you, girl?"

"Hmm?" Tracy turned to look at her, but Muriel could tell she was still elsewhere in her thoughts. Following the direction of where she had been looking, Muriel turned to see what was so distracting. Her eyes landed on an interracial couple cuddling together in the far corner of the restaurant. The rest of the eyes at the table followed hers and studied the couple. Sensing that they were being watched, the couple returned the stares. Muriel, now well acquainted with how they might be feeling, smiled at them, attempting to diffuse their discomfort.

"I just don't get it." Tracy shook her head.

"What don't you get?" Muriel self-consciously turned the diamond on her ring toward her palm as she spoke.

"I don't get the attraction. As difficult as brothers may be, you couldn't pay me to get involved with a white man."

"That's a powerful statement. If you had the choice between being alone and being with a white man, you would just be alone?"

"I don't think I should settle for less than what I want, that's all."

"But if a brother never came into your life and you chose to cut yourself off from other choices, you *would* be settling. You would be settling for being *alone*. And we know you don't want to be alone. Isn't that the bigger issue that overrides what color the man is? How about just wanting a man who loves you?"

"Now that's what I'm talking about!" Felicia had to chime in on that one.

"Tracy, I just think that with the law of averages and statistics on available men being what they are, you have to be more open to sample all the options. And I don't consider that settling—I consider that being realistic. And weren't you the one who was upset by the man availability statistics?"

"True dat to being realistic!" Felicia was truly a vehement supporter, which gave Muriel the courage she needed to build toward her news.

"Think about it. By the time you go down your list of nonnegotiables, there's not a lot of cards left to draw from. First he has to be a born-again Christian—well not for you, but for me he has to be. I know you want a man with integrity and sound character, so wham!—that cuts the pie in half. Then you want him to be financially together or at least have a good job, so wham that cuts off another half of the half you're already down to. Then you don't want him to be gay or on the down low or in jail, so wham, wham, wham, that leaves you with the last ten percent of available men walking around in the world. And there's a whole lot of women looking at this tiny, select group. So what you gonna do, my sister? Still dig in your heels and scream he's got to be black? I would think that would be the *least* of your worries."

"Well, you certainly have thought that one through." Tracy was looking at her carefully now. She then glanced toward the couple across the room again, studying the man for a moment. "To be perfectly honest, I'm just not attracted to white men. They do nothing for me. To me they're just missing that bass note that brothers have, you know?"

"You don't need to be attracted to all of them. Just the one who is right for you. And you might be surprised. If the right one came into your life and swept you off your feet, his color would be the last thing on your mind, girl."

"So you would consider a white man?"

"Yes, I would—if he had what I was looking for."

"I would never have put that together in my brain cells. In fact, it's ironically funny because a while back I was in a cab and I thought I saw you walking down the street with a white guy, headed into a jewelry store. But I decided my mind was playing tricks on me and dismissed it as something that would never happen. Isn't that funny?" Tracy started laughing.

"That is a good one!" Felicia joined her but cut her laughter short when she saw the look on Muriel's face. She was not amused. "You don't think that's funny? You're the one who doesn't have time for men, and I've never known you to care about jewelry so…you, a white man, jewelry shopping…now that *is* a hoot. Unless of course you would do it for a client—but that doesn't seem to be the area where you exercise any great degree of patience." The cloud over Muriel's face darkened, and Felicia hunched her shoulders. "I'm sorry, but it's true!"

"Actually, it was me," Muriel said quietly, while turning the diamond on her ring outward underneath the table. "He wasn't a client, and he was buying me this." With that she extended her hand, positioning it in such a way that the lighting in the restaurant made the diamonds scream.

"Oh, hello!" Felicia said leaning forward toward the light.

Tracy and Adrian's mouths dropped open. Adrian whistled, while Tracy leaned in. "Now that's what I call bling."

"Naw, forget *bling*. That's bling, *blang*, bling! Let's keep it real. Who is this man?"

"His name is Brad Sebastian, and we are engaged."

"What!" they said in stereo.

"When did this happen?"

"How long have you been seeing him?"

"Where did you meet him?"

"What does he do?"

"Have you been seeing somebody all this time and not saying anything to us?"

Their questions tumbled over one another. Finally Muriel held up her hand.

"I will take this from the top. I met him at church. He's amazing, incredible, and beautiful inside and out. He's an entrepreneur and had a very successful business that he recently sold. He relocated to Chicago from Seattle. Carla introduced us…"

"See, that Carla is alright with me. If she could find a man to break you down, that's saying something." Felicia was loving this news.

"He didn't break me down, Felicia, but he did build me up."

"And so you're telling me some brother couldn't have done that?" Tracy wasn't jumping into the feel-good pool right away.

"A brother could have, Tracy, but he didn't. And I'm not down on brothers by any stretch of the imagination. But to be perfectly honest, I don't think a brother would have taken the time to tear down all my walls and deal with my issues. And that's not their fault. Lord knows black men have to deal with enough out there in the world. It's a rare one who still has energy left to wade through a sister's mess on top of that. And though Brad may have his own issues, questioning his manhood is not among them. Because of that, he was able to recognize and get rid of the baggage I was carrying."

"Whoa, this is too deep for me." Felicia pushed back from the table, getting teary eyed. "I mean that's what every woman is really looking for. A man who won't take no for an answer and keeps on coming even if our issues get in the way. The knight in shining armor we all read about in fairy tales. The one who fights for you, kills the dragon, and carries you away. Boy, did we get messed up reading those things—now our expectations are all jacked up."

"You're right about that," Tracy retorted wryly, though still on reserve.

"I beg to differ with you. I truly got a knight in shining armor. He literally rescued me." Now it was Muriel's turn to get teary.

"Muriel, I'm so happy for you. This is truly an answer to prayer. You don't know how many nights I've asked God to put a man in your life who could heal the wounds I knew were there…even though I didn't know what they were exactly," Adrian said.

"You prayed that?" Felicia was incredulous.

"Umm hmm." Adrian nodded, looking quite pleased with herself.

"Adrian?" Felicia looked uncharacteristically shy.

"Yes, Felicia."

"Do you ever pray for me?"

"All the time, Felicia, all the time."

"I'm still salty about him not being a brother. Muriel, have you set a date?" Tracy was still reserved and trying to ascertain how far along Muriel was in her plan.

"Tracy, you are going to have to let that go, you know. I'm thinking about next spring, but Brad says he doesn't know if he can hold out that long."

Tracy frowned, "Hold out on what?"

"Hold out on having sex. I'm a Christian, remember? I'm not doing the sex thing until I'm married."

Tracy and Felicia looked horrified. "You are kidding, right?"

"I wish I were, but I'm as serious as a heart attack."

"Oh, I don't think I could do that. I'm with Brad—you better hurry up!" Felicia looked worried.

"Forgive me for getting all in your business, but don't you need to know if he's any good before you commit long term?" Between the fact that he was white and Muriel was being celibate, Tracy was more than a little worried.

"For some reason I don't think I need to worry about that." Muriel had a conspiratorial smile on her face.

"Aw sooky, sooky now." Felicia was really getting into this.

"So if he rocks your boat that tough, how can you wait so long to sample all of that?" Tracy just didn't understand this form of what she termed self-torture.

"I love Brad, but I love God even more. And here's how it plays out for me. God was there before Brad showed up, and He'll still be there if Brad should choose to go—so it's all about pleasing Him first no matter how in love I am. And all I know is when you do things God's way, you are always blessed. Brad loves God, and in his mind honoring God means honoring me enough to wait. If he values my love that much, then I need to love myself enough to understand my value and not give out free samples. After all, I am not a Sam's Club taste test. I don't come cheap you know."

"Well, from the size of the ice on that ring, we can all see that." Tracy had to concede that perhaps Muriel made sense. Tracy had certainly done things the other way and not gotten anywhere for it. She was ashamed to think of how many times she had given everything to a man…and here she was with no evidence of a return on her various investments. This always came to mind when she watched shows like *Sex and the City.* First of all, she wondered if anyone was really having that much sex. She didn't know anyone who was, at least not since college. Who had time if you had a life that was about anything? She had thought about being celibate, but not for the reasons that Muriel just brought up. It was a rather refreshing way of looking at things. She had to admit she had never considered the value of her body or her love. Or met a man who did either.

After all was said and done, Tracy wondered if she had bought into the hype of sex being far more important than it really was in the scheme of things. How many times had it gotten in the way or distracted her from details about the man that she should have paid closer attention to? And now that she wasn't intimately involved with anyone, she certainly hadn't died. Though she had her moments of longing, these moments passed and life went on. A wave of melancholy washed over her. How sad it took so long to learn such a major life lesson. But perhaps it was all right just as long as she finally did. Tracy looked at Muriel with new respect. It was amazing the things she had learned about these women in the last few months after knowing them for so long. She felt as if they were all finally coming of age, flowering into maturity.

"Earth to Tracy!" Muriel was peering at Tracy, trying to figure out what she was thinking about. "I saaa-aid Brad actually is a brother, so you don't have to feel bad. Even though he looks white, his great-grandmother is African. Does that help you out?"

"Isn't that kind of stretching it to make it comfortable for you? At face value he is white. I saw him, remember?" Tracy didn't know what she was angrier about, the fact that Muriel had held out on her about seeing someone or that the someone she had been seeing and was now talking about marrying was white. In light of her experience with Evan, she just wasn't able to reconcile all this right now. Just because Muriel was happy didn't mean she had to buy into it.

Muriel's eyes narrowed. "Tracy, is this about me or about you? Felicia told me about Evan."

Tracy shot Felicia a nasty look.

Felicia threw up her arms in apology. "Well! I didn't think you would mind. I mean we usually get around to talking about everything, so…"

"We *used* to talk about everything. It seems we have a ton of secrets these days." Tracy looked accusingly at Muriel.

Muriel was getting irritated. "Don't you think you're blowing this out of proportion? I just didn't want it to become an issue until it was worthy of being an issue. It wasn't a matter of keeping secrets, Tracy, and I'm not going to allow you to superimpose your pain on my situation. If you were really honest with yourself, you would admit that Evan cheating on you with a white woman is a small part of the bigger picture. He wasn't worth investing yourself in in the first place, and you know it."

Tracy started backing up her chair and digging into her purse for money at the same time. She was not going to sit and listen to this.

Slapping her money on the table for her drink and food, she said, "Well, I am so happy that you have found someone 'worthy of investing in,' as you put it. However, I don't need a detailed analysis of what is wrong with me or my men, thank you very much. And I will not pay to be insulted over lunch."

Muriel opened her mouth, and then closed it and frowned.

Tracy turned to Felicia. "Tell the waiter I lost my appetite."

"Tracy!"

But Tracy had no more time to listen to Muriel. She brushed past the waiter who was just approaching with their meals.

"Let her go, Muriel. She'll come around." It was Adrian who brought calm reason back to the table.

"She's going to have to because I'm getting married whether she likes it or not." Muriel bit into a carrot with a vengeance. "Hey, this was supposed to be a celebration! One monkey don't stop no show. We're not going to let her ruin our lunch, are we?" Though she did feel a sadness over Tracy's departure, she knew Tracy had to sort out her own feelings. That had always been her pattern.

"Felicia, you all right?" Muriel noticed a change in Felicia, who was quietly watching her.

"I know Tracy will work it out, she usually does. But I was wondering where I'd be right now if I had adopted your attitude earlier."

"Well, it's never too late you know."

"I think I learned that one a little late in the day." Felicia rubbed her tummy.

"Dealing with the consequences of our actions is one thing, but you also have to consider that whatever God allows is for our good ultimately—if we choose to learn the lessons from the experience."

"I guess some of us learn the hard way."

"As long as we learn, that's all that counts 'cause if you don't, then you move over to fool category, and I don't anticipate you going there so shake it off, girl. Everything's going to be alright, and your baby is going to be a blessing to all of us."

"Yes, she is!" Felicia brightened.

"It's a girl?"

"Yup! Found out yesterday."

"Oh my, you know she's gonna be a diva!" Muriel grimaced.

"What would you expect when she's got aunties walking around looking like you all? Just don't blind my child with that ring, okay?" Felicia giggled.

Muriel lifted her hand to the sky, twisting her hand to catch the light just the right way and send prisms reflecting her ring as well as her happiness in the air. The future was both scary and wonderful like any good adventure. Her joy was contagious, and for that moment in time every woman at the table was filled with hope for the future and the incredible possibilities that awaited each of them. There was an anticipation of more pleasant surprises.

Muriel has never looked more beautiful, Adrian thought. She reflected on how faithful God was to answer prayer, and if He answered her prayers for Muriel, then surely He would answer the ones she prayed for herself. She hugged herself and shivered in expectation. She didn't know the specifics of her tomorrows, but one thing she did know—it was all good because of Who held her future.

35

The gallery was lit in such a way that the paintings on the wall commanded full attention. The figures that Adrian had painted on the canvases came to life before the eyes of the chic crowd gathered to pay them homage. Small pockets gathered to discuss this one or that one and muse about which struck a chord with them and why. It was an interesting mix of professionals and eccentric artistic types. Though they were from widely diverse backgrounds, the temperature in the room said that at least in this place they were all on common ground.

"Are you ready to meet your public?" Mr. Morrow appeared more excited than Adrian. He had already said he couldn't remember the last time he had seen a crowd like this at an opening. He was sure it was due to the favorable press around the event. The writers for the art sections of the *Sun-Times* and the *Tribune* had requested earlier unveilings because they were both off to cover a major art exhibit in another part of the country. After viewing Adrian's work they had written long articles proclaiming it as some of the most exciting work to break onto the art scene today. The phone had begun ringing off the hook with people clamoring for entry to tonight's event.

"I'm as ready as I'm ever going to be." Adrian could feel her stomach rumbling.

"Don't be nervous. You're already a hit. All you have to do is lap up the compliments—and hopefully the checks!"

"I could get into that." She giggled at the thought of getting paid to do something she found so enjoyable. It was incredible to think that people could actually make a living doing what they liked as opposed to what was considered necessary. After years of homemaking, a nine to five job was something she didn't feel she was wired to handle. "Did the musicians arrive?"

"They are ready and in place. This promises to be quite an evening. Oh—and I did notice on the RSVP list that Ron is expected. He called to see if he could have an appointment to see your work before the exhibit, but I explained that it's against our gallery policy—with the exception of the press and our regular patrons, of course."

"Really!" Adrian didn't hear the rest of his sentence. She was still stuck on the fact that Ron had made it his business to be present. The papers had arrived announcing their divorce as official. She filed them alongside her faith, choosing to believe that God's will was greater than any one man's decision to have a moment of madness. Her goal had not changed; it just moved to a new place on her list of priorities. She had gotten one phone call from Ron asking when they could get together to talk, but she had wanted to concentrate on finishing her collection first. Not knowing which way the conversation would go, she opted to focus on completing what she had started without distraction. She could not afford to be paralyzed by emotional issues right now. She had deliberately called while she knew he was out to leave a message stating that she would not be available to see him until after her showing. He called to leave a message while she was at Bible study, saying he understood and would be waiting for her call and that he didn't want to pressure her. Obviously he didn't want to waste any words until then.

As she entered the room she was overcome by a deep sense of joy and excitement. This was the closest to heaven she could be on earth— to be standing in a room observing those who had come to see and celebrate her work. Her eyes scanned the room, looking for familiar faces. There was Muriel, standing next to a man she assumed was Brad. Hmm, he was fine, if she said so herself. He didn't look mixed at all, but then that really didn't matter. As far as she was concerned, love came in all colors, and whatever shade you could find it in, you needed to embrace it, celebrate it for all it was worth, and keep on stepping. Life is too short to hinder yourself from getting the love you wanted by insisting on rules that could keep you from getting what you truly valued. Muriel and Brad looked happy. He was totally into her and it showed. *Humph. That's what I'm talking about,* she thought. *It's really not too much to want or expect from the man in your life. It is possible, and I will settle for nothing less.* Adrian smiled to herself as she watched Tracy checking Brad out on her approach with Felicia in tow. Felicia looked like cotton candy in a soft, fluffy, pink number that complemented her natural glow in her skin and highlighted her beauty. More than a few heads turned as she walked by, but she was oblivious so fixated was she on finally meeting Muriel's mystery man.

The gallery manager gently took Adrian by the elbow, leading her to the center of the room, directly in front of her first painting. Turning on his portable microphone he cleared his throat to get everyone's attention. Adrian scanned the room for Ron, but found him nowhere. She turned her attention back to what her host was saying.

"Our expectations for this new artist are boundless. She brings an energy to the canvas that I haven't see in quite some time. She paints from her soul and her passion—she's a consummate artist. Please enjoy what you see!" As he spoke the lights in the gallery dimmed until he, Adrian, and the painting stood alone in a shaft of light. "Our artist has chosen to share her work with you in an unusual way this evening— through song. It promises to be a unique experience. Without further ado, ladies and gentlemen, I present Adrian Sterling."

Her maiden name, though it had the artistic edge she liked, still sounded slightly unfamiliar to her. The crowd applauded and the music began. They stood mesmerized as Adrian swayed in front of the painting, an image of beauty herself. A liquid sheath of silver that hugged every curve of her body without appearing loudly suggestive was topped by a loose organza wrap thrown carefully about the neck and trailing into a wisp of folds behind her. She was a vision to behold. Diamond chandelier earrings and a confection of a wide mesh bracelet sprinkled with diamonds made her an elegant apparition bathed in light that seemed to glow around her, illuminating the painting behind her. She and the woman in the painting became one as she sang of midnight flights and the freedom that came from wearing love as your only garment.

Adrian closed her eyes, feeling the music, painting pictures with her voice. As she ended the song, the light shifted to another corner of the room bathed in soft blue. She made her way across the room, gliding more than walking toward the second painting in the series. Every eye was on her as she took her observers on a magical journey through the tempestuous waters of love, deliverance, and redemption. As she ended the journey and the jazz quintet allowed the last note to linger and fade, her audience stood transfixed for a moment in time and then burst into thunderous applause. Adrian stood still for a moment to quiet her trembling and stabilize herself. When she had first dreamed up the concept of her presentation, all the old performance jitters had almost made her table the idea. But she felt driven to do something unique to make her reviewers experience her work instead of merely observing it. Now she had done it, and their applause and appreciation was all the reward she needed.

As the lights came back up, the first face she saw was Ron's. The pride and desire in his eyes spoke volumes. Then Muriel, Felicia, and Tracy were upon her, with Brad and Adrian's mother in tow. Carla and Al were close behind, and then came a sea of unfamiliar faces. Their words tumbling over one another expressing how incredible she had been. Flawless, beautiful, stunning, on and on. It was absolutely amazing—and that she could agree on. The night became a blur of meeting and greeting and being made to feel way too special. Her mother leaned in to kiss her tenderly on the cheek and whisper she had been perfect. Adrian smiled, thinking tonight perfect was perfectly all right. By the end of the evening she was dizzy with exhaustion and all the various compliments floating in her head. Ron lingered. *Where is Amber?* she wondered. But, then again, she really didn't care. She watched him in deep conversation with Mr. Morrow. *Are they talking about me?* Mr. Morrow's eyes kept glancing in her direction, then back to Ron. She frowned slightly, trying to decide what to do. She was ready to go, but wanted to say goodbye to Mr. Morrow. She headed toward them. They broke off their conversation a bit too abruptly. "What are you two so deep in conversation about over here?" she asked with a smile.

"Oh, we were just in the midst of boring business talk," Mr. Morrow said, appearing to be a bit too fidgety to be perfectly honest, but Adrian decided to let it slide. Obviously she wasn't going to get anything out of them, and at this point she was looking forward to sinking into a good, deep sleep. Her body was aching from the tension of holding herself upright so tightly that now that she had relaxed, her bones felt raw. She arched her back and rolled her neck without thinking, trying to ease the pressure from her joints. When she opened her eyes, Ron was staring at her. For a moment she felt shy and dropped her eyes away from his.

"I see. I was just coming to say good night."

"Are you driving?" Ron asked.

"I was far too nervous to drive and get here in one piece, so I cabbed it."

"Please, let me give you a ride home."

"That won't be necessary, I'll be fine."

"We can't have the star of the evening going home in a cab," Mr. Morrow interrupted.

"That's right," Ron seconded the motion. Then he shyly smiled, putting her on the spot. "Please. The pleasure would be all mine."

Not exactly! she thought as she acquiesced. "Alright then, I would appreciate it."

Ron put his hand against the small of her back and the heat of his hand penetrated through the thin silk fabric of her dress. She shivered at his touch. "Good night, Mr. Morrow. Shall we speak Monday?"

"Most definitely. It was a good night, Adrian. Above our expectations. We need to plan the next exhibit."

"Really?"

"Oh, yes, indeed!"

Ron beamed at her and she, forgetting herself and all that didn't exist between them right now, flung herself into his arms. He embraced her back. She wondered at how comfortable it felt. It was as if they'd never been apart.

"Did you hear that?" Adrian's eyes were sparkling and looking into his. He smiled back.

"Yes, I did. I'm impressed." He raised one eyebrow. For one moment neither of them said anything. Then Adrian remembered herself and pulled away looking slightly embarrassed.

"Sorry."

"There's nothing to be sorry for. It's a night to celebrate. Perhaps we should stop somewhere for a toast on the way home...I mean to your place." Now it was his turn to be flustered. Turning to Mr. Morrow, he said, "I'll follow up with you this week to take care of what we discussed."

"It will be a pleasure. Well, time for me to lock up. Again—congratulations, Adrian."

"Thank you. Mr. Morrow. Good night."

As Ron and Adrian stepped out into the night, she suddenly felt self-conscious. Though this was a moment she had imagined, now that it was happening she felt like a silly schoolgirl unable to come up with one brilliant or witty thing to say. They both walked in silence, sorting out their thoughts.

"Do you think you'd like to stop for a drink?" Ron asked as he opened the car door.

"That would be fine."

Again they slipped into their own worlds, searching for something else to say. But their silence said more than anything they could have vocalized. They pulled up to a small restaurant that, through the windows, looked like it was illuminated by the candles on the table. Adrian watched Ron motioning to the valet and wondered if this was considered an official date. She knew she wanted him back, but what did he want? That was the question. And what type of boundaries would she set for herself now that she had the chance to have a new beginning? She had married him before she became a Christian. After her conversion, he had never voiced interest in joining her in her faith. Now that she was free, should she go back to a man who wanted nothing to do with something that was so much a part of her life? She recalled how lonely she had been at times, feeling more single than married. *Shoot, I can be lonely and miserable all by myself,* she thought. *There is nothing more painful than loneliness inside a marriage. Actually, it was downright excruciating. I don't want to experience that again. No, this time some things will have to be different for sure.* As Ron opened her car door and extended his hand to help her out, she thought how handsome and debonair he looked. But it wasn't enough to go back to something that wasn't working. There wasn't that much fine in the world. Perhaps God was giving her a chance to recalibrate and get the marriage He wanted her to have in the first place, one with a godly mate. Adrian decided not to jump to any conclusions or assumptions. She would allow the conversation and events to unfold.

Settling into their chairs at the table, the candlelight illuminating their faces, they were a striking couple. Ron ordered her drink from memory, and then he settled into his chair looking at her thoughtfully. "So, lady, you really made a name for yourself tonight."

"You think?"

"I know! I was so proud of you. It was like watching a flower open up right before my very eyes."

"Aw shucks."

"No, really. It's like you've transformed into... I don't know how to explain it."

"Ron, what happened to us?" Adrian couldn't contain the question any longer.

"I think what I was feeling finally clicked for me this evening. I couldn't explain it before when you asked me because I hadn't figured it out. On the surface everything had been fine, but something was missing. I couldn't put my finger on it. All I knew was I was miserable. Tonight, as I was watching you and thinking about what an incredible woman you were in your moment, it was like the light came on and I knew what happened. It's not really a good excuse, but it was where I was at the time. I...I was just bored, Adrian."

Ron took a sip of his drink, looked into the glass, and then back to her, trying to read her expression. She simply waited. "I know that sounds immature, and it's a sorry excuse, but it's the truth. I wanted to be living with and making love to the woman I saw at the gallery tonight, but that wasn't who was at my house. There was this woman who acted as if being my wife was a duty. I didn't feel like you wanted me any more. The only things that excited you were your church and your pastor, and all of a sudden I was on the outside looking in. You turned into a church lady." At this he made quotes with his fingers. Then he slumped in resignation. "I was the sinner and you were the holy one. And I didn't want any part of church life because it looked boring. So there I was— bored and in the middle of a contest I didn't want any part of. I felt like a complete failure. I couldn't win for losing. Does that make any sense?"

"Actually it does."

"It does?"

"Mmm hmm. I hadn't really thought about it before, but I did look at being your wife as more of a job than something I enjoyed. It didn't start off that way, and to be honest I don't know when it changed. All of a sudden we were standing at opposite sides of a great big gulf, and I couldn't figure out how to bridge the gap."

"I blame myself for the separation. I should have reached out to you and tried to understand your faith more instead of resenting it. It must have been lonely for you, but understand it was lonely for me too. I didn't want to live with the church lady. I wanted my woman back, and I couldn't understand why I couldn't have her. I couldn't reach you any more, and I resented that. I don't know who I resented the most—God or your pastor. They both seemed bigger than life, and I didn't have a strategy to beat either one at their game. I watched enough brothers living in quiet desperation, dying quietly, and I just was not going out like that…so I fled. And then I thought I saw something that could make me feel the way I wanted to feel, so I went for it. "

"Amber."

"Amber. She was just easier."

"So where is she tonight?"

"We're finished."

"Finished?"

"Done. Kaput. That was just being stupid. I want you back, Adrian."

"What? Little ole boring me? I haven't changed, you know. I'm still living holy."

"Holiness wasn't looking boring tonight, I can tell you that!"

"I'm sorry if I made it look like something other than what it really is. But because my faith was so new to me, I went about things the wrong way. I didn't understand that holiness was something you *are*, not something you do. I let myself get lost in religion instead of letting my relationship with Christ enhance who I was and sweeten our marriage. By the time I knew better, I had settled into some habits that were hard to break. I ended up losing pieces of myself that were pretty valuable."

"Consider yourself incredibly enhanced. What do you say, Adrian? Can we give it another try?"

"Aren't you forgetting something?" Though Adrian wanted him back, she was not about to be a pushover or sacrifice her self-respect.

"What?" Ron looked confused.

"If I have to tell you this one, you're in *big* trouble." She arched her brow and waited, watching him squirm under her scrutiny. Then the light of understanding dawned on his face.

Leaning forward he took her hands in his. Looking into her eyes he breathed, "Baby, I am sorry."

Adrian's eyes began to fill with tears. "You hurt me, Ron."

"I know, but I didn't mean to. I—I was just drowning. I got scared. I didn't know what to do. Adrian, I never stopped loving you. I just couldn't find you. And I know it's not a good excuse for what I've done, but I am truly sorry. Will you forgive me?"

Adrian nodded, afraid for a moment to say anything. Swallowing deep, she answered, "Yes, I do. I'm sorry too."

"It wasn't your fault. It had nothing to do with you and everything to do with me. I—I was just…being selfish." He was beginning to truly look miserable now that he was forced to own what he had done.

"I have to own my part in this too. I'm sorry you couldn't find me. But I'm here now."

"Yes, you are—and better than ever. So what do you say? Can we start over?" He paused. "Perhaps this will help." He leaned back and cleared his throat. Rising from the table, he stood over her, extending his right hand to shake hers. "Hello, my name is Ron. Ron Henderson."

"Hello, Mr. Henderson. My name is Adrian. Adrian *Sterling*." He winced at the sound of her maiden name.

"Adrian. A beautiful name for a beautiful woman."

Adrian lowered her eyes in mock modesty, demurely replying, "Thank you!"

"Would you mind if I join you? You seem like the type of woman I'd like to get to know better."

"Really?" Adrian smiled and hesitated for a beat. "I think I'd like that."

Ron sat down with an expression of exaggerated relief on his face. "Whew! I don't know what I would have done if you had said no. I don't envy anybody who is still out there trying to find a good woman. It's rough."

"Well, I was just getting into this single thing." She laughed, drying the corner of her eyes.

"Were you now?"

"Yes, I was." She laughed again. Then growing serious at his look of dismay, Adrian looked at him with her heart in her throat. "Ron, I love you. I never stopped loving you. However, in order for us to get back together some things have to change, otherwise what's the point? We would just end up here again. If we get back together we have to share the things that are most important to us. The only way for you not to feel you're in competition with my faith is for you to join me. So I think we should start off slow. Kind of like returning to our first love. I want to be wooed and courted. I want us to go to church together. I want…"

"Hey, hold up. How long do we have to go through this exercise?"

"Why?"

"'Cause I'm thinking if you're doing this holy thing, and we're not married that means no…"

"Sex? You got that right, buddy!"

"I knew it." Ron groaned.

"We're starting over, and we're going to do it right this time. Now tell me, what do you want?"

"I told you. I want that woman I saw at the gallery tonight—beautiful, alive, sexy, doing her thing, and taking prisoners."

"That should be simple enough now that I'm back on track. Well, we'd better get going. You still have to drop me off before you can go home."

"You're really going to make me go home?"

"Yes."

"You are wicked."

"Now how can I be wicked and holy at the same time?"

"I don't know, but it's a rather enticing combination. A woman who won't compromise is fascinating. Maybe you should give lessons to your friends."

"I think Muriel has it down. Did you meet her fiancé tonight?"

"Yeah, cool dude. That was a surprise."

"To all of us."

"Here's to more surprises."

"I'm looking forward to them." Adrian knew they weren't finished talking, and there was still more to flesh out, but for tonight it was enough. She remembered that honey was far more inviting than vinegar.

"Me too," Ron whispered.

As they rose to leave, Ron ran his hand down her back then squeezed her familiarly. He leaned forward—a breath away from her lips— looking into her eyes. He said quite seductively, "Are you sure I should go home?"

"I'm sure." She barely breathed, fighting the temptation to give in, knowing that would be a big mistake. She was all about making smart choices for long-term rewards. She knew this was where most women blow it, and she didn't intend to be among that group. The rationalization that he really was her husband and it was all right was snuffed out by a louder voice that reminded her that he had divorced her for another woman. Ignoring her hormones and every womanly instinct within her, she chose to focus on what she ultimately wanted—her husband's respect as well as his love. *Is love a game? Perhaps, to a certain degree.* And while she had no intention of manipulating Ron, she understood that every man needed to slay a dragon and win his maiden fair. Adrian decided to become his greatest adventure.

As Ron led her to the car looking like a little boy striving to be on good behavior, Adrian felt empowered. She would take one day at a time until God told her something different, but for now Ron had to earn her love and trust back. She knew that Ron, with his sports manager mind, believed that anything worth having was worth fighting for. She had no intention of being an easy victory. This time she was playing for keeps.

36

Felicia peered at her mother over the various packages on the table, wondering if there was anything left in the city for anyone to buy. Her mom gave new meaning to the words "shop 'til you drop." Felicia's mother was in town for her annual shopping spree in the big city with her circle of friends. It had taken some convincing to lure her away from them so that Felicia could break the news of her pregnancy to her. By enticing her to high tea at the Ritz, she had managed to procure the private audience she wanted. She comforted herself with the assurance that since they were in a public place her mother would be held at bay from dramatic displays...should she take the news as badly as Felicia expected her to.

Now she was looking rather accusingly at Felicia. "Why didn't you tell me about this sooner?"

"What difference would it have made, Mother?" Felicia had grown beyond caring what anyone thought. She was far too distracted by the changes taking place in her body and the plans she was making in anticipation of the new life that she was carrying. It was all she could do to stay awake and finish all of her projects in the next two months before her delivery date.

"It could have made a lot of difference, Felicia. It's too late to do anything about it now."

Felicia watched her mother take a bite of cucumber sandwich. *How beautiful she is...in a hard sort of way.* Maybe the boredom of being wealthy tightened her features making her perfectly chiseled nose and cheekbones appear sharper than they really are. Others paid to get what she had naturally—and she took arrogant pride in that fact. She took just as much pride in her body that was as slim and taut as a twenty year old's. Usually fanatical about what she ate and her workout routine, Felicia was surprised her mother was indulging in tea cakes today. Her appearance must have upset her more than she cared to admit. Felicia smiled at the thought.

"And what would you have suggested had you known earlier, Mother? That I get rid of my child?"

"It is a rather inconvenient state to find oneself in, don't you think?"

"No, I don't. And since when is having a child a state of affairs? Isn't it supposed to be a blessed occasion filled with wonder at the miracle of life?"

"Yes, if you're married. Felicia, what exactly do you intend to do? You are a single woman. A child literally takes you off the market. You can forget about finding a suitable husband now. The type of man you want to marry is not going to be attracted to that type of baggage."

"Baggage?"

"Yes, baggage. How did you get yourself in this position?"

"Oh, come on, Mother, you know how babies are made. Let's get back to the baggage. Is that what you considered me when you found out that you were pregnant out of wedlock?"

Felicia thought her mother's eyes were going to pop right out of her head.

"Who told you that?" Before Felicia could answer, she practically hissed, narrowing her eyes, "Who told you that?"

Now that Felicia had played her trump card she relaxed, enjoying her newfound power. "No one told me. I overheard Uncle Chester and Auntie Marion talking about it one day. So tell me, how could someone who had been through exactly what I'm going through right now be so callous? Or are you sorry you had me—even after all these years? And it certainly didn't seem to affect your marketability. You ended up marrying rather well since you've never worked a day in your life." She ended her speech by doing a Vanna White indication toward the shopping bags on the coffee table in front of them.

"Don't you talk to me like that, young lady. You have no idea what I went through. And perhaps I wanted to save you from the type of heartache I experienced."

"The only thing that is heartbreaking is how you've treated me as an inconvenience all of your life. Perhaps I wouldn't have made some of the mistakes I made had I found the love I was looking for at home."

"Are you going to blame *me* for your pregnancy? Oh, Felicia, honestly..."

"I'm not blaming you for my mistakes. I am well able and willing to take responsibility for the consequences of my own actions. All I'm saying is that *things* don't equal love, and perhaps if you had given more of yourself I would have been able to make better choices because I would have known what real love looks like."

Felicia's mother blinked rapidly, her eyes looking brighter than usual. "I did the best I could. When I found out I was pregnant with you, I was so frightened. I had no one to go to. Your father laughed in my face when I told him. He said, 'You don't really think I'm going to leave my wife to marry some little black girl and endanger everything I've worked for, do you? I suggest you pretend I never existed if you know what's good for you.' Do you know what it's like to find out that the man you love doesn't really love you and doesn't want you or his own child?"

Felicia fought to keep a straight face. She refused to break down in front of her mother, though this part of the story she did not know. She wondered if her aunt and uncle knew who her father was. How does one deal with the confirmation this late in life that the man you've called Father is not your father and the news that your real father is white? It was a lot to digest. But all of a sudden a lot of things made sense. No wonder she had found herself looking in the mirror, wondering who she really looked like. She could find no resemblance to her mother or father except for her coloring. She had always assumed that she had skipped back through the gene pool to grab her features elsewhere. But no one had been able to account for her gray eyes and her naturally golden, thick, wavy hair. Though the combination was beautiful, their origin had remained a mystery. Now her "father's" careful distance and almost clinical approach to dealing with her was finally understandable. There had been no warm, fuzzy "daddy's little girl" moments for her. How many times had she wondered what it would be like to have a doting daddy like Tracy had? While her mind swirled to complete the puzzle, her mother continued. "When Erwin came along two months later, I still hadn't told anyone. He asked me to marry him right away, and I saw it as the perfect opportunity to give you a father. No one said anything when you came early, but they had a lot to say once they saw you. But Erwin didn't care. He loved me enough to treat you as his own. And now this is the thanks we get? Your sarcasm?"

"Am I supposed to be grateful that you didn't abort me and ended up with a rich husband who subsidized your acceptability with the rest of the family just in case they should ever need a handout? Don't play the pitiful role with me, Mother. It was no fun being the poor little rich girl either."

"You had everything. What else could you have possibly wanted?"

"How about parents who made me feel loved instead of making me feel like a stepchild? Although at the time I didn't know it, I really was one. How ironic is that? Love—that's all most people want from their families. Real simple, and it doesn't cost anything. But then again, maybe hearts are more expensive than I thought."

"What do you want from me, Felicia?"

"Perhaps more than you can give. Maybe you've given everything you have. Maybe it's harder work than I know being married to someone you're really not in love with. Maybe mourning over the love that got away takes more out of you than I know. Or having a constant reminder of what went wrong in your life was more than you could bear so you buried yourself in shopping and avoided me. I don't know. I felt so alone, so unloved for so long. Suddenly I'm very tired of trying to figure out why I can't experience the type of relationship with my mother that Tracy has or that my other friends have. Why is society more appealing than family to you? No matter how unmarketable you think I am, I know I will end up happier than you because I will choose to love my child and not allow my past to dictate and destroy my future. And though I may not end up with a wealthy husband, I will be rich beyond compare because I will know and experience true love."

"I think you've said enough, Felicia."

"I agree."

"You know you've never been very smart. Pretty, but not smart. I tried to give you everything you needed to secure your future so you wouldn't end up like me, and now you've blown it. I will not disgrace myself by trying to qualify this to my friends. If you want to redeem this situation, I suggest you give that child up for adoption and get on with living your life in a more responsible fashion. If you do not do as I've suggested, don't look to us to bail you out." She stopped suddenly. "Does Marion know about this?" The thought that her sister might know about this brought mortification to her countenance. "My sister would love it if I were disgraced. She's always been jealous of the life I've created for myself."

"No, Tracy's parents don't know yet. I asked Tracy not to say anything until I had told you."

"Oh, thank God."

"Don't thank Him yet. They will know because I am keeping my baby, Mother."

Felicia's mother glanced at her watch and reverted back to a business-as-usual voice. "Look, dear, I'm sure after you've had some time to think this over clearly, you will come to your senses. You've worked yourself up into a fine lather, and I've probably exacerbated the entire situation by saying some things that might have been a little painful for you to receive right now." Again she glanced at her watch. "I have to go; the girls are waiting." She stood and gathered her things, and then she stopped to stare penetratingly at Felicia. "Felicia, don't make the same mistake I did. Get rid of it. Life will be easier that way. Call me when you come to your senses. Thanks for tea. It was lovely." Without a backward glance she was gone.

Felicia watched her mother stylishly fade in the distance and concluded her mother was more troubled than she let on. *I'm not angry at her.* Obviously she had done what she had to in order to survive. The shallow world she created for herself is rather pathetic when all is said and done. Felicia would do as her mother asked—she would not make the same mistake she had.

From across the room Felicia was a beautiful picture, a young mother-to-be sitting on a plush couch enjoying her tea and crumpets, though one might wonder why she was talking to herself.

"Well, that went better than I thought it would. Cheers to you too, Mother." With that Felicia lifted her teacup and toasted an invisible companion. She sipped ever so slowly and carefully as the tears began to fall.

37

The workman stood in the doorway impatiently tapping his pen against the clipboard. Adrian looked beyond him to the large crate that was being rolled up the sidewalk. He extended the board toward her. "Sign here, please."

"What is it?"

"I don't know, lady. I just deliver the mail; I don't read it. Came from some art gallery."

Adrian frowned, searching the corners of her mind for what this could possibly be. She hadn't bought anything—certainly not from an art gallery. Inside the phone was ringing. She excused herself to answer it, leaving the man in the doorway propped against the huge delivery.

"Hello?"

"Adrian, I'm glad I caught you!" Mr. Morrow exclaimed. "I hope I'm not too late, I've been meaning to call to let you know to expect a delivery. Things have been so crazy here I realized Suzette hadn't informed you of Ron's purchase."

"Ron's purchase?"

'Yes, he bought the first in the series of your paintings. It should be delivered to you sometime this morning. He went to a great degree of trouble to get that painting too. Someone else bought it, and he tracked them down and made an offer they couldn't refuse. He was determined to have the first one, though there wasn't anything left after the exhibit anyway. Nice to see he was up to the challenge."

"Well, thank you, Mr. Morrow. The deliverymen are here even as we speak. I had better let them in. Thank you for calling."

"Sure thing. And hey, I hope everything works out. Don't be too hard on him. Anyone who goes to that much trouble deserves careful consideration."

"I'll be sure to let you know how things turn out." Adrian smiled. Mr. Morrow sounded quite tickled with himself. She could picture his eyes dancing with anticipation, ready to claim his part in being responsible for her and Ron's reconciliation. Back at the door, the deliverymen had decided not to wait. They had eased the crate onto the foyer floor and were disassembling the protective crate. A card was attached to the box containing the painting. Adrian opened it.

"Here's to no more flights alone at midnight. Let's fly together. I thought this deserved to be in its original home. Enjoy. Love, Ron."

Adrian threw back her head and laughed, clutching the card to her chest. She did a little shimmy step. "Aw sooky, sooky now." Suddenly aware that two pairs of eyes were watching her in amusement, she walked over to them with as much dignity as she could muster and thanked them for their services. She signed the delivery receipt and ushered them back out the door after they had deposited the painting in the living room. She danced back down the hallway to find a knife to begin the delicate surgery of rescuing her painting from its box. Just as she had begun to peel back the protective wrapping the doorbell rang again. Gee, this was turning out to be a busy day full of surprises. She wondered if it was Ron coming to see if his present had arrived safely. She wondered how much he had paid for it. She giggled all over again as she swung the door open to reveal a woman pacing in agitation then turning to stand with her back to the door. She didn't recognize her and was about to ask how she could be of help when the woman turned toward her.

"Amber?" Adrian was taken aback for a moment and didn't know what to say. She took in her disheveled appearance and feared the worse. "What's wrong? Did something happen to Ron?"

"That's a good question. What have you done to him?"

"Done to him? What are you talking about?" Adrian took a step back as Amber took the liberty of entering the house, walking past her and heading down the hall toward the living room.

"Is he here?"

"Are you referring to Ron?" Adrian could feel her blood beginning to boil as Amber stopped to peruse the half unwrapped painting. *Oh no—this woman will not just walk into my house!* "Amber, why are you here, and what do you want?" The tone of her voice snatched Amber's focus back to her.

"I want Ron."

"He is not here, and you shouldn't be here either."

"Don't you have enough?"

"Excuse me?"

"Don't you have enough? You've got a fabulous house—that you didn't have to pay for by the way. Fabulous car, wardrobe, and from what I hear a career now. Do you have to come after my man too? Why can't you just leave him alone?"

"What?" Adrian thought she was going to pass out from the dizzying effect of the blood that rushed to her brain. Truly it was time to deal with this chick head-on. She felt her hand leaving her side and planting itself on her hip. Her feet walked toward the woman who was oblivious to the fact she had stepped over the line. Adrian felt as if she was on the outside of her body observing the unfolding scenario and there was nothing that she could do about what was about to transpire. "Your man?" She inched closer, slowly, deliberately, like a panther stalking her prey. *"Your man?"*

Amber remained silent, hypnotized by the fury in Adrian's eyes.

"Let me tell you something, little girl. You've got a lot of nerve coming where you don't belong looking for something that doesn't belong to you."

"But…"

"Shut up!" Adrian's hand shot up to silence her. "Now you listen to me, and you listen good. My husband, and yes I said *my* husband 'cause a piece of paper means nothing to me. My husband is *not* your man. He never was and he never will be. Don't get it twisted. I'm sorry you made a bad choice and deluded yourself into playing with fire and getting burned. A thank-you for the wake-up call is all I can offer you. What is up with women like you anyway? How can you fool yourselves into thinking you can take somebody's husband and get away with it? And why would you want a man you could take from another woman? Is sleep possible after you pull a stunt like that? Between worrying whether he's going to cheat on you too or just having a messed up conscience about how low you had to go to get somebody, I would think not."

"You don't..."

"I *said* shut up! I'm not finished. You had enough nerve to come over here, I'm going to give you what you didn't come for—some good advice. Have you thought about Jesus? 'Cause Him you can have. Ron you cannot. You need to grow up before you try to dip in grown folks' bizness—as in other people's marriages. It is really not in your best interest to go to a man's wife's house looking for 'your man,'" she made quote signs with her fingers, "who is actually *not* your man 'cause you *might* get *hurt*. Do you understand me? Let's review just in case you're not clear on this. Ron belongs to me, *not* to you. Now I suggest you get out of my house. I may be saved, but I must confess I'm not feeling that saved right now. Got it?"

"Really?" Adrian and Amber spun around toward the sound of Ron's voice, which was coming from the entryway. Leaning against the wall he looked quite pleased with himself as he looked at Adrian. Turning toward Amber, his expression changed and coldness entered his eyes. "Amber, what are you doing here? When I fired you, I told you it was over."

"You wouldn't return my calls, and I needed to talk to you." She was whining, and Ron was looking more removed than ever.

"There is a reason I did not return your calls. There's nothing else to talk about."

"But I think you're confused…"

"No, I was confused when I was with you. I'm very clear on where I want to be now—here with my wife."

"Thank you for that," Adrian said to Ron. Turning back to Amber she spread her hands, palms upward, "Why are you still here? I think we've all said quite enough."

Amber turned toward Ron. "Aren't you going to walk me to the door at least?"

"No, he is not." Adrian made sure Ron knew he was not to move, as men could be naïve from time to time. "You found your way in here, you can find your way out. And trust me—you do not want me to show you to the door."

Amber started moving toward the door. With one backward glance to reveal her wounded pride, she was gone.

Adrian muttered after her, "Let the doorknob hit you where the dog should have bit you."

"Ooo, there is fire in them there hills!" Ron laughed, whether it was more from relief or nervousness it was hard to tell.

Adrian stood looking at him, not cracking a smile. She was not about to let the moment slide. "You know I'm not amused, right?"

"Baby, I had no idea she would have the nerve to come over here like that. I'm sorry you had to go through that."

"I'm not because it puts things in perspective. I was only hard on her because she chose to dishonor me by coming to my home. But the onus is really on you, Ron, because you chose to entangle yourself in a relationship with her."

Ron opened his mouth to say something, but Adrian put up her hand to silence him.

"Let me finish because I am going to say this once, and I am not going to revisit it. I do not intend to rehash past mistakes over and over because that is not what God does with us. As I said, I don't blame Amber for this—I blame you. She could have run after you all day, but you had to make the choice."

"Adrian, we've been through this…"

"Yes, we have, but in light of what just took place I feel I have the right to have my say, so humor me."

Ron lifted his hands in resignation and looked as if he was ready to accept his comeuppance.

"You are the man here, and it is your job as my husband to cover me and protect me as well as provide for me, not just financially but spiritually and emotionally. You put me in harm's way when you decided to uncover me and cover someone else. What if she had really been crazy and came here to harm me? Would you ever have been able to forgive yourself? And I'm not even going to bring up diseases and other unsavory thoughts because that would push me over the edge."

"Adrian, she meant nothing to me."

"I understand that and I am not going to sit around crying about it anymore. *However,* I am not going to excuse it either. It was cowardly and irresponsible. If your needs are not being met, have the decency to say so and we will work it out. If you ever pull that mess again, understand and know there will be no coming back."

"I'm not going anywhere, Adrian. And I'm here, aren't I? I don't know what else to say. I've apologized. I've asked you to forgive me…"

"And I do forgive you, Ron. I just don't want to forgive you again, at least not about the same thing."

"I got that piece, but I don't know what else to do or how to make this better for you. What do you want me to do?"

"I want you to be my prince and not my pain. I want you to talk to me and love me enough to tell me when I'm not giving you what you need. And I want you to never take your needs outside of our home again. I'm willing to do my part if you are willing to do yours."

"You are an incredible woman, do you know that?"

Adrian held up her hand, counted to ten silently, and then took a deep breath, replacing her frown with a smile. "Thank you. And thank you for my painting. Now that was a master move—you get major points for that one. That was a good woo move."

"Mmm, you know I'm just trying to get my woo on."

"And it's workin,' my brotha, it's workin.'"

Ron moved closer to Adrian, taking her in his arms until she was just a breath away. "So how well is it working?"

"Let's just say the pot is on slow simmer. You've got a ways to go to get me to a boil." Adrian smiled mischievously. She was going to take her sweet time and have fun with this.

"I'm up to the challenge."

"Are you now?"

"Oh yes! Never let it be said that Ron Henderson fell down on the job."

They were interrupted by his pager. He grimaced. "Oo, got an appointment. Hey, what are you doing for dinner tonight?"

"Sorry, already got plans," Adrian said casually and smiled. She had plans all right—for a bubble bath.

Ron stopped for a moment and looked at her, comprehending the cat and mouse game. "Oh, I get it. I need to make an appointment, huh? Are you playing hard to get, Ms. Sterling?"

"You can never take a woman's schedule for granted. That's what makes the chase exciting."

"Oh, I got your excitement." He started toward her, and she flitted across the room giggling as she gripped the back of a chair.

"Didn't you say you had an appointment, Mr. Henderson?"

"Yes, I do. We'll pick up on this later. In the meantime I'll have my people check with your people on when we can have dinner. Perhaps Sunday after church?"

"That would be very nice. Have a good day, Mr. Henderson."

"Likewise, Ms. Sterling." Pausing for a moment he looked at her. "Humph." He voiced a grunt of admiration and was gone.

Adrian sank into the chair hugging herself. Truly attitude was everything. She could have been downright evil with him for causing her such pain. But actually out of the pain had come amazing fruit. She had grown as a woman, rediscovered her gifts, and gotten to a better place of honesty with the man she loved. And though it wasn't a perfect world, all in all everything had turned out for the good though she couldn't say she had enjoyed the process. *Whatever works,* she thought. *I am truly the better for the experience. Freer, far wiser, and infinitely surer than ever that God is able to redeem even the deepest mistakes and hurts and make them into something beautiful.*

Truly God had collected all of Adrian's tears and washed her with them, rinsing away the temptation to grow bitter and make wrong choices that could have cost her the very happiness she so longed for. It was so hard not to say everything she was thinking or feeling or to press for the things she wanted. It was even harder to wait for God to unfold things when the time was right, but she was becoming much more aware that timing was everything. *All things in time,* she thought. It was a roundabout way to have her prayers answered, but the bottom line was God was working on Ron, and how long had she been praying for that? But knowing that God never wastes anybody's time in the process, she also realized He was working on her too. Funny how much things can change when you change yourself. She went back to unpacking her painting, humming to herself as she peeled back the layers, "Have thine own way, Lord, have thine own way…"

38

*T*ouch my chicken and you die," Felicia said, her fork raised in the air. This tickled Tracy to no end. She laughed as she pulled her hand away from Felicia's plate.

"Don't you think you need to watch your weight? You don't have much time left to blame your baby for your thighs, you know."

"I don't care. I am going to indulge while I can."

"Spoken like a truly out-of-control woman. Speaking of out of control, I heard your mother was here shopping last week."

"Ah yes, indeed she was. I have such fond memories of our time together." The sarcasm was syrupy and not missed by all in attendance at lunch. Four pairs of eyes stared. Tracy, Adrian, Muriel, and Carla all waited to hear how the news had gone down between mother and daughter.

"How did she take your big news?"

"Let me put it this way. I thought I had a surprise or two up my sleeve that would at least render her to empathy, but no. Once again I was bested by my dear mama. She had some doozies. Talk about some hot revelations that pretty much flattened me—though I didn't give her the satisfaction of knowing that."

"What are you talking about? Revelations like what?" Tracy looked more than a little curious now.

"Did you know that Daddy really isn't my father? That my real father is some white guy who was married and left Mother high and dry when she got pregnant? Is that drama or what?"

All their mouths had dropped open.

Felicia scanned the table. "What? Somebody say something." She went back to working on a chicken bone.

"Alright, since I'm the new big mouth, I have to ask several questions here," Carla said.

"I can always count on you, Carla." Felicia giggled, not too far away from hysteria.

Carla was sitting at full attention now. "First of all, can we ever get together and not have any high-drama moments? Do you all drop bombs on one another regularly or what? Because if that's the case, I'll just prepare myself next time. Second, how could you not know about this? You can't tell me you lived with a man for most of your life and didn't ever suspect that he wasn't really your father. Do you resemble him?"

"First of all, I knew Erwin wasn't my father shortly before I graduated from high school because I overheard my aunt and uncle talking about it. I do have to admit I went into complete denial. Kind of like if I never spoke it, then it wouldn't be true, you know?"

"Shut up! How come nobody ever tells me anything!" Tracy looked completely shocked.

"Second, no, I never thought about it because—I don't know about you guys—but in black families you can have a whole lot of folk not looking like one another because they've snatched back into the gene pool to great-great-grandmother or Aunt Bessie. You can come up with all kinds of different complexions, eyes, and hair textures in one family so people don't really give it that much thought."

"I did because I wanted your hair!"

"Come on, Tracy, get serious."

"I was being serious. But trust me, that was about all I envied. From where I stand, fat wallets equal bankrupt lives. I think being rich is highly overrated. We didn't have much at our house, but we had each other. No secrets, no issues, just lots of love and laughter 'cause we had to entertain each other. I always felt sorry for you—except that year when you got that Barbie I wanted."

"And I always wished that my dad was more like your dad."

"Excuse me for breaking in on your trek down memory lane, but how did all these new revelations make you feel?" Carla was looking pretty befuddled. "I mean how can you just drop all this information in our laps and not process it yourself? It's a shock to my system…and it isn't even my business. I'm sorry, but either you're awfully shut down or superhuman."

Felicia had to laugh at Carla's frankness. "Oh, Carla, at this point in my life nothing that my mother throws at me is a shock. It actually clarified a lot of things and helped me make peace with them. I think not knowing screwed me up more than knowing. So where she thought her news was going to shock some good sense into me, it really made me solidify my decision. It made me sad from the standpoint that I spent almost half my life trying to get love and validation out of a man who not only wasn't my father but was totally incapable of giving me what I needed so badly. As a woman, it seems I've picked him over and over again in all the men I've dated, still trying to squeeze blood out of a turnip, so to speak."

"You know that daddy thing is deep. It really does affect the way we deal with men. You know what they say, women marry their fathers and men marry their mothers." Adrian was in a philosophical mood.

"Yeah, if they manage to get that far," Felicia wryly interjected.

"That's true. But in my case perhaps having a great father messed me up because I assumed that all men were as great as he was. I ended up trusting men that I shouldn't have," Tracy reflected.

"Hmm, that's interesting. But it might also have kept you from getting attached to someone who wasn't deserving of you, Tracy, 'cause you will drop a man like a hot potato if he doesn't treat you right. Notice I've never accused you of being picky. You always seemed to know that you deserved better treatment, so if that's what your daddy did for you, thank God, girl, 'cause there's a whole lot of women not able to because they don't know what love from a man is supposed to look like," Muriel said, quick to put the whole thing into perspective.

"Hmm, true dat. But can we talk about these mothers of ours? Do you think it's a generational thing or what? All these secrets and keeping up of appearances. It's a wonder they haven't all just blown up walking down the sidewalk or something. How could they harbor so much stuff…and for what?" Tracy was shaking her head.

"It's true. My mother is from that same camp. Head held high. Face perfect. Beautiful outfit. Falling apart inside. Don't dare let people see you sweat. That was the mantra of the day. Call it strength if you want to, but that was some serious pride in my estimation. And pride will kill you deader than dead if you don't come clean with yourself at some point. I'm all for letting it all hang out and keeping short accounts these days."

Adrian knew exactly what Tracy was talking about. She told them about her encounter with Amber.

The table came alive with animated responses and reactions that would have been classic to capture on film. No one could believe that dear, sweet, quiet Adrian could go off on somebody like that.

"The nerve of that girl, showing up at your house like that."

"Ooo, chile, I might have hit her!"

"It's a wonder you didn't pummel Ron."

"I tip my hat to you. You're a better woman than I am. I would have lost it."

"I almost did for a minute." Adrian paused to reflect. "But I had to keep my eye on the prize, if you know what I mean. A woman has to use her head these days. If you allow yourself to be led by your feelings, you will end up messing yourself up. You've got to be a thinking woman to get what you want in the end. I knew I had to put her in her place and let Ron know I wasn't going to let that nonsense slide—and then I was cool. Remember, I'm about getting my husband back so I have to pick my battles. I can either be right or have a relationship. I don't see the victory in proving a point and ending up with no man. Trying to prove I'm not a fool and causing me to end up by myself isn't what I ultimately want."

"Humph, that makes sense. I never looked at it that way. I have to confess I've blown Kenny off because of my pride. I felt it was the last remains of something I could salvage for myself. Plus I thought it would be safer for me to dump him before he dumped me. I couldn't take that on top of being pregnant. It was too much with my hormones raging out of control." Felicia looked lost.

"I can understand that, but at some point you need to revisit that because you are going to need help even though you have us. Plus you're having a girl, and there are certain things she needs to get from her father to ground her as a woman. And you know, Felicia, this baby might be just the thing Kenny needs to grow him too. You can at least be open to the idea. If he proves to not be a good father, then at least you tried and you can make another decision on where you go from there. It's not about just you anymore. It's also about that precious little girl."

"I don't know. I still have to think about that one," Felicia stated.

"I have to confess that your situation brought up some deep issues for me too," Carla said quietly.

"You have issues too? I guess we all have stuff, don't we?" Felicia feigned shock.

"Yes, Felicia, white girls need love too." Carla sighed dramatically, and then proceeded to tell them about her evening of realization and disclosure to Al. As the painful events of her own lost love and lack of support from her parents came tumbling out everyone at the table leaned in as if to hold her. Felicia placed her hands on top of Carla's and her eyes were filled with compassion. Even Muriel was uncharacteristically misty eyed, imagining her pain. When Carla had exhausted all the details of the past, silence hung around the table and the atmosphere was tentative. There were no appropriate jokes and chiding for something that cut this deep.

"So what are you going to do?" Felicia asked carefully.

"I finally released the whole thing to God and stopped insisting He do things my way. We're going to start looking into adoption and see what happens."

"You know what's going to happen, don't you? The minute you adopt you'll get pregnant. Funny how that always seems to happen. Do you think sometimes God allows us to get so frustrated we actually end up doing what He wants us to do—and then He gives us what we want as a reward? Think about it. Perhaps God wanted you to rescue some sweet baby in the first place. If you had your own child would you ever have considered adopting?" Adrian was really on a Dr. Phil roll.

"In all honesty, probably not. I would have been happy to stick to what was mine and call it a day." Carla chuckled. "God is something else."

"I'm always fascinated when you people start talking about God. You act as if He's a person."

"Well, He is in a sense, Felicia. Even though He's God and omnipotent and all of that. He's the only perfect Father in the universe." Adrian's eyes glowed at the thought of the pleasure she got from her relationship with the supernatural Lover of her soul.

"The only constant friend, comforter, adviser—you name it. I don't know how anybody lives without the Lord in his life," Muriel chimed in with enthusiasm. "I'm not trying to dis you or anything, but I just don't know how you do it. I'd be a wreck trying to figure out all the ins and outs of my life without God helping."

"I am a wreck at this point. Ain't no need in trying to play it off 'cause I think it's pretty clear to see I am not on top of my game. As a matter of fact, I don't even know what the game is anymore."

"Felicia, you know I've never tried to push Jesus down your throat because I feel everyone has his own personal journey and everyone has to decide on his own that he needs a Savior. But I do highly recommend Him if you ever decide you could use a little heavenly counsel and assistance. Hey! I'm singing at church this Sunday. You should come! Even Ron is coming." Adrian broke into a big grin.

"Ron, huh? I keep working my way back to you, girl…" Muriel broke into song and then exploded into laughter. "Girl, you know you've broken that man all the way down. See, that proves my point. When a man loves a woman he'll do anything to get her. I don't know why women won't get a clue…"

"Yeah, that move with the painting was sweet. Maybe you should see if Ron would be interested in training some brothers. Maybe I can talk him into it on Sunday myself. You know Tracy and I have been talking about coming to church with you, Adrian. Sounds like this would be the perfect time. What do you think, Trace?" Felicia could feel Tracy's reluctance from across the table. She didn't know why she was always so resistant about this. She refused to discuss "religion" as she put it because it always made people upset. What was she afraid of? Did she think God was going to bite her or what? And wasn't He everywhere anyway? Felicia decided she was going with or without Tracy.

"Sounds like a plan," Tracy finally said. Felicia looked at her. Tracy actually seemed all right with going. She wondered what had lowered Tracy's resistance but dared not ask.

"I think we should all make a day of it, don't you? Al enjoyed you so much at the gallery I know he'll be game. What about you and Brad, Muriel?" Carla suggested, always ready to turn an event into a party.

"I'll double-check with him, but I'm sure it will be fine."

"Oh goody! This is gonna be fun! That isn't being irreverent, is it?" Felicia asked.

Adrian, Muriel, and Carla laughed.

"What?" Felicia didn't get what was so funny.

"Oh, Felicia, I think you probably make God laugh a lot. But seriously, God is really not so big a mystery, you know. He wants to be friends with us, and that includes being there through the laughter as well as the tears. He's in for all of it, so yes, to answer your question, you *can* have fun at church," Adrian explained.

She was always so good at explaining these things. It was still hard for them to imagine her telling anyone off, she was always so patient with them. But it was liberating for them to know that she could go there. Suddenly she was more real. Lately they all were sharing and handling their stuff together. It made the burdens so much lighter and the road ahead not so overwhelming. It was a relief to know that everyone had issues, and there was no need for pretense. Who needed to grow old early by keeping all that stuff bottled up inside? It felt so good to let it out.

Felicia didn't know if she was being hormonal or just overwhelmed with feeling awfully good at that moment, but she let the tears flow down her face freely. She laughed as she dabbed at her eyes with her napkin.

"Felicia, girl, are you alright?" They were all a bit alarmed.

"You know, everything *is*. Everything is incredibly alright. I'm just having a feel-good moment. I'm glad Muriel is getting married. And that you and Tracy made up."

Muriel and Tracy both looked sheepish.

"What? We didn't make up. I just wrestled Tracy to the floor."

"I'd say you had nothing to do with it. That Brad is a charmer. I think he made me his assignment at Adrian's exhibit."

"Mmm hmm...look but don't touch, girl." Muriel was grinning widely.

"Don't worry. I don't think I'd want to tangle with the likes of you over anything that was important to you." Tracy feigned fear.

Felicia laughed. "Now that's what I'm talking about. Everything is as it should be. You know what? I really love you guys. How could I have missed it for so long? Thanks for being there in spite of all my madness."

"We love you back." Muriel was misting up again. Blaming it on allergies, she refused to accept that she was turning into a big softie.

"Ooo, I feel a group hug coming on." Carla was the first one up. The rest followed, and Felicia could explain it no other way than to say that wrapped in that circle of love she felt safer than safe.

39

*I*t was a beautiful Indian summer day. The kind where you're tempted to dress for summer, but it's really not appropriate if you're a fashionista. Felicia had no idea what the appropriate dress was for church. Searching for in-between wardrobe when you're seven months pregnant is no joke, but she managed to pull it off in a soft, winter white suit with matching slides. The jacket was three-quarter length with a beautiful organza empire top underneath that peeked from just beneath the hem of the jacket, adding a beautiful fringe to it. The skirt was slim and tapered to just below the knees. Unless you were standing directly in front of her, you would not know she was pregnant. Her hair swept up and back off her face and beautiful diamond studs in her ears that matched the twinkle in her eyes gave her a look of chic innocence.

Waving to get Tracy's attention she quickly paid the cab driver and made her way toward her. Tracy was looking rather lovely herself. Felicia chuckled, wondering if they both looked like little girls playing dress up. She could tell that Tracy also had been careful in her selection, taking a little more thought to all the details. A soft, banana-colored sheath with a matching swing coat made her look as if she were floating when she walked and brought out the flecks of hazel in her eyes. She had on classic pearls and matching drops in her ears. She could have stepped off the pages of *Vogue,* yet it didn't look overdone, just yummy. Yes, that was the word.

"Hey, girl, where are the others?" Felicia hugged Tracy and wondered again why she seemed so uncomfortable when it came to church.

"Adrian is probably already inside, and you know Muriel will be late." They laughed. As they reached the front doors, they seemed to swing open magically as two greeters smiled at them in stereo.

"Here we go. We're off to see the wizard," Tracy murmured.

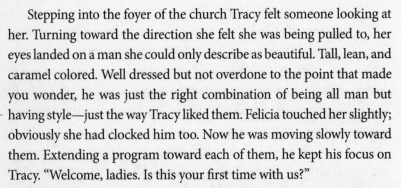

Stepping into the foyer of the church Tracy felt someone looking at her. Turning toward the direction she felt she was being pulled to, her eyes landed on a man she could only describe as beautiful. Tall, lean, and caramel colored. Well dressed but not overdone to the point that made you wonder, he was just the right combination of being all man but having style—just the way Tracy liked them. Felicia touched her slightly; obviously she had clocked him too. Now he was moving slowly toward them. Extending a program toward each of them, he kept his focus on Tracy. "Welcome, ladies. Is this your first time with us?"

"Uh huh." Tracy could have kicked herself, but her brain was blank as she looked into his face. *He has such pretty teeth,* she thought. Boy did she feel retarded.

"Well, please, don't make it your last," he said, still not breaking his gaze from hers. She could feel Felicia trying to move her along, but she felt rooted to the spot.

"Thank you, I'm sure we will come again. I'm Felicia and this is my cousin Tracy. We're friends of Adrian Sterling...I mean Henderson." Tracy could hear Felicia's voice on her left side.

"Yes, I'm sure we will." Tracy was on automatic. The man reached out his hand to shake hers.

"I'm David Grant. I'm an elder here. Please let me know if you have any questions or I can be of assistance."

"Thank you, David." Tracy was finally able to muster a response. She was relieved to hear Carla calling.

"Hey, Tracy, Felicia, over here!"

"It was nice meeting you, David. Will you excuse us?"

"Of course. Enjoy the service."

With that he was off to greet others, but every now and then Tracy could feel him checking her out as she waited in the lobby with Carla and Al for Muriel and Brad. Finally they decided they should go in and find seats.

Entering the sanctuary, Tracy felt sad. Her thoughts drifted back to the times she spent with her father in church. He always loved it, lifting his rich baritone voice in song. Sometimes he would embarrass her, he sang so loud. When he grew ill he would listen to all his favorite gospel songs and draw such comfort from them. Tracy just didn't get it. She felt he had been way too passive and surrendered to death unnecessarily because he was looking forward to being with the Lord far more than wanting to remain with her and her mother on earth. *Why wouldn't God heal someone who loved Him so much?* Tracy wondered again. She had vowed not to adopt her dad's pie-in-the-sky mentality. Those who rely on themselves without depending on the crutch of God seem to work harder and practice more discipline in making life happen for themselves. But could it be that she had just been angry at God all this time for taking away what was dearest to her? And could she have been wrong? Adrian, Muriel, and Carla certainly could not be called passive. They were passionate and down to earth, dealing with their individual struggles realistically. They had never been judgmental toward her, and they had been transparent with their lives and loving as friends. These were all things Tracy pondered as the music began to swirl around her.

Boy, things certainly are different from the last time I attended church, Tracy decided. A lone ballet dancer came on stage bathed in light. Adrian's rich voice sounded as if she were standing directly in front of her singing, "Where would I be, you only know, I'm glad you see, through eyes of love. A hopeless case, an empty space if not for grace....Amazing grace, how sweet the sound. I once was lost, but now I'm found....I was a hopeless case, an empty space if not for grace." She could hear Felicia sniffing beside her but couldn't turn to look at her because her own eyes were filled with emotion overflowing, spilling onto her cheeks as the woman danced in celebration of her brokenness and God's redemption. There was a hush over the sanctuary, and all Tracy could say was in that moment she sensed the reality of God. She could feel His presence in the room. She was wondering if He was smiling because she had finally made it to this place. And then the preacher was preaching, not the stereotypical message with dramatics that she associated with those deeply embedded in religion but just a simple, to-the-point message.

"It doesn't matter where you've been or what you've done, how deep the disappointment, how stupid the mistakes—there is grace available for you. A place of renewing and refreshing. A place of restoration. God knows that all have sinned, have done everything from the ridiculous to the sublime. And yet He graciously says, Come let us reason together, though your sins be as scarlet, I will make you white as snow. Notice He said *He* will do the work of redemption. Some of you might feel that you are beyond repair. That you've strayed so far there can be no way to find the embrace of God. But He stands waiting with arms open wide to claim you, to hold you, to make you His own. Won't you come this morning? Come to the altar and lay down your heavy burdens, lay down your tears, your mistakes, your struggles, and even your questions. God is waiting to meet you here. This is not about anybody around you. This is between you and God. Someone out there may even be angry at God this morning. He can handle it. He says be angry and sin not."

Tracy felt as if her mail was being read, but she didn't care. What he was saying made so much sense. She could feel waves of relief washing over her. Perhaps this had been the missing piece? All the men in the world could not fill the gap created to embrace a holy God. He had made a room in her heart for Himself that no one else could fill. Small wonder complete satisfaction couldn't be found elsewhere.

"Today can be your day to find your way back to Him. To kiss and make up. To experience joy unspeakable and full of glory, the peace of God that passes all understanding. Why does it surpass understanding? Because it equips you to walk through the hard places of life with confidence, knowing He is able to bring you out as not just a survivor but an overcomer. I'm not preaching a lazy gospel. This is not a message to the faint of heart. It takes courage to have faith. Strength to stand firm in the trials of life. To have peace in the face of the fearsome."

So Father wasn't being a coward; he just knew something I didn't. Suddenly Tracy felt ashamed. Ashamed because she realized that her father had more courage than she had realized. He hadn't been weak. He had not abandoned her. Tears of relief flooded her face.

"Won't you come? Come and give your heart to God this morning?" the preacher asked.

The words of the song once again filled the sanctuary. "Where would I be, you only know…" Muriel leaned over to Tracy. Placing her hand on top of hers she looked into her eyes gently questioning, "Would you like me to go up there with you?" She indicated the altar where some were already gathering. Somewhere in the back of Tracy's mind she wondered when Muriel had arrived. She hadn't felt her slip into the seat beside her. A tug of war began within her. Part of her longed to run to the altar and throw herself on God's mercy. Another part still felt unworthy. And though she knew there was nothing she could ever do to earn God's mercy, the greater culprit in dissuading her from giving into whatever it was that was tugging on her heart was a flood of uncertainty. Uncertainty of her ability to honor her commitment to God. She was overwhelmed by the irony. She who longed for a committed relationship more than anything was finding it difficult to commit herself. She hung her head, admitting to herself that it was she who was the coward. She quietly shook her head, unable to meet Muriel's eyes. She simply wasn't ready. Glancing toward Felicia she found the seat empty. Felicia was already on her way toward the altar sobbing loudly and held in Carla's grip.

Felicia thought her heart would burst. All the accumulated pain of years gone by had grown like a massive pimple in the center of her heart to the point where it could be contained no longer. Intellectually she felt completely embarrassed that she had been unable to contain herself. Even before she reached the church she had felt the heaviness begin to grow in her chest and the pit of her stomach. It was as if a well stream had opened up from the depths of her soul. She had felt the flood growing within her as she made her way into the sanctuary.

As the first words of the song penetrated her heart, she could keep it in no longer. She needed God's grace. She wanted that grace. She was so relieved to know she could have it. The pastor was speaking to her. As if he had overheard her fears, witnessed her disappointments, been privy to all her stupid mistakes, and yet he was so tenderly offering her a respite in the desert of her soul. As she walked toward the altar she could feel the pressure building in her stomach. In fact, it took her breath away for a moment. She stopped. Carla looked at her with concern. Felicia steadied herself and continued walking. Taking deep breaths to clear her head she repeated the prayer, "Forgive me, Lord. Come into my heart. Be my Lord, my Savior…" All of a sudden the pressure increased until she was bowled over. Grabbing her stomach, she cried out, "Help me, God!" And then the dam broke. In horror she looked down at the wetness on her legs and passed out.

When she came to she was being wheeled through the doors of the church on a stretcher. The faces of Tracy, Muriel, and Carla were hovering over her. "What happened?"

"Your water broke."

"What? But it's too early. I can't lose my baby now…"

"Felicia, you are not going to lose your baby. Everything is going to be alright. Just remain calm. We'll have you at the hospital in no time. I've already called your doctor." Leave it to Adrian to always be the calming force in the midst of the storm.

As they lifted her into the ambulance Carla grinned mischievously. "Leave it to you to bring a dramatic close to the service! But at least you'll never forget the day you gave your heart to God, that's for sure."

"No, I guess I won't." Felicia smiled weakly, then the ambulance doors were closing. "We'll meet you at the hospital!" Tracy yelled over the siren and the vehicle took off.

Everything seemed to happen so fast. A thousand things were going through Felicia's mind. Clients to call, things not yet done. The half-ready baby room. Kenny. God. The song that kept going through her head. And then the doctors were surrounding her. Pushing and prodding. And the pain was making her eyes cross. A familiar face with a mask was peering down at her through the haze of all the others in attendance. "Well, well, what have we here?"

"Kenny, what are you doing here? Aren't you on the wrong floor?" Felicia grit her teeth.

"Nope, I'm right where I'm supposed to be."

"How did you know I was here?"

"I'm a doctor, remember? I know other doctors, including yours. Since you wouldn't call me back, I told her to let me know when it was time."

"But…ooo!" Another contraction hit, rendering her silent.

"But nothing! Hey, this is great. I finally have you where I want you— flat on your back, unable to talk back."

"Kenny, I don't need you…"

"Yes, you do, Felicia. And like it or not, you are not getting rid of me.

This is my baby too. When are you going to get it through your thick, pretty little head that I do love you? I want to be here for you, but I am not going to let you rearrange who I am—so cut a brother some slack, okay?"

"What! But I thought…"

"As my mother would say, 'Do you know what thought made a man do?' Now is not the time to tell you, but what you think and what is really true are two different things. And if you would pick up your phone and call somebody back so a body could get a word in edgewise, you might find out some things you need to know instead of assuming."

Another contraction hit Felicia, and all she could do was look at him while the tears spilled out the corners of her eyes and onto the pillow. Kenny smoothed her hair back from her face and looked at her tenderly. "Look at you. Don't mess with me, I've got a praying mama, and she didn't raise no deadbeat dads. Looks like you're stuck with me, girl, so I suggest you concentrate on pushing that baby out instead of pushing me away."

In the waiting room Tracy paced back and forth. "I can't believe this! I'm supposed to be in there. What do you mean I can't go in?" The nurse was shifting nervously.

"I'm sorry, miss, but the father said he would prefer if no one else was admitted in."

"The father!" Tracy's eyes narrowed. "And who would that be?"

"Dr. Kenny…"

"Kenny? Kenny is in there? Oh, this is priceless."

"I think it's great," Adrian's voice quietly broke through the highly charged atmosphere. "After all, Tracy, it's where he belongs. Good for him. And who said there weren't any good brothers left? Just when you thought it was over, one steps up to the plate strong."

"We'll see…" Tracy said, not so sure of how things could possibly be going between Felicia and Kenny without her to run interference.

Forever felt longer than usual as the friends waited impatiently for the new arrival. Finally Kenny came out to let them know that everything had gone well. The baby was fine but under observation. Felicia was sleeping soundly. They could wait for her to wake up if they liked. Watching her sleep, Tracy thought of how sweet and childlike she looked. There was a vulnerability about her that wasn't there when she was awake to defend and protect herself. She was beautiful. Tracy wondered if all the attitudes and thoughts they harbored were always that apparent on people's faces, even when they weren't aware of them. How many men had they scared off if that was the case? A soft knock interrupted her thoughts. She turned to see David Grant entering the room.

"Is everything alright? Pastor was wondering…"

"Everything is fine. Thank you for coming."

"No problem. Is there anything I can do for you while I'm here?"

Kenny stepped in. "You must be Tracy. It's good to meet you." He shook Tracy's hand in a professional manner that signaled he was claiming his territory. "Listen, why don't you go on home and get some rest. She might be sleeping for a while, and I've got this. I'll let her know I sent you home." He looked at David as if to give him a cue. David took it.

"Why don't you let me give you a ride home?"

"Are you sure?" Tracy looked at Kenny. Kenny nodded.

"I'm sure. Go on. You can come back later. I promise you won't miss any more excitement."

The rest of the room was stirring.

"Maybe we all need to go and come back later. Let Felicia have a little time to regroup." Muriel was following Brad's lead.

"Why don't we get a little something to eat and meet back here at seven? Same place, same bat channel?" Carla's stomach was rumbling.

"Sounds good to me." Al was ready to go.

"I know just the place." Ron whipped out his cell phone then hesitated, looking at Adrian. "You are still available for dinner, aren't you?"

"Oh, most definitely!" Adrian smiled.

Suddenly Tracy looked from Adrian to Ron and smiled, her faith growing by the minute for a beautiful future. To her and Felicia's relief, God had worked things out for Adrian—perhaps it was because Adrian had worked with God. Suddenly Tracy felt very tired but happy. "You all go ahead. I think I really do need to take a nap. It's been quite a day. I think I need some time alone to absorb everything." With that she turned to David and smiled. "I'm ready."

These were loaded words as the possibilities were endless. Though she hadn't taken that walk up the altar, Tracy felt a sense of relief knowing that God was waiting. The ball was in her court, and she felt ready for a change. Ready for new beginnings. Ready for love. Ready for any and everything that God had in store. Looking at David, the statistics on the lack of men didn't seem so daunting anymore. After all, she only needed one man, not a dozen. Perhaps her focus had been wrong. It wasn't about trying to find the diamonds among the scraps; it was about being a diamond herself and waiting to be found at just the right time. It wasn't about what was unavailable and out of reach; it was all about what she was going to be anyway with or without anyone by her side. She was part of the last ten percent of eligible women who were the total package—a good thing that a man could celebrate finding. Yes, Tracy liked that idea. She was ready for that.

40

*M*ama, were you asleep?"

Tracy's mother denied that she had been deeply wandering through her dreams for quite some time.

Tracy chuckled. She always woke her mother up, and her mother always denied that she had been asleep. It was their personal ritual.

"Just thought I'd let you know Felicia had the baby prematurely but everything is alright. She's beautiful and very, very tiny, but she's a little fighter."

"Just like Felicia."

"Yeah, I guess that's true."

"Does Florence know?"

"Would Florence care, Mama?"

"Somewhere beneath all the designer fashions and jewelry the heart of a mother beats. I'll give her a call, and see if I can convince her it's not a crime to soften up a bit."

"I will be happy to leave that chore to you."

"You got it, baby girl."

"Mama?"

"Yes."

"I love you, you know that?"

"I know that."

"No, I mean I really, really love you."

"Are you alright?"

"I am great. Over the moon. And so grateful that God gave me to you."

"So am I. What's this all about?"

"Oh, you know, you just get to a place in life where things happen around you that put everything into perspective. You can't help but be supremely grateful for even the things you thought you were thankful for but really had taken for granted until you see how someone else completely missed out."

"I see…"

"Actually you don't, and it would take way too long to explain all the specifics, but just know I thank God and I thank you for all you did when I was a child and all you do now as my mom and my friend."

"That is so sweet. You're welcome. I guess you'll get around to letting me in on the details at some point."

"I will. And Mama?"

"Yes, Tracy?"

"I think I finally get it now."

"Get what now?" Tracy's mother was fighting to stay awake.

"The whole peace bit. Remember when I asked why you didn't want to get married again after Daddy died? I couldn't understand how you could just settle into being alone, and you said that you had become well acquainted with peace and you weren't interested in anyone disturbing it. Remember?"

"Mmm hmm. I remember." Tracy's mother yawned into the phone. Tracy chuckled again. Like mother, like daughter. Their body clocks were serious. The Stewart women had to have their sleep.

"I'm not going to hold you any longer. I just wanted to let you know I finally know what you're talking about."

"That's a very important lesson to learn."

"I know! 'Cause otherwise you can make a lot of bad choices that rob you of even more peace. It's a vicious cycle."

"What do you all say? 'True dat!'"

"You better watch yourself trying to get hip on me! Get some sleep, Mama. I'll talk to you tomorrow."

"Okay, baby. Good night."

Peace. A profound concept and an even greater feeling. Who da thunk it, that she'd finally arrive in this place? The phone jolted her from her thoughts. It had to be Derrick.

"Yo, bro, where you been? Missin' all the excitement. Felicia had her baby!"

"Really? That's great. I was off wrestling Shirley to the ground. I finally got her to agree to marry me."

"Wow, Derrick! That's great." Tracy thought about how they had jokingly said that if they weren't married in another five years they'd marry each other. Oh well, she was on her own now. She smiled, realizing that actually that was all right with her. "That really is great!"

"Don't sound so excited—it's like you're happy to be getting rid of me."

"Oh, Derrick! I'm not getting rid of a brother, I'm gaining a sister." She was placating him now.

"Yeah, right. So we're going to do this in a month. Any chance you'll be off your man fast or whatever you call it? I think I have someone I want you to meet."

"Really? I don't know; I'll see how things go. I'm beginning to enjoy the space I'm in. I might want to hang out here for a while."

"Well, don't stay there too long."

"I don't think I can. Actually I met someone interesting today. Someone I might want to check out, but I'm gonna take it slow."

"Whoa! What's up with you, girl? You trying to grow up on me?"

"Something like that. You know, Derrick, I've made this major discovery. Peace is a beautiful thing. It takes all the pressure and rush out of life. No more struggle, no more fear of drowning in loneliness. I'm just floating—and it's sweet."

"Well you float on, my sistah, I've got an early morning meeting with you know who. Gotta get some shut-eye."

"I know you're not rushing me off the phone, Mr. Late Night Talker. Oooh I get it, Mm, mm, mm. It's starting already. Now that you're getting married, I better get used to you not having time for me. Another one bites the dust."

"That is not even true."

"Yes, it is, but you know what? It's all good. It's just another part of the journey. And you have my blessings."

"Whatever! You are getting too deep for me. I'll see you tomorrow."

As Tracy hung up the phone and settled into the depth of her bed, she considered all that had transpired that day. She revisited the church service in her mind, reliving the moment that hope had flooded her being. Her heart had sprouted wings. She could feel herself soaring above all the things and feelings that had bogged her down before. Life was good and could only get better, though nothing about her situation or her single status had changed. Something greater had occurred. She had changed. Her outlook had changed. And suddenly the same old situations looked altogether different. Reaching for her journal she wrote quickly, following her stream of consciousness.

Dear Diary,
　The beauty of love
　　　like a rainbow that everyone can see
　　　　and pray to grasp
　　　Is all the beautiful shades
　　　　that are not
　　　　　so far out of reach after all.
At the tip of our fingers

always available
   promising covenant
      warmth and strength
   The beauty of love is
         you have more power than you thought
      when you discover
            that love begins with you
      begins with God
            begins with you...

41

Felicia stood looking at the new life on the other side of the glass. An attending nurse smiled as she adjusted the little cap on her baby's head. She was so tiny, so helpless. Oh how she could relate to feeling that way! The doctor had told her she was holding her own, calling her a little fighter. "Just like you," Kenny had said. Mother love flooded her heart as she watched her and settled on her face. Eyes shining above a smile that could not be contained, she made her way back to her room.

As she swung the door open she stopped short. "Mother!" There was her mother in deep conversation with Kenny. *What has she said to him? He seems none the worse for wear from his encounter with her—so far anyway.* Her mother swung around to face her. Felicia took note of the large box placed at the foot of her bed.

Her mother's eyes followed hers. "I brought some things for the baby. Hopefully her clothes will not join the things I've sent you at the back of your closet."

Felicia lowered her eyes as if she had been caught with her hand in the cookie jar.

"Hey, where's my niece?" Tracy stuck her head in the door, and then eased into the room upon spotting Felicia's mother. "Aunt Florence! What...?"

"What am I doing here? Why wouldn't I be here, Tracy?"

"I don't know. I just thought..."

"You know the women in your family do a lot of thinking," Kenny interrupted, looking straight at Felicia.

Felicia giggled, thankful Kenny was there to run interference should the need arise.

"You all need to watch that. You know what thought made a man do, don't you?" Kenny remarked.

"Hey, that's my line." Felicia's mother smiled a brilliant smile at Kenny before turning her attention back to Tracy and Felicia.

"I had already started shopping for the baby. When Marion called me first thing this morning, I caught the next plane I could. I am your mother, you know!" she said, looking directly at Felicia.

"So you're excited about being a grand…?"

Felicia's mother held up her hand to silence Tracy.

"Don't say it! I may be grand, but I will be 'Nana' to…" She stopped and frowned at Felicia. "What is her name, anyway?"

"Celeste, Mother. Celeste Amor."

"Speaking of Celeste, would you like to accompany me to see her?" Kenny asked, before turning to Felicia. "Baby, you need to rest. Your mother and I will be back shortly."

"Are you sure?" Felicia was uncertain of how much of her mother Kenny should be subjected to.

Kenny headed toward the door, and Felicia's mother followed behind. She turned before going through the door. "I like him," she mouthed before disappearing through the door.

Tracy laughed. "Well, will wonders never cease? Who'da thunk it? Grand…I mean Nana Flo showing up after all she put you through. And Kenny! Large and in charge and handling her. I'm glad I got to see it 'cause I don't think I would have believed it if you told me."

"You better believe I'm pinching myself." Then Felicia got a mischievous glint in her eye. "Hey, let's open the box and see what she brought Celeste." Then stopping with a worried look on her face, she said, "You don't think St. John makes things for babies, do you?"

"If they do, you know Aunt Flo found it." They both laughed.

"You couldn't possibly be having so much fun without me being in the mix," Muriel said as she entered the room, followed closely by Brad, who was carrying an incredible bouquet of flowers.

"Wow! It looks like a flower shop in here already. Somebody's got good taste!" Brad looked at the other bouquets with admiration.

"That would be Kenny."

"Kenny, huh? The same Kenny who was missing in action? He's suddenly Mr. Responsible? That's interesting."

"Actually, he wasn't missing in action. If I had gone to the library I would have found him. He was studying to get his certification in a specialized area of his practice." Felicia looked a little sheepish.

"Well, there you have it!" Brad dramatically said with a sweep of his arm as if he were an attorney making his case.

"There you have what?" Adrian asked as she held the door for Ron to make his way through the door with a basket filled with baby articles.

"Never mind!" Felicia was not about to rehash how silly she had been in the presence of other men.

"Never mind what? I haven't missed anything have I? How's the baby?" Carla came bursting through the door, followed by Al.

"She's doing fine. She has to stay here for a while, but I get to go home tomorrow."

"Alright! So that means we need to coordinate the troops to help out. We'll need to get you home and settled in and make sure you have some meals…"

"I've got the going home part covered." Everyone's eyes turned toward the door to see Kenny and Felicia's mother standing there.

"I think I can handle the meals part," Felicia's mother answered. All eyes were on her.

Felicia broke the awkward silence with a round of introductions. "Everyone, this is my mother. And you've already met Kenny."

There was a quick flurry of mumbled hellos and then silence again.

"She's a beautiful baby. She looks just like you when you were a baby." Felicia's mother's eyes were misting.

Al gave an uncomfortable cough. Carla chimed up. "Hey, I think it's high time we saw little Miss Celeste." There was a collective seconding the motion as they all started moving toward the door.

"Go all the way down the hall and then to the left," Kenny instructed. Catching a look from Felicia's mother, he moved toward the door. "As a matter of fact, I'll show you."

Felicia stood still as her mother crossed the room toward her. Slowly she smiled. No longer did she wilt beneath her mother's gaze. Perhaps it was because she was now a mother herself. She had someone to live for who was completely dependent on her. She felt strong. She felt good. She felt like a woman on even footing with her mother. She was free because she finally realized she had nothing to prove to her or anyone else anymore. Suddenly she felt sorry for her mother.

"Felicia, I know I said some hurtful things that last time…"

Felicia put a finger to her mother's lips, shushing her. "Mother, it's alright. I understand. You did the best you could with what you had to work with."

"Yes, I did. But I shouldn't have expected a child to understand that."

"But I'm not a child anymore, and I get it." Felicia laughed. "Thank goodness for growing up, huh? Hey, that means that one day Celeste will get over all the foolishness I subject her to."

"Perhaps because of what you know now you can keep it to a minimum." Felicia's mother laughed. "You're off to a good start, Felicia. You have a good man who loves you. Wonderful friends who seem to be there for you. You're actually ahead of the game."

"Wait a minute! Kenny told you that he loves me?"

"Yes, he did. But you need to know he's his own man, Felicia. You won't be able to force his hand. He has very definite ideas about how life should go. Just give him the room he needs to get all his ducks lined up and you all will be alright, okay?"

Now it was Felicia's turn to get teary. All her life she had waited for this moment. All she had ever wanted was a mother to share motherly advice and intimate exchanges. On impulse she grabbed her mother and hugged her. Her mother stiffened at the uncustomary burst of affection, and then relaxed and returned the embrace. *When was the last time Mother hugged me,* Felicia wondered. "Thanks, Mama." She sounded like a little girl. Slowly her mother extricated herself from Felicia's arms. She self-consciously wiped the corners of her eyes and glanced at her watch.

"Oh dear! Look at the time. I promised Lorraine I would meet her at the Zodiac room. I'll check on you later, okay?" She turned back at the door. "And Felicia? I do love you."

"I love you too." Felicia watched her go, the tears flowing freely. Her mother was looking slightly uncomfortable at her display of emotion. As the door closed behind her, Felicia took a deep breath and surveyed the room. The flowers. The baby basket. Her mother's box…

Tracy poked her head in the door. "Is it safe?"

"It's safe." Felicia absentmindedly wiped her eyes.

"You sure you're okay?" Tracy was almost tiptoeing into the room and was followed by the rest of the gang.

"Everything is perfect. I feel as if I've been given a whole new life."

"Actually, that is exactly right," Adrian said. "When you said that prayer on Sunday, even though it was interrupted…" They all laughed. "When you said yes to Jesus, He gave you not only new life but a new beginning. 'Old things have passed away; behold, all things have become new.'"

"It's so ironic that you would be born again and your baby would be born on the same day. Talk about a double whammy blessing!" Carla was practically vibrating.

"Wow! That's true! God is amazing, huh Adrian!"

"And the most amazing thing of all is that an amazing God loves us no matter how unamazing we can be at times."

"That's why its called 'amazing grace'!" chirped Carla.

"Humph! I always thought grace was a person in that song."

"You are kidding, right?" Muriel was frowning. Felicia laughed as everyone looked at her with great concern. "Of course I am, you silly goose!"

"Oh, I feel a group hug coming on." Carla led the pack. As all the men watched, the women encircled Felicia.

"I love you guys!" Felicia averred.

"We love you back." Tracy's voice was muffled.

Felicia sighed. Life was good. But the best parts of life were moments like these—when you learn that all the love you'd been looking for was there all along.

The Last Ten Percent
Discussion Questions

1. What did you think of the communication between Tracy, Adrian, Felicia, Muriel, and Carla? What obstacles do you encounter when you communicate with your close friends?

2. What support system do you have in place to help you during difficult times? Why are transparency and accountability so important among close friends?

3. Felicia and Tracy longed for a committed love. Carla longed for a child. Adrian longed for her husband to return. What is your heart's deepest longing? What has kept you from obtaining what you desire?

4. Felicia and Tracy gave in to momentary pleasure, only to face the consequences of rejection and hurt. What have you given in to in the past that you presently regret? How can you keep from making the same mistake in the future?

5. What did Adrian do when she realized how narrow her life had become? In what ways can you move beyond your comfort zone?

6. How did hiding the truth hinder Muriel's emotional and spiritual growth? How would her life have been different if she had confided in her friends earlier?

7. What would it take to make you decide to break unhealthy patterns in your life? What unresolved needs affect your choices in your significant relationships? In what ways have your fears caused you to sabotage the obtaining of your desires?

8. Were you able to relate to the interaction between Adrian and her mother? What generational habits have you embraced in your own life? What were the results of repeating the same things your parents did? How might the outcome have been different if you had done something different?

9. How did Adrian's faith in Jesus help her cope with her husband's infidelity? Where do you draw strength when you feel vulnerable?

10. How open are you to the unexpected ways God might bless you? What do you fear most about surrendering the details of your life to God?

11. Carla finally forgave herself and accepted God's forgiveness for her past mistakes. What mistakes or bad choices can you give to God right now to experience freedom? What mindset can you adopt in order to forgive yourself?

12. Tracy and Felicia's families were very different. How did their upbringing shape their attitudes about love? What experiences and encounters have been the most instrumental in shaping your opinion of love?

13. What are your views on interracial dating? How has insisting on a specific type of man perhaps limited your opportunity to get the love you want?

14. Which woman did you identify with most? Why?

15. What causes you to enter into situations you know are not good for you? What will you do to make more heart-smart choices?

16. How did facing the consequences of her choices change Felicia? What experiences in your life have changed you for the better?

17. What plan did Adrian have to reconnect with Ron? What can you actively do to secure the love and life you want?

18. Have you experienced pain like Muriel, Adrian, Tracy, Felicia, or Carla? How does this pain affect your present? Your future?

19. What constructive steps can you take toward healing during times of emotional upheaval?

20. What silver lining can you find in your past pain that's made you who you are today?

Other Books by
Michelle McKinney Hammond